I0691651

The Connelly Chronicles

FAMILY CONNECTIONS

N.J. NIELSEN

FAMILY
CONNECTIONS

Dedication

To Max, the one person who listened to me through so many renditions of Viv and Ray's love affair—it's finally here. And to any family member who thinks they might be in here somewhere—suck it up—'cause you probably are. You know I love you all, but admit it, some of the crazy stuff that happens in our family needs to be shared to be believed.

To Kyle, who was the basis of my inspiration for this book in the first place—hard to believe it's been twenty-six years since you passed away. I'll always be your knight in tarnished armor as you'll forever be my damsel in disgrace—miss you.

Chapter One

"Hey, yeah, yeah, yeah, what are you doing to me? Hey, yeah, yeah, yeah, what are you waiting to see? I loved you more through all of your games..."

Viv snapped his head toward the stage as the young male singer's melodic voice filled the room and drowned out the chatter among the other nightclub patrons. Why this song after all they had been through? Why did memories of her have to come back and haunt him now? Even if it was through the lyrics of a stupid song, sung by a total stranger. Viv had thought he was finally getting over Grace. Especially after the last time she had decided to hurt him by screwing with his brother Daniel's life. Even though he had once loved Grace with all his heart, Viv never wanted to see her again. "Oh my." Daniel turned to Viv and smiled sardonically. "Now there's a blast from a very fucked-up past. This song makes me hate the fucking bitch even more than I already do. Mind you, at least this guy's way sexier than Grace ever was."

Both men ignored Brie's unsympathetic laugh at Daniel's statement. Daniel's current girlfriend in Viv's eyes wasn't much better than Grace.

By the venom in his brother's words, Viv knew without a doubt that Daniel was still as fucked now as he had been before at the hands of Grace and all her stupid mind games. Once she had been so sweet, then it seemed as though she'd changed overnight. What she'd done to Daniel had destroyed what she and Viv had shared. Viv always had the feeling Brie had somehow been involved in what had happened to Daniel, but he couldn't prove it. Hence, the reason Brie was still in their lives.

Daniel studied him, and Viv realized his brother saw all the emotions he couldn't quite hide as he listened to Grace's favorite song. Viv suspected his present girlfriend of being part of the group that had drugged Daniel and uploaded the video to the Internet for the world to see. Viv blinked away the unwanted tears of anger and humiliation at the memory of Grace and all the pain she had repeatedly inflicted. She was the reason he no longer dated seriously. There was no way in hell he was letting anybody get that close to him again.

"Yeah," Daniel mumbled more to himself. "He's much too pretty."

"Daniel, sometimes the shit that comes out of your mouth amuses me and has me wondering what the fuck you're on?" Viv chuckled as he tried to divert the attention away from his own unwanted show of emotion over the coincidence of a stupid song. Even though he had never meant for what he'd said to hurt, pain flashed in Daniel's eyes.

God give me strength.

Silence fell between them for a moment and, as much as he tried, Viv couldn't seem to take his eye off the young male singer. Viv thought he was very pretty—for a man. His short, dark and spiky hair stood up in odd angles all over his head, as though he had been frustrated and had only moments before scrubbed his hand across his scalp. He also had a pencil-thin mustache and beard stubble. Facial hair looked strange on him, yet in a weird way, Viv rather liked it. The guy's build was lean, but not overly thin. Sweat glistened on his face under the stage lights, and by the way he was singing, he obviously enjoyed what he was doing—he looked happy. More than a few people in the crowd, both male and female, were turned toward the show ogling the singer, which amused Viv, as the guy seemed oblivious to them.

"What did I say?" Daniel asked, his attention also riveted to the stage.

Viv studied his brother and got the feeling that Daniel was reflecting over everything they had talked about and again, Viv had to agree with Daniel's earlier comments. The singer really was pretty, and if Viv had to be honest, he was better looking than Grace. Daniel had been right about that. He was probably somewhere between Daniel's twenty years and Viv's own thirty-two years. He wondered whether the guy was straight. In his opinion, he didn't think anyone so damn pretty could be straight, and he gave off the 'I'm too sexy to be single' vibe.

Where the hell did that thought come from? I'm not gay. I'm not attracted to men, no matter how damn cute they are. More than likely some handsome young man is waiting on the sidelines for him to finish, so even if I was attracted, there is nothing I can do about it. So let's close that door and move the hell on.

Daniel sighed, and Viv had a feeling his brother was already infatuated with the man on stage. For some strange reason, Viv didn't like how his brother watched the guy. Part of him wanted to remind Daniel that he had a girlfriend sitting at the table with them — a fucking pain in the arse girlfriend, but Dan's girlfriend nonetheless — and to keep his eyes off someone he wasn't dating.

"Just forget it. I didn't mean what I just said. I don't want to talk about Grace." He said his ex's name with more than a touch of bitter hatred. "I'm sorry I took my frustration out on you." Viv stared at the singer once more and aimed an intense amount of dislike at him. In his own mind, the stranger entertaining the crowd was the reason he and his brother were now at odds. Well, not odds exactly. More that he was the reason Viv was taking his hurt and self-hatred out on his brother over bringing Grace into their lives in the first place.

Even as he funneled his misguided resentment toward the stage, he knew his reaction didn't make sense. He didn't know this guy from Adam. After tonight, he would probably never see him again. Was it fair to blame the entertainer for his own stupidity? Maybe this was a blessing in disguise. Still, he couldn't seem to take his gaze away from the fellow. And crazier still, his imagination told him the guy was looking right back at him. Viv nearly laughed aloud. For a moment, it felt as though his heart was pounding in time to the thumping music.

How crazy is that?

Viv had never classed himself as homophobic, though many people still saw him that way. Why? He never really knew. For him the issue was simple — he preferred girls. Girls were soft in all the right places.

Sure, once or twice — okay, maybe a few times in the past — he had thought some dude was good-looking, but that was as far as those thoughts had ever gone. Never once had he acted upon them. This guy was definitely handsome, but realizing this didn't make Viv gay, did it? Viv was used to being around gay men and women and it never really bothered him in the least, especially living with Daniel, who didn't seem to care who he loved, as long as he was loved in return. Maybe his brother felt that way since he was only twenty and not ready to settle down. Most of Daniel's relationships had been based on lust with a tendency to burn out fast. No matter what, Viv loved his brother exactly the way he was, even if, at times, Daniel's antics frustrated the hell out of him.

He couldn't say the same for some of the people his brother chose to be with. Daniel's current and longest fling was starting to go sour, and Viv hoped Brie would soon leave the picture. He was sure that Daniel had only stayed with her for as long as he had because he knew how much she pissed Viv off. His brother had always enjoyed making Viv as uncomfortable as possible, and this girl certainly did the job well. He couldn't stand the bitch. She was sly, and his gut told him she was bad news.

Not only that, Brie was rude, crude and very uncouth. Viv glanced at her and rolled his eyes. She also seemed mesmerized by the singer on stage. The lust was written so plainly on her face. He wondered if she would hit on the poor guy like she had with other band members who played at Declan's. Not that Daniel knew what his precious Brie had been doing. Viv wanted to tell her she was wasting her time. The guy wouldn't be interested in her anyway. The only thing stopping him from speaking up was the fact that he didn't have a clue what type of person the singer preferred sexually. And he couldn't bring himself to speak to her, as it would only end in another argument. Maybe he should tell Daniel how often his girlfriend had hit on not only Viv, but also every other male in the near vicinity for the seventeen months Daniel had been with her. No, he couldn't say anything. If he did, it would only end up hurting Daniel more.

Why the hell did Tony hire this band anyway?

And what was with the group's name? Darkness Crawls?

He shook his head at the other two occupants sitting at the table with him. Viv could see the handsome guy on stage was going to become Daniel's new obsession.

Oh, what joy.

Not.

Viv could only imagine his near future inundated with the presence of a man who was already confusing Viv's body enough to make him want to run for the hills and never look back. He didn't know whether he would be able to bear to witness Daniel being with this guy without giving himself away too.

His thoughts came back to the here and now when Daniel kicked his foot under the table and growled, "Viv, you know what? You can kiss my arse."

A smile tugged at the edge of Viv's mouth as he turned to his brother and saw Daniel gearing up for a fight without once taking his gaze off the stage.

Tonight's finally going to be the end of Brie. Halle-fucking-lujah! Well, I hope it's the end of her, since there is no way Dan could be really mad at me. Dan's never mad at me, no matter how much we fight. I almost feel sorry for the poor, dumb bitch. Wait… Nope – not sorry at all. I'll argue all Dan wants, especially if it gets me what I want.

The song kept bringing his focus back to the stage, and the feelings he had no right having for a perfect stranger were doing some sort of happy dance right in the middle of his gut.

Why does he have to sing this song? Why now? Is this some sort of a sign? And if so, what's the message?

Viv was a big believer in signs. It was something taught to him by his father who had always said, 'Everything happens for a reason, so make sure you're listening'.

He sighed. *Please don't let Grace come back and ruin everything. Why do I always turn into a total fucktard the minute she smiles at me?*

Viv couldn't chance his ex getting anywhere near Daniel. Not after what had happened last time. Viv closed his eyes. He prayed he was wrong. But the way his luck was running lately, she would be turning up shortly just to fuck with his head again. In the past, she'd come into his life at yearly intervals and here the year was nearly up since her last stint of hell-raising.

As Viv slowly opened his eyes again, his gaze drifted back toward the stage. He froze when he realized the singer was still staring at him. There was no doubt in his mind that the man was looking at only him. His breath caught when he saw a crooked smile flash shyly in his direction. A strange warmth ran through him, one he didn't want to understand. A vibration settled in the pit of his stomach as he fought to get his thoughts into some semblance of order.

Stranger still, he couldn't stop himself from smiling back.

What the hell am I doing?

I am so fucked.

"Well, that's a first," Daniel blurted out in apparent shock. "If I didn't know better, I would think the singer was coming on to...well...you. And if my eyes aren't deceiving me, I would say you're flirting back." Daniel stared at Viv.

Daniel bit his lip, and Viv wondered if his brother sensed the weird shit swirling inside him, messing everything up. Daniel's eyes widened further and his jaw dropped open when Viv shrugged then turned back to the stage and grinned at the singer again.

"When you got it, flaunt it." Viv grinned, not sure why he was taking delight in Daniel's inflammatory statement of the guy flirting with him. So, he did the only thing he could think of and blew it off as a joke before adding, "Honestly, he's probably staring at you anyway."

"Viv," Daniel asked quietly, worry written clearly across his face, "do I really piss you off?"

Viv should have known his brother would come back to his stupid comment from earlier. "No, Dan. You don't. I'm sorry I said what I did." Sometimes Viv hated the way his mouth shot off and, nine times out of ten, his poor brother copped the brunt of one of his rants.

"Sometimes I feel like you're always disappointed in me," Daniel admitted sadly.

Viv fell silent as he watched Daniel's apprehension. There were twelve years in age between them but they were close. They'd always stood up and fought for each other when needed. In the last seventeen years, he'd raised Daniel without any help whatsoever from his mother. She had dumped the then three-year-old Daniel in his lap and had taken off on a road trip with Daniel's father.

Apparently, having to raise a child hadn't fitted in with their plans.

"No, Dan. You could never disappoint me." Viv stroked his brother's arm. Daniel seemed to brighten with his next words. "You're like a son to me. I'll always be proud of you, no matter what I say otherwise." He reached out again and patted his brother's cheek in comfort and reassurance. "And I'll always love you."

Sometimes Viv thought his brother had the attention span of a flea. Now that he'd been reassured he was still wanted and loved, Daniel had moved on to the next subject at hand, and truthfully, Viv welcomed the distraction from his own current and disturbing thoughts. For once, he would be willing to listen to whatever his brother wanted to ramble about, especially if this conversation kept his thoughts and hormones away from where they had no right going.

"Did I tell you about the most intriguing—and also the strangest—girl I kind of met today?"

Viv shook his head and waited for Daniel to go on.

"I was heading across the street to buy Tony a burger, and this girl walked by me. She was laughing aloud to herself. I was fascinated, so I followed her."

Viv watched him curiously. "You stalked a stranger?"

Daniel shrugged. "No, I didn't stalk a stranger. Well, not stalked exactly. I kind of followed her into the music store and watched her while she was looking through all the CDs. I couldn't help myself. I needed to watch. She was so fucking beautiful," Daniel said, and his eyes lit up. "You know, she was one of those people who is beautiful without even trying to be and more than likely, doesn't even know she is. I could have stared happily at her all day."

When his brother sighed dramatically, Viv tried not to laugh. "And how's that not classed as stalking? The music store is four blocks from here."

Daniel rolled his eyes. "Anyway, what I'm getting at is that she saw me and put down the CDs she was holding, then she stood and stared right back at me for the longest time. She pushed her sunnies up on top of her head to reveal amazing, big blue eyes that were twinkling and happy. When I thought it was about time I got the hell out of there, she started rummaging through her bag and pulled out a packet of photos. She sorted through them, picked one out and said, 'What's your name?' And after I told her, she scribbled my name across the bottom of the photo, put a heart with an S at the bottom and said, 'Here's a photo. It lasts longer'."

A slow smile crept across his brother's face seconds before he spoke again.

"Then before I could think of anything to say back, she grabbed me by my neck and pulled me toward her so she could kiss me. And I mean it was a full-on, no holds barred kiss. When we were finished, she asked for her mint back as it had ended up in my mouth. Then she winked at me as she popped the lolly back into her own mouth while paying for her stuff. Before my brain had time to think straight, she started laughing to herself again and walked out of the store. I really wanted to keep following her around town all afternoon — but then *that* would have been stalking."

Viv wondered if Daniel even realized he had sighed and was now wearing a big, goofy grin. Brie, on the other hand, snorted in what could only be disbelief, though an angry frown seemed to be quickly forming around her eyes. She folded her arms in front of her and listened as she glared daggers at Daniel. Daniel was purposely ignoring her, and the shit was about to hit the fan. Viv couldn't wait.

"So what did you do then?" Viv asked, knowing he was only furthering Brie's anger. And didn't that just make him happy?

"I was too stunned to do anything but stand there, and by the time I'd got outside, she was gone. So, I walked back and got Tony's burger, after I'd bought a frame so I could put the photo on my desk in the office. Remind me to show you before we go home tonight." Daniel shook his head in awe at the memory of the girl, a smile settling on his face. "I might even get it blown up so it's bigger. She's dressed up like a hippie in shades of purple and her golden hair looks like a halo. If I find her again, I might ask her to marry me, before she has a chance to walk away."

"So what was the name of this beautiful girl you want to marry?" Viv asked curiously. He could almost see the anger pouring off Brie as she fumed over the turn the conversation had taken. The sour look on her face was an indication of an imminent explosion. Viv wanted to usher them into the office, so he stood and gestured for his brother to stand. "Come and show me the picture now. I want to have a look at the woman who stole your heart."

The band was just finishing their set as Viv stood up. Daniel nodded and led him toward the staff entrance to their office. He knew Brie was following but Viv didn't care, as long as her hissy fit took place behind closed doors. The argument was going to be epic.

An even angrier Brie slammed the door shut behind them as Daniel walked over, picked the frame up off his desk and handed it to Viv. Surprise filled Viv when he realized that the woman was every bit as beautiful as his brother had claimed.

Daniel shrugged and pointed to the signature. "I don't know her name, but it has to start with an S."

Their conversation abruptly ended when Brie began furiously yelling obscenities at Daniel. Maybe they should really have saved this particular conversation until the club was empty, because pounds to peanuts the patrons of the nightclub would still be able to hear her through the walls, despite the music. Viv listened to her colorful language about exactly what Daniel could do with the photo of this oh so fucking beautiful girl. Viv was impressed at how Daniel stood so calmly through her whole tirade with one eyebrow cocked as he looked at Brie.

This was the end. Viv knew exactly what was going to come out of his brother's mouth next. He had heard this speech a few times before and could practically say it word for word with Daniel. This time Viv happily waited for Daniel to speak. He had to bite the inside of his cheek to keep from smiling.

Daniel shook his head in mock dismay, his voice dripping with sarcasm. "I love you... No, wait. On second thought, I don't. Things were good while they lasted, but you and I both know we're going nowhere. So don't call me, and I definitely won't call you— ever."

Without so much as a second glance, Daniel turned back to Viv and resumed the conversation about the strange and beautiful girl he'd met earlier that morning. Neither of them even looked up as Brie continued to curse profusely before she stormed out of the office.

Was it wrong that Viv wanted to jump up and down and shout out his happiness to the world? Luckily, for everyone involved, he was too mature to act like a giddy schoolgirl. But he did give his brother a nudge on the shoulder accompanied by a manic grin before they walked back out onto the main floor of their nightclub.

"Come on. Let's go out and meet the band." He felt safe to do this now, seeing as the singer had rushed out of the place as soon as they'd left the stage for a break. Wherever he was going, he was in one hell of a hurry.

Talking to the musicians was something they usually did whenever they had a live group performing at Declan's. This was when they found out if everything was running smoothly. Though tonight would be a little different since Viv knew Daniel would bring up the singer in the conversation, wanting to know where he had gone and when he would be coming back.

It's not like I haven't been keeping track of him all night and wondering the same thing.

* * * *

At end of the last set, Ray un-slung the guitar from around his shoulders and placed the instrument on the stand. Then he really looked at what Beth was wearing. He couldn't have stopped the manic grin from forming as he helped Beth step off the stage at Declan's. Why she was wearing that particular pair of heels when she had so much trouble walking in them, Ray couldn't understand. Especially since every nightclub they'd played in had some sort of stage she had to step down from. Why the hell hadn't he noticed them earlier?

Right, because I was too busy checking out Mr Tall, Dark and Sexy to pay any attention to anything else.

"They need to go in the bin so you can never be tempted to wear them ever again," he joked as he pointed to his friend's feet.

"Shut up, Ray. I'll swap with Girly when she gets here. You know they're my favorites," Beth said as he led her to the table where Josh and Jasper were already waiting.

"I'll be back as soon as I can," Ray promised as he pulled out his phone and read the message he'd received during the last song.

Dad, you're late. I'm waiting.

He chuckled softly. At least Girly was ready. He messaged back.

On my way. Meet me out front, please.

After only a few seconds, her reply came.

Already there. You owe me. GG says hi, slacker.

He loved his grandma more than anything in the world, but lately *every* time she'd seen him, she'd started in on him. Tonight he didn't want to have the same old argument with her. Ray exhaled slowly as he pulled up in his grandma's drive to find her waiting out front with Girly, so he'd had to listen to her anyway. Typical.

During her whole spiel, Ray's thoughts kept drifting toward the guy he'd been watching. He smiled to himself and wondered if his grandma would leave him in peace if she could read his thoughts. Was it so bad that he'd had an instant attraction to a total stranger? Ray had found it fascinating to watch while the object of his desire was talking to the younger man whom he sat with. Well, the younger one was talking, and the guy was listening. Whatever he'd heard must have been good, as it had made him smile. The stranger had such a nice smile. His whole face lit up, making him look even more stunning, if that was possible.

Everything from the olive tones of his skin to the dark, blue-black hair curling loosely to his shoulders fascinated Ray. If the guy's hair was any longer, it would probably fall in ringlets. And wouldn't that be sexy as all fuck. His fingers actually itched to run through those silky locks. It would have been awesome if the man had stood so he could see just how tall he was. Ray was partial to a man taller than himself. Okay, so he was more than a little excited. His heartbeat raced to a thrash metal tempo and certain other parts of him were growing hard as rock.

His imagination ran wild as he thought about what he would've said had he had the guts to introduce himself. 'Hello. My name's Ray, and I'd just like to say I think you have a beautiful smile. Oh, and would it be all right if I touched your hair?'

Man could he sound and act any more like a frickin' girl? Being gay did not give him the right to ogle every good-looking guy who crossed his path. Even though he was kind of disappointed, knowing he had to leave, and he'd hoped the guy would still be here when he got back. Maybe then he would've had the balls to go over and introduce himself.

Nah, maybe not.

* * * *

Daniel and Viv both introduced themselves and sat. Viv waved to a waitress and offered to buy everyone a drink—like he normally did on any other live entertainment night. The band members all thanked him, put in their orders and introduced themselves as Beth, Jasper and Josh.

"Where did the other guy go?" Daniel asked with disappointment in his voice.

Beth stared at Daniel for a moment before she answered, "Ray? He went to pick up Girly. They'll be back soon."

Her feet were in Jasper's lap as the man undid what Viv would've described as hooker heels. They had to be at least six inches high.

"So, Daniel and Viv," Beth asked. "Who are you, exactly?"

"We own this place." Daniel gestured around them. "You spoke with Tony about doing the gig here. He runs the live entertainment side of the business." Daniel pointed to the tall, dark-skinned man standing behind the bar talking animatedly to a patron. "The club used to belong to Viv's dad, hence the name Declan's. But we changed the place a lot since we took over." Daniel's train of thought switched gears mid-topic. "I really liked Ray's voice."

"Has your band been together long?" Viv asked. He tried steering the conversation in a completely new direction before Daniel started asking more questions about Ray or let loose with his theory of how Ray and Viv had been flirting during the band's last set. His brother had never had a brain-to-mouth buffer. If Daniel was thinking about something, then soon everyone was going to be hearing about it. The trait was both endearing and annoying as hell.

"Yeah," the blond bassist, Josh, answered. "We all met in high school. Back then, we were just a garage band. Jas, Brent, Girly and Ray were already friends, and when Beth — I call her B — and I moved here, Ray took a real shine to our B, so we all hung out for a while and have remained friends ever since." Josh stared at Beth, who had pulled the straw from her drink and flicked it at him. "What was that for?" As if realizing what he'd done, he added, "Guess I'm sharing too much information again. B, you are my sister, after all. Although I have to tell you, we used to get the best cakes and biscuits at Ray's grandma's house. I think she loved having us around. Man, I miss those garage band days."

Beth and Jasper started laughing. "What are you talking about, idiot? We went to Grandma's house only last Monday. For the love of God, no wonder you don't have many friends. Nobody actually wants to know our life history," she teased him affectionately.

"I know, but thinking about those cakes makes me hungry."

They were all still sitting there chatting away when Ray walked back in with his arm around a young woman — a very beautiful young woman whom Viv thought looked very familiar. Viv was riveted as they went straight onto the dance floor.

Daniel's mouth dropped open and he elbowed Viv in the side. "That's her! That's the minty chick who gave me the photo. Didn't I tell you she was beautiful?"

Beth turned and stared where only Ray and Girly were currently dancing like lunatics, and Beth started laughing. "Sounds like Girly. I bet she told you it lasts longer."

Daniel was too busy staring at the two people to answer. So many emotions flowed across his face, and Viv could almost hear the thoughts in his brother's head. He knew Dan would be thinking, 'Of course she would have a boyfriend. If the guy she's dancing with is her boyfriend, then he definitely isn't gay, either.' Disappointment would be running through him twice over both losses. Viv knew this, for strangely, he was also feeling some sort of loss and he needed to work out why.

Viv watched Ray dancing and bit back a groan as the warmth that had settled in his stomach was now starting to churn like raging rapids. He hoped he was only getting sick. Anything else would just be a complication in his life—a complication he wasn't ready to acknowledge in any way, shape or form. Ray and Girly were both singing along to the song playing over the sound system. It made Viv take notice of the actual way they were dancing. Somehow, it gave him the impression that they weren't boyfriend and girlfriend, but he could tell they were very close. Maybe they were brother and sister.

Daniel spoke, asking the same question.

"Is she his girlfriend?"

Viv brought his glass to his lips as he watched and was relieved when Beth shook her head.

"No, she's his daughter."

The answer given wasn't what he had expected. Viv choked on his drink, and Daniel pounded on his back as Viv blurted out before he could stop himself, "She's too old to be his daughter."

Jasper answered, "Sara's his sister's kid, but everyone calls her Girly. Izzy died when Girly was nine. Ray was only eighteen. Izzy left her to Ray, and his dad said she was his responsibility, so he arranged for Ray to adopt. Though, seriously, he's been looking after her ever since she was born. Izzy wasn't exactly the best parent in the world, and when she met a new guy, she dumped Girly and ran."

Now didn't that sound familiar? Viv shook his head. This sounded so much like his mother's operating procedure. Viv had been surprised that his mum hadn't brought him more kids to raise over the years. Maybe she'd never had any more. It would be sad to think he had other siblings out there he'd never know, and that they, in turn, wouldn't know anything about him and Daniel. He doubted his mother would want to advertise her past and explain about the kids she'd given away.

"That's just fucking crazy," Daniel whispered.

Beth explained, "You have to understand the Connellys are a very old-world money family. Somewhere along the line, Izzy—Isobel—did something that got her disowned by her parents. In the end, she only talked to Ray, because he still loved her, no matter what she'd done. Their father, Liam, had a hard time claiming Girly as part of the family when she was a baby. On her birth certificate, the father is listed as unknown, but they all knew who the man was. The guy in question was married at the time. He even had a child of his own a year or two older than Girly. That didn't matter to Ray and he couldn't let Girly go. She was his last link to Isobel and had already been like his kid for nine years. Izzy didn't want to be a parent and fobbed Girly off onto Ray's family every chance given. Ray once said she was always his responsibility. He had been babysitting her since the day she was born."

When Ray and Girly headed toward them, Daniel spoke quietly as he asked, "He won't get upset that you told us, will he?"

"Nah. Girly will tell you anyway. She's so proud of him. They're the best of friends," Josh chipped in.

"Hello, Dan. Fancy meeting you here," Girly said. She brushed her lips across Daniel's before she sat on his lap. She reached into her bag and pulled out a packet to hand to Josh. "GG sent you some dessert, you big kid."

"GG?" Daniel queried.

"Great-grandma is too much of a mouthful," Girly explained.

A smile broke out across Josh's face as he opened the bag and looked inside. "All right! Love you, Grandma." He started scarfing into the piece of chocolate cake from the bag.

"Brother of mine, you are gross." Beth laughed.

"So, if I heard right, you two are brother and sister?" Daniel asked, his arm wound tightly around Girly's waist.

The sight made Viv smile. Fingers crossed that Girly didn't turn out anything like Brie had.

"Yeah." Beth laughed again. "We were born in the same year, but we're not twins. No sooner had he popped out when Mum fell pregnant with me, but most people think we're twins."

"As a plus, we both get to celebrate two birthdays every year," Josh added, as he stuffed the last of the cake in his mouth.

Ray's whole body tingled and he nearly had a heart attack when he and Girly headed for their table. As freaky as the notion was, the guy he'd been checking out earlier was now sitting there talking to his friends. His face flamed as they were introduced.

Fuck. This guy is too gorgeous for words.

And, as luck would have it, the only available seat was right next to Viv. Ray nearly wet himself in nervous excitement as they were introduced. Even as he tried to act cool, calm, and collected, inside he was a screaming, raving mess of nervousness.

Ray thought about running. Being this close to the guy was once more making his body react inappropriately. He wished he would stop responding this way, especially when he was still pretending to the rest of the world that he liked girls. Connellys were never gay. At least that's what his grandfather had always told him. Glancing at Viv, he tried not to be obvious about what he was doing. His heart fluttered as he saw how green Viv's eyes were. They were the color of grass and made his face look even more beautiful close up. Ray fought the urge to rub the pad of his thumb across the guy's full lips as he sat and half listened to the conversation around him. Fighting desperately not to keep sneaking peeks at Viv, Ray admitted defeat. Really, he would have been quite willing to sit and stare at Viv for the rest of the night. The only thing stopping him was fear of getting yelled at, or, worse, punched in the face.

Giving himself a good inner shake, Ray came back to the conversation at hand and realized that Jasper was staring at him. He knew by the looks on everyone's faces that Jasper had been trying to get his attention for a while.

"What?" Ray blushed.

"So, does Grandma still want you to hurry up and get a boyfriend?"

Ray nodded. "I keep telling her I'm not gay, but she won't listen." The little white lie slipped out as easily as it always did.

Both Girly and Beth rolled their eyes at him, while Josh and Jasper tried to hide their smiles. Ray grew even more nervous. He wasn't ready for his friends to know the truth yet, and he definitely didn't want to talk about his sexuality in front of Viv and Daniel.

"What?" Ray tried to act nonchalant.

Girly leaned across Viv and patted Ray's cheek. "She knows what she knows. I think you should take some random guy around to meet her. Maybe then she'll be pleased and will get off your back. You want GG to be happy, don't you?"

Ray looked at her in disbelief. "Of course I want her to be happy, but what am I supposed to say? 'Hi. My name's Ray. Look, my grandma wants to see me settled down with some nice, young man. So do you think you can pretend to be gay with me for the next twenty years so my Grandma can die content?'" Embarrassment consumed him. "I'd get punched in the mouth before I'd even finished talking."

"You know there are guys out there who would be willing to date you in a heartbeat, right?" Daniel said.

"He's still pretending to be straight," Girly answered. "My great-grandfather had some pretty fucked-up notions when it came to sexuality, and Dad has a hard time being open about who he is."

Ray wished she would shut the hell up and stop airing his life to the world. He scowled at her, hoping she would take the hint.

"I'll do it. I'll be your boyfriend for her," Daniel said sincerely.

Everyone stared at him in disbelief, especially Ray, and he couldn't help but notice how Viv was glaring at his brother.

What the hell is that about?

But Girly spoke before he could answer. "No, you bloody well won't. I have plans for you myself."

Daniel looked like a stunned mullet.

Ray hoped that would be the end of it, but Girly didn't seem to be in the mood to let it go.

His daughter turned her attention back to Ray. "Dad, you should do it. I love GG, and she loves us. Please, all she wants is to see you happy. Well, happy — and she wants you to have more kids," she ended with a grin.

Ray shook his head in frustration. "Let's talk about this at home. You know you only confuse the hell out of me when you start arguing her side all the time. And you also know why I can't be gay." He didn't need this right now. Not when they still had a gig to finish. "And if I was gay, how the hell would I have more kids for her? Steal them?"

Ray stood and walked back to the stage before anyone else could add their two cents. He picked up his guitar and began strumming, then looked back at the table in time to see Viv get up and leave. He rolled his eyes when he saw Beth and Girly exchanging shoes.

Those damn shoes have to go.

All through the next set, Ray found himself looking for Viv as Viv drifted around the club talking to people. Once or twice Viv actually turned and stared right back at him, and Ray dropped his eyes in mortification at being caught. A few minutes later, he would find himself looking for the man again.

Finding out that Viv was the owner of the club was an added bonus. He knew it meant Viv wasn't going to be leaving any time soon. Well, he hoped he wouldn't. Ray loved being able to lose himself in the music and, just for a while, forget about the maybes and what-might-have-beens. Being gay sucked when he couldn't be honest about who he really was. He was shit at keeping secrets and everyone knew it. Ray was still amazed that his parents had never figured out he was gay. Not that he had actually lived with his parents since he took custody of Girly, and maybe he had misled them when he took women to functions he had to attend in the Connelly name.

By the end of the gig, Viv had come back to their table and was talking to Girly, who was once again sitting on Daniel's lap. Ray didn't even hesitate as he took the seat beside Viv and listened in on their conversation.

"Dad, Dan has invited us around for dinner tomorrow night."

"I think he invited you, not me," Ray said affectionately to her when she rolled her eyes. In moments like this, she reminded him so much of her mother. It was almost like having Izzy back. But he was lucky that looks were the only part of her mother she seemed to have. Ray had no worries that Girly was going to do a runner on him.

Daniel was the one who answered with a smirk, "Viv will be there as well, so you aren't going to be a third wheel. It'll be more like a double date. Now doesn't that sound like fun? You can practice having a boyfriend."

Glancing at Viv's astonished expression for a moment, Ray then focused on Girly again. With a grin, he said, "Maybe you should also invite Grandma. Me on a date with Viv would definitely make her happy. He's cute as—" Ray suddenly realized what he had been about to say and turned to Viv, blushing in embarrassment. "I'm sorry—I didn't mean anything by what I said. I was just..."

"It's okay," Viv said hesitantly.

Heat suffused Ray's body. *How stupid can I get? Way to go. Scare him off before I even have the chance to get to know the man.* If he had looked any more like a moron, he would've repeatedly smacked his head on the tabletop.

Ray sat for the remainder of the night watching the very complex and somewhat confusing man, thinking about everything he had learnt about him so far. He found himself liking both Viv and his brother. They seemed honest, and Viv was funny when he opened up. Still, Ray couldn't believe Daniel had so willingly agreed to play gay for him.

Ray thought that after tonight—well, at least after the dinner tomorrow night—he probably wouldn't ever see the brothers again as they weren't really the type of people he normally associated with. Sadly, this was because Ray found it so hard making friends that he only stuck with the same group he'd known since high school. Maybe their being here had been a spur of the moment thing after the intended band had canceled, but hell, he was glad things had turned out the way they had.

Chapter Two

Viv was pleasantly surprised when Daniel began cleaning the house with a vengeance, and for once, Daniel wasn't complaining. He even volunteered to clean the toilet and bathroom, which shocked the shit out of Viv. Would wonders never cease? Their house wasn't messy as such, but their home definitely looked lived in.

The surprises kept on coming as Daniel took over cooking the roast dinner. He'd never seen Daniel behave this way with any of his other conquests, especially only having met her a few days beforehand. Maybe he really liked this girl or was very much in lust with her, or maybe Ray was the one he was after. Strangely, the thought of Daniel and Ray together made Viv's stomach lurch. A frown touched his lips as he watched his brother preening in the reflective glass of the kitchen cabinet. He would have to pay close attention and see who his brother was striving to impress then deal with the after-effects.

"Do I look okay?" Daniel asked.

Viv appraised him up then down. "Depends which person you're dressing for."

Daniel shrugged. "Either, or — they're both pretty sexy. If I'm honest, Girly intrigues me more. I want to know what makes her tick, but I'd also like to know what Ray's thinking. He seemed so genuine and really funny. Which one do you think I should pursue?"

"You look fine, and my only advice is to just follow your heart," Viv answered as the doorbell sounded. With a genuine smile, he added, "Go and let your guests in. I'll check on dinner to make sure it isn't going to be a complete disaster."

As soon as his brother left the room, Viv ran a hand through his hair and adjusted himself to make sure his clothes were neat and tidy before checking the stove. Not sure how he should dress, he'd settled on jeans and a long-sleeved band T-shirt, with a button-up shirt open over the top. He relaxed when Daniel led them in and he saw Ray dressed similarly. Girly had on a purple maxi skirt and a gray tank top.

"Dan said you had a preference for red," Girly said as she offered him a bottle of wine.

Ray carried a small cooler bag, and when Viv raised an eyebrow in inquiry, Girly supplied the answer.

"Dad only drinks beer — Hahn Premium Light. So if we go anywhere, we find it easier to take our own."

Ray remained silent and shrugged. However, his eyes seemed to drink Viv in, and that look alone was starting to mess with Viv's ability to think coherently.

Sheesh, think of anything except the man in front of me. I do not need my body spilling secrets I don't want anyone knowing. Do not look at Ray and see what's never going to happen.

"Dinner's still about half an hour away. Let's go into the lounge room," Viv announced, as normally as he could.

Viv found he couldn't take his eyes off Ray. He watched as Ray walked over and began reading all the titles of their music shelved in the entertainment system. Ray bent over and ran his fingertip along their spines. Smiling at one, he pulled the disk out.

Girly took one look at the cover, rolled her eyes and said, "Put it back, Dad. No Bowie tonight."

Ray smirked at her but slid the CD back into place.

"Do you like Bowie?" Viv asked in surprise. It wasn't often that he found someone with his own musical tastes.

Again, it was Girly who answered him. "Dad's a Bowie freak with a capital F. I think we have all his CDs and quite a few DVDs, books and movies."

Ray turned then and looked straight into Viv's eyes. For a moment, Viv's breath caught in his throat. He had to concentrate just to have everything still make sense when Ray finally spoke.

"There's nothing wrong with Bowie. The man is brilliant, and he'll always be my hero."

Girly rolled her eyes again, though she smirked when she retorted, "Like I said, Dad's a super freak."

Daniel chuckled. "Then I guess we both have one. Viv's a huge Bowie fan as well, though I usually make him keep the rest of his crap in his bedroom."

Ray turned abruptly and stared at Viv, as if appraising him in a completely new way. Viv felt warmth spread through him again like he had the night before.

"What's your favorite song?" Ray asked.

Viv looked deep into the eyes staring back at him. He couldn't determine whether they were gray with blue flecks or blue with gray flecks. Whichever they were, they sure knew how to suck a person in completely. Viv shook his head to clear his thoughts.

"*Silly Boy Blue*," Viv answered. "And yours is?"

"*Let Me Sleep Beside You* and also *Lady Stardust*," Ray answered with a shy smile. "It would seem we both like the oldies the best."

Daniel got up and pulled Girly to her feet. "Come help me with dinner, before we both get bored to tears."

They laughed as they left the room.

"Can I...? Can you show me your other CDs to see if you have anything different from mine?"

Viv hesitated, trying to remember how clean his room was, but when Ray flashed him the same crooked smile from the club, he immediately got to his feet. He almost took Ray's hand, but caught himself in time.

"Just ignore the mess in my room. It's my maid's day off," Viv joked as Ray followed him to his bedroom.

One quick glance around told him the clutter wasn't too bad. At least he had remembered to make his bed that morning. Viv led Ray over to the wall unit where his stereo was and waved at the many shelves of CDs.

Ray pointed at the stereo. "Who are you listening to at the moment?"

Viv hit the remote and the music began to play softly. "Some Scottish guy. His name's Paolo Nutini. Tony gave me his CD to listen to." Viv picked it up and handed the cover to Ray then snatched his hand back as soon as their fingers touched. "Sorry about that. I have a tendency to zap people."

Ray blushed shyly. "I don't mind," he said as he walked over and sat on the edge of Viv's bed where he began reading the song titles. "He's got a nice voice—kind of mellow, soothing—and even romantic."

Viv crossed the room then sat beside Ray, ever conscious of the fact that their legs were touching. Why he was sitting so close, he didn't know, and only found himself leaning in more when Ray never moved away. They both studied the case, and Viv was finding it difficult to keep from staring at the side of Ray's face as they talked about the songs.

They both looked up as Daniel stuck his head in the door and grinned. Viv jumped away, blushing.

Crap, that's all I need—for Daniel to get the wrong idea. Well, maybe *the wrong idea—fuck I'm so screwed up.* He needed to work it all out in his own mind first before others started adding their two cents.

"Hope I'm not interrupting anything, but dinner is served," he said, bowing formally in their direction before he straightened and left. Daniel's laughter followed him out of the room.

Viv shook his head. "Did I mention how much of an idiot my brother can be?" Ray chuckled as they went to eat.

* * * *

Days later, Ray was taking a well-earned timeout. He lay submerged to his shoulders in a steaming bubble bath as he thought about everything that had occurred. Luckily, Girly had driven them home from Viv and Dan's that first night, because Ray would surely have blown the bag when they were pulled over to be breathalyzed. As Girly chatted to the policemen, Ray had simply sat and let his mind wander back over the evening.

Daniel had been so caught up in Girly and seemed oblivious to him and Viv. So Ray found himself left to socialize with Viv all night—not that he minded. In fact, he liked talking to Viv a lot more than he'd thought he would. They found out they had a lot in common.

Ray had been surprised when, toward the end, Viv had asked if he could come around and see his Bowie collection. Before Ray even had a chance to reply, Girly had quickly invited them for dinner the following Wednesday night. When she gave them the address, Viv's eyes had widened a fraction. Ray hoped it wasn't in a bad way. Sometimes, when people found out how well-off Ray's family was, they fell into two categories. One, they ran and never looked back. Two, they tried to use Ray or Girly as a stepping stone in their lives. Ray immensely disliked the ones who fell into the latter group. For once, he just wanted someone who would love him for him and not for what his last name offered. He wondered which group Daniel and Viv would fall into.

Ray sighed as he remembered the hug he'd gotten from them both as he and Girly had left. Daniel's was firm and full of confidence, and Viv's seemed shy, as though he wasn't quite sure about what was going on or where to put his arms. His reflections shifted again. Not only had Viv looked amazing that night, and the same again when they'd come here for dinner, he smelled...wonderful. A shiver ran through his body. He considered that maybe he should've been having a very cold shower instead of a relaxing bath. He mulled over why Viv affected him so much. No one else had ever made him feel this way before—not even Beth, and back then, he'd believed he'd been in love with her.

"Dad?" Girly called as she walked through their house.

She would find him sooner or later, so he stayed in the bath, slowly sipping from a bottle of beer and staring at the wall in front of him. He needed this time to take stock of what would possibly happen in his life and wishing he had someone other than Girly to share everything with. He loved her, but sometimes she was too in his face and trying to run his life, as though she could do a better job. Maybe she could. Who knew? He certainly didn't.

"Dad, I've been calling you, like...forever," Girly said as she stuck her head through the partially opened door.

"I'm naked in here," Ray said in exasperation. "Can't a man have any freaking privacy anymore?" Luckily, the bubbles covered everything important.

"Gross! You're my father. I would never look at your body in that way. Besides, I've seen you naked way too many times over the years to be affected now," she retorted with a flip of her hand.

"What do you want, Girly?" Ray placed the empty beer bottle on the floor and motioned for her to pass him a new one.

"Dan's coming to pick me up, and we're going over to GG's. Do you want to come?"

"Who?" Ray asked, pretending he couldn't remember the guy whom his daughter had spent every waking hour with since the dinners. The fact that Dan wasn't here now was the only proof Ray had that they weren't actually conjoined twins.

"Dan... You know... The guy from the club the other week. The one who offered to be gay for you, remember? We went to their house for dinner, and they came here."

Ray frowned, still pretending to be confused until she rolled her eyes when she cottoned on to what he was doing.

"You're an idiot. So do you want to come or not?"

He shook his head. "You go and have fun. And say hello for me."

"You're the one she wants to see. She's hurt because you keep avoiding her. You need to just suck it up and go there."

He hated when he made Girly or his grandma upset.

"I'll see her soon. I promise. Today I have some thinking to do."

"You're acting like an idiot, you know. Great-granddad is dead, and GG doesn't care that you're gay. Nobody cares, except you." She squatted beside the tub. "Dad, I love you, and I want you to be happy. You haven't been in a serious relationship since B. I'm a big girl now. I know about sex and won't get grossed out if you're in a relationship, no matter what sex the person you're with is. I don't know why you're still holding onto a persona that isn't even close to the real you. Grow a set and get the hell over it already."

"And what's that supposed to mean?"

"It means GG is right. You're gay. I've always known you are, and so have all of our friends. You seem to forget we all have eyes. Sometimes when you think no one is paying attention to you, you watch other men. You watched Dan's brother a lot, not only at the club when we were there, but also when we had dinner with them. I've never really seen you act that way before, not even with B. Don't you think it's about time you're finally true to yourself, and for once, live your life to make *you* happy and not to please everyone else?"

"Don't be bloody ridiculous. I don't need to have someone in my life to be happy." Ray knew he was lying, yet he couldn't stop himself from doing so. "Besides, I have you. What more could I possibly need?"

"But you can't sleep with me, Dad. You can't take comfort in my body. That's what GG wants for you. That's what we all want for you. There has to be someone out there for you. You shouldn't be alone. You were always there for me when I was growing up and looking out for me. Now, it's your turn. You need someone who can love you back in a whole different way from how the family does."

"Well then, maybe I should've taken Dan up on his offer," Ray snapped. He hated it when they argued. He always said things he didn't mean, and once they were out in the open, he couldn't take them back.

"Maybe you should have," Girly snapped right back as the doorbell sounded. "Why do I always have to sort out your problems for you?" she added as she stood and left the bathroom.

"Stay out of my love life, Girly. I'll work things out on my own. I don't need you or anyone telling me how to live my life," Ray yelled.

Before she slammed the door shut, Ray thought he heard her say 'Yeah right.'

Frustration rolled through him like an unsettled wave. He fought it and went back to staring at the wall. He didn't want to think about what Girly had said to him. But think about it he would. He always did.

Ray laughed at how ridiculous everything they had argued about seemed. He stared at himself in the water and groaned at how his body reacted to just the memory of Viv. He felt the heat rising up in him as he remembered the exact green color Viv's beautiful eyes were. He recalled the curve of Viv's lips when he smiled over something they had talked about or done. Ray's heart raced when he recalled the hesitant touch of Viv's hands when they'd said goodnight.

Crap, now all he wanted to know was what Viv's mouth would feel like against his. Would it be firm or soft and warm? Ray gripped the side of the bathtub with one hand as he slowly and steadily stroked his rigid and aching cock with his other. His firm grip, as his thumb pressed against the leaking slit, had his balls drawing up close to his body and sent the tingle that started in the base of his spine tearing through him like a storm about to break loose. Ray shuddered in pleasure as he gave in to his release. Well, that was one hell of a way to end drinking beer in the bath and staring at the wall.

Standing up shakily, Ray emptied the tub then stepped into the shower to rinse off. His body still hummed from the gratifying act he'd performed moments before. He stared at the palm of his hand and wondered what it would be like to have someone else's hands on his body. His sexual encounters of the male persuasion had been few and very far between, and kept away from the prying eyes of his family or anyone else who knew him. Hell, with his paranoia of being found out, Ray never even gave people his real name. Everyone only ever knew him as Alex, the shortening of his middle name, Alexander.

He grew angry with himself all over again. Why did he always have to listen then think about whatever Girly said to him? Damn stupid Girly and damn her stupid ideas. Why did she have to make him think that it would be okay for him to fess up and step out of his self-imposed closet?

* * * *

Later that same day, Ray stood in the kitchen making something to eat and listening to David Bowie's *Changes* CD full bore when Beth and Jasper sauntered in. They sat at the table and waited for him to join them. They had a bag of takeout, so he didn't offer to make them a sandwich. He wiped away his tears as he turned to face them and saw the sympathetic looks in their eyes. His tears didn't stay gone for long.

"So, we ran into Girly and Daniel when we were up at the store getting lunch. She told us about your little talk in the bathroom. When they left, we came straight here in case you needed someone to talk to," Jasper said hesitantly.

Ray stared at them belligerently. "Look, if you're here to discuss my sexuality, then keep your mouths shut. I don't want to hear it." He took another swig of his beer, deciding whether to ignore the presence of his friends then cursed himself for giving them a key to his house in the first place. Glancing at Beth and seeing the look of determination on her face, Ray knew she was going to pick up where Girly had left off.

He didn't need this right now, not when everything was still a big, festering ball of confusion in his own head.

Beth reached across the table and patted his hand. "It makes no never mind to us if you're gay. We've known that you are for a long time now."

"Known what exactly? For crying out loud. I want to know why everyone thinks I'm gay. And if I am, why they think it is any of their fucking business, and why they all have a right to run my fucking life?" Ray shouted. Secrets he'd kept for so long started tumbling down around his ears.

Jasper started laughing in a weird way. Ray knew his friend was trying to lessen the heat of the moment.

"If you didn't want anyone to know then maybe you shouldn't drink," Jasper stated. "And maybe you shouldn't be anywhere near Viv."

"What are you talking about?" Ray snapped. There was no way they had ever seen him out with another guy. It wasn't possible. And what the hell was the comment about Viv?

"Drunken men tell no lies," Beth added as she scrutinized his every movement.

"What?" Ray shook his head as fear started to fill him. He sensed that she was going to tell him something he should remember.

"Ray, we love you. You know that, don't you? You're like my best friend and a brother all rolled into one. You're my family. Well, the only family I *care* about," Jasper said, laying a hand on Ray's arm.

He could only nod. He didn't like where this was going.

"So I need you to believe me when I tell you that we have known for a very long time that you are, in fact, gay. Beth, Josh and I have all seen you in action."

More fear flooded Ray's system, drowning him. "W-what...? What are you talking about?"

"Do you remember when we did that gig for some chick's twenty-first about three years ago? We had to drive for fucking hours. Remember the pub was right out in the middle of nowhere?" Jasper asked cautiously.

"Yeah." Ray dreaded where this was heading and tried desperately to recall some of the finer details that night had included. His memory was a little suspect, since he had gotten really drunk that night... Shit!

"Well, at one stage I went outside to take a leak and saw you leaning against a wall with your arms wrapped around some young guy, and you were thoroughly enjoying every minute of his tongue being stuck down your throat. Your hands were all over him, and by the time I got back with Josh and B, let's just say things had well and truly progressed."

The red suffusing his friend's face let Ray know exactly what his friends had witnessed.

"I don't really remember the night too well." Embarrassment washed over Ray. He tried harder to recall the incident, but he couldn't remember much after the band had stopped playing. Flashes began to emerge of some pretty, young blond eagerly handing him beers as they had played.

"Well, believe me when I tell you we kept asking you if it was something you truly wanted. Your reply was to punch me in the mouth. The guy kept calling you Alex. After you slugged me, you told us all to fuck off because you were busy. We left you there to finish what you had started."

Ray folded his arms on the table in front of him and laid his head on top of them as flickers of memory began to inundate his mind — memories of him leaning against a wall while a beautiful blond man was down on his knees before him. Ray could almost feel how his fingers gently held the guy's face to him. He remembered that he pulled the man up and pushed him against the wall before he shoved the fellow's trousers down and returned the favor. Ray couldn't remember if things had gone further, but if they had, he could only hope to hell he'd remembered to use condoms.

He felt sick.

"Why…? Why didn't you bring this up with me before now?"

Beth came around the table and embraced him. "Ray, it really is okay in this day and age to be gay. No one will care if you are. We're all still going to love you anyway."

He didn't lift his head as he answered her but spoke into the hollow of his arms. "Try telling my father that and see how far it gets you. I've had it drummed into me for years that no Connelly could ever be gay."

"Sorry, darlin', but that bullshit was your grandfather, not your father. Only you can tell your parents what's going on in your life. I'll come with you for moral support, if you need me to, but as much as I want to save you the stress, I can't say the words for you." Beth caressed the nape of his neck with her fingertips.

After Jasper and Beth had left, Ray crossed the living room to the bar and grabbed another bottle of beer before he collapsed into the leather couch to figure a way out of this mess. For so many years, he had lied to everyone around him, thinking that no one could see the real him, when, in fact, everyone he'd ever cared about already knew the truth about him. Once more, tears slowly escaped as he tried to reconcile his old self with the self his friends were giving him the opportunity to be. Could it be as easy as everyone was telling him it was?

Somehow, he doubted that very much.

By the time Girly and Daniel came home, a growing number of empty bottles littered the coffee table in front of him.

"Dad, what are you doing?" Girly asked as she sat beside him. Worry filled her face.

"Drinking." Ray chuckled as he held up a half-empty beer. He was completely skunked and didn't care.

"Why?" She brushed his hair out of his face. "Dad, I'm sorry I said all those things to you this morning."

She sounded as worried as she looked, and Ray didn't even have the energy to comfort her.

He looked at his daughter and started laughing, which ended up sounding like a strangled sob. "Jas and B came around and tol' me stuff. No"—he shook his head—"they 'minded me about stuff..." Tears rolled freely down his face. "Apparently everyone knows I'm gay." He lay on the couch until his head rested on his daughter's knee. "Tell me what I'm s'posed to do, Girly."

He sobbed softly. He didn't complain when she took the bottle out of his hand and placed it on the table with the others.

"Well, for starters, you can stop drinking." She stroked the side of his face as he closed his eyes. "Now we just need to find you a boyfriend," she whispered.

"Want Viv. I like Viv," Ray mumbled before he started snoring.

Chapter Three

Two weeks later, and after a few more visits to GG's house with Daniel, Ray found out exactly what Girly and Daniel had been up to. Even then, Ray realized, she was enough of a chicken to make Daniel be there with her while they confessed. She'd explained that Daniel was every bit as much to blame as she was. Ray had been a little wary when he'd accepted their invitation to lunch.

When he finally arrived at the restaurant, he saw Viv sitting with Girly and Daniel. As he took his seat, he noted that there was an extra chair at the table, and his insides began to churn. His heart raced when he saw Viv's green eyes look his way, and Ray hated it. Girly looked nervous, and he immediately jumped to the very worst conclusion.

"You're pregnant, aren't you?" he said in exasperation.

She looked at him in shocked silence for a long moment before she could find her voice. "No, I bloody well am not... But you're right, we do have something to tell you both."

Ray's gaze dropped to her left hand as another conclusion leaped into his head, but her finger was still bare.

His reaction didn't go unnoticed.

Daniel remarked on his gaze. "In case you're wondering, we aren't about to get married, either."

Viv sighed at the exact same second he did, and this made both Daniel and Girly laugh nervously. If it wasn't a pregnancy or marriage then Ray wasn't sure what could be worse.

"Then what do you have to tell us?" Viv asked.

Daniel spoke. "Christopher, do you love me?"

Christopher? Who the hell is Christopher?

When Viv nodded, Ray realized it must be Viv's real name. Why hadn't he ever thought to ask before? Christopher—he liked it. Though Viv suited him better.

Girly reached for Ray's hand. "Dad, do you love me?"

"You know I do, Girly."

"Well, we should tell you GG will be joining us for lunch in about twenty minutes."

She wrung her hands with obvious apprehension. She refused to look at him, and some sort of warning began seeping through his body.

"Now remember, Viv," Daniel added. Even he sounded nervous. He moved just a little farther away from his brother. "You have already said you love me, so don't get angry at me…because—because I told GG you were Ray's boyfriend," he ended in a rush.

Right then, Ray's heart began beating out of control as Daniel jumped up and moved so that the entire table was between Daniel and his brother. Horrified, Ray stared open-mouthed at his daughter then at Viv. Embarrassment washed over him. The way Girly grabbed his arm to stop him from taking off, or doing something worse, wasn't helping. He cringed inwardly when Viv shouted "What?" so loudly the whole restaurant turned in their direction.

This can't be happening.

Ray chuckled. To top it all off—Grandma was early.

Trapped, Ray found it difficult to breathe.

Daniel walked around and resumed his seat beside Viv. Ray heard him whisper, "I'm sorry, Viv. Please, can't you go along with it for today?"

Everyone stood as Grandma approached the table.

"I know I'm early," she said, "but I couldn't wait to meet Christopher. Ray, you should sit near your young man. Let me sit next to this delightful child." She smiled warmly as Daniel held a seat out for her.

She took a moment to study Viv as she sat, and Ray knew that look. She was assessing whether or not Viv was good enough. She must have liked what she saw. She winked at Viv and patted his arm.

Ray was relieved when Viv didn't come right out and tell her what was going on.

This was all too confusing. Ray couldn't bring himself to meet his grandma's eyes, but he finally looked up as Viv took his hand and squeezed gently. When he let go, Ray moved his hands below the table to hide their trembling, in both guilt for lying to Grandma, and excitement. When Viv had touched him, an electrical current had run through him and brought all his synapses to life.

"So, Christopher, your brother tells me you both own a nightclub," Grandma said, "and most people call you Viv?"

Viv agreed. "That's right. My last name is Vivvens. Dan and I have different fathers."

"It's good you are so close, then. So how did you meet my Ray, and was it love at first sight?"

By the mischievous twinkle in her eye, Ray knew they were in for a round of thirty questions—if not more. His grandma could be relentless when she wanted to find something out about someone.

"Surprisingly, yes," Viv chuckled. "Ray's band played at our club in an unexpected change of bands, and he caught my eye by smiling at me."

Ray looked at him in surprise, and Viv grinned. He tenderly caressed Ray's cheek with the backs of his fingers. Ray realized Viv was one of the smoothest liars he'd ever met, and he felt even guiltier lying to his grandma, even though the lies were making her happy.

He was more than a little confused. As the meal progressed, he found the way Viv touched him so easily was in direct opposition to Viv's earlier reaction to hearing what Girly and Daniel had done. Mainly they just held hands, then, unexpectedly, Viv laid his arm along the back of his chair so his fingertips curled around Ray's shoulder. All Ray could do was lean back into the touch.

At the end of the meal, Ray paid the bill. The least he could do was pay, seeing as Viv had graciously gone along with the stupid plan. They all walked Grandma out to where her limo and driver waited. Viv stood behind Ray, and as Grandma looked back at them, he wrapped his arm around Ray's waist so he was leaning back against Viv's chest. Viv's heart pounded so hard it slammed into Ray's back, and Ray wondered if this was what the physical part of anger felt like. He knew Viv had to be angry about the deception. He froze in place as Viv brushed his lips across the side of Ray's throat. Panic filled him as his body reacted to Viv's intimate touch. He sighed as he brought one of his hands up to rest it over Viv's and patted it in understanding and comfort.

No sooner had his grandma's car turned the corner when Viv suddenly let go and stepped away. Before he left, he pointed at his brother's chest and said, "You and I will be having words." Not looking back, he jumped into his car and took off.

It shocked Ray how easy it had seemed for Viv to pretend to be his boyfriend. His throat tingled from where Viv's kiss had touched his skin—fiery hot.

"I'm sorry, Dad," Girly whispered as she pulled Ray into her embrace. "Things kind of got a little out of hand. Once the ball was rolling, I didn't know how to stop the damn thing."

Upset, Ray trembled and as he drew away from her to stand a couple of feet away. "I told you to stay out of this, didn't I? I told you I would work things out for myself. How am I ever going to face him again? Did you even think of that, or did you think about what I'll have to say to Grandma? What the hell am I supposed to do if she ever wants to see Viv again? I'm a grown man, Girly. I don't need you taking care of me. You're my daughter—not my wife!"

Girly finally spoke a little shakily. "Dad, you will always need me to look after you. You know you would be hopeless without me around. Who would you get to do up your ties?"

Ray sighed. "You really should have butted out. You've only made things worse. What if she tells Mum and Dad? How do you think your grandparents are going to take the news about me being gay?"

"Dad, you should tell them the truth. They'll love you no matter what, but maybe—no definitely—you should tell them before GG does."

"Tell that to your mother," Ray grumbled. "Being family doesn't mean they'll always love and support you." He felt horrible. How was he supposed to face his parents with this bit of news? Then reality hit him, and he stared at his daughter with a horrified expression. "What if they want to meet Viv?"

Daniel smiled brightly, which Ray found strange.

"Your father's one of Viv's heroes, and he's been trying to get a meeting with him for about a year now."

"What about? I mean, what does Viv want to talk to my father about?" Ray asked, his curiosity piqued. Then he chastised himself silently for sounding too interested.

"He wants to join some department your father has in his company. Sounds boring to me, but he wants to work there. Funny, though, how Viv hasn't realized the very man he wants to meet is your father."

Ray rubbed his face feverishly. "Could this get any more fucking complicated? Who should I talk to first, Dad or Viv?"

"If it was up to me, I would talk to Nan and Pop first," his daughter said.

* * * *

On the drive to their house, Ray deliberated hard over what he was going to say to his parents. Girly and Daniel had decided to come with him for moral support. Well, more since, he was sure, Girly wanted to make certain he was going to talk to them and didn't chicken out.

Ray found them in the pool house. His anxiety shot through the roof when he realized his grandma had beaten them there. His face burned in shame as he watched his parents. This was not good. Everyone was right. He should have been the one to tell his parents and not let them find out second-hand.

"Where's your nice young man?" Grandma said as Ray kissed her on the cheek.

"He had to go back to work, Grandma."

"I was telling Liam and Claire all about Christopher, and they didn't know anything about him."

Ray took one look at his father's expression—a mixture of confusion and hurt—and froze. Words failed him.

Girly broke the silence. "Hey, Nan, Pop. Guess what? Surprise! Dad's gay."

Ray relaxed only slightly as his mother smiled and spoke softly. "We've always known. Do we get to meet this friend of yours?"

Ray watched his father and waited until he had spoken before he could even think of answering.

"How long have you been this way? Why were you afraid to tell us?"

"All my life, I guess. I was born this way. I wasn't scared, exactly. I just needed to work it out in my head first." Okay, so that right there was a fib.

His father's face relaxed somewhat. At least he was no longer looking as hurt, even though Ray had an inkling that his Dad wasn't quite as easy-going as his mother seemed to be. His suspicion was confirmed with his father's next words.

"Have you tried not being this way?"

Ray answered honestly. "Yes, I tried very hard, and even though I am this way, I'm still your son," he ended in a whisper.

His father didn't speak for a very long time. Finally, he said, "Yes, you're still our son. So, like your mother asked, when will you bring this Christopher around to meet your mother and me? Will six o'clock be convenient?"

Ray thought his father's voice still sounded strange, and he knew his father wasn't taking no for an answer. This whole scene was enough to make Ray want to jump straight back in the closet, slam the door shut and lock it for all eternity.

"Can I let you know? I have a few errands to run. I'll ring you up by three to tell you one way or the other." Ray was only half relieved when his father nodded. Now he would have to convince Viv and hope to God that Viv didn't knock him on his arse. Ray wouldn't blame him if he did. This whole situation was fucked up. The sad part was that he knew he would use his family connections to get Viv to agree.

"We're staying here," Girly said as she pulled Daniel toward the changing rooms.

Once again, Ray found himself driving across town, wondering what he was going to say when he got to Declan's. Daniel had given him his set of keys to the club, where he would supposedly find Viv. According to Daniel, Viv was a workaholic.

As he pulled into the lot, he saw Viv's car and his heartbeat accelerated. This time he experienced more fear than anything else. How was he going to apologize for dragging Viv into this? His stomach churned and he fought the urge to throw up. Using Daniel's keys, he knocked on the door then let himself in.

* * * *

Viv looked up in surprise as someone knocked on the door—flustered, especially since he'd just been thinking about Ray, and the way the man had felt in his arms as he'd held him out the front of the restaurant.

"What can I do for you, Ray?"

"Can I come in?"

Viv pointed him to a seat.

Ray hesitated. "I'm sorry you got dragged into this whole stupid mess. I honestly had no idea Girly and Daniel were going to do what they did. If I had known, I would have tried to stop them. But now that it is done, I have a problem."

"What are you sorry for, exactly? Us being tricked and used by our families or because it's all a lie? Or is it that your supposed boyfriend's straight and not interested in your body at all?" Viv teased. His mask nearly dropped as pain washed over Ray's face. He found himself wanting to reach out and comfort him, but restrained himself.

"No, I have a bigger problem than even that."

Ray looked so embarrassed Viv knew he wasn't going to like what he was about to hear.

"So what's this bigger problem?" he asked as Ray blushed even harder. Viv realized then that he was sort of cute when he was embarrassed. He dropped his gaze to his desk. *What the hell am I thinking?*

"My father wants to meet you. Grandma told my parents about you. I'm so sorry Viv, but I'm a big coward where my father is concerned. I always have been."

Viv raised one eyebrow in disbelief before turning back to his paperwork. He needed to get his jumbled thoughts under control. He also couldn't help but think that Ray was as weak as piss if he was afraid of his own father.

"You don't say no to my father. Believe me, I've tried," Ray stated. "Not many people in this world can deny the high and mighty Liam Alexander Connelly and survive to tell the tale."

Viv's eyes popped wide as he snapped his head up to stare at Ray. Holy fuck. The notion had never occurred to him, when Beth had said the Connellys were old-world money, just who Ray was related to. "Your father is Liam Connelly? Head of the Connelly Corporation?"

Ray nodded.

"This means the woman we ate lunch with today is Christine Connelly."

Ray nodded a second time.

"*The* Christine Connelly?"

Ray shrugged. "I call her Grandma."

"I've been trying to get an appointment with your father's corporation for nearly a year now," Viv said in disbelief. He'd sat right next to one of his heroes at lunch and hadn't even realized it. She'd looked familiar, but confusion over Ray's nearness had fudged his brain. *How fucking stupid can I be?*

"Well, you can meet him at six o'clock tonight, if you want to," Ray said tentatively.

Viv stared at him. "But only if I pretend to be your boyfriend again, right? I get to meet him if I keep pretending to be gay?"

Ray shrugged. "You are a boy and you are my friend... Well, sort of... So technically we're not really lying to them, except for the whole part about us being in a relationship."

Viv continued to stare at him, thinking and weighing the pros and cons.

"I wouldn't ask you to do anything you're uncomfortable with," Ray added. "We don't have to hug or hold hands like at lunch today. Please come over to my parents' place and meet Dad once, and I swear that will be the end of things. Then I'll do anything you want. I'll stay away from you, and you will never have to see me again. I promise."

Pain shot through Viv at the thought of Ray keeping his oath.

"Okay, Ray. I'll do this on two conditions." Viv's mind had jumped into overdrive.

"What?"

"I'm not gay, but if I have to play gay then I'll play the part well, so there's no fear they'll know the truth. You need to hurry up and find a real boyfriend to take my place so we can break up. I don't like lying to people, especially those I admire and respect. And secondly, I want an interview at your father's corporation."

Something akin to true pain fleetingly washed over Ray's features, and Viv almost took back his request. But he really wanted that interview.

"So, is that a yes? I told my dad I'd let him know by three if we could be there or not. He—" Ray's phone rang in his pocket. "Hold on. It's him. I have to take this," he said before answering the phone. "Hello... Okay, I'll ask." Ray ended the call and embarrassment appeared to wash over him anew as he turned his gaze back to Viv. "My father said if you're nearly finished here, we could go there and join them now. They've decided on having a pool party and Dan is..."

"Daniel's at your parents' house right now?" Viv asked in surprise. "Why are they swimming? It's winter, for crying out loud."

"I think he's been there a couple of times with Girly. He already had board shorts there, and as to why a pool party? It's because the pool is indoors and heated."

Viv considered the situation for a moment before he stood. "Fine. Let's go."

"Really?" Ray sounded amazed.

"We'll have to stop and buy swimwear. Believe it or not, it is the one piece of apparel I don't own." Viv locked the club as they left. "We'll take the one car. It will be easier. You can follow me home so I can drop mine off."

Viv hated the fact that he was going to be lying to Liam Connelly when he wanted to get a foot in the door at the Connelly Corporation. At least Ray knew this love affair was platonic. The question remained — could Viv really act convincingly? He hoped he didn't flinch from touching Ray, especially in front of the others, but secretly he was hoping he didn't embarrass them both by trying to jump Ray's bones in front of everyone. Which, at this stage, was looking more and more like a distinct possibility.

* * * *

"The neighbors are here," Ray said as they pulled up in the parking garage. He wondered why they would be there and realized his dad would've probably been straight on the phone and gossiping with Uncle Matt, telling him that Ray had finally come out of the closet. "Sorry, I didn't know there were going to be other guests."

A second later, Viv's phone rang. They stopped long enough to answer it. Ray watched as the color drained out of Viv's face. For a moment, he thought Viv's knees were going to give out. Ray had decided to give the man some privacy when Viv hung up.

"Ray, wait," Viv said and grabbed his arm. "I think we may have another problem. Daniel told me Grace is here. She arrived on the arm of the neighbor's son. Holy fucking hell. I can't believe she's here."

"What? Who's Grace?"

"My crazy ex-girlfriend."

"Oh." Embarrassed, Ray wanted to give Viv an out if he needed it. "Would you rather leave? I'll take you home, if you want." He gestured toward the car.

Viv shook his head. "I'm not running away—not when I'm this close to finally meeting Liam Connelly—but she might call me on the whole not being gay thing. I wanted to warn you, so don't act too surprised by anything I might do to you. I mean, the worst she could ask me to do is kiss you, right?"

Ray watched him closely. He saw the war waging inside Viv. Hurt rolled through Ray when he had the confirmation that Viv fell into the second category of how people reacted when they found out who he really was—they used him for their own gain and to get closer to his father.

"Do you think you could be convincing when kissing me?" Ray blushed, but he needed to know. "Look. This is too much trouble. I should just take—" His heart started galloping as Viv stepped toward him, a look of determination on his face.

Viv didn't let him finish as he gently took Ray's face in his hands, leaned down and brought their lips together, his tongue tenderly probing until Ray let him in. Electrical shocks coursed through Ray. The moment their tongues touched, the kiss intensified. Dropping one hand and snaking his arm around Ray's back, Viv pulled him closer. Ray brought his arms up to encircle Viv's shoulders. Pushing up onto his tiptoes, Ray lost himself in the kiss.

The bag containing their board shorts dropped to the ground. Right then nothing else in the world mattered. Ray sensed Viv pulling away, so he held him closer still, letting his hands run up under his jumper and over his back. His fingertips craved the slight touch. His heart raced full speed ahead, but he didn't know whose was beating the hardest—his or Viv's. When the kiss finally ended, Viv took two steps away and looked at him in total confusion. Ray knew the other man hadn't meant for things to get so out of hand. Viv obviously hadn't intended to kiss him so thoroughly and seemed a little shocked that he was the one who had initiated everything.

To cover his apparent embarrassment, Viv cleared his throat and said, "Do you think he will be convinced?"

"Yes," Ray whispered hoarsely as he stared back, bewildered. His body was burning hot from the closeness they'd shared.

Viv took hold of his hand as they made their way around to the pool house.

Might as well get this show on the road. If they were going to convince everyone they were in love, then a kiss like the one they'd just had would leave them all believing the little ruse. Ray took a deep and calming breath as he silently wished that Viv would kiss him again. As they neared the outside entrance to the pool house, Ray's mouth still tingled from Viv's kiss. It amazed him that Viv had interlaced their fingers.

As the door came into view, Ray stopped them.

"I've changed my mind, Viv. I'll tell them the truth. You shouldn't have to pretend like this. If you still want an interview at Dad's company, I'll get you one. I'm sorry I talked you into this. Look, this is my problem, not yours."

Ray's blood heated as Viv embraced him, kissing him again. This kiss was enough for Viv to explore his mouth thoroughly. Ray vibrated with need. He suspected that Viv was only practicing in case he had to kiss him in front of the others, confusing Ray even more. It seemed more than only practicing, especially when Viv's hands started wandering again.

"I wish you wouldn't kiss me like that," he said breathlessly as they broke apart.

"Why?" Viv asked hoarsely.

Ray was having trouble thinking coherently, so he answered honestly. "Because I'm getting turned on," he whispered against Viv's chest.

He was surprised when Viv chuckled and retook his hand. "Of course you are. You're gay."

For some strange reason, that comment should have pissed him off and didn't. The first person Ray heard as they joined everyone was Girly—who didn't sound happy at all—and when Girly was unhappy, she didn't suffer in silence. She was talking to a petite blonde woman who was staring intensely at Viv and him as they held hands.

Whoa.

So, this was Grace. He would have to get the full story from Viv later, and if Viv wasn't forthcoming, then Daniel would be sure to spill the beans. Secrets were not that man's forte.

"See? I told you I wasn't lying about Viv being my dad's boyfriend. Don't they look handsome together?" Girly beamed at them both and waved.

Daniel, on the other hand, was talking to Brent, Ray's neighbor and close friend, and Daniel was ignoring Grace completely.

Ray pulled Viv toward his parents and the neighbors.

"Mum, Dad, this is my Viv," Ray said a little breathlessly. "Viv, these are my parents, Liam and Claire Connelly."

With his free hand, Viv shook hands with Ray's father. It surprised Ray when his mum kissed Viv's cheek.

"It's nice to finally meet you both," Viv greeted them. "Ray has told me so much about you."

Ray couldn't speak anymore as Viv began caressing the back of his knuckles with his thumb in a circular motion.

Liam introduced the neighbors as Susan and Mathew King before adding, "Daniel was telling me you are interested in research and development, so I thought I would invite Matt over and you two can talk. We're always looking for bright, young, new up-and-comers."

Viv nodded and answered, "Thank you, sir. That is very kind of you, but I don't want to make a nuisance of myself on your and Mr King's day off. I would be willing to make an appointment to see you at your convenience, if the offer still holds."

Mathew King started laughing. "Son, there's no such thing as a day off anymore, but if you would like to talk in more depth than we do today then call my secretary. Better yet, get young Ray to bring you in and we'll talk. I'm going overseas next week and won't be back until the beginning of August, so if you like, we'll make an appointment for soon after."

"Come on." Ray tugged on Viv's hand as soon as they had set up the meeting time and place. "Let's get changed."

They both kissed Grandma's cheek as they passed her. Ray could tell Viv was very impressed with meeting Uncle Matt and his father.

At least he gets something out of all of this, though it would have been nice if he were here because he's truly interested in me and not because he got roped into a game of pretend.

When they reached the dressing rooms, Ray didn't expect Viv to follow him inside the one he was using. Viv pulled off his clothes and stood before him, naked. Ray froze. He didn't take off his own jeans, owing to an erection, and didn't want to humiliate himself again. He also didn't want to embarrass Viv by his body's behavior.

"Aren't you getting changed?" Viv stood, holding his swim shorts in one hand, still completely naked, and apparently uncaring as he removed the tags from the item of clothing.

"I think I'll wait." Ray dropped his gaze.

Viv placed his hand under Ray's chin and tilted his head until their eyes met. "I've promised to play gay for you until you find yourself a real boyfriend and until I have my meeting, so you'd better get used to this. I mean, *this* as in us being in situations like this." Viv kissed him on the nose before he pulled on his boardies.

When he was done, Viv leaned back against the door, watching, as Ray slowly got undressed.

The awkwardness stepped up a notch when Viv added, "It's not my fault if I thoroughly turn you on." He stood smiling.

He got the feeling Viv teasing him was fun for the guy, even if it was torture to Ray.

He turned his back so that Viv couldn't see how much he was affected by his proximity. He inhaled sharply when Viv stepped up behind him, ran the palm of his hand slowly and, strangely enough, very erotically down his back and over his bare hip. His heart fluttered with desire when he heard Viv groan.

Man, I am so screwed.

Ray didn't quite understand what was going through Viv's mind as he touched him this way, and Ray couldn't help but tremble beneath his touch. He bit back a moan as Viv used his thumb to caress Ray's flesh, but it didn't stop him from breaking out in goose bumps when Viv leaned in and breathed warm air across the nape of his neck.

Ray stopped Viv's hand from sliding farther down his body. "Viv, I think you should stop, because very soon, I won't want you to."

He shivered as Viv wrapped his free arm around him and pulled his nakedness tightly back against his own body.

"You're only playing at being gay," Ray whispered hoarsely. "Remember?"

Ray couldn't understand what was happening. Why was Viv acting like this? There's no way this was all show for Grandma—she couldn't even see them. Hadn't Viv only just finished telling him no more than two hours ago that he was straight and not interested in Ray's body? This was becoming too confusing, especially when the hardness of Viv's erection pressed up against his arse.

He heard Viv sigh, then whisper, "Yes, I'm only pretending."

This only further confused Ray. Viv kissed the nape of his neck before he released his hold and leaned back against the door again.

Ray's fingers shook as he finally managed to clothe himself and tie up his shorts. "Are you ready?" he asked nervously when he realized how intently Viv had been watching him.

He got slightly flustered as Viv looked him up and down slowly then smiled. It seemed to Ray that Viv's gaze lingered on Ray's still-evident erection. Butterflies filled his stomach when Viv stepped toward him and brought their mouths together again. Ray couldn't stop his own traitorous arms from sliding around Viv's waist. Ray loved the tautness of Viv's body. He must work out a lot, as he had strong muscles in all the right places and six-pack abs that any guy would kill for. Ill at ease about his own not so muscled physique, Ray was shaking when Viv let go and took his hand.

They made their way to where Daniel and Girly were sitting on the edge of the pool. Ray sat beside his daughter.

"Hey, Dad," she said as she laid her head on his shoulder.

"Hey, Girly." He hoped she couldn't feel his shaking.

The petite blonde was still staring at them in an unsettling way. "Is she *really* your daughter?"

Ray nodded. "So her adoption papers say. Do you have some sort of a problem with that?"

She shook her head. "You seem nearly the same age."

Ray was surprised when Viv spoke up. "They are. Ray's only nine years older than Girly. Isn't that right, love?" Viv caressed Ray's cheek

All Ray could do was nod.

Emboldened, he rested his arm against Viv's lower back. To everyone else, they'd look like they were cuddling. His act was reinforced when Viv leaned into him in an intimate manner. Viv released his face and dropped his hand onto Ray's thigh, moving his fingertips gently over the pattern on his board shorts.

Ray wondered if he was even aware of what he was doing.

Someone finally introduced the girl to Ray as Grace Kennedy.

They studied each other a long time before she turned to Viv and said frostily, "So when did you decide to turn gay?"

Viv smirked at her. "The moment I first saw Ray."

Ray turned to stare at Viv and was rewarded by a misplaced kiss, which must have been aimed for his cheek, but landed right on his open mouth. More bewilderment washed through Ray as Viv's tongue sought entry. Aware that Viv wasn't going to stop until he gave in, Ray opened his mouth as the kiss intensified. This was turning out to be one fucked-up day of Ray not knowing what the hell was going on. Viv tenderly brushed his fingers over Ray's body as though seeking comfort. Ray was taken completely by surprise when Daniel pushed both him and Viv into the pool in the middle of the kiss, laughing his head off as he did.

Ray managed to get out of the way seconds before Daniel grabbed Girly and dive-bombed into the pool. Water sprayed up all over the Kings and Grandma, and they all squealed. He resurfaced, laughing.

"Sorry, guys. Sorry, GG," he added with a wicked gleam in his eye.

Daniel didn't get a chance to say any more. Viv jumped on him, dunking him under the water. "I told Mum to drown him at birth." Viv laughed. "Looks like I'll be the one to get the privilege."

Girly swam toward Ray then wrapped her arms around his neck. "That was one interesting kiss, Dad. I thought I even saw more than a little tongue involved."

Ray frowned. "He's only pretending so he could meet your pop. Don't go making more of this than it is."

She looked at him incredulously. "Sometimes you're so blind, Dad. I personally think he's just as much into you as you are him. Dan said Viv hasn't stopped talking about you since the night they had dinner at our place. That's kind of why we told GG he was your boyfriend."

Ray started laughing at the absurdity of her thoughts. "I don't think so, Girly. You're way off the mark. I think I would know a gay man if I saw one. Besides, I'm not into him," Ray lied. He knew his daughter never bought it at all.

She cocked an eyebrow. "Dad, everyone has tried to convince you about yourself, and you still refused to believe what we've been saying. The way he has been touching you is too much to be pretending. And as for the kiss, well—wow. I wish I had friends like that. And yes, you *are* into him. You're only fooling yourself if you believe you're not. You asked Dan and me if you could have him the night you finally owned up and accepted the truth about yourself. Yes, the very same night you decided it would be a good idea to drink yourself into oblivion."

"I think you're wrong," Ray said. His little voice inside his head was making itself heard. *Then why did he touch me and kiss me in the changing room where no one could see us together? And Girly's right. Those kisses seemed much too real to be pretend.*

She patted his cheek. "I know what I know."

Why is Grandma always watching? What does she know that I don't?

Their conversation came to an abrupt end when Viv came up behind Ray in the water and slipped his arms around his waist. Daniel had done the same to Girly, and Grace and Brent came to join them too. Ray thought it was a little strange how Viv and Daniel were still ignoring Grace as much as possible and she, in turn, was staring at Viv with such intensity that Ray thought Viv might burst into flames. He wanted to reach across and bitch-slap her into next week. He wanted to tell her Viv was *his*. The only thing stopping him was the truth. Viv really wasn't his—and never would be. Yep, definitely screwed.

Brent looked at Ray then Girly. "We're all going up to the lodge in August when Dad gets back from Europe. Are you guys coming? Dad and Uncle Liam reckon they're finally going to catch old Reg this time. Me? I can't see it happening, but I'm not going to rain all over their delusions."

"Old Reg?" Daniel asked curiously.

Girly giggled. "He's a mythical fish. Pop and Uncle Matt swear he lives in the lake up there. They'll spend the whole weekend fishing and catching everything but old Reg."

"Is Grandma coming?" Ray asked.

Brent nodded. "So is mine. It's her first outing after Gramps."

"We'll come. Sounds like fun. Right, love?" Viv said enthusiastically. "If there's room for us, I mean," he added then trailed his lips in gentle butterfly kisses along Ray's shoulder and up the side of his throat.

Brent, Girly and Daniel looked on in amusement as Ray tilted his head to the side to give Viv better access.

Grace fumed.

Turning, Brent called to Ray's father. "Hey, Uncle Liam, is there room for these four up at the lodge?"

Liam nodded, once. "Did you find out whether Jas, B and Josh are coming with us? I rang them and left messages, but they haven't got back to me yet. We have to give the staff up at the lodge twelve weeks' notice to make sure the place is guest free and ready for us."

"You might want to think about this for a minute, Viv," Ray murmured as he turned in Viv's arms. Not wanting the words to come out sounding like he didn't want Viv to come, he thought this might just be another added complication. Ray was still shivering in a nice way under Viv's mouth, which wasn't helping in the least.

"Don't you want me to come?" Viv asked quietly, brushing his lips up the side of Ray's throat, again making Ray tremble.

"It's not that. Come with me. Let's go for a walk." Ray got out of the pool, grabbed a towel and headed for the doors leading out onto the covered patio. They had been in the heated pool so as the air hit his wet body he instantly broke out in goose bumps. He didn't stop walking until he was far enough away that no one would overhear them talking. His grandma's attention followed them. She never missed anything.

Viv placed his hand on Ray's shoulder and turned him so they were facing. "Tell me why you don't want me to come?"

Ray thought Viv actually sounded hurt, and his heart lurched. He watched Viv for a moment.

"I don't mean it that way," he told Viv. "I would love for you to be up there with me. I thought you should know the lodge isn't just a car ride away, but a whole plane ride away. If you come, we'll be in the same room to sleep together—in the *same* bed," he emphasized. "A weekend at the lodge means going Thursday and coming back Monday. Once, a weekend at the lodge lasted two weeks. Can you leave the club for that long? And finally, you have your meeting with Uncle Matt. You don't have to keep pretending anymore. After tonight, you can go back to your life, and I'll no longer be an interruption. You can forget you ever met me." Pain rushed through Ray as he thought about never seeing Viv again.

Viv smiled. "And disappoint Grandma? I don't think so. I told you I would be your boyfriend until you find a real one." He pulled Ray into his embrace and held him close.

As strange as the situation was, Ray was comfortable with Viv's arms wrapped around him. They seemed to fit together so well and this closeness felt really nice, especially when he closed his eyes and pretended that Viv truly was his.

Ray whispered against Viv's bare chest, "Then we're going to have a problem. You turn me on too much for any good to come out of this. I think we should stage a breakup as soon as possible, with or without a real boyfriend. I don't want to fall in love with you. Neither of us needs this." Deep down, Ray already knew it was too late. He already loved Viv more than he should.

Viv didn't say anything, nor did he release Ray. They stood like that for what seemed like ages. Ray moved his face so that he was staring out over the vast lawns. He shivered as Viv caressed his back in silence. His actions felt so good, and Ray didn't want him to stop.

"Ray, we're going, and that's all there is to it."

Ray looked up as Viv spoke and was rewarded with a deep kiss. He wondered who was watching them for Viv to embrace him like this, but then didn't care as he lost himself in the moment.

Chapter Four

Viv sat on the couch smiling as he watched Ray and Girly dance. Their actions were a cross between *Swan Lake* and Muppets gone wild. Josh cranked up the music and whistled as Ray twirled Girly like a crazy ballerina. Not long after, Ray walked toward him, laughing when Daniel took over. Viv made room on the couch next to him, but disappointment ran through him when Ray opted to sit on the arm of Beth's chair and chat with her. Eventually he came to give Viv his presents to open and sat by him.

"Happy birthday, Viv."

Ray's living room, featuring a tiki bar and palm trees aplenty, had been transformed into a mock beach party—minus the sand—so they could celebrate Viv's thirty-third birthday. Ray had given him a book on David Bowie, *Moonage Daydream*, and a voucher for the music store, explaining that he didn't know what he was meant to buy a pretend boyfriend, and he hoped that what he had gotten was appropriate and not too intimate. Viv's heart melted at the thoughtful gift.

Viv placed the presents on the coffee table, pulled Ray into his embrace and held him against his body. He closed his eyes as he pressed his lips against Ray's throat.

When he opened them again, he saw Beth and Grace staring at them.

Ray tried to pull away, but Viv refused to let him go.

He whispered in Ray's ear, "I'm going to kiss you now."

It seemed like his whole body had been charged with electricity as he began to kiss Ray. Part of him didn't understand why the touch of Ray's lips affected him this way. All he did know was that he liked the feeling and wanted more. Thankfully, the shirt he wore was long enough to cover his body's reactions.

Ray's lips were doing wonderful things on Viv's, and he never wanted things to end. Ray, Girly and Daniel all knew the romance was only make-believe, but kissing Ray like this felt so real, and somehow it seemed right. More to the point, he was starting to believe that he wanted this feeling to be real. He wanted Ray to love him, and he was sure he was falling madly and desperately in love with Ray. But he had to be sure before he said anything.

"I think," Ray said as they broke apart, "I need to walk away from you now, in case I do something I'll regret, and that you might want to hit me for. I'm going outside for some air."

"What?" Viv asked curiously. The happiness inside him was so vibrant, the sensation made him wonder if his skin was aglow. A huge grin split his face while he stared at Ray's arse as he followed Ray into the backyard.

"Believe me. You don't want to know," Ray said with a grin.

Viv pinched Ray's arse as he went. "It's my birthday. The least you could do is tell me what you meant," Viv said, pouting. He caressed Ray's cheek.

Ray shook his head and chuckled. "Uh-uh, no way. I value my life too much to tell you. I've finally admitted I'm gay, so I'm allowed to think these things, but you're straight and would hate me for thinking them. Especially when I'm thinking them about *you*."

Ray stared at him with such passion that Viv blushed.

"Maybe when I have a real boyfriend, I'll tell you," Ray added, "but not now."

Viv tugged on Ray's hand as he walked over and sat on the garden bench. The weather was freezing outside, but like it always did any time he was near Ray, heat assailed him—hot, with a capital H. Ray always made him feel as though he was on fire.

"Have you found a real boyfriend yet? Or anyone with potential?" Viv asked, not sure if he wanted to know the answer.

Ray remained quiet for a long time. Finally, he replied, "I'm working on a plan. I have a date with this guy named Angus next Friday night. Actually, he's meeting me at your club so we can go out after we finish our gig. Josh set things up for me. I've talked to Angus on the phone a couple of times, and he seems okay."

Viv's stomach clenched, and he forced a smile. "Do you think you'll hit it off?"

Ray shrugged. "To be honest, I'm not really sure. Part of me is excited, but there is this other part of me that feels like I'm cheating on you."

Ray rolled his eyes at Viv's surprised look.

"Don't look at me like that," Ray added. "I know we're only pretend, and I'm a little bewildered is all.

You confuse me too. Truthfully, sometimes you confuse me a lot. I suppose once I'm actually on the date with Angus, I'll feel okay about the situation. As to whether we'll get along will depend on if he's a good kisser. I like kissing, as you probably already know. Then there's this whole other part of me that's terrified he won't even show up or that he will hate me. I'm not that good at getting close to people. I always seem to end up disappointing them somehow."

Viv watched as Ray tried to explain what he was feeling and wished there was some way he could help. He stood and pulled Ray to his feet. "Come on. Let's go back in before we both freeze to death." Viv draped his arm around Ray's shoulders as they headed back into the party.

Ray's upcoming date had given Viv a lot to think about.

"It's still okay for me to crash here for the night, right?"

Viv relaxed somewhat when Ray nodded.

* * * *

That night finally arrived. Guilt slapped him hard in the face like a jilted lover as he watched Ray on his date with Angus. Yes, he knew he should walk away and give Ray all the privacy he needed, but part of him wanted Ray to see him. He didn't quite understand why he wanted Ray to notice him, but he just did, and he had even stooped low enough as to pull some strange girl out onto the dance floor while the band played. Since he had absolutely no interest in her whatsoever, it only doubled his guilt.

I'm such a fucking arse. Ray needs to move on and I need to let him. Why can't I?

As they were dancing, Viv looked up and saw Ray watching them. Viv grinned, and Ray frowned. When the song ended, Viv led the woman back to his table and got her a drink. When he realized that Ray's gaze had never left him while on stage, he felt better. When Ray was off stage, well, that was a whole other story.

In Viv's opinion, Angus would have been classed by most people as a very good-looking bloke. He was attentive to Ray and didn't seem to mind when Ray asked him to dance – even going so far as to wrap his arms around Ray while they swayed to the DJ music during the band's break. In reality, Viv seethed, wondering what he was going to do if Ray and Angus kissed – or more to the point, what he was going to do when they decided to leave together. He couldn't exactly follow them without coming off as a stalker. Part of him was ready to run over there and rip them apart, right now.

Angus is definitely all wrong for him. Why can't Ray see that?

* * * *

As much as he tried, Ray couldn't seem to get into the mood of the date he was supposed to be enjoying. Angus was a very interesting man – a very attractive man. And Ray wanted to know more – really, he did. What stopped him from getting to know him better was that he sensed Viv watching them, and this confused and frustrated the hell out of Ray. But it was probably his fault for having the date in Viv's place of business. For some unknown reason, he felt like Viv was purposefully trying to sabotage his date night.

Girly had whispered to him that she thought Viv was jealous. There was no way possible that that was what Viv was feeling. While he danced with Angus, it felt nice, though not nice like when he had danced with Viv at home.

He couldn't help but stare at Viv, wondering who his female companion was and if Viv was planning on taking her home. The thought upset him, and tears sprang into his eyes. Furiously blinking them away before anyone noticed, he ignored the shame heating his cheeks when he realized Angus knew he was upset and had probably guessed why. His date turned and looked toward Viv as they went back to the table.

At the end of the night, Ray stood beside his car and talked quietly with Angus. Even though he knew Angus wanted to kiss him, he wasn't sure he could let that happen—mainly since he'd prefer Angus to be someone else. Someone who, at that very moment, was sitting inside probably kissing some strange girl he'd only just met tonight.

Life isn't fair.

"You're not really interested in me, are you?" Angus asked quietly.

Fiery heat crept over his face. "I'm sorry. You seem like a very nice person. It's just that—"

"That guy, the one who kept staring at you all night, is he your boyfriend? Or your ex, maybe?"

Ray shook his head. "No, Viv isn't my boyfriend. He isn't even gay." *Well, he says he's not.*

"But you would like him to be?" Angus guessed.

"Yes," Ray whispered, blushing as he finally admitted it aloud to someone who wasn't family.

Angus gently caressed Ray's face. "Well, if you ever get over him and think you might be interested, give me a call." He patted Ray's cheek before he got into his car and left.

I'm the biggest frickin' idiot. He was nice, and I let him walk away. What the hell is wrong with me? He walked back into the club. Everyone would be wondering what had gone wrong. He wasn't going to admit how pathetic he was. *Why did I just blow off someone who is probably terrific? Why am I pining after someone who will never want me like I need?*

Ignoring the table, he went to pack up his guitar and began unplugging everything. He would take the instrument with him tonight. The staff would put the rest of his gear in the storeroom for him.

"What happened, Dad?" Girly said as she helped him.

When Ray didn't answer, she guessed.

"Viv."

"I don't want to talk about it," Ray stated as he stood. Pain hurtled through him when he realized that Viv and the woman had come to join their table. His insides screamed with the need to lash out and hit someone. Ray didn't even look in Viv's direction as he said goodnight to everyone, kissing both Girly and Beth on their cheeks before heading out to his car. Tears burned in his eyes with his desire to get home, away from Viv. One way or another he was going to get Viv out of his system.

"Ray, wait."

Ray didn't turn, but sped up as he heard Viv call out to him. All he wanted was to get away before he made an even bigger fool of himself.

"*Ray*." Viv put his hand on Ray's arm to stop him from getting into the car.

Damn!

"What do you want, Viv?" Ray leaned against his Mercedes, purposely avoiding eye contact. If he looked into the man's beautiful eyes, he knew he would be begging Viv to give him something—some sort of hope.

"I wanted to see how your date went," Viv spoke quietly.

Ray stared at him for a moment in disbelief, tears again pricking his eyes. "You're kidding, right? I'm going home alone, so I guess you can figure out for yourself how frickin' well my bloody date went."

"Didn't you like him?" Viv asked.

"Yes, I liked him. Viv, I really don't think I want to talk about this with you. I'm feeling bad enough without having to relive what went wrong. You should go back in to your girlfriend. She'll be lonely," Ray said, coldly hoping that Viv would walk away and leave him the hell alone.

"She's not my girlfriend," Viv whispered, blushing as he spoke.

"Well, from where I was standing, she sure as hell looked like she was." The threatening tears finally began rolling freely down his face, and Ray was kicking himself for showing how upset he really was.

"Not jealous, are you?" Viv chuckled.

To Ray, Viv's response sounded off.

Ray took a deep breath, wiped the tears from his face, and decided to answer honestly. Viv deserved that much. "You know I am. You're not fucking stupid. You know I have feelings for you, that I care for you more than I should. I told you once before, neither of us would benefit if I fell in love with you."

"Ray—"

"I gotta go, Viv. Please, try to forget I said anything."

Viv grinned. "Don't go. Come back inside with me and I'll be your date by proxy." He took Ray's hand in his. "Come on. Let's have some fun."

Ray shook his head. "That won't help the situation. I'll only end up feeling worse, and my being there will probably piss your friend off."

"I don't care about her," Viv said, seeming discomfited. "What about if we grab some beers and go back to my place and watch movies?"

"I don't think so. I think I'd rather go home." He tried to free his hand, but Viv wouldn't let go.

"Fine, then I'll come with you," Viv said, determined.

Ray looked at him in exasperation. "What part of 'I don't think my being near you is going to help matters' don't you understand?"

"You're upset, and I'm not going to let you be alone like this." Viv caressed Ray's cheek with his free hand, wiping away the last of Ray's tears with his thumb.

"Okay," Ray snapped. "Let's go and watch damn movies, but we're going to my house." He fought the urge to smack himself upside the head when Viv grinned. Self-loathing hit him in a tidal wave as he couldn't help himself from leaning in and kissing him briefly before Viv went back inside to tell the others he was leaving with Ray.

Ray stared after Viv. *Why does he have to confuse me so damn much? Why can't I tell him no? Why does he always act like a total jerk then turn around and be so damn nice? Daniel has told me so many times that Viv usually doesn't act this way. Am I so special I bring out the inconsiderate arse in him? And yet, I'm letting him come home with me anyway. How fucked up is that?*

* * * *

Viv woke up somewhere close to dawn, still lying on the couch with Ray. After noting the way he was lying half on top of the poor guy, he flushed with mortification. Ray's face was turned in his direction, and before Viv could stop himself, the need to gently cover Ray's mouth had him giving in to his desire. He slowly slipped his tongue between Ray's lips to taste the man while he had the chance. The slight movement was enough to make Ray respond, and the kiss that followed was extremely erotic and did strange things to Viv's anatomy. He couldn't stop himself from sliding his hand down Ray's body to cup Ray's semi-hard cock, squeezing gently through his jeans. The erection fitted so perfectly into his palm, he couldn't stifle his groan.

Why does this feel so right? I'm so screwed.

Ray slept through the whole thing, even if he did moan at Viv's touch and press closer to him. Viv's heart pounded crazily as they broke apart. His breathing and heart rate seemed to take forever before returning to normal, and somewhere along the way, he drifted back to sleep, still wrapped around Ray's body.

* * * *

Ray woke when he felt movement beside him and was happily surprised to find he was still lying on the couch with Viv. Someone had covered them with a blanket, but he couldn't get up with Viv's body pinning him to the cushions. Ray heard Girly and Dan talking in the kitchen, and he moaned happily as the smell of bacon wafted out to him. His stomach rumbled in appreciation.

Viv looked so peaceful lying there asleep, his dark hair sticking up in all directions. The man really was beautiful. His skin possessed a nice tanned appearance, coming from his Latin lineage rather than from spending endless hours baking under the Australian sun. His mouth was a tad too wide but even in sleep, his lips curled up in a slight smile. Ray had never noticed before how long Viv's eyelashes really were. His nose was perfectly straight. His ears, well, they were simply gorgeous.

Ray gently ran his fingertip along Viv's jaw line and was taken by complete surprise when Viv kissed him—too bad he was asleep and missing all the fun. Ray smiled into the kiss just as Viv's eyes flew open and he jumped away.

"Don't look at me like that. You planted one on me all by yourself." Ray grinned. "The least you could do is finish the job."

Viv pushed himself up and stumbled as he got off the couch. Ray couldn't help but laugh at him.

"Can I use your shower?"

"Do you want me to wash your back?" Ray joked. He grinned as Viv blushed deeply.

"I think I can manage," Viv said.

Ray nodded as Viv fled the room before Ray picked up his phone to check his messages then stopped when he saw the picture. The grin was still there as he slipped the phone into his pocket. This one he would definitely keep. He'd have to thank Girly and Dan later.

* * * *

Two weeks later, Viv waited as everyone walked into Declan's. The only person he didn't see was the one person he was looking for.

"Where's Ray?"

"He's gone to Flashes." Girly giggled, though she seemed to be closely scrutinizing Viv's reaction. "Dad said he's tired of being the only one not getting any action, so he's gone to get laid."

At her words, panic slammed through Viv.

"Bet he chickens out." Josh laughed. "Ray wouldn't know what to do if some guy hit on him."

"Not unless he was totally pissed. Remember Marissa's twenty-first? We should go spy on him." Jasper grinned. "It's going to be frickin' hilarious watching Ray trying to hook up with someone. He's always so awkward around strangers."

"Nuh-uh," Beth said. "Ray's gorgeous. Men will be falling all over themselves to be with him." Worry filled her eyes. "I hope he finds someone nice and not a total creep or a weirdo. I wouldn't want to see him get hurt."

Viv stared at Beth, knowing she was right. Ray was too good-looking. Men and women would be throwing themselves at him. What was he going to do now?

"We are *not* spying on him," Daniel said forcefully. "Let him try this on his own. First pickups can be quite awkward. We're not going to show up there and embarrass him. He'll do enough of that by himself."

"Spoilsport." Jasper chuckled.

Viv sat listening as they joked about Ray's sex life. He wanted to tell them all to shut the hell up. He didn't like the idea of Ray picking up a total stranger. It worried him and he knew without a doubt that Ray needed someone there to watch his back in case the worst happened should he actually go home with someone. The very idea had Viv wondering if he needed to man up and explain to Ray how he felt about him and how much Ray meant to him. If Viv could be honest, Ray wouldn't be out there now looking for someone else. Although he was beginning to understand what he truly wanted, he still feared admitting it to the world. He was going to deny everything for as long as he could and hope no one found out his secret.

Viv sat for as long as he could stand it then got up and walked away, not even saying goodbye — though, as he left the club, he alerted Tony that he was leaving in case they got worried. He hoped they didn't work out where he'd gone. During the half-hour walk to Flashes, he convinced himself that he was only going to make sure Ray was okay. After twenty minutes of standing outside to work up the courage to enter the premises, he'd convinced himself that Ray wasn't interested in anyone at all.

Please don't let him be interested.

In the end, he needed help going in. Two women grabbed his hands and pulled him in after them.

One woman looked at the bouncer and said with a smile, "This one's a first-timer." She held out his hand to get it stamped.

Viv made his way over to the bar and ordered a drink. He let his gaze wander around the room, finally coming to rest on what he'd come there for. Ignoring the guy wandering over to sit next to him, and who then tried to start chatting him up, Viv only sat and watched.

Ray sat at a table with three women and two guys. They were all laughing at something the short redhead next to Ray was saying. Anger washed through Viv as one of the men caressed the whole length of Ray's arm and Ray smiled shyly at him.

That is my *crooked smile, damn it. Why is Ray smiling at someone else like that?*

An hour into Viv's vigil, the guy pulled Ray up and out on the dance floor. The sensual way they moved was like a kick in Viv's stomach, especially when Ray leaned over and kissed his dance partner.

He slammed his glass down on the bar. He had seen enough. Ray was perfectly capable of looking after himself.

"What's your problem, man?" the bartender asked angrily.

"Nothing," Viv all but shouted, not taking his tear-filled eyes off Ray. Hurt and anger coursed through him.

* * * *

Ray instantly froze the instant he looked toward the commotion at the bar. His gaze locked with Viv's, who looked so hurt. Ray stepped away from his new friend and apologized. "I'm sorry, but I have to go."

"Is he your boyfriend?"

"Something like that, but not really. Look, it's hard to explain," he said with a sigh.

The guy shrugged and went back to his friends.

Ray headed toward Viv. "What are you doing here?"

"Obviously making a huge mistake," Viv spat coldly.

Ray grabbed Viv by the upper arm and pulled him away from prying eyes. Anger flooded his system too as the words tumbled from his mouth. "I'm only doing what you told me to do. I thought this was what you wanted."

"No, Ray, this isn't what I wanted. I told you to find a boyfriend, not go and fuck the first loser who comes along."

Ray's voice rose. "And what do you expect me to do, when every time I turn around, you're there watching me? How am I supposed to find someone else when you're always in my line of sight?" he exploded. "You don't want me, but you don't want anyone else to have me! I can't keep playing pretend forever, Viv. No matter how much I enjoy what we do, I want more, and you can't give me more because you obviously still don't know what *you* want."

Viv pushed Ray who then stumbled backward into the wall. "Tonight I'll be your boyfriend. You can kiss, hug and feel me up as much as you want. I won't have sex with you in any way, shape or form, but I'll do whatever else you want. Please, don't go home with one of these losers, and tomorrow you can go back to finding a real boyfriend."

Ray heard the desperation in his voice and Ray's resolve failed. What was Viv doing to him?

"Please, Ray."

Viv's mouth was only inches away from his. Ray couldn't resist and brought his hands up to caress the back of Viv's neck and Ray kissed him.

Knowing he was losing himself in Viv wasn't exactly helping. How was he ever going to be able to have a real relationship with anyone if Viv kept stopping him?

Ray was too embarrassed to say goodbye to the people he had been sitting with. Instead, he took the coward's way out and let Viv take him home. He wanted so much from this man but deep down he understood that tonight was going to make or break their pseudo relationship.

He never once complained as he stood and watched Viv undress then clumsily do the same for Ray. If this was going to work, then Viv had to be an active participant in what was happening.

"Ray, come to bed," Viv whispered as he pulled the cover back.

The way he appeared so shy was a contradiction to how he usually was. Ray was starting to believe that this wasn't even happening. Maybe this was all just some freakish pain-in-the-arse dream that was going to break his heart more than it already had.

Goose bumps sprang up all over his skin as Viv lay back on the bed and held his hand out to Ray. The heated look in Viv's eyes urged Ray to move to him. Viv freely offered his body, and Ray wasn't stupid enough to say no—and he wasn't going to feel guilty for anything that happened tonight.

Without hesitation, he crawled up over Viv and lay flush against him. Using his knees, he pried Viv's legs apart and positioned himself between them. Rocking slowly, he pressed his erection against Viv's as he leaned down and devoured his lips. Part of him understood that this was all new to Viv. Fuck, it was new to Ray too. He'd never actually gone beyond kissing and a blow job, let alone being full-on naked and in bed with someone. The heat generating between them was like a bonfire slowly building before it went crazily out of control.

Breaking away for air, Viv labored to breathe as he locked gazes with Ray. He knew Viv was feeling the exact same thing.

"You do realize I'm going to make you come many times over before we're done here, don't you?" he ended by grinding his cock forcefully against Viv. He loved watching the way the man fought as if he was trying to keep quiet. Ray wanted Viv to be loud and scream his passion to the ceiling. He also wanted Viv to see how good things could be between them. If he did this right, then Viv would want to be with him.

Was he selfish? Maybe.

Did he care? Hell, no.

"Ray, I'm gonna..." Viv's gaze seemed to flutter all over the room as though he couldn't settle on one thing.

Ray liked the way he was affecting his lover. "I know. It's okay. Let yourself go. I will catch you when you fall."

Watching as Viv did exactly that was an amazing thing to behold. The way his eyes clenched tight as his body froze in place seconds before cum shot out of him and landed on his chest.

"Fuck... That was so hot," Ray whispered.

He dropped down to cover Viv once more and latched onto the man's neck with his mouth as he quickened his pace. He was determined to suck up a mark everyone was going to see. Viv might never admit who had done it, but at least Ray would know.

"Ray... Please..."

The way Viv was moaning was like a symphony to Ray. His body danced in time to every beautiful note. Pinpricks of heated pleasure ghosted over his sweat-slicked skin. His balls drew tighter to his body the closer he came to his orgasm. The expression 'true pleasure was like seeing the stars' must be accurate, because in the second of his release, Ray saw the whole bloody galaxy and everything beyond.

Only as he was coming back down to earth did it even register that Viv was saying his name over and over in some sort of mantra. Letting go of Viv's neck, he took the opportunity to thoroughly kiss the man. If just rubbing off against Viv was this good, he wondered what actual sex would be like — mind-blowing, for sure.

Ray went to slip to the side, but Viv held him in place. "Don't. Just stay here for a little longer."

"I'm not going anywhere. You promised me all night, and I plan on collecting." It was the truth and Ray was ready to admit to it. "I was just going to grab something to wipe us down before we stick together." As erotic as sex was, the aftermath was a little messy — it must mean they had done something right.

Viv grunted as he finally let Ray move. "I'll get it. This is my house, after all."

The way he spoke was a little confusing. If Ray wasn't mistaken, Viv had been just as into what they had just done as Ray had been. Maybe Viv was pissed off that he had enjoyed it so much.

If he's so against this, then why is his dick already trying to stand up and say hello to me. It's as if the man's body wants me, but his brain hasn't quite caught up to what's going on between us. I intend to spend a lot of quality time tonight trying to bring the two into alignment. Why would he have given me this night if he doesn't want it?

The moment Viv got near enough to touch him, Ray grabbed a hold of Viv's hips. He flashed the man a smile before leaning in enough to suck down Viv's manhood. His brain short-circuited at the flavor that hit him. Ray moaned as Viv fisted his hair and slowly thrust into his mouth. If there was anything better in life, Ray wasn't sure what it would be — right now it was being here and loving Viv.

"I'm close."

Viv's words filtered through seconds before his cum filled Ray's mouth. The taste was slightly bitter and spicy all rolled into one. As soon as Viv pulled free, Ray pushed him face first onto the bed and straddled the backs of his thighs.

"Ray, what are you...?"

"Shh, I'm not doing anything you didn't agree to." Leaning forward, he planted his hands on the bed on either side of Viv's shoulders and slowly rubbed his cock along Viv's crease. God, the man's arse was a work of perfection. He wasn't going to last. Leaning down even further, he whispered, "You're so fucking beautiful."

A tremor rolled through Viv at his words. Ray couldn't resist licking the shell of Viv's ear, making the man buck against him. That one small movement was enough to rip Ray's orgasm from his body. He collapsed on Viv's back and lay there for what felt like an eternity. The sound of Viv's breathing lulled him into sleep.

* * * *

By morning, Viv seemed a little distant and a little colder toward him. Ray straddled Viv's thighs and gave him one final, deeply tender and lingering kiss. Regret and sadness washed over him. Sighing with pent-up desire, he got out of bed, dressed, then stopped at Viv's bedroom door to look back at him still lying in bed.

"I had fun. It's a pity you can't admit the same. I promise I won't tell anyone what happened between us, so your secret's safe." Viv still hadn't said anything. "If you want, I'll stay away from you from now on, but I need you to do the same for me. I'll only come around if the family asks you to join us on something."

"You need a real boyfriend, Ray, not a one-night stand."

"What I need is none of your business, and I'll never get a real boyfriend if you keep stalking me on my dates. I meant what I said last night." Ray said it coldly, regretting his remark when he saw the wounded look in Viv's eyes.

"Ray, you're my friend and…"

"I don't need friends, Viv. I have friends. I need somebody I can make love to. Do you know how much you confuse the hell out of me? What you say you want me to do and what you really want me to do are two completely different things. Do you know our friends think you're in love with me? What a joke." He shook his head as he turned and left. When he thought about everything they had done then he thought about everything he would like to do, that's when his tears fell. Ray wanted to run back and throw himself into Viv's arms and beg to stay.

* * * *

Ray finally found the courage to go out on a proper date, which, thank God, none of the family knew about. This was only some random guy he'd met standing in line at the bank. They had gotten to talking when the guy asked if he was gay then asked him out. Ray didn't want to tell anyone, as he wasn't taking the chance of Viv finding out and ruining this date.

"Where are you going, Dad?" Girly asked when she saw him all dressed up.

Ray grinned. "Out to dinner with a friend."

"What friend?"

"None of your business." He chuckled at the look of concern on his daughter's face. "If you don't know the details, then you won't tell Dan and then Viv can't find out and ruin things."

"At least give me a first name," Girly asked.

"Tomas. His first name is Tomas." Ray grabbed his jacket and keys, leaving before she could give him the third degree.

* * * *

Ray waved when he saw Tomas standing on the corner waiting for him. Thankfully, Tomas looked genuinely happy to see him, which relieved Ray greatly.

"So where are we eating?" Ray was expecting some little out-of-the-way café, but was surprised when he was led into the Atrium Restaurant at the Hilton. The Atrium was a little more upmarket than he was expecting and Ray was glad he had dressed nicer than he normally would for the occasion.

"Ray, do you want the good news or the bad news first?" Tomas asked softly and somewhat nervously.

"Hit me with the bad first." Ray answered, though his stomach was a swirling, twisting ball of knots.

"My roommate has decided to crash our date, and he has brought some of his uni buddies. David has had a crush on me since forever and doesn't appreciate me going out with you tonight." Tomas looked uncomfortable with his confession. "I'm really sorry about this. Other than his jealousy, he's really a sweet guy."

"Then the good news would be?" Ray forced another smile.

"You look absolutely gorgeous." Tomas chuckled then winked. "Good enough to eat."

"Why don't we ditch your friends and run off somewhere quiet?" Ray whispered into his ear as they entered the restaurant. As soon as he saw the people waiting, he halted. "I don't fucking believe it."

"What?"

"See the guy over there? Please tell me he isn't your roommate." Ray pointed to the table.

"No."

Ray sighed with relief.

"The guy sitting beside him is," Tomas added, staring at Ray. "What's wrong?"

"I know one of his friends."

Anxiety nearly choked him. The fucked-up thing was that Ray had had the feeling all day that something was going to come along and screw up his night. *It'd be easier to turn around and walk away, but when have I ever taken the easy route?*

"Which one, Frankie or Chris?"

"Viv. I mean, Chris."

Tomas' smile brightened. "Well, then, I don't have to warn you he doesn't like gays, or so everyone says."

"And yet, here he is," Ray grumbled.

"Everyone, I would like you to meet Ray." Tomas held lightly to his arm as they approached the table.

Viv's eyes grew round in shock as he looked up at Ray's frown.

"Ray, what are you doing here?" Viv blurted out in surprise.

"I was under the assumption I was on a date with a very good-looking and single man," Ray all but snarled.

Tomas seemed to glow with the compliment.

David scowled at Ray. "Now you're on a date with four very good-looking men."

Glancing at David, Ray quickly returned his attention to Viv. "Yes, but there is only one man I'm interested in."

The tension around their table grew heavier as the dinner passed. Ray sighed gratefully when Frankie did the smart thing and excused himself. No need to involve anyone else in their drama. Shit-faced, and apparently pissed off, Viv threw dark looks at him all evening. Between Viv's drunkenness and David's smart-assed mouth, Ray couldn't wait to get the hell out of there. What made matters worse was that Tomas seemed just as shell-shocked as he was.

By the time he'd dragged Viv home, his own anger had resurfaced. Girly and Dan looked startled as he carried Viv inside.

"Hey, how did your— Is that Viv?" Dan asked. He got up and opened the bedroom door wide so Ray could carry Viv across the room. Pissed off to the hilt, Ray dumped Viv unceremoniously onto the bed.

"Should we ask?" Dan tried not to smile.

"No," Ray spat as he began taking off Viv's jacket, shoes and socks. Lifting Viv off the bed, he got Girly to pull down the doona.

* * * *

Ray woke in the morning with Viv wrapped around his naked body. Somewhere during the night, Viv had lost the remainder of his clothes. Pushing him away, Ray sat on the side of the bed, pissed off and very frustrated. Somehow this whole being gay thing was too hard to do. He was getting less sex now than when he was pretending to still be straight. At least then he'd had a few one-night stands, even if they had only consisted of groping and kissing. The closest he got now was the frigid naked git currently asleep on the bed behind him who kept saying he was straight but sure the hell didn't act like it.

"Ray?" Viv asked in confusion when he woke up. "How did I get here?"

Ray turned and looked at him coldly. "I brought you here because you were drunk."

"Thank you." Viv started to touch his back, but Ray stood before Viv could make contact.

"Yeah, whatever. I think you should go have a shower, get dressed, then get the fuck out of my house." Ray walked into his closet, re-emerging moments later fully dressed.

"I didn't know you were going to be there, Ray," Viv said from where he was still lying in bed. "I honestly didn't."

"But you didn't leave either," Ray spat back as he headed for the door.

"It's not my fault, Ray." Viv jumped out of bed and grabbed Ray's arm to stop him.

Ray stared at the floor for a long time before he looked deeply into Viv's eyes. "Viv, are you gay or straight?"

"I'm straight," Viv said softly.

Ray nodded, once, then he pulled out of Viv's grasp and walked away. "Don't be here when I get back. I'll stick to our agreement. I'll deal with you only when it's necessary, but other than that, I don't want to see you anymore. It's not good for me. You're not good for me."

Ray turned to leave again, but Viv threw himself into his arms and pressed Ray up against the wall.

"Don't be angry with me, Ray. Please. I promise next time if you're on a date, I'll walk away." Viv kissed him lightly.

"What the fuck are you doing, Viv?" Ray asked forcefully as Viv began pulling him back to the bed.

"Kissing and making up—what the hell do you think I'm doing?" He pushed Ray back onto the bed and lay beside him. "I really am sorry, Ray. What's going to make you feel better?" He kissed Ray again.

"*Sex*," Ray answered honestly. "Sex will make me feel better."

"Ray." Viv pulled back and frowned at him.

"I know… I know… You won't, so I have to find a real boyfriend, I'm trying… Believe me… I…" He didn't get to say any more as Viv kissed him, and Ray forgot why he was angry with the man in the first place.

The way their tongues danced for dominance was powerful, and Ray's body betrayed him, selling him off like a two-dollar hooker to the first person who came along. The longer the kiss went on, the more feral it became. It ended when Ray caught Viv's lower lip between his teeth and bit down hard enough to leave marks but without breaking the skin.

Ray shuddered as he stepped away. "We can't keep doing this."

Chapter Five

A week later, even though he was still confused over the whole Flashes night and the Tomas debacle, Ray went to see Viv.

Brent was turning twenty-seven and Ray was supposed to invite Viv to the Kings' place. Every year since they were about eight years old, they'd always had a sleepover movie night and, for this one night, they all got to be kids again.

Ray was nervous, as he hadn't seen or spoken to Viv since they'd spent the night together after his date with Tomas. He'd explained to Viv what was happening, and now he was waiting for the man to respond.

"So, you're telling me we'll basically be staying in their lounge room in sleeping bags?" Viv asked with a smirk.

"Yes, but Aunty Sue makes us party in the pool house now because we get too noisy — especially since we began having booze at them." Ray grinned at Viv's amusement. "Though now, as much as I hate to admit it, we're all soft and we use air mattresses for comfort.

If you don't have a sleeping bag, you can always share mine. I have a double," Ray joked and blushed.

As hard as he tried to stay away from Viv, there was some insane need to be near the man any way possible. His emotions acted like a yo-yo where Viv was concerned, bouncing from anger to something close to desire every time they were in the same room. No wonder Viv walked all over him the way he did. He knew he was as much to blame for this whole screwed up *faux* relationship as Viv was, yet he couldn't seem to stop himself.

"Who else is going to be there?"

"There'll be B, Jas, Girly, Dan, Josh, whatever girl he has picked up for the night, Brent, Grace, me... And you, if you want to come," Ray said as he ticked off the party members on his fingers.

"Okay," Viv said softly. "What should I wear? I mean, is it a full-on pajama party or is it normal clothes?"

"Well if you're sharing with me, then boxers. Two bodies in the one bag gets very hot. If you're sleeping by yourself then wear whatever the hell you want."

"Are you sure there isn't anyone else you'd like to take? Like maybe a date, perhaps?" Viv inquired.

"Why would you even ask that? You know damn well I haven't found another boyfriend," Ray whispered, refusing to look at him. "I'm not forcing you to come. I know with Grace being there, things will be awkward for you, but I would like you to at least think about it. But if you don't want to come, I'll tell everyone we broke up. I'll even call and ask Tomas if he wants to go. Maybe trying a second date would be good."

Viv got up, walked over to Ray and placed his hands on his shoulders. Using his thumbs, he gently caressed the sides of Ray's neck, and Ray cursed himself as he leaned into the touch.

"I already said I would go, Ray." Viv smiled.

"Okay, then I'll see you tonight." He pulled away from Viv and made a hasty retreat.

* * * *

Ray knew he was a glutton for punishment when he saw Viv enter the party without bringing a sleeping bag. He wanted to cheer when Viv willingly climbed in his bag beside him. Viv had even taken the time to change into boxers. As hard as this was, deep down, he realized he was a sucker where Viv was concerned. Although his brain said no, his heart said yes. In fact, his heart had already claimed Viv. Ray understood that he was the one who was going to be hurt in the end.

During the third movie, Ray moved enough to get comfortable and wound up with a sleeping Viv with his head on Ray's chest. Viv was gently snoring and draped around Ray's body. Ray tenderly wrapped his arms around him, confirming his previous decision that he liked the feeling of being this close to Viv a little too much. His heart raced out of control as he kissed the top of Viv's head. Glancing across the room, he had to smile at Beth who was watching them with something akin to amusement.

As the night wore on, Ray began feeling uncomfortable when he realized Grace kept staring at them. By the look on her face, she was fuming. The hatred poured out of her and all of her fury was aimed at him. It was so tangible he was drowning under the intent behind her emotion.

* * * *

When the end credits finally began to roll up the screen, Viv woke with a start, but relaxed when he realized where he was, snuggling closer to Ray. Ray whispered into his ear about Grace. Instead of answering, Viv hugged Ray close, bringing their mouths together in a gentle kiss. Ray shivered as Viv hooked his leg around him and held Ray in place. It reminded Viv of the Flashes night, except this time he was holding Ray and they both had some clothes on.

As the others got up to stretch their legs during the break, Viv didn't immediately let Ray go. He froze when Ray slid his hand into the waistband of Viv's boxers and cupped Viv's arse, drawing him closer still. The motion had a very swift reaction on other parts of his body. *How is it Ray can make me instantly hard? It's like my body has morphed back to a teenager's with my first full-on crush. If I'm not careful, I'm going come in my pants.* He wondered if Ray realized he was actually feeling him up as well, since Ray was so engrossed in what he was doing.

"I'm sorry," Ray whispered, pressing his lips against Viv's shoulder and sliding his hands back out. "This is a mistake. You can have the sleeping bag, if you want. I'll use a blanket."

"Don't be an idiot, Ray. This was an accident. I know you didn't mean anything by it," Viv said quietly. He willed his body to stop reacting before Ray worked out how much he had actually been turning him on. Kissing Ray wasn't supposed to give him an erection, so why did he have this problem every single time they touched?

"Liar. You know I totally meant to feel you up," Ray whispered low so the others wouldn't hear. Before he backed away, he added in a louder voice, "I'm going for a leak before they put the next movie on."

"I think I'll join you."

Grace was still watching them, so Viv held Ray's hand as they walked outside. He wanted her to get the hell over whatever was running through her mind. Viv knew her mental gears were cranking and soon they would find out what she was really up to. Not for one moment did he actually believe she was still interested in Brent. Anyone with eyes could see she wasn't fully committed. She was definitely scheming something, and he hoped like hell that neither he nor Daniel was in her sights.

Before they got back into their sleeping bag, they made hot chocolate with marshmallows. Girly complained loudly and repeatedly when she was forced to get up and make her own. As they got comfortable, Viv wrapped his arms around Ray and held him against his side so they could have more practice at kissing, if the opportunity arose. Viv assured Ray that this was only because of Grace. Ray didn't seem to believe him. Viv couldn't bring himself to complain as Ray let his hands roam over Viv's body. Strangely, he was somewhat disappointed when Ray kept away from his more intimate areas. Well, most of the time he did. Sometimes the temptation for Ray was apparently too hard to resist.

When Viv felt uncomfortable, which was code for 'I'm getting way too turned on here', he turned so Ray was spooning him. Ray rested his hand lightly on his hip, and when he was sure Ray was asleep, he took hold of that hand and pulled Ray's arm around him. He bit back a whimper when Ray's erection pressed against his arse—though a smile graced Viv's lips as he drifted off to sleep.

Viv woke some time later to the sound of Ray's ringing phone. He answered it before the noise had a chance to disturb Ray or any of the others as they slept. Ray moaned as he snuggled back into Viv's side.

"Hello. Ray's phone. This is Viv speaking," Viv whispered into the cell. He tensed when he recognized the voice on the other end of the line.

"No, Tomas, Ray isn't available to come to the phone, or to breakfast." Viv turned enough to gaze at Ray as he listened to Tomas' request. "I think you should know that right now he's lying in bed wrapped around my body. Ray's mine and you need to get over him." Viv said it coldly and hung up.

Viv put Ray's phone back down beside them, totally shocked by what he'd just done. What was Ray going to say the next time Tomas called him? How much was Ray going to hate him for what he'd told Tomas? Viv moved his arm enough so he could hold Ray closer as he lay there and worried if he had ruined their friendship.

I am so fucked in the head sometimes. Fuck! Why can't I learn to shut my mouth and let things go? What right do I have screwing with Ray's life?

The longer they lay there, the more guilt ate at Viv. What the hell was happening to him? He swore to himself then and there he was going to stay away from Ray and let the man move on like he wanted to. Then a little nagging voice in his head laughed at him and said, 'Yeah, right. Like hell you will'.

* * * *

Ray looked up from the pictures he was going through and smiled as Jasper and Beth walked in and collapsed on the couch beside him.

"Your grandma says hi. She also said to tell you to stop being a slack arse and go visit her—and bring your nice, young man," Beth said with a smirk.

"So how's the pretend relationship working out for you?" Jasper asked as he tossed Ray a beer from his Esky.

"We hardly ever see each other"—Ray shrugged—"so he isn't interested in seeing me other than when he has to. The last time we were actually in the same room was at Brent's party. For the last couple of weeks, he's either been busy or he is avoiding me."

Beth watched him curiously. "Have you fessed up to being in love with him yet?"

He shook his head and smiled shyly. "That's our secret. He doesn't want to believe the words. I've told him often enough, but he thinks I'm only joking around."

"Has he fessed up to being in love with you yet?" Jasper asked as he sipped his beer.

Rolling his eyes at his best friend, he explained, "It's not like that for him. Viv only agreed to be my pretend boyfriend so he could get an interview at Dad's company. That's all. Besides, why would I want to be with someone who would willingly use me that way?" Ray was really beginning to think they were right. He added, "He doesn't want to be gay."

"That's bullshit, Ray, and you know it! In the last three months whenever you two are together, he gets too into you for this all to be pretend. Look at how he was at Brent's party. I didn't need X-ray vision to see his hands and mouth were all over you. I bet he's as much into you as you are him. There is no way in hell any straight man would kiss a gay man like he's been kissing you. I know I bloody well wouldn't, and you're my best friend," Jasper replied.

"Girly and Dan think so as well," Ray confided, "but I still think you're all wrong. Viv's only doing this for his own reasons, like the job at Connelly Corporation. He keeps asking me if I've found a real boyfriend yet. That doesn't sound like the actions of a man who's interested in me."

"Have you?" Beth asked.

Ray grinned. "If I have a real boyfriend then Viv will stop pretending, so why would I even bother? I'll keep on enjoying things while they last, though I do have other options in case everything goes down the crapper."

"Other options? With who?" Jasper and Beth asked simultaneously.

Ray grinned and shook his head. He'd forgotten that only Girly, Daniel and Viv knew he'd been seeing Tomas. "Just a friend," he answered.

Beth picked up the pictures scattered across the coffee table. "What's all this?"

"I've been reminiscing. Girly's all grown up now, and I kinda miss having a little kid around to dote on," he confessed as he took a photo of a nine-year-old Girly and smiled fondly.

"Do you think you'll ever have more children?" Jasper asked.

"I'd love a heap more. I loved everything about being a father," Ray mused. "But I doubt I'll ever get my wish. Kinda gay now, remember?"

"Being gay doesn't stop you from having more kids. You could always adopt or get a surrogate mum," Beth said, replacing the photos on the coffee table in a neat pile.

Jasper burst out laughing. "I can see the headlines now—Gay Man Seeks Fertile Woman to Have His Babies."

"You would be surprised at how many women would put their hands up, especially if there was a picture of Ray in the ad. He's kinda gorgeous."

"Thank you, B. I think you're pretty gorgeous too. Girly offered to carry one for me, but I thought that was a little too weird. I could see those headlines— 'Girl Gives Birth to Her Own Sibling. How long do you think it would take before I wound up in jail?"

"I think it's hilarious you're talking about being a father and having more kids when you're still a virgin." Jasper ducked as Ray threw a cushion at his head.

"I'm not a virgin, you fucking idiot. B was my girlfriend long before she became your wife."

Jasper laughed. "I tend to forget. I block out those mental pictures, but thanks for giving them all back to me."

Ray leered. "Any time, arsehole."

Beth joined in the teasing. "You know, even back then I had begun to think you were gay. In English, you would stare across the classroom at Harley... What the hell was his last name?"

"Dunne." Ray snickered. He hadn't thought about Harley Dunne in years. "I used to worship that guy. I didn't realize back then I had a crush on him. I wonder whatever happened to him."

"Who cares? He wasn't cool enough to hang with us anyway. Have you forgotten how mean he was?" Jasper asked.

Beth spoke softly, "We went and had all our tests done yesterday."

Ray had known B and Jas had talked about being tested to see if something was wrong with either her ovulation or Jas' sperm count. His friends had been trying to conceive for the last couple of years with no luck.

Reaching out, he took Beth's hand. "What did they say?" He hoped the news wasn't bad.

Jasper's face fell. "The doc says I might be shooting blanks."

"We get the results back in a few weeks, so there's always hope." Beth smiled at her husband as she used her free hand to squeeze his hand in comfort.

Ray raised his beer bottle. "Here's to hope."

"Hope," both Beth and Jasper said at the same time, as they raised their glasses.

"Where's Girly?" Jasper asked.

Ray shrugged. "Probably out with Dan and Viv. She hangs out with them a lot now. She has thrown me over for someone better looking. Well, two someones who are better looking." He shook his empty beer bottle and indicated for Jasper to throw him another one.

Beth watched Ray for a while. "Hon, I think you should think about finding a new boyfriend. Since Mr Green Eyes came into your life, you have been drinking way more than you used to."

Ray stared at her and said, "Seriously? I finally admitted my whole life has been a fucking lie. I was kinda freaked when you all forced me out of the closet. So what if I'm trying to drown the part of me that still wants to hide who I am from the rest of the world."

"All right!" she groused. "Calm down. Geez Louise, I was just saying is all."

Ray looked chagrined. "Sorry, B. I didn't mean to take this out on you. I'm still confused by some of the shit going on in my life right now."

"And we all know what that is," Jasper mumbled into his beer bottle, before adding 'Turn up the radio. Let's take this party to a whole new level."

They were in a middle of a game of 'Name That Song' when Girly, Dan, and Viv entered the room. Viv walked straight over, sat beside Ray and kissed him. Ray was a little shocked when Viv grabbed his beer out of his hand and took a mouthful, before handing the bottle back. Ray turned Viv's face as he saw Beth approaching with the camera. She'd obviously been looking through his room again. Every time he hid the camera in a new spot, she always found it. As she went to take their photo, Viv moved so he was closer to Ray then wrapped his arms around Ray's shoulders. Ray laughed as Viv snuggled in, making the peace sign.

The smell of pizza filled the air. Someone had turned the radio low as they all sat around the living room chatting. Viv was so attentive, and in some ways, it confused the hell out of Ray. As the night progressed, Ray saw that everyone was having fun. He also realized they were all watching how tender Viv was with him. He wondered if they were just as confused as he was.

Ray was a little nervous, but mostly amazed when he woke up in the morning to find he wasn't alone in his bed. He was beginning to get a little too comfortable with this habit of randomly waking up with Viv beside him. Even though he'd promised himself he'd never go there again, he had gotten the idea stuck in his head that this time was different. Last night Viv was the one who again had chosen to share. He had practically dragged Ray to the bedroom the moment Jasper and Beth had gone to sleep in one of the spare rooms.

Ray shivered at the lack of blankets. He looked down toward the end of the bed where they'd kicked the quilt, saw that he and Viv were once again starkers—and smiled. Viv lay beside him with his hand on Ray's crotch so his fingertips were resting in his pubic hair. Viv woke up with a start, and Ray quickly closed his eyes, pretending sleep. He was determined to give the man an easy out if he needed it.

Ray could hardly keep still when, instead of removing his hand, Viv gently fondled Ray for a few moments. Viv's breathing grew ragged and his erection tapped against Ray's thigh. Ray almost jumped off the bed when Viv turned his face enough to kiss his shoulder. His bed partner was so close, yet still so far out of reach. Ray found it difficult to breathe as images claimed him of Viv waking up and taking Ray to the outer limits of space and back as Viv pounded him through the mattress. The very thought overwhelmed his senses.

This was going to lead to heartbreak and depression—mainly for Ray—though he wondered what was going through Viv's mind right now. Ray stirred slightly, and Viv quickly removed his hand, pulled the blankets up over them, and rolled away from Ray who pretended he knew nothing about what had occurred. He stretched then got up and headed for the shower, fully intending to finish the job Viv had started.

* * * *

Viv opened his eyes and stared at the ceiling when he heard the shower start in the other room. He was fucking stunned by what he had just done. Why did he keep touching Ray intimately? What would he have done if Ray had woken up mid-grope? He knew the answer. Ray had hardened beneath his touch, and Viv liked the feeling. This was different from being with a woman. What did this all mean? Was he now leaning toward homosexual tendencies because he had pretended to be gay for the last three months? Hanging out with Ray was starting to screw with his brain, and the strangest part was that he was the one who always came looking for Ray. Viv desperately wanted to remain straight, but the thought of Ray now naked only a few feet from him was making his body react in strange ways. He knew he'd soon find more excuses to wind up naked and in bed with Ray with every intention of touching him again. Viv wished he'd participated more the night he'd given Ray free rein of his body, and he would have liked to have the guts to get up and join him in the shower now too.

Ray smiled at him as he emerged with a towel wrapped low on his hips, and Viv's heart fluttered.

"Shower's free. The towels are in the cupboard under the sink."

Viv nodded as Ray walked into his wardrobe to dress. Viv got up and headed for a cold shower—well, as cold as the weather would allow. He needed to get Ray out of his head. Ray re-entered the bathroom as Viv stepped into the stream of water.

"There are new toothbrushes in the second drawer and help yourself to my clothes. Dan usually does."

Viv could only nod as Ray proceeded to brush his teeth before leaving. After lathering up and rinsing thoroughly, Viv shut the water off, dried himself, dressed then headed downstairs. By the time he reached the kitchen Girly, Daniel and Ray were in the middle of making breakfast.

"Hey, that's my favorite shirt," Ray exclaimed with a mock pout.

Jasper and Beth both sat at the kitchen table telling stories about some of the gigs and things they had done over the years. Viv listened as Daniel asked how they had gotten together, and Ray answered.

"Funny enough, we were up at the lodge, and B and I were going out at that stage. We were all sitting there talking, and Jasper stands and announces to everyone he was going to marry my girlfriend."

"What?" Daniel leaned forward, obviously eager to hear the rest of the story.

Viv felt the cold rush of jealousy run through him as he stared from Ray to B and back again.

"Well, B looks at him and says, 'Jas you're an idiot'. And they have this huge rip-roaring argument in front of our whole family, as well as the Kings. Everyone started taking bets on the outcome. Then, at the end of the fight, she agrees to marry him and moves all her stuff into his room," Ray reminisced. "I won two hundred bucks off Josh that day."

"When did this happen?"

"Dad was twenty-three at the time," Girly explained, "so four years ago."

Viv asked, "Didn't you get angry at them? How long had you been going out?"

"I think about three years?" Beth estimated.

Ray nodded.

"Even back then he was gay," she said. "He just didn't know it. He didn't get angry, and he loved us both very much, so he ended up being our best man at the wedding."

"Did you two ever...?" Daniel wiggled his eyebrows.

Beth burst out laughing. "Of course we did. Ray was my boyfriend in every sense of the word. I enjoyed every minute. He was very gentle and sweet." She ended with a dramatic sigh.

Viv itched to reach across the table and slap the affectionate look off her face.

"Would you bloody stop putting the freaking mental pictures in my head? I suffered for four years to get rid of them. I don't want them back—ever!" Jasper hit the side of his head.

Ray laughed.

Frowning, Viv sat as he watched Beth get up and wrap her arms around Ray's waist. She leaned against his back, and again jealousy ran through him at the intimate scene. He wanted to tell her to get away from Ray. She was married, for Christ's sake. Why couldn't she keep her hands off the guy who wasn't her husband?

"Remember when we used to sneak out and go skinny dipping in the lake near the lodge?"

Ray only smirked, but Jasper burst out laughing.

"Remember when Grandma caught us and we thought she was going to go off?" Jasper said.

"What did she do?" Daniel asked.

Viv shook his head. Daniel would drop everything to listen to a good story.

Girly started laughing so hard she nearly fell out of her chair. "She stripped and joined us."

"No way." Daniel gasped.

"If you don't believe me, ask her. She'll tell anyone who will listen. Skinny-dipping at seventy-three was a huge delight for her."

"Dad and Mum weren't as impressed when she told them, though. They wanted to ground the lot of us." Ray cackled.

"Except me. You said I was your daughter, and you would be the one to decide whether I got grounded. And because you were also skinny dipping, you didn't think I should be punished." Pride resided in Girly's voice. "I was fourteen, so this was all kind of sexy, especially looking at Josh, Jasper and Brent. They were the only other guys I had seen naked besides Dad. Actually, come to think of it, I've seen those guys naked a lot over the years. I should find that disturbing, but somehow they were like three overprotective big brothers."

"Maybe we should go skinny dipping when we go up next time. And maybe Grandma will even join us again." Jasper guffawed.

When the time came for them all to leave, Ray stood at the front door and began hugging and kissing everyone's cheek as they passed him. When Viv got to him, Ray hesitated for only a moment before his lips aimed for Viv's cheek but Viv turned into the kiss, holding lightly to Ray's waist as he did. Viv sighed when Ray gently pushed on his chest and stepped away.

He knew Ray had feelings for him. The conversation he'd had with Ray the night of and the morning after Flashes kept running through his head. Also, Ray was always telling him to stop when things got too heated between them as he was getting turned on. The main giveaway was that he still hadn't tried to find a real boyfriend. It didn't matter that Viv wasn't really letting him try. Whenever anyone had ever shown any interest in Ray by asking Viv about him, he told them Ray was already in a serious relationship. This always made him feel bad afterward, but he just didn't think they were Ray's type. He kept telling himself he was only looking out for his friend—even if it was a big, fat lie.

Man, life sucks!

Viv looked back and waved as Ray and Girly watched them drive away. Part of him wanted to go back, take Ray into his arms and announce to everyone that he wasn't pretending. But he still wasn't sure if he was lying.

Daniel looked at him and smiled. "I didn't think I would ever see the day you would willingly climb into bed with another man. You've slept with him, what, five times now? Maybe there's more to this pretend relationship than you're letting on. So, did anything happen I should know about? Also, the goodbye kiss you gave him looked really intense."

"Do you honestly think I would tell you? And the kiss was nothing. We were practicing for the lodge." Viv shook his head. He didn't want to correct Daniel. Ray had kept his word, so no one knew about the Flashes night, and there was no way Viv was going to tell them.

Chuckling, Daniel continued. "You won't, but Ray and Girly don't have secrets, so he'll tell her and she'll tell me, and I'll find out eventually. So you might as well tell me now and save us all the hassle."

"Nothing happened. There. Are you satisfied? He's still gay, and I'm still straight." Though now he worried if Ray truly had kept his promise.

"Oh, well, maybe when you share up at the lodge."

"Not going to happen. I'm not interested in his body," Viv lied, staring out of the window so he didn't have to meet Daniel's gaze.

"Sure you're not. You always wrap yourself around every naked man you happen to be sleeping with," Daniel teased.

Viv growled at him, and Daniel quickly changed the subject.

* * * *

As they closed the door, Girly rounded on her father. "Dad, you can be a real nong sometimes."

Ray looked at her, perplexed. "What have I done now?"

"Viv practically threw himself at you all freaking night and you completely ignored him. Even when he went and hopped into bed with you again, both of you as naked as the day you were each born, I reckon you still woke up a gay virgin." Girly patted his cheek. "Dan thinks the whole thing's hilarious. Viv supposedly doesn't like gays, and now he's falling in love with you. His preferences are obvious to us all. Though why he wouldn't like gay people is beyond me, seeing as his brother is bisexual. I know everyone says it's true, but I don't believe that for one minute. I think people just don't know the real Viv."

Ray's heart fluttered as he stared at her. He wished with all his heart that she was right. "No, he's not. I keep telling you, as soon as he has his interview and gets his job, this is all over. I can lust after him all I want, but I'll still get nowhere. He doesn't want me in that way. He's already told me he isn't interested in my body. You can't get much clearer than that."

Ray was going to comment on the fact that he wasn't a gay virgin at all, but somehow he didn't think blow jobs and hand jobs were really classified as sex, so he kept his mouth shut. There was no way he was discussing that part of his life with his daughter—some things were better left unsaid.

"Uh-huh, then why was he holding your dick when I looked in your room this morning?"

"What?" He decided to pretend to know nothing about it. "When I woke up, he had his back to me. Why the hell were you in my room anyway? Haven't you ever heard of a little thing called privacy?"

Girly laughed. "Whatever. I know what I saw, Dad. His hand was in your crotch."

"Damn, wish I'd been awake for that." Ray laughed as he made the joke. "It would have made my day. Was he awake?"

"No," she conceded. "But nothing changes the fact of what I saw."

"Well, next time—if I'm so lucky—I'll try to be awake and see for myself, or you can wake me up."

Chapter Six

Ray knocked gently on the door of Viv's office and smiled as Viv looked up. They needed to move on since their pseudo relationship was nearly at an end. Ray wanted to put the past wounds behind them and pondered if they could turn their *faux* love affair into some sort of friendship, seeing how Girly and Daniel seemed to be getting serious.

"Hey, I was wondering if you're free for lunch?" Ray asked.

"What, you and me?" Viv said rudely.

Ray nodded and blushed as he realized he was about to make an idiot out of himself all over again, but he couldn't stop himself from talking.

"We can invite other people to join us. I thought it might give us a chance to talk before we go to the lodge next week. We've supposedly been going out for three months now, so maybe we should actually learn a bit about each other in case someone asks us a personal question." When Viv didn't answer, Ray got even more nervous. "If you want, we don't have to do lunch. We could talk about things here. You don't have to be seen in public with me if you think someone will get the wrong idea."

Still silent, Viv stared at Ray as though he'd just had the stupidest idea in the world. Ray shook his head and turned to leave. He didn't realize how being alone with him was going to be too much for Viv to bear. The fucked-up thing was that this seemed to be in total contradiction to the way Viv acted when they were around family, or when they were completely alone with no chance of anyone walking in on them. Sometimes his pretend relationship was too confusing to work out.

"Sorry I mentioned it. We don't have to talk. No one will ask us anything anyway, and if they do, we can wing it. I'm gonna go now and let you get back to your day," Ray ground out.

Ray left, feeling like a complete loser and a total freak. So much for everyone's theory that Viv was into him. He wondered what they would say if they'd witnessed that little scene.

Pulling out his phone, he called someone who *would* like to be seen with him.

Viv caught up with him at the front door. Ray noticed how Viv made sure not to touch him in case the staff, Tony, Alli or Jeff were watching. Ray kept right on talking and making dinner arrangements with Tomas. He needed to be honest with Tomas and set him free. In all of this, he realized he was doing the same thing to Tomas that Viv was doing to him — stringing him along. However, if possible, he would like to try to keep Tomas as a friend.

The moment he placed his phone back in his pocket, Viv spoke.

"Sorry, Ray. I was rude. Of course we can go out somewhere for lunch."

When he stepped outside with Viv, Grace drove around the corner and into the parking lot. Upon seeing Viv with Ray, she glowered as she got out of her car. Ray wanted to ask her what the hell her problem was, when Viv leaned closer so only Ray could hear.

"Now it's your turn to play gay for me. Whatever happens, please don't leave me alone with her. I'll explain later." His mouth lingered on the skin behind Ray's ear and Ray smiled.

Ray shivered as Viv ran the tip of his tongue along the edge of his lobe.

"What can we do for you, Grace?" Viv said coolly, still a little confused by his own reaction to Ray's nearness. The feeling usually wasn't this strong. He placed his arm across Ray's shoulders as Ray slid his around Viv's waist and leaned against his chest. Since the doors to the club were solid steel, Viv wasn't worried about being seen by any of his staff.

"I thought, if you weren't busy, we could have lunch." She spoke only to Viv, ignoring Ray completely.

He shook his head. "Sorry, but we already have other plans."

"Can't you change them?" She smiled sweetly.

He frowned. "Well, I could, but honestly, I don't want to. I could spend the next couple of hours talking to you, or spend those same couple of hours naked in bed with Ray and actually enjoying myself. Now which do you think I'm going to choose?" Viv snorted.

As though to piss her off even further, Ray brought his mouth up and nibbled on Viv's ear, probably to repay him for earlier. It brought a smile to Viv's face.

"Hold that thought until we're home, baby," Viv whispered against Ray's flesh.

Viv didn't wait for a reply as he steered Ray toward his car. Ray got in behind the wheel then he waited for Viv to walk around and climb into the passenger seat before asking where they were really heading. Viv kissed him again, knowing Grace was still watching them. He gave himself over to the kiss, enjoying every moment as Ray explored his mouth, and he wished this could last forever. Ray was a fantastic kisser.

When they finally parted, Viv apologized. "I know I'm treating you like a fucking toy. I'm sorry you have to put up with all my shit."

Ray smiled brightly and asked again, "So where are we really going?"

"To your place. I wouldn't put it past the bitch to follow us. She's been known to do crap like that before." Viv studied Ray. "Don't nibble my ear again. I'm ticklish."

Ray grinned, and Viv reached across to tug playfully on Ray's earlobe.

Ray wasn't surprised to find Girly and Daniel there, but his insides thrashed around as his daughter and her boyfriend stared at him and Viv. Ray quickly explained the scene outside the nightclub and, with each word, his anxiety grew to epic proportions. They had only been inside for about ten minutes when the doorbell started ringing crazily.

Viv shook his head. "That'll be her."

Dumbstruck, Ray stared. "She wouldn't really barge in here, would she?"

"Yep, I told you. She's done this before."

"She, who?" both Girly and Daniel said together.

"Grace," Viv answered angrily. "She wanted to have lunch with me, but I told her I couldn't since I was going to be too busy having sex with Ray."

"Well, in that case, you two go have sex, and I'll answer the door. Make sure you strip down to make things nice and convincing now." Girly winked at them.

Daniel smiled then his face became hard as he headed to the front door with Girly.

Ray appeared shell-shocked as Viv grabbed his hand and dragged him the whole way to his bedroom, leaving the door ajar so everyone could hear what was being said. As soon as he heard Grace's high-pitched and irritating voice, Viv began stripping.

"Well, are you joining me or not?"

Viv frantically helped Ray pull off his clothes. They climbed into the bed, pulling the doona across enough to be obvious still that they were both bare-arsed with Ray lying on top of Viv.

"Why are you smiling?" Viv asked quietly.

"It's not every day a good-looking and very sexy straight man strips us both naked, jumps willingly into my bed and asks me to feel him up—even if this is pretend. And you've done it how many times now? So don't get angry with me when I get turned on and come all over you."

"Shut up, Ray," Viv said as he pulled him down onto his chest.

Ray snickered as Viv kissed him, hard. He needed some way to shut the man up before he begged him to do just that.

The way Ray shivered when he ran his hands lightly over his skin was erotic. Viv slid his hand slowly down Ray's back and cupped his arse cheeks, squeezing gently. Ray moved so he was kneeling between Viv's thighs, and Viv wound his legs around Ray's waist, holding him in place. Viv's eyes widened when he felt exactly how turned on Ray really was. The steel rod pressing against his cock was doing wonderfully wicked things to his insides. Every ounce of heat his body held immediately hurtled through him to pool in his groin. He whimpered with each little movement Ray made.

Viv broke the kiss and whispered, "Get ready, but be careful where you stick that thing." He pushed up into Ray's crotch. He bit his lip to keep from moaning aloud when Ray mimicked the gesture.

Ray grunted. "It didn't seem to worry you after Flashes." He pretended to thrust gently, as though they were making love. Ray focused his gaze on Viv's full lips. And Viv poked his tongue out at his friend.

"You're a very beautiful man, Viv," Ray whispered.

Just as they started kissing again, the bedroom door flew open with enough force that it bounced off the wall. Grace stood in the doorway glaring at them, followed very closely by an irate Girly. A smiling Daniel took in the scene. Viv knew his brother would give him the third degree later.

Not for the first time, Viv didn't want to stop kissing Ray, nor did he want to interrupt the way Ray was grinding against him, even if only long enough to look in frustration at the three intruders. Viv pushed himself up onto his elbows as he spoke to Grace. The doona slipped sufficiently and flashed Ray's bare arse.

"What? Didn't you believe I was taking Ray to bed?" Viv sneered. "You should remember from when we were together I'm not a liar. Now if you will get the hell out, I'd like very much to get back to what we were doing." He turned his attention back to Ray's lips. He pulled Ray closer to him as Daniel and Girly dragged Grace out of the room.

As soon as they heard the door close, Ray went to pull away, but Viv took another long moment to end their kiss before he was ready to let go. Moving to lie on the bed next to Viv, Ray didn't complain when Viv rolled toward him and placed a hand across Ray's chest, fingertips caressing him gently.

"We'll stay here for a bit. Daniel will let us know as soon as she's gone," Viv said as they heard screaming from the other room.

"Are you going to tell me what all this was about?" Ray asked.

Viv frowned, trying to work out how to tell his story without sounding like a complete moron for the way he'd allowed Grace to treat him. "Grace has been my on and off girlfriend a lot over the last six years. It never works, and she causes me a lot of heartache, but every time she wants me back, she smiles and I'm stupid enough to let her back into my life—only to have her fuck with me again."

"So, you think pretending to be gay with me is going to solve your problem with her?" Ray asked quietly.

"No. There's no solution, but this allows me enough time to work out how to be strong enough to say no. I can't go back there again," Viv said honestly.

His voice sounding a little odd, Ray said, "If you keep caressing my nipple with your fingertips, you won't be pretending to be gay anymore. You'll have turned me on so completely I'll have no other option than to ravish your very beautiful and extremely sexy body."

"Oops! Sorry." Viv let go as he pushed himself up, leaned against the headboard and gestured for Ray to join him. "I'm sorry if I made you uncomfortable by pretending with me, but I couldn't think of anything else to say to make her leave me alone."

"I'm not uncomfortable. A little turned on maybe. Actually, right now I'm a lot turned on," Ray replied. "I love being gay with you. I know you're probably feeling a little out of sorts about being here like this. Dan told Girly how you don't like gays, and even Tomas warned me about the same thing. But why would you, seeing as Dan is bi." Ray frowned in thought. "Don't you get freaked out by how much we end up kissing and hugging or by how often we wind up naked together in bed?"

Viv thought for a moment. "Strangely, I don't mind it. You're a good kisser, though the naked part I could do without."

Ray chuckled. "Thanks. So are you. Sometimes I think you're a little too good. I kind of like being able to talk honestly with you this way. It makes things easier, if that makes sense."

Viv nodded. "So let's talk about us. What deep dark secrets are you going to tell me in case someone asks when we're on the family vacation?"

"What, besides the fact I'm madly in love with you?" Ray fanned his face as he joked. "I don't know. What do you want to know? I guess I'll start with the obvious, I suppose."

So Ray began telling Viv all his likes and dislikes, about all the things he wanted to accomplish in his life. He told him about Isobel and about raising Girly. At some stage during the telling, Viv took hold of his hand. He listened as Ray told him how fucked up he'd been when he was finally forced out of the closet by their friends.

"Didn't you ever think that maybe you were entitled to be happy?" Viv asked. He couldn't understand how

Ray had managed to keep that side of himself hidden for so long. Or maybe he was just grateful that he wasn't the only one who was doing so.

Ray shook his head. "I blocked it all out and refused to take notice of my own wants. When I saw you for the first time, it blew everything out in the open. I couldn't take my eyes off you, and apparently everyone saw exactly what I was feeling," Ray admitted. "They staged an intervention to yank me kicking and screaming out of the safety of the closet where I was happily living in denial. I can tell you I took things really hard, then when my mum and dad were accepting, I realized I was finally free to be me." He squeezed Viv's hand. "Why don't you tell me about you now?"

Taking a deep breath, Viv slowly began telling Ray all about himself—how he didn't get on with Daniel's father, so he'd left home when he was only fifteen. He'd gone to live with his own father and had worked hard to put himself through the remainder of high school and university, and he was still doing some classes, mostly online, but he also attended a few lectures as well. He explained why he wanted to work for Ray's father's company. Viv confided in Ray how when Daniel had only been three years old, he'd been dumped on his doorstep by their mother. She had waited a whole two weeks after he'd left home to decide she didn't want the responsibility of raising Daniel.

They talked about how many things they actually had in common. Especially, how they had both raised other people's children. And like Ray, he now thought of Daniel as his son and not his brother. Viv liked telling Ray about how he had inherited the club after his father's death, and over the last couple of years, he and Daniel had worked hard to turn things around from the rough nightclub it once had been to a now very successful venture.

Then he told Ray all about Grace.

"Do you think you'll ever find the right person?" Ray asked.

"One day, maybe, but usually the ones I want turn out to be the very worst people for me. Even when they're absolutely the right person, I'm too stupid to take the next step. I'm scared to death of what other people will think of my choices. I'm not talking about my sexuality, but about my life in general — if that makes sense."

Ray nodded. "I know what you mean. I find it hard being in a relationship. I never think I'll meet the other person's expectation of me," he admitted.

"Do you think you'll find the right person?" Viv asked the same question.

"I found the right person, but since he's not interested in me whatsoever, I doubt anything will ever happen. So for now, I'm happy playing pretend with you." For a moment, Ray sounded really sad.

Viv felt the gnawing twang of jealousy as he turned Ray's face to look at him. At Ray's statement, both Angus and Tomas jumped into his mind, and he could see how Ray would be attracted to either of them. "If this guy had the brains God gave him, he would fall in love with you immediately. You're a good person, Ray Connelly." Without thinking, he leaned across and lightly kissed Ray's mouth.

"Thanks."

They both turned as the bedroom door opened and Daniel poked his head into the room. Viv let go before Daniel could see that they were holding hands. Guilt ran through him for being such a coward.

"She's gone... She's pissed off big time, but at least she's gone," Daniel stated then left the bedroom again.

Ray sat there as Viv got dressed. "I think one day you will find the perfect person for you," he whispered. "So with that in mind, I think after we get back from the lodge, I'll take you to have your meeting with Uncle Matt then you can get on with your life. I'll tell my family the truth then I'll go out and find a real boyfriend so you won't have to play pretend anymore. My problems shouldn't have to fuck up your life. I'm so sorry, Viv. I never meant for you to ever get tangled up in this whole sorry mess — and I'm sorry that I've let things drag on this long."

Viv looked at him in bewilderment but he nodded. "Are you going to get dressed?"

Ray took the offered jeans, pulled them on then grabbed his shirt as he followed Viv back out to the lounge room where Girly and Daniel waited.

"Man, that chick really doesn't like Dad, does she?" Girly said to Viv. "I thought she was going to jump on the bed and kill him. What's her freaking problem?"

Viv smiled sadly. "She thinks she owns me and I usually let her walk all over me. She does it knowing that I won't stop her."

Ray sat quietly and listened as Daniel began filling Girly in on his brother's past relationship with Grace. He'd already heard the story, but it was different hearing it from Daniel's point of view and was enlightening in a whole new way.

"Grace is a total bitch! The last time they were together, she got me so high I didn't know what I was doing, then she got her male friend to come over and they both had their way with me. They took a heap of very explicit photos, and a video, and put them on the

Internet. The police couldn't do anything about it. Grace said the sex had been consensual. She lied and got away with everything."

Well, that part was new. Ray glanced at Viv, who nodded in affirmation.

Girly wrapped her arms around Daniel and asked, "How long ago did this happen?"

Daniel thought for a minute. "About eighteen months ago. Viv came home, found them, and hit the roof big time before throwing them both out. We hadn't seen or heard from her until she showed up with your neighbor. I wanted so much to warn the poor bastard, but I was too ashamed. What they did to me isn't something I like announcing to the world."

"You're telling us," Girly said as she stroked his back.

"Yes I am, but I'm going to marry you one day, and we shouldn't have any secrets between us. So, I don't mind telling you."

She tightened her arms around him. "And when you ask me to marry you, I'll probably say yes." She turned toward where Ray sat with Viv. "Then we have to get these two married off."

Daniel chuckled. "If they keep playing pretend for much longer, they'll wind up marrying each other."

"Idiot," Viv said under his breath.

"You know you love me, so you'll forgive any stupid thing that comes out of my mouth. Though sometimes I'm not so stupid. As GG would say, 'I know what I know'." Daniel rested his cheek against Girly's breast and looked at his brother.

"I'll always love you, Daniel, no matter what." Viv turned to Ray. "Do you want to give me a lift back to the club?"

Ray stood up and grabbed his keys as he followed Viv out of the door. His thoughts were deep as he drove. He had a lot to think about. Ray jumped when Viv placed his hand on his arm.

"We didn't end up having lunch. Do you want to stop somewhere and pick up some takeout? We could eat it back at the club."

"If you want." Ray had so many thoughts running through his head that he couldn't think of a word to say. Instead, he drove through the drive-thru at KFC and bought their food. They went back to the club and ate in Viv's office.

"Viv, I think after what happened today, we need to end this. I know we talked about it back in my bedroom, and I…" He tried to get out exactly what he wanted to say.

"Ray, I don't mind being your boyfriend for a bit longer. There's no need to stop right now," Viv said quietly.

"No, Viv." Tears sprang into his eyes. He was breaking his own heart in the process of letting Viv go. "I don't want to do this anymore. This isn't fair to either of us. I won't go out and look for a boyfriend if you're always here for me, and soon people will begin to think you're gay as well. I want a real relationship, Viv. One that will lead beyond the hugging and kissing we do. I want the sex too, and I'm tired of pretending. Things will be better for the both of us if we just end everything now, so your life can go back to normal." He found it difficult to look at Viv while he spoke. "Okay, because of everything you've done for me, I'm happy to take you to your interview, and also willing to keep up the charade to help out with Grace while we're at the lodge. When we come back, I'll need to let you go and try to move on."

A short burst of music interrupted them and Viv swore. "Shit!"

"What's the matter?"

"Grace is here. The music they played was to warn me," Viv spat. "It's something the staff and I worked out the last time I broke it off with her."

Ray didn't hesitate as he quickly straddled Viv on the couch and began kissing him. Viv swiftly undid the buttons of his own shirt then began on Ray's. As he pushed Ray's shirt off, he let his lips wander along Ray's collarbone, then Viv dropped his mouth to Ray's nipple. Viv flicking the tip of his tongue back and forth across the nub caused something inside Ray to burst into life. He switched nipples, and Ray gasped as he leaned into Viv's mouth. Grace pushed the door open and walked in as though she had every right to be there.

"What the hell do you want, Grace?" Viv asked, exasperated. He rested his hands on Ray's waist, caressing his thumbs over Ray's hips just above the waistline of his jeans.

"I want him to leave so I can talk to you in private," she said coldly.

"Not gonna happen, Grace. I have no secrets from Ray. In case you haven't already figured things out, I'm in love with him, so if you want to talk to me, you can talk in front of him."

"Fine! I don't believe you're gay at all. I think you're acting this way because I'm back, and you're trying not to want me. You and I both know I'm the person you need. I fulfill all your deepest desires. You can play make-believe with him all you want, but you'll come back to me in the end. You always do."

Viv's grip tightened on Ray's waist as Viv grew angrier.

"No, I won't!" Viv snarled. "Not this damn time. Why can't you get this through your fucked-up head? I don't want or need you in my life, especially after what you did to Daniel. Why can't you fuck off and leave me alone? You have a rich boyfriend now. So go and fuck with his life and stay the hell out of mine."

"It's simple," she sneered. "I know what you want. Brent is convenient. He's not my ever after," she said with a note of finality.

"I want Ray. Why can't you grasp what I'm telling you? I don't want you. I'll never want you again and if you keep harassing me, then I'll tell your new boyfriend exactly what you're capable of." Fury filled Viv's words.

"Bullshit. You, Christopher Vivvens, belong to *me*. You will always belong to me, and I *will* have you back. So he"—she pointed her finger in Ray's direction—"can fuck the hell off and leave what's mine alone." She left, slamming the door behind her.

Ray slid off Viv and picked up his shirt to put back on. "That is one more reason we need to end this. You say everything I want to hear, and now I've gone and fallen head over heels in love with you! You, Viv. No one else. But you're only pretending. You can't see the real me and will never be able to love me how I want you to. I meant what I said, Viv. If you don't want me then you need to stay the hell away from me, because I'm dying inside." Ray wiped at his tears. "You say you're straight, but you're my boyfriend in every way except for the sex. Our friends all think one good push would have you tumbling out of the damn closet that you're so desperate to remain in."

Viv dropped his head into his hands. "I'm sorry, Ray. I wish—"

"Don't, Viv." Ray took a step toward the door when Viv said his name again. "Just don't. Forget about the vacation. You can still come if you want, but it will be as a friend and not as my boyfriend. I don't wanna play house with you anymore. I want the real thing."

"Please, Ray."

"I think I should go. It's best if I don't see you again until we leave." Ray quietly shut the door behind him.

He threw his drink and half-eaten lunch in the first trashcan he found. Nausea rolled through his stomach. How could I let my life become so fucked up in such a short time? He rang Tomas back and canceled their plans for the evening, positive that there'd be no future dates. Ray couldn't deal with any more bullshit tonight and no matter what, it wasn't fair to string Tomas along.

Ray drove aimlessly, not knowing where he was headed until he landed on his grandma's doorstep.

"Ray, what are you doing here?"

Ray knew he had to confess. "I've come to apologize, and tell you I've been lying to you."

His grandma patted his cheek then led him into the sitting room. "I expect this is about your young man," she said as they sat on the couch together.

Ray's tears spilled over as he nodded. "Viv isn't really my boyfriend. He never has been. Dan and Girly got carried away and things snowballed, then Viv agreed to go along, and so did I, and now it's all just one huge freaking mess and I don't know what to do anymore."

"So, if you got Viv pretending to be your boyfriend, then what did he get?" She rubbed soothing circles over his back as he lay his head in her lap.

"He got an interview with Uncle Matt. I'm supposed to take him when we get back from the lodge. I told him a little while ago that I want to end everything and go back to our own lives."

"But you're in love with him?"

He nodded. "Yes, I'm in love with him. I've been in love with him from the first moment I saw him."

"What does Girly have to say about all this?"

Ray sat up and faced his grandma. "That's the thing, Grandma. She, Dan, Jas and B all think he has feelings for me. It's so confusing. I know he doesn't feel that way. Too many people have told me how Viv dislikes gays. But then Girly said that can't be true or he and Dan wouldn't be so close. Dan's told everyone he's bi. I don't know what to think anymore."

Grandma laughed, which startled Ray. "Well, he puts on a damn good show. I wouldn't rule out that he does have some sort of feelings for you."

"What am I supposed to do, Grandma? How am I supposed to tell Mum and Dad I've been lying?" Ray started crying again. He didn't know how he was going to make any of this right.

Grandma wiped away his tears. "We won't tell them anything. Let your young man come to the lodge then have his interview. At least he deserves that much. Things always have a tendency to work out for the best. After that's done, we'll find you someone more worthy of your love."

"He's worthy, Grandma. Viv's a very good man, but the whole situation is wrong. I hear him say he loves me and wants to be with me, and I want to hear the words. Then I remember he's pretending and it tears me apart inside." Ray laid his head back on his grandma's lap. "Can I stay here tonight? I need to be somewhere I can think without any interruptions."

"Of course you can. You know where your room is." She rested her hand on his back.

"I love you so much, Grandma." Ray rose and headed for the room that had always belonged to him.

"Ray," Grandma called to him, "Antonio will bring you something to eat later."

"I'm not really hungry."

"I know, but he'll bring some food to you anyway." She waved her hand, gesturing for him to go on to his room.

With a sigh of relief, that's exactly what he did.

* * * *

Ray had lain awake all night thinking and by the morning, he was resigned to the fact that he had to let Viv go and move on. His grandma had already left for a charity breakfast by the time he had gone downstairs, so he quietly made his way home. An angry reception waited for him, which he hadn't been expecting.

"Where the hell have you been, Dad?" Girly was pissed off big time. "I've been bloody worried sick all freaking night. Dan and I rang every hospital to see if you had been admitted to any of them. Dan's still out there now, driving around looking for you. Why didn't you answer your damn phone? They are called mobile phones for a reason, you know."

"Sorry, Girly. I was at Grandma's. I was tired so I decided to sleep there. I told her the truth about Viv now that he and I have stopped pretending. You should call Dan and let him know that I'm okay. I'm going to lie down for a while. I haven't had much sleep and my phone is dead. I forgot to charge the stupid thing."

Girly wrapped her arms around her father. Her anger rolled away like the many tears he'd shed. "Oh,

Dad, I'm sorry. Dan and I were so sure he was in love with you too. I didn't ring GG, or Nan and Pop. To be honest I didn't want them worrying about you as well."

"It doesn't matter. You should call Dan, baby." Ray headed to his room. His bed was still messed up from playing pretend with Viv yesterday. He closed his eyes and inhaled the lingering scent of Viv's aftershave on the linen. As he drifted into sleep, he cuddled the pillow Viv had used

* * * *

Viv was suddenly very angry about everything, and every single person who crossed his path was feeling the sharpness of his temper. Daniel had come by looking for Ray, as he hadn't gone home last night. That pissed Viv off. He wondered who Ray was with and what they were doing. Hadn't he made things perfectly clear when he told Ray he wasn't supposed to have one-night stands?

To cap off his morning, Grace had turned up again and they'd gotten into another huge argument about Ray. She wanted him to break up with Ray and he didn't want to. The situation was fucking him up. In that argument, he finally realized he really didn't want to end this thing with Ray. Even now, his knees buckled every time those words flashed inside his brain. He loved spending time with Ray. Pretending to be in a relationship with the guy gave him the perfect opportunity to work out what he wanted. He needed to find a way to explain all this to Ray so the man understood. It was difficult when he still wasn't sure he was ready to admit that part of himself.

Then the delivery guy had fucked things up by taking their order to a completely different club. After that fiasco, Tony accidently dropped two trays of glasses.

And now, when he didn't think things could get any worse, Ray was refusing to answer his goddamn phone! Viv threw his phone against the wall in frustration and heard it shatter into dozens of irreparable pieces.

"Fuck!" he screamed into the empty room.

Grabbing his keys, he yelled at Tony that he was heading out. His anger never abated as he drove to Ray's house. He was only a little cooler when Girly answered the door. "Where the hell is he?"

"He who? If you mean Dan then he's not back yet, and if you mean Dad, then he's asleep."

Viv didn't even ask as he pushed past her and walked through the house to Ray's room. Relief flooded through him when he found Ray alone, looking so peaceful. At first, Viv thought about leaving again, but he couldn't bring himself to walk away. Instead, he gently tucked the doona in around Ray, kicked off his shoes then slipped under the covers. He lay down beside Ray, holding him while he slept.

Viv's body shook with want and this terrified him.

* * * *

After an hour, Viv had calmed down enough to leave. Gently he kissed the still-sleeping Ray on the mouth before he left. He didn't say anything to Daniel or Girly, though he knew they were watching him as he strode out of the house and drove back to the club.

He was surprised to find Christine Connelly sitting in his office when he returned. Taking one look at her face, he knew that Ray had already told her. "Hello, Grandma."

"Christopher." Grandma nodded as Viv sat behind his desk. "I think you understand why I'm here."

"Ray." Viv sighed, vigorously rubbing his hands over his face as he did so.

"Yes, my grandson came to me last night very upset and told me a little story you and I both know isn't true."

Confused, Viv wondered if maybe Ray hadn't told her the truth after all. "What did he tell you?"

"Everything he believes is the truth. Even the part about the interview for my company with Matt King."

Viv ran a hand across his eyes and was surprised to find tears there. "I'm sorry. I don't have to have the interview."

"No, you don't. I have spoken to Felix Bennet in the employment department. He is organizing the paperwork as we speak. You will be starting with the Connelly Corporation when you get back from the lodge. I did some research on you, Christopher, and you do have all the right qualifications, so the job is yours, especially with the courses you are doing at uni. I would like you to undertake a few others as well, which the corporation will pay for, of course."

"Why would you do this for me after what Ray told you?"

"My grandson believes he's in love with you, and he thinks you deserve this chance. For his sake, I looked into your qualifications, but I'm giving you the job because I think you will do well."

"What do I have to do?"

"Unlike you and Ray, I do not trade favors. I'm doing this purely for him and not you, though I do have a few words of advice for you and I think you should listen very carefully, Christopher. You need to search deep inside yourself and find out exactly what you do want. More to the point, you need to work out who you want. I know my grandson has promised to be with you at the lodge, so you won't have problems with that Grace woman, but I do not want, and will not tolerate, my grandson getting hurt. Ray is like my very own child."

"Maybe I shouldn't go," Viv said quietly.

"You will go. We haven't told Liam and Claire the truth, and they'll ask questions if you're not there. But you do not get to hurt my Ray any more than you already have." Grandma studied him for a moment. "Do you love him? If you do, you should tell him the truth before you lose him to someone else."

"I don't know," Viv said.

"Then think about what you want. I'll expect an answer by the time we get back from the lodge. You will still have the job, regardless of the answer, but answer me, you will."

Viv stood as Grandma got ready to leave. He walked her to the car and was surprised when she made him kiss her on the cheek and hug her before she drove away.

* * * *

When Ray woke, he felt worse than when he'd gone to sleep, and he would swear the scent of Viv in his room was stronger than it had been before. This made him feel sad all over again.

"I'm acting like a girl. I need a cup of frickin' coffee." He chuckled as he realized he was talking to himself.

When he entered the kitchen, Daniel and Girly were sitting at the table playing gin rummy.

"Watch her. She cheats," Ray said as he walked over to the kettle.

"You had a visitor while you were asleep," Girly said as she placed her cards on the table. "Gin."

"Who?" Ray pulled out a mug and sat on the bench.

"Viv came to see you. He was really ticked off, and he went and hopped into bed with you for about an hour. Then he left."

Ray was stunned. "What did he want?"

Daniel shrugged and began dealing out the next hand. "Don't know. He didn't say."

Ray nodded, but Daniel wasn't finished.

"I'm sorry I said I thought he's in love with you. I still think it's true, but me knowing it and Viv admitting it are two totally different things. I think he's such an idiot sometimes. If he just opened his eyes, the truth would jump up and bite him on the arse."

"Don't worry. Once we get back from the lodge, I'll be able to let go and move on. Now that Grandma knows the truth, I'm feeling a lot better. This whole thing with Viv was a balls-up right from the start. When I come home, I'll start over." Ray smiled sadly. "I told him I wanted him, but he doesn't feel the same way, so I need to man up, face the facts and stop pretending."

Daniel shrugged again. "Well, let me know when you're ready and I can set you up on a few dates and see how you go from there. Maybe you could give Angus another call. He seemed like a nice guy. And there's always Tomas."

Ray laughed at the thought of going on a blind date again. "Thanks, but I think I'll pass. Every time I try, Viv seems to somehow step in the way."

"Well, you're going to be my father-in-law one day, and I think I want to keep in your good books. Just don't hold it against me. I've told you before my brother's a complete moron," Daniel said sincerely.

Ray burst out laughing. As he went back to making his coffee, he smiled at them both. "With you two in my life, I don't even need to be in a relationship."

Girly smirked. "Yes, but then you would be missing out on all sorts of kinky sex. That's the whole point to being in a relationship."

"Girly, way too much information. No father wants to hear his daughter is having kinky sex, especially when her boyfriend has already offered to play at gay for him."

Daniel stared at him in amusement. "Didn't Girly tell you? I wasn't pretending. I would have been happy to be either of your boyfriend. I find you both extremely attractive, and you already know I swing both ways, but Girly staked a prior claim on me by a couple of hours."

Ray's eyes opened wide and his jaw dropped.

Girly rolled her eyes. "No, Dad. I won't share him with you."

"You're sick and twisted, Girly. Must be why I love you so much." He ruffled her hair as he left the kitchen and headed out to listen to Bowie, wondering when Girly would come out and change the music. Probably about two hours, which was usually her tolerance limit, but today he didn't turn the volume up as much as he normally would. The music was still loud enough to be heard in the kitchen, and he chuckled to himself at the sound of both Daniel and Girly groaning.

Chapter Seven

Daniel sat on the edge of Viv's bed and watched him pack for the weekend with Ray's family. "Viv, can I ask you something?"

He didn't stop packing as he answered, "Sure. You know you can ask me anything you want."

"Viv, are you gay? I mean, I never thought you were because I've never actively seen you pursue a man before, but watching you with Ray, and even though you are adamant everything is all pretend, it still makes me wonder."

Viv's hands froze on the zipper. "Makes you wonder what?"

"Well, I have eyes and can see Ray's a very beautiful and extremely sexy man, so I understand the attraction. Hell, if the truth were known, I'm still a little infatuated with him myself. But when the two of you are together, you're the one who's always touching him. I've never seen him try to kiss you, but you always seem to be kissing him, hugging him, or just holding his hand. And you've climbed into bed with him at least six times now that I know of, but he's never climbed into bed with you." His brother looked into his face as though he was trying to read Viv's expression. "Having been gay on more than a few occasions myself, I know the signs, and to me, you've been showing them all. In the last three months, I think maybe you've swapped sides."

Shakily, Viv replied, "I'm not gay. I'm doing a friend a favor." He finished zipping up his bag, even though he knew that Daniel was probably right. Stupidly he still wasn't ready to admit his feelings to anyone else yet. Viv also didn't want to admit how he was lying to himself. Since the very first time he'd kissed Ray at his parents' house, he'd found so many other reasons to kiss Ray again and again.

"You do know Ray's fallen in love with you, don't you?" Daniel said quietly.

"Yes, I know. He told me. We intend to break up as soon as we get back home, but until I actually start the job on our return..." Viv held up his hands in a gesture saying things will remain exactly as they are. He was sounding like a total arsehole, but with Dan confronting him like this, his answers were a knee-jerk reaction. Why couldn't his brother let him be? Viv knew he always did better when he worked things through in his own time. This weekend ahead would either make or break his *faux* relationship with Ray.

"So you're using him?" Daniel's tone seemed bitter. Anger and disgust washed over his face.

"We're using each other. He needed a boyfriend and I want the job with his family's corporation." Viv ran his fingers through his hair and winced. Saying it aloud like that sounded bad—very bad.

"Well, in that case, Girly and I would like you to tame things down a bit before her father's heart gets broken more than it already is. As for whatever this thing is you two have agreed upon—this relationship—and I don't care if you're only pretending, you're the first relationship Ray has been in since B. We don't want to see him get hurt. I really like Ray and I love Girly, so please don't fuck this up for me. I want to marry this woman one day. I also believe if you opened your bloody eyes, you would see you're in love with Ray as much as he is with you."

"I'm not—" Viv began to argue.

"Bullshit! I saw the fucking stamp on your hand and know you followed him to Flashes. I've heard you tell guy after guy that Ray was not available. I've seen the way you look at him. How fucking stupid do you think I am? You're always telling him to move on, and the minute he tries, you're right there stopping him. All it's doing is fucking him up." Daniel didn't say anything else as he got up and left. Shame and remorse filled him. This time Daniel was the one telling him to cool down his relationship before the other person involved got hurt. Every other time that had always been his job. If he was honest with himself, Viv knew he more than liked Ray, and he really didn't want to cause him any pain. He also knew Daniel was mostly wrong about him being gay. There was really no desire to have sex with Ray. Well, not a lot of desire, but he didn't mind the kissing and the touching so much. Was he in love with Ray? Even though he wasn't sure, he could imagine falling in love with him so easily. Ray truly was a beautiful person, with a smile that frequently made him go weak at the knees. And he loved the way Ray felt beneath his hands, but was it enough to change everything about himself to see what it could be like with Ray?

He sat staring at his hands for a long time and thinking about life. He hated knowing he was using Ray, especially when Ray was so willing to end the charade. Now, with Grandma knowing the truth, it made things twice as hard. Then there was the part of him that actually liked hanging out with Ray and doing the things they did—besides the intimacy. The normal friendship stuff was the real reason he was still in this pretend relationship. Regardless, he knew he wasn't ready to say goodbye. Once they broke up, Viv would have no excuse to be in Ray's life anymore, and everything they'd been doing would just stop.

No, that was something he was definitely not ready for.

So many thoughts ran through his head. Like, if he wasn't in love with Ray, then why did he enjoy getting naked with him, no matter how much he pretended he didn't? Why couldn't he admit his feelings? The answer hit him like a bolt of lightning. Deep down, he thought Ray was too good for him. He realized with sudden clarity that Grandma was right. If he didn't do something soon, he was going to lose Ray altogether. This trip to the lodge was his last chance to fix this problem. How? He had no fucking clue.

From another part of the house, Daniel yelled that the car had arrived to take them to the airport. Downstairs, it shocked him to find a stretch limo waiting. Some of the neighbors were staring, probably wondering what the hell was going on. Viv waited while the driver put their bags in the boot and was surprised to see that there were already some in it. He knew they weren't traveling alone, and from the look of some of the luggage, he knew at least one person in the limo. He quietly swore to himself.

As Viv climbed into the car, the first person he saw was Grace. She smiled at him, and he was almost quick enough to disguise the disgust he felt at her being there. He couldn't believe he put up with her nearness all because of a job—and Ray. He couldn't forget about him. Ray was definitely a big part of the reason Viv was on this trip.

"Hey, Dan, Viv, are you all ready to go?" Beth smiled and patted the seat beside her.

Viv gratefully sat. Daniel had to sit near Grace and her damn smile. Viv felt doubly bad. He knew how much Daniel hated her. Daniel's anger and disgust lay close to the surface. To his credit, Daniel ignored her completely, preferring to call Girly and talk to her the whole way to the waiting plane.

As the car started off, Beth resumed her conversation with Jasper. Viv was still amazed that they were married and that Ray wasn't pissed off over how everything had gone down. "I'm sure if I approach him right, he'll agree to help us."

"I don't know, B. Ray has a lot on his plate right now." Jasper took her hand and his eyes flicked toward Viv then back to his wife.

Why do I get the feeling this has something to do with me?

"It's Ray for crying out loud. How often has he told us he wants more children? I reckon he'll jump at the chance."

Viv listened, though he pretended not to. He wanted desperately to know what he had missed in the conversation and was surprised when Beth reached out and held his hand.

"Do you like kids, Viv?"

"Sure." Viv wasn't sure where this line of questioning was going. He also wasn't sure if anyone had told them he and Ray weren't the real deal, and he couldn't say anything in front of Grace, either.

Beth didn't say any more. She spent the rest of the drive in deep thought, still holding onto his hand as though it was a lifeline. Maybe, like Daniel, their friends were seeing more in the relationship between him and Ray.

Are they right? Am I in love with Ray? If I am, why didn't I see it sooner?

Then the conversation that he'd had with Daniel at the house before they'd left flittered into his mind.

I'm an idiot, that's why. I didn't see I had the perfect person standing in front of me all along. I'm too damn scared of how people will look at me instead of worrying about who is good for me. Mentally he rolled his eyes. *Ray really is too good for me. I'm such a screw-up.*

When they finally arrived at the airport, Beth spoke again. "I think I'm going to ask him. Viv already said he likes kids, so asking can't hurt."

Jasper only sighed.

* * * *

Ray's heart accelerated as he watched Viv climb out of the limo, looking gorgeous, just as he always did. Honestly, he thought Viv would end up not coming after everything that had happened over the last few weeks. Ray smiled and waved as Viv finally saw him and grinned. Even though the pretend was all for show, he both liked and hated the fact that Viv walked straight over and pulled him tightly against his chest.

Ray went to kiss his cheek, but Viv turned into the kiss so their lips met fully. Without hesitation, Ray opened his mouth, moaning in pleasure as he tasted Viv's tongue. These last few days he'd been granted with Viv were something he was planning to enjoy as much as possible—making memories, enough to last Ray a lifetime without the man. When they stopped, Viv pulled Ray away from everyone else so they could talk.

"Didn't you tell Jas and B that I'm not really your boyfriend?" Viv asked as he snaked his arms about Ray's waist.

Ray guessed he wanted everyone to think they were hugging and talking like any normal couple. For some reason, Viv seemed different. Maybe, like him, Viv was getting ready for their breakup.

If that's the case, why is he still all over me like a rash? Even at the end he's going to drive me nuts — and, as usual, I'll let him. God, I'm pathetic.

Ray looked at him in confusion as he tried to answer what Viv had actually asked. "Jas and B know... Why?"

Viv shook his head. "It doesn't matter. I must have misunderstood what she was talking about." With his fingertips, he'd begun tracing patterns over Ray's back.

It felt nice, so Ray relaxed into the touch.

"What did she say?" He stared up into the green depths of Viv's eyes. They looked troubled.

"It doesn't matter. I only heard half the conversation, but I think she wants to ask you something."

A range of emotions washed over Viv's face, and all Ray could think about was kissing him again. He had truly fallen in love with the beautiful man who was currently holding him in his arms.

He frowned as Viv kissed his temple. They both stared toward the others. Beth, Girly, Daniel and Grace were all watching them, so he wasn't surprised when Viv tilted his face and kissed him again. Viv had been telling the truth when he'd said he would play his part well. Viv played his part a little too well. And while he did, Ray knew he had absolutely no interest in finding a real boyfriend. With every touch of Viv's lips and with each caress of his fingertips, Ray felt himself falling deeper and deeper in love with him.

Life definitely isn't fair.

When they boarded the family jet, Ray sat in an aisle seat, preferring to let Viv have the window. That way Viv didn't have to talk to him if he didn't want to. For all intents and purposes, Viv could spend the whole trip gazing out of the window. Pretending was something Viv did well. After what Viv had said to him on the tarmac, he wasn't surprised when he found Beth and Jasper sitting opposite them. She looked determined, while Jasper seemed worried. Ray tried to smile reassuringly at them.

Beth waited until the plane was in the air before she finally spoke. "Ray, I want to ask you something, and I don't want you to answer me straight away. I really need you to seriously consider what we are going to ask."

He nodded.

She took a deep breath and went on. "Do you still want more children? If you do, I have a proposition for you. Jasper and I want a family—maybe not this year. We want to finish the house first." She inhaled another deep breath. "We got the results back, and it looks like babies aren't going to happen for us. Jas has a low count, and after he and I talked about it, I came up with a solution—though Jas thinks it's too much of an ask."

Confused, Ray said, "What's too much of an ask?"

"I'm willing to have a baby for you, but I expect you to pay all the medical side of things. Then next year, when we're ready, I want you to donate sperm to me. Jas and I can then start our own family."

Ray was stunned. He actually dropped the drink he was holding — a fact that didn't even register until the hostess came to clear up the mess.

"Please, Ray. Just think about helping us. You're the closest person Jas and I have to family and we couldn't ask for a better donor."

During the conversation, Ray sensed Viv staring at him, but for the life of him, he couldn't bring himself to turn toward the man.

When he could finally manage to speak, he said quietly, "I'll think about it, B."

Beth dropped to her knees in front of Ray and kissed him tenderly. Her kiss felt so familiar, but now a kiss from a woman, any woman, felt so wrong. Her kisses no longer made him feel the way they used to. They did nothing like what Viv's kisses did to him. He wondered if her feelings would be hurt if he pushed her away. If he was going to be kissing anyone on this trip, he wanted it to be Viv.

"Thank you, Ray," she whispered as she brought their lips back together for an instant.

Ray watched from the corner of his eye as Viv clutched the armrests of his seat very tightly and remained there until Beth let go of him. The man even played jealousy to perfection.

"Hey, what's going on back there? I thought you were now a screaming queen?" Uncle Matt teased when he witnessed the last kiss. "And what the hell are you doing kissing a married woman? Especially since she's supposed to be your best friend's wife."

Ray couldn't help grinning broadly so he'd looked like a total deviant. "It's okay, Uncle Matt. She wants to make babies with me." In that second, as the words left his mouth, he realized he was going to be a father again. This time, he was going to experience it all, so he stood and held his arms out wide and announced. "I'm going to be a daddy!" He laughed as he pulled Beth to her feet. She jumped up into his arms and wrapped her arms around his neck and her legs around his waist, holding on for dear life as she smothered him with kisses. Jasper had tears in his eyes as he slung his arms around them both. They were soon joined by Girly, who was jumping up and down in excitement.

When everything finally calmed, Ray couldn't seem to wipe the smile off his face. Finally, he had something wonderful to look forward to, something to focus on. It didn't matter now if he had no boyfriend. Soon he would have someone else to give all his love to, and they would love him back unconditionally.

After a while, he realized that Viv was very quiet and staring fixedly out of the window. "Is everything okay?" he asked softly as he laid his hand gently on Viv's arm.

Viv turned and glared at him. "We could have at least discussed the situation before you announced to our whole family we're going to become parents. It would have been nice if you had actually talked to me first—or have you forgotten I'm in this relationship too?"

He found Ray's selfishness hard to believe. He was being so dominant about their whole relationship. How were things ever to work if Ray made all the decisions? This whole thing was supposed to be an equal partnership—that's how relationships worked.

I'm so fucking stupid. Why the fuck am I so upset? It's not as if... Oh!

It was when his emotion came bubbling to the top like a volcano about to erupt—it hit him. Ray was acting like this because he didn't know things had changed.

Confused, Ray looked at him. "What the hell are you talking about? We're not in a relationship, remember? We aren't doing anything. *I'm* becoming a parent—a single parent. When we get back and you have your damn job, you won't need anything more from me. You will finally be rid of me like you want. I'll be out of your life, and yours can go back to normal. I'll be nothing but a bloody bad memory." Anger laced his words.

Hurt by Ray's words, Viv wondered how Ray could possibly think that? "No, my life bloody well can't, Ray," he snapped back.

"Why?" Ray appeared both shocked and upset.

Viv stared at him. Why couldn't Ray see what was happening? What *had* happened? How could Ray be so fucking blind?

"Because it can't, Ray. My life can never go back to what was before, no matter how much I *might have* wanted."

"Why?" Ray demanded a little more loudly this time. Tears filled his eyes. "Why, Viv? I don't understand. Why can't you—?"

"You know bloody damn well I'm in love with you, that's why," Viv said softly, but evidently not quite low enough.

Daniel and Girly, who were now sitting opposite them, focused on them with interest. Viv turned back to stare out of the window.

And Ray dropped his second drink.

"Took you long enough to realize that you love him." Daniel grinned.

"Shut up, Dan." Viv blushed, both from finally admitting aloud that he was gay and from Ray not seeing what had been happening between them.

Ray gently turned Viv's face so their gazes locked. "Tell me that again."

"I've fallen in love with you." Viv's heart jumped around in his chest like a crazy-arsed kangaroo as he confessed. "I love you, Ray."

"That's what I thought you said." Ray stood in total shock before he walked the length of the plane, locked himself in the toilet and cried.

He jumped when a knock sounded on the door and Girly said, "Dad, are you okay in there? Open the door and let me in."

He flipped the lock with his thumb so she could join him.

"Dad, what's wrong? I thought you liked him?" She wiped his tear-stained face. "Why are you crying?" Concern filled her eyes.

Ray shook his head. "I don't know. The tears, they just happened. I don't know what to think."

"Don't you want Viv to be in love with you? I can tell you I think his little announcement staggered him. Dan and I think he never even realized how he truly felt until he said it out loud, even though the rest of us have known since the very beginning."

Ray wound his arms around Girly and asked, "What am I supposed to do? I wasn't prepared for him to love me back. It never even crossed my mind he would ever feel this way about me."

"All you have to do now is be happy, though the whole thing is a little weird."

"What do you mean?" He held her away from him so he could look at her.

She rolled her eyes. "Well, my father, who was my uncle, will be my brother-in-law. If that isn't bad enough, my brother-in-law will be my father. Can you imagine when the next one comes along? His or her uncle will be their dad, their sister and brother will be their aunty and cousin and uncle, and then they'll have full-blooded brothers and sisters belonging to a completely different set of parents."

Ray smiled. "When you say it like that, it is pretty twisted, isn't it?"

They were still chuckling as Girly led him back to his seat.

"But we'll cope, and we'll love him or her, no matter what," Girly stated.

When Ray sat, Viv was again staring out of the window and didn't turn, though his hand reached out and took Ray's, holding on tightly for the rest of the flight. Ray didn't force Viv to speak, and for once, he was happy just to sit with him in silence.

Ray winked at Grandma, who was watching them both intently. Bringing Viv's hand up, he kissed the back of the man's hand, and Grandma smiled at him.

* * * *

A couple of hours later, whilst they were getting settled at the lodge, Viv had a massive attack of the nerves. He and Ray were shown to their room to unpack and clean up before dinner. The thing that stood out the most was the huge bed. Sex was not a direction he had ever intended taking this relationship in, and to be honest, he was more than a little bit terrified of what was going to happen. When he had finally calmed himself, he realized Ray looked exactly like he felt — scared and maybe a little excited all rolled into one.

"Ray, I know I finally admitted I've fallen in love with you, but I don't know if I can... You know." He gestured toward the only bed in their room. "I don't know if I'm ready for that."

Ray seemed to breathe a sigh of relief. "I understand, but you do realize I will want to eventually, don't you? I want the sex as well as the friendship."

"So what do we do?" Viv asked quietly.

"We can lie there and hold each other for a while. Would that be okay?" Ray asked shyly.

Viv pulled Ray down onto the bed and held him, then he rolled Ray to the side and spooned him, kissing the nape of his neck. "I've already learnt to crave being with you this way. Holding you was never a problem." Viv patted Ray's hip. "Turn around and face me."

He lay there, staring into Ray's eyes. "You can hold me back if you want."

Viv exhaled slowly as Ray moved closer and wound his arm around Viv's body. Viv hooked his leg over Ray, swooped in and captured Ray's mouth in a kiss, which had Viv's heart reverberating throughout his whole body. Ray began shyly exploring, and Viv welcomed his touch. Ray's worked his hands up under Viv's shirt and traced lightly over his love's skin. The intimacy seemed so different from every other time they had pretended. This time it was real.

Ray looked a little confused when Viv pushed him away, then smiled as Viv took off his shirt and waited for Ray to do the same. The whole thing was awkward, clumsy and funny, and they persevered right up until Ray started laughing and couldn't stop.

"What's so funny?" Viv asked, kissing him gently.

"We kinda really suck at this," Ray joked.

Viv stared at him. "I thought the kissing was going pretty well."

Ray lay there smiling as he ghosted his fingertips over Viv's mouth. "The kissing is perfect, but we've had a lot of practice in that department. It's everything else to do with the foreplay we suck at."

Viv chuckled. "Well, they do say practice makes perfect." He let his hands drift lower to Ray's pants, where he undid the fly. "Wanna get naked again and push our luck a little more?" Viv wiggled his eyebrows.

Ray didn't answer, but lifted his hips and allowed Viv to slide his jeans and underwear down his legs. Pulling them off completely, Viv tossed them onto the floor before removing his own and tossing them onto Ray's. Viv sat looking at Ray's body for a long time, and Ray admired him with the crooked smile Viv loved so much.

"What are you doing?"

Viv stroked a finger lightly down the length of Ray's torso, starting at the hollow at the base of his throat and ending at the tip of his cock. He smiled as Ray hardened beneath his touch.

"Just looking. Your body is as beautiful as your face. Did you know that?" Viv believed this was the make or break point for him. Yet, as he touched Ray's bare skin, he realized this was no different from touching a woman. Okay, so the parts might be a little different but the sensation of skin against skin was the same— and he wanted more. Before, when they had been in similar situations, it had felt as though Viv was standing on the outside watching. Now fully engaged with what was going on, he liked it.

Ray shook his head. "Thank you. I didn't know I was beautiful."

"Very," Viv whispered.

He moved until he was lying on top of Ray and began ravishing his mouth again. Viv whimpered the moment Ray wrapped his legs around Viv's, holding him close. The slight rocking motion and the sensation of their hardened shafts rubbing against each other overwhelmed Viv. His need built beyond the point of control, and he gave in to what he had been denying himself since he'd first met Ray and started the whole fake relationship. In a moment of pure bliss, he knew what heaven was like as he began shuddering in Ray's arms. The warmth spreading between them must have been enough to send Ray keening over the edge as he joined Viv in an orgasm.

"That was... Was..." Words were denied him as he slowly came down from the high.

He tried to move so Ray wouldn't be squashed, but Ray held him tightly, seemingly unwilling to let go.

"I never thought it could be like that," Viv added.

Ray chuckled and grabbed one of the towels lying out on the bottom of the bed. He wiped his stomach, then Viv's. "I didn't either. I may be gay but that doesn't mean I've actually fucked anyone, or been fucked by them. I want to, but my whole experience has been hand jobs, blow jobs and kissing."

Sighing dramatically, Viv got up and reluctantly pulled his jeans back on.

Ray caught his arm. "Can we explore some more tonight?"

"If you want to." Viv pulled Ray into his arms. "I think I definitely like your plan of exploring."

"Thank you," Ray whispered against Viv's throat.

Once they finally were able to step away from each other and finish dressing, Viv wound his fingers through Ray's as they went to join the family. Grandma was watching them curiously, and Viv smiled at her, trying to answer her question without actually verbalizing it. She gestured for them to join her.

"Do you have names picked out for this baby you're planning on having?" she asked when they sat beside her.

Funny, Ray didn't appear to have to think about this. "If we end up with another girl then she'll be Isobel Christine and if a boy, then he'll be James Liam. I've had those names picked out for many years."

Tears welled up in her eyes at the mention of her husband's name. "Thank you, Ray. The gesture is very kind, but we all know your grandfather would never—"

"I loved Izzy very much and I want the name James to not leave a bad aftertaste in my mouth. I want to cleanse that name in our family," Ray said quietly.

Viv could only wrap his arms around Ray in comfort when Ray turned enough to embrace him.

Grandma looked at Viv. "And how about you, young man? What do you think about becoming a father? And do you have an answer for me yet?"

"If I'm with Ray then I'll enjoy the whole thing immensely. I'm grateful I'll get to experience this with such a loving person, and my answer is, yes," Viv said softly.

Grandma watched them both for a long moment before cackling. "Then I think I'll put off dying until my next great-grandchild is born. God knows I need another Connelly to spoil. It's been way too long since Girly was that young."

They were interrupted as Girly and Daniel walked into the room.

Daniel called to Grandma, "Hey, GG, we're going skinny dipping! You want to come?" He winked at her suggestively.

"I am seventy-seven years old, child, and I still say I would look better naked than you would," she said with a straight face.

"Oh, yeah." Daniel dropped everything in his hands and started stripping. "Bring it on, GG."

He didn't stop until he was down to his boxers, and she burst out laughing.

She turned to Ray. "And you're going to let him marry our Girly?"

"Apparently so. He hasn't officially asked her yet. It could have been worse. I could have ended up with him. He did offer to be my boyfriend for you, and he told me and Girly he was attracted to us both at the beginning," Ray admitted.

Viv tightened his arms around Ray and whispered into his ear, "Mine."

Grandma looked at Daniel in surprise. "Is that true?"

"Sure," Daniel said as he pulled the clothes back on that he had removed. "I mean, look at them. They're both as sexy as hell. What's not to love? Lucky for Girly, she kissed me first, though I broke up with my girlfriend when I saw Ray... Even if he did only have eyes for Viv."

Viv saw that Girly didn't look surprised, He figured Daniel had probably told her all this before. All she did was snicker through the whole conversation.

When Granny King came in, she was shaking her head. She ignored them all as she said to Grandma, "You know, I'm not entirely sure I like Brent's new girlfriend. She seems like a money grubber to me."

Daniel was the one to answer her. "No one likes her. She's a horrible, mean and nasty piece of white trash."

Granny King looked at him, and Daniel hid his trembling hands.

Grandma was the one who broke the silence. "You kids go for a walk and keep Grace distracted, and we two grandmas can have a nice long chat." She looked first at Viv then at Daniel. "Do you mind if I share your story?"

"Anything to get rid of her. Tell whoever you want," Daniel spat. "Come on." He tugged on Girly's hand.

He and Ray kissed both grandmas' cheeks as they followed the others out of the room. There was something wrong with the whole situation, and as they walked, he fell silent.

"What's the matter? Have you changed your mind about us?" Ray asked quietly, so the others couldn't hear.

Guilt tore through him at the thought of Ray thinking he wanted out of their relationship so soon. Viv pulled Ray over to sit on the shore beside the lake.

"No, I haven't changed my mind about us. I love you and want to be with you. I just think if she loses Brent, she'll double her efforts on me. What happens if I cave in?" *God knows I've done it before.*

Ray leaned over and kissed his cheek. "I'll be your bodyguard."

"But you won't be with me twenty-four-seven. What about when I'm at home alone?" As strange as it was, Viv was actually worried about this. He didn't want to screw up what he had with Ray.

Ray stared into the lake for a long time then called Girly and Daniel over to them. Brent, Grace, Jasper and Beth followed.

"How would you feel about Viv moving in with us?"

"I couldn't leave Dan," Viv said, but his heart raced at the thought of waking up every morning in Ray's arms.

"Daniel already practically lives at our place more than he does at yours. I think he's slowly been moving in for a while now."

Girly pretended to think about it before she grinned at them. "As long as all that kinky sex remains in the bedroom then I'm fine with you living together."

Beth settled the issue. "If you're going to be parents, then you should be living in the same house and sharing the same bed—much less confusing for the baby."

Viv smiled at her and nodded then kissed Ray before saying, "Well, looks like you lost a pretend boyfriend and gained a de facto one." He wasn't prepared as Ray knocked him down and pinned him to the ground.

Their friends and the world were forgotten as the kissing began.

When the others had wandered off, Ray stopped long enough to whisper, "Did you mean what you said, or are we pretending again?"

Guilt ate at Viv. "I meant every word. I do want to be with you. But I also know I'm a total mind fuck where Grace is concerned. So I'm asking you to forgive me now for anything I may end up doing. I would never willingly hurt you, but she has always been able to fuck with my brain."

Ray kissed him deeply. "There's only one thing I don't think I would be able to forgive, which would be if you had sex with her. Seriously, if you're not fucking me, then you shouldn't be fucking her, either."

Viv moved him so they could sit up. He knew Ray had said what he had half in jest, but he also knew there was more than a touch of truth ingrained into his words.

"We will do it... I promise."

They sat there kissing until the sun began falling below the horizon. Viv didn't want to go back to the lodge but he started laughing as Ray's stomach growled.

Viv stood and pulled Ray to his feet. "Come on. Let's go eat before they send out a search party for us."

He was still chuckling as they got back to the lodge. The trip seemed to take forever. Ray kept stopping them on their journey to kiss him. Eventually their kisses had turned into mutual fondling and blow jobs. And to his dying day, Viv knew he would always remember the look on Ray's face as he dropped to his knees and took the hard cock in front of him into the depths of his mouth. That was the one thing he knew would show Ray he was telling the truth. By the time he'd swallowed around the pulsing cock, he released the flesh enough to taste the very essence of Ray. When he'd finished, Ray had pulled him to his feet and returned the favor. This was more than lust. This was the start of the rest of their lives and Viv was determined to enjoy every damn minute of it. Was it the best blow job he'd ever had? No, but it was the first one he'd been given when he knew the other person loved him unconditionally.

"About time you two got back," Girly growled as they walked into the lodge. "Pop wouldn't let us eat without you."

Without even thinking about it, Ray and Girly sat on each side of Viv and Daniel sandwiching them in so Grace couldn't sit near either of them. Then and there, Viv understood that they would do this for the remainder of the stay.

* * * *

Ray was more excited than nervous as he and Viv showered before bed. At least with the weather still cold, they had a great excuse to be wrapped up in each other's arms all night long. Ray stared into the flames of the fire and watched as Viv threw two more logs into the fireplace before climbing back into bed.

Lying beside him, Viv said quietly into the semi-darkness, "I feel kinda stupid being so scared. I mean, why should I be so terrified to do something Dan finds so easy?"

Viv's arms tighten around Ray's waist as Viv pulled him back against his chest.

"I actually asked Dan about gay sex," Ray whispered. "I wanted to know if it hurt."

"What did he say?"

Ray turned in Viv's arms, wanting to look into his eyes and to read the expression on his face. "After he stopped laughing his arse off, he told me at first there was a little bit of pain, but when you get used to the feeling, everything changes. He explained when relaxed and really in the groove, things begin to feel fantastic. He got this blissful look on his face and said doing it to the other person is a pleasure that's indescribable. Then he went out and bought me a bottle of lube, just in case. His final words of advice were 'lubricate before any penetration—and lubricate well'."

Viv vibrated against him with laughter before searching for his lips. Finally, he asked, "I don't suppose you brought the bottle with you?"

"No, I didn't, but surprisingly, it ended up in my toiletry bag anyway, so I have either Dan or Girly to thank."

Ray's pulse raced as Viv climbed over him, stopping long enough to kiss him thoroughly before he went to find the toiletry bag and said bottle of lube. He also carried a new and unopened box of condoms. He opened both and placed them in readiness on the bedside table.

As he climbed back across Ray, he asked, "Did my brother have any other words of wisdom?"

Ray grinned. "He said make sure all oral sex was over and done with first. Apparently lube doesn't taste too good... Even if it's flavored."

Viv ran his fingertips across Ray's flat stomach, and Ray's muscles quivered under Viv's touch.

"So," said Ray, "are we done with all things oral or will we be practicing a bit more before we lubricate well?"

Ray heard Viv's sharp intake of breath when Ray snaked a hand down between Viv's legs and caressed him gently before becoming more demanding. The memory of what Viv's mouth had done to him earlier was enough to make him instantly hard again.

Ray's breathing was labored as he whispered, "Lubricate well, please."

"Who goes first?" Viv asked breathlessly.

"You. I want to feel you inside me." Ray's never stopped his hand as he fondled Viv's cock and balls.

Beside him, Viv moaned deeply. "Are you sure you want me to go first?"

Ray had trouble speaking as Viv moved him into position. He shuddered as Viv's now lubricated fingers pressed against his hole, wanting in.

"Tell me what you are thinking? I need to know," Viv asked

Ray couldn't answer at first so he pressed himself against Viv's fingers. "Do it, Viv, before I chicken out." Ray winced as Viv breached his body, slipping a finger inside him and stretching him. With each new finger Viv added, Ray's body heated up another notch.

Oh, God in Heaven… It burns, but there's no way in hell I'm telling him to stop when I'm this close to having it all.

When Viv sat back on his haunches and covered his cock with a condom, Ray's heart almost faltered as a whimper of need escaped him. The perception of being torn apart increased momentarily when Viv's cock replaced the fingers that had been inside him. Yet, with the first pull back and plunge in, Ray came unglued as the pain morphed into ecstasy. The sensation of Viv moving inside him had Ray pushing up to meet Viv's every thrust. Hell, if he had known having a cock up his arse would have felt this good, he would have seduced Viv long before now.

"Don't stop," Ray whispered as he stared up into Viv's face. He lifted his legs, wound them around Viv's waist and locked them together. Sweat glistened on Viv's skin and the sight was as erotic as what they were actually doing.

Ray knew Viv was trying to be gentle, but with his next deep, penetrating drive, Viv leaned forward and latched onto Ray's mouth. Ray knew he wasn't going to last much longer. All he could think was that Viv was now truly his. Ray gripped Viv's hips tightly and screamed as he came. With each wave of release, he wanted Viv to be deeper inside him, and by God he swore that was exactly what Viv was trying to do. Ray bit his lip to stop his continual cries of pleasure, but it was useless. At that moment, he didn't care if the whole damn lodge heard him. Viv's rhythm slowed and his grip loosened on Ray. After gently withdrawing from Ray, Viv lay beside him. Ray turned to face Viv as they both fought to get their breathing under control.

"Did I damage you too badly?" Viv asked.

Ray's voice shook as he spoke. "You didn't damage me at all. Dan was right. There was pain at first, but not unbearable. Then… Holy Fuck! You touched something inside me, and I almost passed out with pleasure. How was it for you?"

Viv couldn't seem to find the right words to describe what he felt, so he gave Ray an earth-shattering smile as grabbed the bottle of lube and poured a generous amount on Ray's fingers. Ray stretched Viv by doing exactly the same thing as Viv had done to him earlier. One finger became two, the fear and pain on Viv's face changing the second Ray twisted his fingers enough to rub against the bundle of nerves he was searching for.

Once he had Viv sufficiently stretched, Ray had to grit his teeth and ride out the need to come again. It wasn't helping how Viv was gazing up with those beautiful as fuck, lust-filled eyes. Opening a condom, he sheathed his cock in readiness, adding more lube before slowly and methodically pushing into his lover in small increments when all he really wanted to do was thrust home with all his might.

"Ray, what are you doing?" Viv panted and his question turned into a deep guttural moan as Ray slowly rotated his hips in small movements.

Ray reached between them, wrapped his hand around Viv's cock and set the same rhythm he was using with his hips. "I'm trying to savor you for a little bit longer."

With every tug of his hand, Viv tightened around him and Ray groaned as his lover came, Viv's cum flooding between their bodies.

Ray gritted his teeth as he rode Viv through his release. The tightness had him voicing loudly exactly how he was feeling. "You're so hot... So tight. Oh, fuck, Viv. I'm so close." All it took was three balls-deep thrusts before he followed Viv into bliss.

He hungrily devoured Viv's mouth with his. When he finally had got enough to be able to stop, he asked, "So do you think you will want to do that again at some stage? Or was once enough for you to turn straight again?"

Ray slowly pulled out of his lover and reached for the cloth to clean them both off. Removing the condom, he then knotted it and tossed it toward the bin beside the bedside table. Sufficiently clean, Ray lay back on the bed.

"You're an idiot, Ray." Viv chuckled and pulled Ray against his side. "Though to be honest, when you first penetrated me, I nearly wanted to be straight again, but what followed made me understand without a doubt. I'm never letting you go. What about you?"

Ray shrugged. "I loved the feeling of you inside me. I felt you filling me up, touching everything so deeply—knowing you were somewhere no one else had ever been before. I thought the feeling was wonderful... It felt right, like you've always belonged there."

They lay there silently for such a long time, Ray thought Viv had fallen asleep.

Suddenly, quietly, he heard, "I really do love you, Ray."

"I love you too." Ray kissed Viv's chest as his eyes closed. He listened to the sound of Viv's heart rate slowing to beat normally again, then Ray drifted off to sleep, lost in the wonder that was Viv.

* * * *

Viv rolled slightly so he could watch Ray sleep, unable to resist the urge to run his fingertip around the contours of Ray's lips. They were so soft and made him want to kiss him, but he thought he'd better at least wait until Ray was awake enough to enjoy his kisses.

His heart sped up as Ray smiled in his sleep. He was so beautiful. He turned as he heard the door open then pulled the doona more snugly around them. Snatching the lube off the bedside table, he hid the bottle beneath his pillow a second before Grace stepped into the room.

"What are you doing in here?" Viv asked coldly.

Ray moved in his sleep and wound his arm further around Viv. In the same movement, he brought his cheek up to rest on Viv's shoulder, his leg came up over Viv's. Viv moved his arm to run the length of Ray's spine.

"I came to see if you're still playing pretend with him."

"For the love of God, when are you going to get it through your head? I was never playing pretend. I love Ray very much."

Ray stirred slightly. He hoped Ray would wake up.

"You know you don't really want him. You know you need me." She sat on the edge of the bed and reached up to caress Viv's cheek, but before she could make contact, Ray's hand shot up and stopped her.

Ray opened his eyes and glared at Grace, anger clearly written all over his face. In one fluid movement, he got up off the bed, still holding onto her arm, and used it to march her out of their quarters. Viv followed, though he snagged a towel and wrapped it around his waist before leaving the room. He caught up to them at the same time that Ray threw Grace toward Brent, who had just entered from outside and was staring at Ray's nudity in shock. Viv realized Ray was so caught up in his anger that he hadn't even realized he was completely naked.

"Keep your fucking hands off my boyfriend and, while you're at it, stay the fuck out of our room." Ray looked over at the table. "Good morning, Grandmas," he said politely, inclining his head in their direction before he turned and strode back to their room, slamming the door loud enough to wake up the rest of the family.

Viv quickly followed his lover back to the bedroom.

"Thank God, you finally woke up." Viv breathed a sigh of relief as soon as he had closed the door again.

Ray shook his head. "It was pretty hard to stay asleep with you pinching me like that." Ray indicated the red patch on his lower back.

"Sorry. Do you want me to kiss your boo-boo and make it all better?" He smirked.

"Bloody idiot." Ray chuckled. He hurried over then dragged him back to the bed. He ripped away the towel covering Viv before they climbed in and lost themselves in kissing for a while.

"I think we should get up. I'm getting kinda hungry. I might even put some clothes on this time before we face everyone again. Besides, if we don't get up, we won't be alone for much longer."

No sooner had the words left his mouth when Girly and Daniel burst into the room, followed closely by Beth and Jasper.

"GG told us all what happened out there. Now tell us what happened in here?" Girly demanded as they all jumped onto the bed.

Ray rolled his eyes as he sat up. Viv pulled him close to make room for them all.

"Don't you want to at least let us get dressed first?" Ray demanded.

Beth laughed. "We've all seen you naked enough times not to be bothered by the sight of your skinny white arse."

Ray laughed before he stood up and pulled his jeans on. He picked up Viv's jeans and tossed them to him. "You better get used to these people seeing you naked, my love. Our family doesn't have a problem with walking in on you at any time." Ray turned to Beth and grinned. "Remember when you and I were in the middle of having sex and Brent and Jasper walked in and had a full-on conversation until they realized we weren't just kissing?"

Jasper looked toward Viv and said in all seriousness, "And the worst part is, I sat on the bed with them and was patting B on the leg. Or rather I thought it was B's leg, but it turned out to be Ray's." He burst out laughing.

Viv hesitated for a moment longer before he stood and pulled his clothes on as well. After they'd settled back on the bed, Viv told them about Grace coming in and how Ray had stopped her. "What's she doing now?" he asked, finishing his story.

"Well, Brent dragged her toward the lake. Outside, you can hear them in the middle of a freaking huge screaming match. Matters weren't helped when Dan decided now would be a good time to tell Brent exactly what she had done to him. Brent didn't want to believe him at first, so Dan got on Pop's laptop and Googled the pictures. It's pretty hard to deny something when it's right in front of your face."

"I hate that bitch," Daniel whispered softly. He looked at Viv and Ray and smiled. "Though strangely, Granny King and GG were giving me some interesting but very disturbing tips on sexual positions in case something like what Grace did to me ever happens again. I think your family is kind of cool, Dad... Or is that brother-in-law? No, it's definitely Dad. Viv told me I was like a son to him. It's all kinda confusing, right?"

"Stick with Ray for now. Let's go eat. I'm sure the grandmas want to take the piss out of me for my little nudie run before."

As they walked out of the bedroom, both grandmas, Ray's parents and the Kings started clapping and wolf whistling. Viv snickered when all Ray could do was curtsey in their direction, which seemed to crack them up even more.

"Where is she?" Viv asked as he flicked on the kettle.

"Still yelling," Liam said. "How are you, Viv?"

"I'm fine, thank you. Your son saved my virtue." Viv smiled as Ray came up, wrapped his arms around his neck, and kissed him dramatically before Viv continued. "Grace has a tendency to mess with my head."

Matt looked at them. "Didn't anyone think to warn Brent earlier than this?"

"Uncle Matt, I did warn him," Girly said in exasperation, "but he refused to believe that she's evil and he blew me off."

"Bloody idiot." Matt shook his head.

"That's what I called him." Girly laughed.

Brent walked in with Grace and forced her to stand in front of Ray and Viv and apologize. Everyone fell silent.

When she'd finished, Ray looked at her coldly and said, "Stay away from my family, which includes both Dan and Viv. Don't come near them again. Am I making myself perfectly clear?" Ray turned to Brent. "You're like family to me, but keep her the hell away from what's mine, or you and I will have a serious falling out."

"Don't worry. As soon as we get home, she's history," Brent said in disgust as he turned to Girly. "Sorry I didn't believe you when you told me what she was like."

"Bloody idiot," Girly told him. She shook her head as she walked into the kitchen and began making breakfast. Daniel followed her.

Viv watched Grace for a while before he could bring himself to speak. "Please try to understand. I'm happy with Ray. Everything works so well with him and me. Nothing ever did, and never will, with us. I need you to stay away from me."

* * * *

As the weekend dragged out into a full week, Ray started feeling sorry for Grace, since everyone completely ignored her. Grandma had refused to hear about them returning from the vacation early and told them all that Grace would have to endure it in her own way. Leaving Viv to talk with his father, Brent and Uncle Matt, Ray strolled down to the part of the lake where Grace was spending all her time. She sat on the edge with her feet dangling in the water.

Ray didn't say anything as he took off his shoes and sat beside her. They both stared off across the water. After a while, Ray pointed off to the other side where fish were coming to the surface to feed. She turned and stared at him.

"What do you want, Ray?"

"I thought you could use some company."

"Why? It's not like we're friends or anything," she retorted icily.

"You're right. We're not friends, but I don't like seeing you all by yourself. You must get bored having no one to talk to."

"If you want to talk about Viv then just say so." She went back to staring out over the lake.

"Okay, let's talk about Viv. Why are you so determined to break us up?"

"Honestly, I don't think you're really together. I think the whole thing is a big show."

"Why would you think that?" Ray asked curiously.

"I know how much Viv detests people like you. There's no way in hell he would become one." She glared at Ray with pure hatred. "Not even for someone as pretty as you."

"In the beginning he wasn't, but I chased him for a long time until, in the end, he let me catch him. As for him not turning into a gay man, you're wrong. He's very energetic, if you get my meaning. To be totally honest, being gay isn't a choice. Somewhere inside Viv, he must have always been this way. People are born gay—not made or turned."

"I don't believe you."

Ray shook his head sadly. "I'm sorry to hear that, but I don't think I'll be inviting you back into our bedroom any time soon to watch us in action. I do want you to know that I won't be giving him up. I love him, and for some strange reason, he loves me back." Ray stood and put his shoes back on. "Please believe me when I tell you we're happy. Do you think we would be about to start a family if we were playing pretend?"

Finally, she turned and stared at him. "And I'm just as sure he'll be in my bed soon. You say you won't give him up and now I want you to understand—neither will I."

"You can try, but it doesn't mean you will succeed."

Ray left her sitting beside the lake and headed back to the house. Somewhere deep inside him, his insecurities all fought to be the center of attention.

When he entered the lodge, he found Viv still talking about the assignment he was doing, and Ray thought Uncle Matt was giving him a few pointers. Ray listened in for a moment, but then went and sat with his grandma. "Hey, Grandma."

"What have you been up to this morning?"

"I was trying to talk to Grace about Viv, but she still refuses to see the truth."

Grandma patted Ray's cheek. "So how's everything going between you and your young man?"

Ray smiled brightly. "He's finally decided he really does love me as much as I love him, so at the moment, things are going great. He's so smart, kind and very good-looking, and as Dan would say, what's not to love?"

"I could say the same about you." Grandma laughed. "He's lucky to have someone like you who can return his love."

"True. I am kinda perfect," Ray joked.

"Ray, you remind me a lot of your father when he was younger, even to some extent your grandfather, or what he was like when I first met him, so I don't miss James as much when you're around."

"I'm always here for you, Grandma." Ray reached out and took her hand.

"I know you are and I love you for it."

Chapter Eight

Three months had passed since he and Viv had pulled their heads out of their arses and got together. Ray was amused because Viv was still excited about working in Uncle Matt's department in his father's corporation. At night, as they lay in bed, he loved listening to Viv whilst Viv told him about his day. Daniel and Girly had taken over running the club full-time, although Viv still would go over the books once a month to make sure they were still heading in the right direction business-wise.

Today Ray had come to the club with Girly and Daniel so he could talk to Viv. He had some fantastic news they had both been waiting for and he couldn't wait to share it with the man he loved. He'd even brought him a congratulatory present.

Ray was nervous and excited as he left Daniel and Girly at the bar talking to Tony. He headed back toward the office, feeling as though he was on top of the world and smiling widely as he was about to give Viv his good news in person. They were now finally pregnant! B was expecting.

His hands shook as he reached for the door handle to go inside. As soon as he did, he wished he hadn't.

What the hell?

Ray's eyes filled with tears as he dropped the flowers he was holding. Skin touched skin. The sounds of sexual release bounced off the walls. He spun on his heel, and fled. *I can't deal with this. Please God, turn back the clock so I can unsee what's happening in there. Viv didn't even realize I was there – how could he not see me?*

Ray didn't have the energy or brain function to say anything to Dan or Girly as he walked out, tears streaming down his face. All he could think of was getting away from this place before he went back and thumped the stupid bastard. Hell, at this stage, he wanted to punch them both.

How can I tell Girly how fucked up everything is when I'm not even sure if this isn't all a big hallucination. Viv wouldn't cheat on me – he wouldn't – but he did.

Devastation ran through Ray as he headed to the one place he knew he could find comfort. He needed his grandmother.

"Dad! What's wrong?" Girly jumped up and followed him while Dan raced for the office.

Ray didn't stop when Girly ran out after him. He was so upset he nearly had a collision pulling out onto the street. His every thought was to get as far away from Viv as he could. He needed enough time to go home, get his things packed then get out. He wanted to be gone by the time everyone else got home. He couldn't face them all. He had to get out of there, even if it was his house. How could he have been so stupid as to think he deserved a happily ever after?

* * * *

When Girly returned to the club, she heard shouting. Daniel was screaming in Viv's office. She sprinted in the general direction of the room and came to a standstill in the doorway. She saw Viv, naked, lying on the couch and a half-dressed Grace standing in the middle of the office. It was obvious what they had been doing. Grace wore a smug look on her face. Girly's chest hurt as she realized what her father had walked in on. It had to be only sex. There was no way Girly was going to believe these two had made love. For Christ's sake, Viv looked as though he was drunk as a skunk — or high — or something.

"*Shit!*" She now understood why her father was so upset, and she knew exactly what he was going to do too.

"I'm going home. Dad will need me. I'll have to stop him."

* * * *

Viv's gaze dropped to the flowers on the floor. He grabbed his head as the room spun out of control. He didn't understand what all the yelling was about. He tried to move but his leaden body wouldn't let him. He tried to speak, but no words would form on his lips, and his heart raced a mile a minute as he tried to work out what was going on. Sliding off the couch, he tried crawling to where the flowers lay on the floor. For some reason, he needed to touch them. Tears blurred his eyes as he reached for what he wanted, fell short and collapsed. He was so fucking cold and he wanted Ray to come and find him. Ray would make everything better. He always did. Viv started to shake uncontrollably as Daniel was screaming above him.

What the hell have I done? And why is Daniel so angry at me?

The needed to hurl assailed him as he felt a hand slide down his skin.

What happened to my clothes and why am I naked?

He tried to think back but everything was such a weird blur. Again, his head started to spin.

Sirens. He heard sirens, and pain shot through his gut as he lay trembling on the floor. Somewhere in the distance, he also heard someone arguing with Daniel and Viv wanted to tell them to stop. Whoever sat beside him kept telling him to stay awake and shook him every time he closed his eyes. The constant rocking had him convulsing moments before he vomited all over himself and the floor.

Someone maneuvered him onto his side. His whole body was on fire. He was being twisted inside out and it hurt like shit.

God, if I'm dying, please let it be quick.

* * * *

Daniel's heart was going to explode with a million warring emotions battling inside him as he sprinted toward the office and saw what was happening. Fury burned through him only a second or two before he registered Viv's glassy-eyed stare. "Get your skanky arse away from my brother."

His hands shook as he picked up the office phone and called 000. He quickly told the operator what had happened before he crouched beside his brother, yelling for Tony as he did so.

"Get her dressed, but don't let her leave. She needs to tell them what she gave Viv." He had just enough time to move before Viv expelled most of what was in his stomach. The room stank with the large wet mass lying on the floor near his brother. Hopefully now he wouldn't overdose. His anger returned in a rush with each painful whimper that fell from his brother's lips.

"From now on, I want that slut to be kept the fuck out of my club."

"This is Viv's club and he wants me here. Don't you, baby?" she crooned from across the room.

"It's *my* club," Daniel ground out. He stood and moved to the side when the paramedics entered the room and took over his brother's care. The arrival of the police made Daniel smile at the same time that it made Grace pale even further than she already was.

Getting everything explained and sorted out with the police took far longer than Daniel had ever dreamed it would. Yet by the end, he was happy to stand and watch as Grace was led away in handcuffs. She was in full denial mode, crying and telling them they had it all wrong. Daniel had happily supplied the web address to where it proved she had pulled this before.

What the fuck was he going to do about Viv? He needed to be at the hospital, but he knew he also needed to go home and sort out the whole mess before it got out of hand. He grabbed Viv's keys from out of the top desk drawer and called Girly as he headed out to Viv's car. He tried to explain to his girlfriend what was happening and where he was heading, and she agreed to meet him there.

By the time he finally made it to the hospital, he found Girly sitting on a chair in the emergency room, crying. In her hands, she held a note that she gave to Daniel as soon as he dropped into the vacant seat beside her. The first note was addressed to Viv, and Daniel's heart broke from what he read.

You should have told me I wasn't enough. I would have let you go. I told you at the beginning I wouldn't be able to forgive you for this. I loved you so much, and you threw it all away.

Daniel neatly folded the letter and put it in his pocket before starting on the second one addressed to him and Girly.

Girly and Dan,
I'll miss you but I won't be far, I promise. I'll ring you later, after I've had a chance to think. Girly, I forgot to tell you, you're going to be a big sister. I wanted to tell him first. But I guess now it doesn't matter. Soon I'll have someone else to love as much as I love you both.
Dan, sorry I messed up your birthday.
Dad xo

The fact that today was his birthday had completely slipped from his mind with everything that had unfolded. The party they'd planned for tonight was nothing compared to what was happening.

"I rang Brent. He's going to search for Dad. He said he'll let the rest of the guys know as well." Tears leaked from her eyes as she laid her face against his shoulder. "This is so fucked up."

"Grace is in custody. Tony is going to run Declan's tonight so we don't have to go back."

"What about your birthday?" She sniffled beside him.

"We'll postpone it until next week or the week after. Today we need to concentrate on making sure our family doesn't fall apart." He spoke softly and hoped like hell that what he said was the truth.

"I tried calling Dad, but he left his phone at home. I saw it laying on his bed." Her voice broke as a fresh wave of tears hit her. "I should be with him, but I need to be here. I don't know what I'm supposed to do anymore."

"Shh," he whispered soothingly. "Everything will be okay."

He looked up anxiously as a doctor strode through the door and called for those waiting for Christopher Vivvens. When he motioned, the doctor walked toward them and introduced himself as Doctor Walker.

"Your friend is very lucky he vomited and expelled some of what he'd ingested. As it is, he had enough left in his system to start messing with his organs. We needed to pump his stomach to rid him of the rest of the drugs. At the moment, we have him in an induced coma until everything has worked through him. We will monitor him here for a few days." The doctor wiped his face before continuing. "Whatever was in the cocktail he was given must have been something he was allergic to. His airways started shutting down. We had to intubate him and he will remain that way until the swelling starts to recede."

Daniel trembled as he listened to what the doctor was saying. All that kept floating through his mind was how close he'd come to losing his brother, all because one spiteful bitch couldn't stand the fact that Viv had fallen in love with someone else. If it was the last thing he did, he was going to make sure Grace Kennedy paid for causing hurt to his family.

"Can we see him?" Daniel questioned.

"He needs his rest, so you can stay for only a few minutes."

Daniel nodded as he and Girly followed the doctor. In Viv's room, they found Viv tucked in bed with more tubes and monitors attached to him than Daniel had thought possible. His brother did not deserve this, and he vowed he would do everything in his power to set things right.

* * * *

"Ray?" Grandma met Ray's gaze as he stood on her doorstep with bags in his hands.

"Hello, Grandma. I've come to stay for a while, if that's okay."

She took one look at the tears streaming down his face. "What did he do?"

"Grace, Grandma." Ray choked out a bitter laugh. "He did Grace." Ray let her pull him into the parlor. He sobbed uncontrollably as she hugged him.

"What are you going to do, Ray?" Grandma rocked him gently.

"I think I might cry for a bit longer then I'll work out what I'm going to do. He asked me at the lodge to forgive him for anything he did where she was concerned. I told him I could forgive everything except if he ever had sex with her." Ray sat up and wiped his face on his shirtfront. "I should have known it was all too good to be true."

His grandmother looked at him skeptically.

"Are you sure about Viv? He didn't seem the type to cheat on you."

"I'm sure, Grandma." Ray swiped at his eyes. "He was supposed to love *me*."

"Ray, no one can tell you what to do about Viv. That's something you'll have to work out for yourself.

You'll have to figure out if you love him enough to be able to forgive him."

He stared at her. "I love him enough, but I hurt so much. Why did he do this? I thought he was happy with me." Tears ran freely down his face.

Grandma caressed his cheek. "Cheating always hurts. I felt the same way when I found out your grandpa had his little indiscretion, but I talked things over with him, calmly. Then I thought very hard about everything, and I told him how it was going to be from then on. We were happier afterward, right up until he died, and he never strayed again."

Ray looked at her in disbelief. "Who?"

"Who he or she was doesn't matter, but the point is, you have to think very hard before you decide what to do. Don't jump into any decision. Because I can guarantee at some point you'll be asking yourself if you made the right choice and you'll live forever with the what-ifs."

"Can I live here with you, Grandma? Just until I work out what I want to do."

She patted his cheek. "You know you can stay as long as you like. You're always welcome here."

He smiled. "I do have some good news."

"Tell me your good news."

Ray smiled and it was as if the warmth of a thousand suns had settled in the center of his chest. "I'm going to be a daddy. We got the results back this morning. B's pregnant! Four weeks."

Grandma's smile lit up her whole face. "We should celebrate."

Ray's face fell. "We're meant to be going to Dan's birthday party tonight. I don't really want to go now, but I shouldn't punish Girly and Dan for what Viv has done. Looks like you'll have to be my date tonight."

"I'll be the envy of everyone, as I'll have the most handsome man there." She chuckled.

"I know, I know. I am pretty damn perfect."

Someone yelled Ray's name from the front door. A harried Brent entered the sitting room and locked gazes with him. Ray's stomach plummeted. He knew something was wrong.

"What is it? Is it Girly?" His voice shook.

"Ray, it's Viv. He's been rushed to hospital. I don't know all the details yet, but what I do know is that bitch drugged him and he had an adverse reaction to whatever she used. Girly and Dan are at the hospital and I was sent to look for you," he said as he sank into a chair. "From what Dan said, it's pretty bad."

Ray jumped to his feet and headed to the door with Grandma and Brent on his heels. He climbed right into Brent's SUV and let his lifelong friend drive him to the hospital. By the time they arrived, the waiting room was packed with family and friends and even two policemen who were asking questions of Girly and Daniel. Ray made a beeline to where they were standing.

"I need to see him," were the first words out of his mouth. Girly nodded and led him through some doors and down a hall to the room where Viv lay. Ray rushed over and grabbed Viv's hand. He brought it to his mouth, planting a kiss on the back of his knuckles.

Viv looked so vulnerable. Ray pulled the only chair in the room up to the side of the bed so he could sit and watch over him. The longer he sat there, the more he thought about what he'd actually seen upon entering the office earlier and tried to work out how he could've got the whole thing wrong. Questions still remained—what was Grace even doing there, and why was she alone in the room with Viv in the first place? Especially since Viv had promised Ray that he wouldn't talk to her without him being there or at least Daniel or Tony to back him up.

His mind was a jumble of so many things as he sorted through what he really wanted to know. Ray knew he wouldn't get answers until Viv was conscious. His thoughts came back to the present when a nurse arrived to check Viv's monitors.

"He's going to be out of it for a while. You should go home and try to get some rest. Tomorrow he should be awake and able to talk to you." She smiled kindly at him.

Ray nodded as he got to his feet.

Everyone looked at him expectantly when he joined them in the waiting room.

"We should go home and come back tomorrow," he stated.

"The doctor says there'll be no permanent damage and he should be back to his same old self in the next couple of days," Girly reassured him as they all made their way toward the parking lot.

Ray didn't have to look behind him to know that they formed a convoy back to Grandma's estate. He also knew every person would have a say about what had happened and what they should do next. All Ray wanted to do was go home, crawl into bed and completely forget this day.

The sound of so many car doors slamming behind them and the murmured whispers of family followed Ray as he grasped Grandma's arm and led her inside. Not that she needed help getting there. It was more Ray needing the comfort of her nearness.

Girly broke the tense silence that had fallen as they entered the sitting room. "Grace is being charged with willful bodily harm of another person and rape—

though she is claiming it was consensual. If she can come up with the money, she'll be released on bail. Dan has already applied for a restraining order to make sure she can't come anywhere near him or Viv. If she does, then she will go straight back to jail until her court date."

"Do you know why they were in the office alone?" Ray asked.

Daniel shook his head. "Tony told us that he and Viv arrived together and he never saw Grace enter the premises. His best guess would be that she was already inside when they arrived."

None if this made any sense to Ray. "How would she have got in? Does she have a key?"

"Not to my knowledge. I know neither Viv nor I ever gave her one, and I seriously doubt any of the staff would have either. They all know how Viv and I feel about her. The only thing I can think of is that she must have stolen Viv's, or maybe mine, then had a copy made when she and Viv were still together."

The fury on Girly's face matched Ray's as she spoke. "Viv is going to be so angry when he wakes up and realizes what's happened."

Again, Daniel shook his head. "When Viv wakes up, he'll be ashamed of what's happened and will pull away from everyone."

"How do you know?" Ray asked.

"It's exactly what he did when Grace did this to me. Viv took the blame upon himself. It was about three months before he could even look me in the eye. Even today sometimes I'll catch him looking at me strangely and see the guilt written on his face." Daniel focused on Ray. "I know this may sound backward, but if he distances himself then comes looking for forgiveness, don't give it to him straight away."

Ray thought he knew what Daniel was trying to say, but he needed clarification. "What do you mean?"

"I mean, Viv will feel guilty for hurting you, even though it wasn't his fault. I don't know, maybe... Maybe you could somehow pretend like you're hurt and angry and give him an ultimatum or something. Make him work for your forgiveness."

"Isn't that a little extreme?" Jasper asked.

Daniel shrugged. "I know Viv, and he will forgive himself a lot faster if he thinks he has to earn Ray's trust. I know it sounds like we're tricking him, and to some extent, we are. I don't want to lose my brother over something that was beyond his control."

Ray stared at the floor for a long time as he decided whether he could lie to Viv for his own good. The answer was simple. "I'll do whatever I have to."

* * * *

The next several days were the hardest Ray had ever had to endure in his life. Daniel had been correct when he'd said Viv would retreat into himself. The others had kept him abreast of what was going on in Viv's life—like the fact that Viv had tried to resign from the family corporation. Grandma had stepped in and told him that his resignation was unacceptable and he needed to get back to work and school.

In the week that followed the whole Grace fiasco, Viv had kept as far away from Ray as possible. The request Daniel had made a week ago was looking better and better. Tonight, when they belatedly celebrated Daniel's twenty-first birthday, Viv was going to get a talking to, whether he liked it or not.

Nervous, Ray walked into the nightclub with Grandma. She must have sensed what he was feeling.

In her own way, she did everything to make him laugh. The instant she heard the driving beat of the music playing, she made him take her straight out onto the dance floor. They must have looked funny dancing to Good Charlotte's *Keep Your Hands Off My Girl*. Since everything that had happened, Ray knew Viv wouldn't come near.

Jasper and Beth were dancing nearby until Jasper cut in and Ray found himself in Beth's arms.

"Dan told us how Viv's still avoiding you," she said as she wrapped herself around him. After a while, she added, "Am I supposed to still pretend I hate him? You know I will if you want me to, but it's hard to see him so sad and withdrawn."

Ray shook his head. "You never had to pretend to hate him, and as for Viv, well, he's doing something he feels is right, even if it is stupid." Ray led her back to a table, knelt, and kissed her still flat-as-a-pancake stomach. "Be safe, my baby."

"Why are you still staying at Grandma's?"

"To be honest, Viv still isn't ready for us to be together again." He sat on the seat beside her and gently caressed her belly.

Beth stopped his hand. "If you keep rubbing me, you know I'll have to pee. I can't seem to do anything else lately."

He chuckled. "Sorry, but you'd better get used to my hands being on you again. You've got my baby in there."

Jasper was laughing when he came to the table with Grandma in tow. "Grandma, you're a dancing demon!" He winked at Ray. "Are you done feeling up my wife?"

"For the moment, but remember, I have eight months left of feeling her up." Ray grinned then looked up as Daniel and Girly joined them.

Girly sat on his lap and threw her arms around him. "Are you okay?"

Daniel knelt beside him. "I understood if you don't want to be here. I know how much of a fucktard my brother is being."

Ray turned and kissed him fully on the lips. "Happy birthday, son. Grandma and I didn't want to miss the party." After a moment, he added, "Is he here?"

When they nodded, Ray's heart pounded with mixed emotions over what was to come.

"Where?" he asked. He looked toward the table they pointed to where Viv sat talking quietly with Brent and some strange girl. Viv looked miserable, and Ray's heart went out to him. "Who's the girl?"

Girly grinned. "Her name's Tarni. Brent and I did some therapy shopping this week. We walked into a dress shop where Tarni was and we watched as her friends teased her about not being invited to someone's party. They were saying even if she had been, she wouldn't get a date, and could never afford a new outfit. They were really mean. She just stood there taking their shit, even though everyone saw she was really upset. They teased her about being fat. She may not have been as skinny as their skanky arses, but she's beautiful, and in no way fat. I personally think she looked better than all her friends combined — and Brent said she has real curves. Then Brent got this weird look on his face, walks up to her, puts his arms around her, kisses her on the mouth and said, 'Sorry I'm late, babe, but you know what Girly's like — never on bloody time'.

"All her friends stared at her open-mouthed as he led her over to me, then to her friends' astonishment, he got her to try on clothes with me. After a while, one of her friends came over and told her they were leaving. Brent introduced himself as her new boyfriend. Their eyes nearly popped when they heard his name, and written on their faces they believed there was no freaking way Tarni could score someone like Brent King. He said they could leave, but Tarni was staying with us. The entire time he was talking to them, he had his arm wrapped around Tarni's waist, and she smiled at them all.

"As they got to the door, they turned back, still looking at her in disbelief and Brent full-on kissed her in front of them. So, she spent the day with us, and has every one since. Brent reckons I need some female friends, and he chose her. Really, I think he likes her. She's very shy but funny. Brent has spoiled her rotten ever since."

They all looked back toward the table.

"So I guess now I have a new best friend," Girly finished.

Ray got to his feet.

"Where are you going?" she asked as he stood her up.

Ray chuckled low. "I'm about to do the one thing Dan said I should. I'm going to make Viv face up to what happened. I'm tired of being alone when he is so fucking close at hand."

Before Ray left, Daniel took his seat, pulled Girly onto his lap and said, "This should be a good show. We should have thought ahead and sold tickets."

Ray went and stood beside Viv, who jumped when he realized Ray was standing there. The second he moved his chair back to stand, Ray promptly sat on his lap and wouldn't let him up. Viv looked at him, and Ray saw the confusion and guilt written so clearly on his face. Hesitating, he cupped Viv's face and kissed him. Viv froze. For a moment, Ray thought Viv was going to push him away, but was surprised as Viv exhaled slowly and with so much emotion that he locked Ray in his embrace before kissing him back.

When they finally broke apart, Ray heard Brent talking.

"Don't worry about what you're seeing. Ray's not a perverted freak who walks up and kisses random strangers. He's actually Viv's boyfriend, and he's also Girly's dad. You'll get used to him in time. Ray, stop being ignorant and meet my beautiful, new girlfriend."

Ray turned and looked at the young woman sitting beside Brent. Her gray eyes were wide as though she was in a little bit of shock as she stared at him. He didn't understand how anyone could think she was fat. She may not be the perfect size ten, but Brent was right, she did have some very nice curves. He might be gay but even he could tell when a girl was gorgeous.

"Ray, this is my Tarni. Tarni, this is Ray. He's one of my best friends."

"Hi." Ray smiled across the table. "It's nice to meet you. Now, if you will excuse me, I need to take Viv away for a moment." From the sharp nod Brent sent his way, Ray knew his friend must have guessed what he was up to.

Ray returned his attention to Viv. "Let's go somewhere and talk—somewhere that's not the office, shall we?" He didn't even give Viv a choice to protest as Ray pulled him to his feet. Taking his hand, he led Viv toward a door marked 'Staff Only'.

The silence between them grated on Ray's last nerve, yet he didn't say anything until they had reached the stock room and had tugged the door firmly closed behind them.

He snapped the overhead light on, took a deep breath to ready himself, turned and confronted Viv. "Now explain to me why the hell I should still be with you after what I walked in on last week?" Ray stepped back and folded his arms across his chest, settling a frown on his face as he waited. He didn't want to act like the prick he knew he was portraying, but he also understood this was exactly what Viv needed.

Tears sprang into Viv's eyes. "You shouldn't be with me. I don't deserve you after what I did. All I can say is that I am so sorry, Ray. Honestly, I never meant to do that. It just happened."

Faking confusion for a moment, Ray asked, "So what you're saying is you never really loved me, and you don't want to be my boyfriend any longer?"

"No! Yes! I really do want you."

Viv took a step toward Ray, but Ray backed away. He knew for Viv to forgive himself, he had to hold out a little longer.

"Then I don't understand. If you really do love me, then how could you possibly have sex with her? Or have I been deluding myself into thinking we've been in a real relationship? Has this still been pretend for you? Has fucking me every night for the last three months been nothing but a big joke to you?" Anger laced his words and he saw Viv flinch. Fuck. He hated doing this.

Viv broke down, and Ray's heart melted.

"I'm so sorry, Ray. I'm so fucked in the head. I messed everything up, and now I've lost you.

Everyone's angry with me, and I don't know how to fix anything."

Ray sighed. "You haven't lost me—yet. And as to how we fix this, I don't know, but we'd better work things out soon. We have a baby coming in eight months. Unless, of course, you want out, then only I will have a baby coming." He pulled a hanky out of his jeans pocket and handed it to Viv.

"Tell me what I'm supposed to do, Ray, and I'll do whatever you want. I'll do anything to make this right. I know I'm meant to spend my life with you. My heart knows that."

Ray sat on a box and gestured for Viv to do the same. "I can't tell you what to do, but I can tell you what I want. Then we try to compromise."

"What do you want?"

"I want you to start by letting go of what happened and moving on—together. If you can't do that then I'll need to let you go. Soon it isn't going to be just you and me. Don't you think this baby on the way deserves two people who love each other as much as they will love him or her?"

Viv nodded.

"I also want that thing between your legs to be for me—and only me," Ray continued as he studied Viv's face. "They're my only wants... No... I have one more. I don't want to be hurt ever again, not like this, and not over someone like her. I need you to testify against her in court so she can't do this to you or anyone else again. I heard she was out on bail and I don't want her to remain free. She needs to pay for what she's done to both you and Daniel. I'm sure Dan told you that he's already stepped forward and had his own charges laid against her." When Viv nodded again, Ray continued, "I'm still going to stay with Grandma for the moment and I need you to think about what I've said. If you truly love me, you'll do everything in your power to win me back." He stood. "I love you so much, Viv, and I hope to God you choose me."

Ray walked out and left him sitting there crying. Ray fought the urge to run back in, take Viv into his arms and tell him he was forgiven—like his heart wanted him to. In reality, life didn't work like that, and for once Ray had to pray to God that Daniel was correct and this ultimatum shit would snap Viv out of it and help him move on.

Once he had returned to the main floor, he grabbed Tarni's hand. He needed to do something normal to take his mind off what he had just put Viv through.

"Come dance with me, Tarni," Ray said as he pulled her out onto the dance floor. He watched as Brent went to Viv. Ray was glad Viv and Brent had become friends, even if it was strange how they had bonded over the whole Grace fiasco. He was relieved that Viv had someone to lean on.

"So, how are you finding all this craziness?" he asked Tarni. "Have we scared you silly yet?"

She smiled shyly. "At the moment, I'm treating it all like a trip to Wonderland. You know, nothing's real, and soon I'll wake up and be boring old Tarni Williams again. I'll go back to my friends who don't really like me, and this will all be a happy memory to pull out when I'm feeling down."

Ray burst out laughing, which seemed to shock her, so he explained. "I guess no one told you about Brent. If he's telling people you're his girlfriend, then that's exactly what you are to him. In Brent's world there are no gray areas—everything is black and white."

Her eyes widened even further. "But he's Brent King."

"And I'm Ray Connelly and you're Tarni Williams. To Brent, nothing else matters, and he won't even care if he only met you a couple of days ago. Just be prepared to be spoiled. He treats his women extremely well. So welcome to the family." Ray chuckled as she laid her head against his shoulder. When the song ended, Ray led her over to where Grandma was sitting and left her there as he headed to the stage. He picked up his guitar and strummed as Beth, Josh and Jasper were getting ready to play.

Ray adjusted the microphone stand. "Okay, this one is for my—at some stage—future son-in-law and current birthday boy. A little birdie told me this was his favorite song. If I'm wrong then blame Girly." Ray grinned toward the table where most of his family sat.

Viv and Brent had finished talking and were now sitting next to Grandma, who was holding Viv's hand. Oddly enough, this song would have different meaning for most of the occupants at their table.

"It was a lie that took you away from me. It was a lie I couldn't see. I turned my back on you for so long that in the end you were gone." Ray almost started laughing as everybody at the table got up as one and started slow dancing, Grandma included.

Through singing, Ray had always found he could forget all the problems filling his life. His grandma was right. The question was simple. Was he willing to let Viv go? The answer was the hard part. Now everything was left up to Viv, and all Ray could do was wait and see what the man he loved decided to do.

During the set, the rose lady came around, and he saw Viv buy Grandma a rose. Tarni seemed dazed when Brent bought her one as well, and even Daniel got in on the action, purchasing one for Girly. Ray let the last chords drift away and was happy to finish singing for the moment.

As he left the stage, he groaned as he watched everyone returning to the table. Beth, to his amazement, was once again wearing her hooker heels. Ray touched her arm to get her attention and said, "You know you'll have to give these up before you harm yourself or my precious baby."

"Yes, I know." She sighed dramatically.

When she sat, Ray unbuckled them and handed them to Girly. "Don't let her have them back. At least not until after our baby is born." He bent and kissed her stomach again. "I won't let anything happen to you, my darling."

Girly was giggling as she traded shoes. "Dad, you're acting like a dork."

He poked his tongue at his daughter. "I don't care. I was exactly the same when you were inside your mother, wasn't I, Grandma?"

His grandmother nodded, but Ray could tell she was getting tired.

"I think that's why Isobel left her to you. She knew you would love her."

"I do love her." He smiled fondly at Girly. "You're the best gift I was ever given."

"I love you too, Dad." Raw emotion filled her voice.

"I know you do, Girly."

Ray smiled as Viv handed Beth a rose. "This is for you. I wanted to say thank you for carrying something precious to both Ray and me." Then he gave a single red rose to Ray too. "Just because I love you, and I am so sorry I hurt you."

Ray accepted the offered flower and recognized the first five words. They were what he'd written on the card for the flowers he'd brought the morning that all this bullshit started.

Ray gave him a smile. *Well, this is a start.*

His smile widened as Viv took his hand and pulled him out onto the dance floor.

Heart racing, this was more than Ray had ever hoped for. He was even more surprised when Viv took him in his arms and slow danced with him. By the time Viv kissed him, Ray's heart was jumping like a demented pogo stick. Ray thought the beat of it sounded louder than the music and wondered if anyone else could hear what was happening. Tony and the staff stood at the bar looking relieved. "I love you, Ray, and I'll do anything to make things right between us. Please forgive me and give me another chance to prove I'm worthy of your love. I want you back." Viv kissed him again.

This time the kiss was gentle, lasted longer, and by the time it ended, Ray didn't think his legs would hold him up.

Ray froze in his arms at the rip-roaring taking place at the table where everyone was sitting.

Ray sighed. "I think you still need to sort some things out." He saw pain wash over Viv as he saw Grace standing there. She was trying to give Daniel a present, but he was ignoring her, and her voice was becoming very shrill when no one would talk to her. In reality, Ray wanted to knock her fucking block off, but that would only cause more problems.

Movement at the bar caught Ray's eye, and Tony mouthed 'police' in their direction.

* * * *

"I'm sorry," Viv whispered as they walked over to the table. He grabbed Grace by the upper arm and steered her toward the front doors.

As she went to pull away from him, Brent seized her other arm.

"I can't believe you're back to playing pretend. I thought we sorted all this out last week. Seriously, why did your stupid brother have me arrested? When all this settles down, you and I need to have a very serious talk about us, and the boundaries we need to set where Daniel is concerned. He's under the assumption he has way more power than he does. He won't be smiling when you fire his arse."

Viv couldn't believe the delusional world Grace seemed to be living in. How in the hell did she think Viv would ever forgive her for what she'd done to him? She'd violated him in the worst way possible. There was no way he was ever going to be with her again. Brent's voice was the only thing stopping him from slapping some sense into her.

"The only thing sorted out is that you're a slut," Brent said forcefully.

Viv winced.

"Get this through your head!" Brent continued. "No one here wants you. We've all moved on from you."

"*He* wants me," she shouted.

Brent's face filled with disgust. "No, he doesn't. You are breaking the law. I know for a fact there is a restraining order against you. You shouldn't even be here. Now listen carefully to what I'm saying. Byron King is my uncle and a very good lawyer. I already have him looking into what other charges can be laid against you. If that's too much for you to comprehend then I'll have the appropriate papers served on you tomorrow, just so you see how serious I really am."

Viv couldn't believe how in control Brent was.

When they got her outside, Grace threw the present against the wall. Glass broke and the smell of cheap aftershave reached them.

"Why them? What's so special to make you all stick up for Viv and Dan? It's not like they're rich like the rest of you."

Brent's voice rose. "I'll tell you why. Unlike you, they have never asked for a goddamn thing except to be loved. You're a manipulating control freak who wants it all—every fucking little thing that doesn't belong to you. You finally managed to screw him again and still didn't break up him and Ray, and as for why I think they're so special? It's probably because they made me see what you are—white trash!"

The police vehicles, with sirens blaring, pulled into the parking lot. Their appearance brought a smile to Viv's face as Grace panicked. Before she could run, Brent grasped her arm again and waited for the police. The authorities took her away as she was still screaming at them both.

They turned back into the club.

Brent growled at the bouncer, "For fuck's sake, if she ever comes back, don't let the crazy bitch in."

When Viv returned, Ray was saying goodbye to everyone.

"Are you leaving?" Viv asked. His heart stuttered in pain.

Ray nodded. "I'm taking Grandma home."

"Please come back," Viv pleaded.

With a shake of his head, Ray said, "I don't think so. I need to think about things and I believe you need to do the same."

Viv's face fell.

Pulling Viv into his arms, Ray said, "I'll call you tomorrow."

Ray kissed him, and even though Viv wanted more, he knew he had to stop.

Ray leaned in and whispered in his ear, "Remember, think over what we spoke about earlier."

"Can't I come with you?"

Ray smiled. "It's your brother's birthday. I think your first priority is here tonight. Besides, you need to look after our baby capsule." He pointed at Beth.

They hugged for a little longer.

"Okay, Ray." Viv sat next to Beth.

She reached over, took his hand and placed it on her stomach. Viv leaned down and kissed her tummy. "I'm here to look after you, our precious baby."

"Come on, Grandma. Let's get your tired tushy home and into bed." Ray slung his arm around her shoulders. "What do you think Mum and Dad are going to say when they hear I took you nightclubbing?"

Viv didn't hear what Grandma's reply was, but whatever she said made Ray throw his head back, laugh then lean over to kiss the top of her head.

Girly stared at Viv and shook her head. "Tell me he isn't going to be hurt again."

He sat there, meeting her gaze, before bravely saying, "He won't."

For a moment, Viv didn't think she was going to believe him then Girly nodded.

She leaned across the table and motioned for Viv to do the same. She whispered, "If you hurt him again, I'll cut off what's most important. I love my father very much, and you have lived with us long enough to know I'll do exactly what I threaten."

Viv understood her reasoning and wanted to reassure her, but didn't know how.

Brent picked Tarni up from her chair and moved her onto his lap. "Babe, remind me never to get on Girly's bad side." He slid his arms around her waist and pointed toward the door where her friends had just walked in. "Aren't they your friends?"

"Yeah, they're my friends." She turned in Brent's lap. "Thank you for a very interesting week. Maybe I'll see you again sometime." She went to get off his lap but he held her in place.

"Haven't you heard me tell everyone all night you're my new girlfriend?" Brent said.

She nodded.

"Then if you're my new girlfriend, I have to ask why you'd think I'd let you go back to your old friends who aren't worthy to even breathe the same air as you?"

Tarni's eyes widened. "I thought you were only joking. Ray said you weren't, but if so, then why would you pick up a complete stranger?"

Daniel joined the conversation. "Strangers are simply friends we haven't met yet."

"You do know I'm poor, right?" She shook her head. "You know I haven't got the money to even try to keep up with any of you?"

He laughed. "And now you have a very rich boyfriend—and an heiress as a new best friend."

Girly shrugged. "Dad and I are as rich as sin and will inherit even more later on. Don't let that blind you, though. I really am a nice person. Don't hold my money against me."

"Your friends are staring at you," Viv pointed.

The other group all stopped and turned in their direction.

Viv watched as Brent spun Tarni so she was sitting sideways on his lap. "So, now that we have established that I'm not joking and that you are now my girlfriend..." He studied her for a moment. "I suppose I should have asked you if you wanted to be my new girlfriend. I mean, I wouldn't want to force you or anything."

Beth started laughing. "You never asked her?"

He grinned. "B, we've had a very busy week. We had so much to do, and I got a little sidetracked with what was happening so fast. I can't be expected to remember everything." He looked into Tarni's gray eyes. "So how about it? Do you want to be my girlfriend, or am I making an arse of myself? If the answer is yes then kiss me now."

The whole table started clapping and whistling as Tarni leaned down and kissed him. When she'd finished, all her former friends were staring at her open-mouthed. "If I wake up tomorrow and this has all been a dream, then I don't want to wake up. This may be the best damn dream I've ever had."

Brent laughed quietly. "If you want, you can wake up in my arms."

* * * *

Girly pulled Tarni out onto the dance floor. "I was getting a little queasy hearing him talk like that, but I can't deny he does look good naked." She grinned at Tarni's shocked look.

"Were you and he...?"

"Me and Brent? Good God, no. He's one of Dad's friends, so he's like my big brother or an uncle or something, but we've all been skinny dipping a few times over the last eight years. We sort of have an extended family. The Connellys and the Kings have been friends since forever—and Dad's band are all family. Also Dad and I have Viv and Dan, and now we have you."

All Tarni seemed capable of was nodding. "Then I hope I don't do anything to screw things up."

Girly started laughing. "Not a chance. I won't let you. You're the first girl close to my age, apart from B, who's been accepted into the group. I'm tired of being surrounded by overprotective men."

* * * *

Brent left the table and took over dancing with Tarni as the band moved back on stage. Viv watched in amusement as Girly smiled at Daniel and blew him a kiss. She went with them and picked up her father's guitar. With the first few chords, Viv's eyes popped wide when she played nearly as well as Ray had, though she left the singing up to Jasper.

By the end of the night, they took the party back to their house. Brent seemed happy that he was going to wake up with Tarni in his arms. Viv was still pretty bummed about having to sleep alone, until his phone rang and he heard Ray wanting to say goodnight. He sauntered off to his room talking as the rest were also happily heading off to their own beds.

Chapter Nine

"Ray?" His grandma said as she glowered across the breakfast table at him. "Have you decided what you're going to do about your young man? You know you shouldn't leave him dangling. It's been six weeks. It's time to stop the pretending and go be with him."

Ray grinned in her direction. He loved her to death but, by God, she could drive him to distraction with her incessant meddling. He tried again to explain what was going on. "Grandma, I have nothing to forgive Viv for, but he has to forgive himself. Other than that, I like living here."

"Well, maybe you should invite Viv to come and stay here as well," she said, slowly stirring her tea.

Ray couldn't help but snicker at those words. "You just want him here so I won't leave. Admit it. You like having people around."

She smiled fondly at him. "I'd have all you young ones live here if I thought you would stay."

"I'm in no hurry to go anywhere. I'll ask Viv if he wants to move in, but he might not want to leave Dan.

How about if I invite him to spend the night here first and slowly work his way into moving in?"

"Whatever you think is best, dear," she said with a knowing smile.

He chuckled again. "They should all be leaving home soon. I better go ring up Girly and remind her to have the house calls forwarded to your place, and to pick up Granny King on her way here."

Ray left the room. The house had been decorated for Christmas and everything Antonio and the rest of the staff had done looked artsy and tasteful. Christmas was probably one of Ray's favorite times of the year. There was only one thing he needed to make it perfect. He walked over to the phone in the hall and rang home. The moment Viv answered, Ray's heart melted.

"Hello, Connelly, Vivvens and Marshal residence. This is Viv speaking."

"Hello, Viv speaking," Ray said as seriously as he could. "This is Ray calling."

"How are you, Ray calling?" Viv joined his joke.

"Actually, I was wondering if you wanted to stay here with me tonight. I'd like to wake up Christmas morning with you in my arms. Your presence would probably be the best gift I could get."

"Really?" Viv sounded hesitant.

Ray's stomach flipped. "Don't you want to spend the night with me?" If Viv stayed tonight, it would be the first time—if all went well—for them to make love since Grace. Ray needed this contact as much as he believed Viv did.

Viv was silent for a very long time, and Ray slumped heavily into the phone chair. Why was he always an idiot, just assuming that everything was going to go back to normal?

"Sorry if I put you on the spot. It's okay. You don't have to stay. Look, forget I asked. I really rang to remind you to pick up Granny King on your way over, and to make sure Girly had the house phone calls forwarded to Grandma's. See you when you get here. Bye." Ray hung up before Viv had another chance to talk.

He felt like an idiot as he headed back to his room to wait. He didn't want Grandma to see him. She would immediately know that something was wrong. Before he could face her, he needed time to get his emotions under control so when Viv and the others got here he would be able to function normally. His world wasn't perfect, which he had well learned by now. Really, it wasn't hard to understand why Viv was reluctant. It saddened Ray that Viv was still finding it so difficult to move on.

He must have dozed off. When he woke, Viv lay on the bed beside him.

"I know this isn't exactly Christmas morning, but I thought we might practice waking up with each other," Viv said, just before he kissed Ray and pulled him closer.

Ray snuggled against Viv's side. His heart began frantically racing like a freight train the very second Viv started removing their clothes.

Viv's nervousness was evident when he asked, "Please tell me this is what you want, and that I'm not making a complete dick of myself?"

Ray couldn't answer, as he was too busy helping Viv in the effort to strip each other. This was going to be sex, pure and simple. There would be no lovemaking involved at all. This was them claiming each other again. Making love would come later tonight if Viv stayed. Ray grabbed lube and condoms from the bedside table he had stocked when he'd first arrived at Grandma's, hoping he and Viv would eventually get to use them. Now, with mind-numbing passion, he was glad they were at hand. Hurriedly, they both rose and undressed. Ray barely had time to think straight before he found himself tossed onto the bed.

Heat permeated every microbe of his body as he met Viv's gaze. The fire in his lover's eyes stole his breath away. "You're always so beautiful when you look at me that way."

Ray arched his back, trying to entice Viv closer. It wasn't until his spread his legs wide, offering up the space between them, that Viv finally joined him. "Need you so much."

By Viv's silence, Ray knew without a doubt that his lover was swamped in so many emotions of his own. He wasn't going to pressure Viv into communicating, quite happy to do all the talking necessary.

"Need you to stretch me out… Want you inside me, filling me up."

Viv bit him gently on the shoulder. Ray almost lost it as the pain, mixed with the tender caresses he was receiving, jolted through him, zipping here and there in tiny sparks of electrical energy.

"Fuck!" Ray gasped as Viv breached his body with his fingers. "More… Please, don't make me wait any longer."

Perspiration shone on both their bodies. Ray loved knowing it was there from their arousal. Somehow, sweat generated from sex was better than any other kind.

"What do you need, Ray?"

"You, dammit. I need you. I want you to fuck me hard so it replaces all the bad memories."

The air whooshed out of him as Viv pulled his fingers out and, with one well-aimed thrust, Viv buried himself deep inside Ray.

"Move," Ray begged.

His words came out incoherently as Viv did what he'd asked and used his body. No love. Just lust and need—and exactly how he wanted it. The turbulent pace electrified his whole nervous system. He used his legs in a strangle hold on Viv's body, trying to draw him deeper still.

"Close... Not gonna last." Viv's name tore from his throat as his orgasm yanked him over the edge. Still, he couldn't let go and held on until Viv had followed him into bliss.

Ray was determined there was nothing in the world that was going to fuck up their lives again.

They lay in a tangle of arms and legs as they clung to each other. Viv finally stopped kissing him long enough to be able to speak. "We should go downstairs. Girly was only giving me an hour with you. She said if we didn't make an appearance, she was going come looking for us."

Ray brought their lips back together and distracted Viv for a moment before he broke away again. To be honest, Ray didn't want to give this closeness up, even if it was to be with their family.

"Well, if you're not ready to join the others, can we at least get dressed and clean up before we end up with everyone in here with us again?" Viv's words came breathlessly.

Ray sighed but reluctantly did as Viv had asked. This wasn't over. Now that they had broken the ice, Ray was determined to do it all over again, as many times as possible. The thought hadn't even finished formulating in his head when the door burst open.

All their friends and family crawled onto the bed with them.

Ray winked at Tarni. "Nice to see we haven't scared you off yet."

She smiled shyly. "Not yet, but you have come close a few times." She started giggling as Brent began nuzzling the side of her neck.

"I had a very interesting conversation with Grandma this morning," Ray said, moving so he was sitting up with his back pressed against Viv's side.

Viv wrapped his arms around him, and Ray loved every second of their closeness.

"Well, are you going to tell us or keep us all in suspense?" Jasper asked.

"Grandma thinks we should all move in with her."

Ray let the words sink in.

"When you say all..." Brent started.

Ray nodded. "I mean all, even Josh. Well, I think she wants the rest of you to move in. I'm already here, so this isn't about me."

They all stared at him, stunned.

"It's something for you to think about at least." He turned to Beth and Jasper. "B, I would really like for you and Jas to move in. That way I get to be hands-on during our pregnancy, even if only for part of the time. The upside is that you could renovate your house and not have to live there at the same time."

Beth grinned. "That would definitely be a plus, but I'm not the only one to decide. Jas has to have a say."

"I'm not asking you to share my bed." Ray smiled. "I just want you to stay here with us. Besides, four in a bed would get too squashy, especially when you become as big as a house."

"I don't know, Ray. We have eight fitting in here quite comfortably. Might've been squashy if Josh had come here instead of flying Stateside over Christmas with a girl he picked up last weekend. I suppose we could all stay here until after New Year's and show Grandma what a house full of young'uns is really like. I bet she'll change her mind," Brent said as he kissed Tarni's neck again. "What do you think, babe? Want to move house for a week or two?"

Tarni blushed. "I don't think the invitation was meant for me."

Girly pushed her on her friend's arm. "Dad said all, so that means all."

Tarni blushed redder.

Standing, Brent pulled her off the bed. "We'll be back soon. We're going to pick up Tarni's parents. They're coming tonight. Hope we don't scare them or they might not let me have their daughter anymore."

As Tarni's blush deepened even further, Ray grinned up at her.

Brent didn't miss the exchange before he hurled at Ray, "See you soon, and for God's sake, I like this girl and want to keep her, so let's all try to make a good impression on Mr and Mrs Williams."

As they reached the door, Girly called out, "Then warn them about our screaming queens. You know gayness has a tendency to freak some people out."

Brent was laughing as he left, towing Tarni after him.

"You know what? I think Brent really likes the girl. This is the first time he's ever invited a girl's parents to one of our family parties." Girly turned to Daniel as her train of thought shifted. "So will we be moving house?"

"Sure. GG is cool." Daniel was playing with the hem of her shirt as he lay beside her.

"Okay, I'm sorry to have to break up the party, but this Easy Bake Oven needs to pee," Beth said. She knelt up on the bed, hiked up her shirt, and showed her slightly rounded baby bump. "On the third of January I'm going for an ultrasound to see if there is more than one little pumpkin growing inside here. My doctor thinks I might be having twins."

Ray grinned broadly as he reached out and caressed her tummy. Viv put his hand over the top of Ray's. To Ray, it was perfect.

"Twins would be so cool," Ray whispered.

Beth stood. "I'm not saying anything to anyone else until after I've had the ultrasound, but I needed to tell you. I know Ray would tell Girly anyway, so I figured you wouldn't mind me sharing this with Girly and Dan too. You're both still coming, aren't you?" she asked him and Viv.

Viv smiled. "We wouldn't miss out on it for the world. That's our baby in there."

Jasper watched Beth as she headed for the bathroom, and all Ray saw was the love in his friend's eyes.

"Jas, this whole surrogacy thing isn't weird for you, is it?" In anxiety, Ray lightly traced Viv's thigh with his fingertips.

Jasper thought about the question for a second. "I think more to the point is if you, being the father of my future children, will feel weird for you? My future children will be full-blooded siblings to this one or these two you're about to receive."

He shook his head. "You're going to make a great daddy. I couldn't ask for more than that. Like you said, they will be your children, not ours, and they'll be close, no matter what. We'll always be family. What about me being gay? You won't go blaming me if they follow in my footsteps, will you?"

"What if yours turn out complete and utter nutters like B?" Jasper countered.

Ray laughed. "I love B. Besides, she's not a nutter…most of the time."

"I heard that," Beth said as she came back from the bathroom. "Let's go down and be with the family. Grandma needs to see you two are really back together."

The last part of her speech was aimed at Viv. Ray felt his lover tense beneath his hand.

Ray waited until they had left before he pulled Viv back down onto the bed for a further round of hot and steamy kisses. He knew they had to join the others, but this was too good to pass up. Standing, Ray straightened his clothes, making sure he looked respectable. The problem was before they even made it out of the room Ray found himself half naked and having the hottest mutual hand job ever up against the back of the bedroom door. It was going to be super quick, and in Ray's opinion, one of the most erotic things he and Viv had ever done together. The way the man's cock felt pressed up against his own as Viv's hand enveloped them, tugging in a fast and furious pace, was turning Ray into a big pile of gelatin. This time they didn't speak. The only sound was the soft grunts as they came closer to completion. Slamming his eyes shut, he thrashed his head against the door as cum coated Viv's hand and their stomachs.

"Think I might need to change." Ray snickered.

Viv devoured his mouth in a hot and hungry kiss.

Taking the time to clean up, Ray kept a good arm's length away from Viv so they didn't get sidetracked again.

* * * *

When they finally went downstairs, Girly rolled her eyes at them. Ray blew her a kiss as he pushed Viv into an oversized armchair and sat on his lap.

"So, Grandma, have they told you they're all moving in after New Year's?" Ray snorted at her as she clapped her hands in joy. "I don't know about Brent and Tarni yet. They left before they gave me an answer. I suppose you can always ask them when they get back."

The festivities wore on, and it wasn't long before Brent returned with Tarni and her parents. Brent introduced them to everyone as Corazon and Hugh. Ray couldn't stop staring at Tarni's stepmother.

She returned his stare as though he was making her feel uncomfortable. Bluntly, she asked, "Are you staring at me because I'm black? If I make you uncomfortable, I can leave."

Everyone sitting near her turned to watch with amusement. Ray smiled as he saw the confusion in her eyes. "Sorry, I don't mean to be rude or make you feel uncomfortable, either. I keep staring at you only because you're so beautiful. Your face is...exquisite."

"Then... I guess... Thank you very much," Corazon replied. Her smile was slow as it crept across her face.

Ray's eyes widened even more as her beauty intensified ten-fold.

"Beautiful," he whispered, more to himself.

Girly leaned over and patted Corazon's arm. "In case no one has warned you, not only is Dad gay, but he's a bit of a dork. You'll get used to him, in time."

Corazon, who had insisted that everyone call her Cora, laughed a very strikingly-timbered laugh.

This, in Ray's humble opinion, only added to what there was to like about Corazon. He thought she was so very graceful in her movements. She seemed to be out of place next to Tarni's father, Hugh, who was so normal, but every time they looked in each other's direction, Ray sensed the love between them was exactly the way he felt about Viv.

If he admitted it to himself, Viv would have to say he was a little jealous as he watched Ray staring at Cora. The phone rang, and he was surprised when Antonio entered the room to say the call was for him. He was grateful when Ray followed him into the hall as he took the phone.

Viv collapsed into the chair as he listened. He couldn't believe what he was hearing and never in a million years would he ever have thought these people would be back in his life. When he hung up, Viv was shaking and he couldn't say anything as he stood. He needed to find Daniel.

"We've gotta go. There's been an accident. Mum's in the hospital." Viv turned to Ray. "Please come with me. I don't think I can do this alone."

Ray looked over at his grandma. "We'll be back as soon as we can," he said as they left the sitting room.

On the way to the garage, he grabbed his keys from his jacket, still hanging in the hall closet. Girly and Daniel followed close on their heels.

No one spoke as they drove to the hospital.

"Do you think *he'll* be here?" Daniel asked quietly as Viv parked the car. "I'm not sure if I want to see them. Not after what they did."

Viv knew Daniel remembered only flashes of his parents. As always, he would be remembering his father hitting Viv and their mother doing nothing at all to stop him.

He looked at his brother. Even Daniel didn't know the full reason behind Viv leaving home all those years ago. The feeling of almost being raped by the man who was supposed to be his father was something he'd never found the courage to confide in anyone, not even Ray. His mother had never done anything to stop Jeff from doing what he'd done, but after Viv had left, for whatever reason, she gave Daniel to him. At least this way Jeff hadn't been able to move on to the next easy target.

Pushing away the thoughts of hatred, he spoke. "They wouldn't tell me anything. They said we would talk when we got here. They got my contact details from my records from when I stayed here." Viv held Ray's hand as they walked into the hospital. At the administration desk, they were directed to the ER, then someone led Viv and Daniel into a cubicle. Their mother lay on a bed, covered in blood.

Her eyes filled with tears as she saw them. "My boys," she said softly.

Viv gently took her hand, his tears falling too. Seventeen years had gone by since he had last seen his mother, and, even though she had never been a true parent, in some strange way he still loved her. They turned as a nurse came in, carrying a sleeping infant in his arms and handed him to Viv. Viv stared at the baby. He could be no older than a few months. Sighing heavily, he slowly returned his gaze to his mother.

"Take care of him," his mother whispered. "You raised one of my sons and now I give you another. His name is Benjamin." Her voice sounded frail as she fought to speak.

A doctor asked to talk with Viv. All he could do was follow the man to an office. Unable speak, he looked down as Benjamin stirred in his arms.

"Mr Vivvens, I assume you want to know what happened."

Viv nodded.

"From what we understand, there was a head-on collision. I'm sorry to inform you that your stepfather died on impact. Your brother was the lucky one in all this. His capsule saved his life. He doesn't even have a scratch on him, though, after his examination, it is obvious he is malnourished. With time, young Benjamin will recover nicely. Your mother, on the other hand, is critical and refused treatment until we could track you and your brother down. We also—" A code blue rang out and the doctor jumped up as.

Viv followed him as he raced back to his mother's room. Standing there, he watched dumbstruck as medical staff rushed into the cubicle. They forced him and Daniel out into the hall as the staff went to work on their mother. Ray wrapped his arms around Viv and the sleeping child.

"What about Dad?" Daniel asked as he came to stand beside Viv. His hand shook as he rested it on Viv's arm. "Why isn't that bastard here?"

"It was a car accident, he didn't... He didn't survive... He..." Viv fell silent as the doctor exited and gravely shook his head.

"I'm sorry, son. There wasn't much we could do. She waited too long."

This time, when the doctor led Viv away, the others followed. There was a lot of paperwork for Viv to look over and sign. He reluctantly handed Ben to Ray. The baby woke up and began crying, and Viv heard Ray singing softly as he rocked the small boy back to sleep.

What seemed like hours later, they were finally allowed to leave. Ray still cradled Ben in his arms as they headed to the car. When they reached it, Viv looked at his watch and said quietly, "Merry Christmas."

Girly took the keys from Viv's hand and drove them home. Along the way, she pulled into an all-night mini-mart and ran in, coming back with diapers, bottles, a pacifier, formula, baby food, and a ton of little toys.

When Viv looked at her inquiringly, she said, "It's Christmas. The baby will need presents too."

Viv was surprised when everyone was still up and waiting for them. By the time they got inside, Benjamin had woken and was looking around wide-eyed, smiling when he saw the huge Christmas tree covered in lights. It made Viv think that maybe his littlest brother had been left often with different people. Any other child would be upset and crying by now.

"We'll be back in a tick. I think we need to go and change his nappy," Ray said.

Viv grabbed the nappies from Girly and followed Ray up to their room. Viv sat on the bed and watched as Ray changed Ben.

The doctor had been right, Ben was a little underweight, though Viv knew some of the infant clothes he had already bought would probably fit him. Ray must have had the same thought as he left Ben lying on the bed beside Viv and he went and got some pajamas that looked as though they might fit. Ray must have stopped in the bathroom on the way back because he also carried a warm, damp washer to bathe the baby with.

Viv was looking at Ben as Ray dressed him. "I wonder how old he is. We don't know anything about him. What's his middle name? What's his date of birth?"

Ben giggled as Viv reached across and tickled his tummy while Ray put powder all over him.

"We know some things," Ray said as he lifted Ben into his arms. "He's alive, he's happy, and probably hungry.

"Do you want to carry him or shall I?"

Viv took Ben. "We also know he's ours now."

"And he's the best Christmas present either of us could ask for," Ray whispered. "Sorry about your mother.

"You being here for me is what I need. I haven't been close to my mother for a very long time. I'm not exactly sure myself what I'm meant to feel. Come on. Let's head downstairs." Viv wasn't ready to tell Ray the whole truth about his lack of concern for his mum.

Girly must have been thinking the same thing. When they reached downstairs, she had a bowl of mashed food, a bottle warming in a jug and a towel to catch any mess.

Everyone listened as Viv told them what had happened. Uncle Matt said he would get Byron to looking up what they could find out about Ben, explaining this would also allow them to make discreet inquiries into the family.

* * * *

Christmas was a quiet affair. The funeral for Viv and Daniel's parents was set for the twenty-eighth of December.

Viv was getting Ben ready for the day when Ray asked, "Do you think he'll remember any of this?"

"God, I hope not. I sure wouldn't want to be reminded how my parents didn't love me enough to properly take care of me."

Ray never got a chance to answer as his phone rang. When he finished speaking, there was a strange look in his eyes. "We're needed downstairs."

As Ray led Viv into the room, Antonio entered behind them with a woman and child. The little girl, who appeared to be between one and two years old, squealed in delight.

"Baby!"

Viv stared in shock as he looked down into Daniel's eyes. He was saddened as she also looked underfed, and apparently, no one had washed or brushed her hair in a long time. It was filthy and matted.

"Christopher." The woman stared at Viv.

"Gwen," Viv retorted.

"I figured I'd find Ben with you. I went to the hospital and they gave me this address."

"What do you want, Gwen?" Viv asked his stepfather's sister.

Gwen pointed at the little girl. "I was supposed to have her for a week. That was nine months ago. I can't afford to look after her, and you seem to have come up in the world, so you can take care of her as well. I loved your mother, and I know my brother was a jackass, but Millie should be with you and your brothers. I'm assuming Daniel's still with you. I don't know if you realize this or not, but I was the one who forced your mother to drop him on your doorstep all those years ago."

"I'm still here," Daniel said from the doorway. He didn't greet her like family.

Viv knew there was no love lost between any of them, though he was shocked by Gwen's revelation of how he came to have Daniel all those years ago.

They fell into an awkward silence.

Finally, Ray spoke. "Could you please tell us their full names and dates of birth?"

Gwen looked at Ray curiously. "Millicent Jane Marshal, born January ninth, two thousand six, and Benjamin Christopher Marshal, born June eleventh, two thousand seven. If you want, I will find out what medical treatments they've had and send all the information to you. I've kept up with Millie's, but I don't know about Ben. Knowing my brother, their medical visits will have been few and far between. Everything else was more important than his own family."

"Thank you. We greatly appreciate what you're doing," Ray answered.

Viv was never more grateful to have Ray as part of his life.

Gwen stared at Ray curiously. "May I ask who *you* are?"

Viv was the one who answered abstractedly, not even realizing what had slipped out as he stared at the little girl. "Ray's my husband."

Disgust ran across her face then she turned her attention back to Viv. "I'll see you at the funeral, then. I assume there will be one."

Viv told Gwen where and when the service would be. She didn't look back or even say goodbye as she left the house.

As her aunt left, Millie didn't seem to bat an eyelid. Viv knelt beside Millie and she smiled.

"Hungry!"

"She didn't bring any clothes," Ray said, when he noticed the absence of bags.

"Dad's family is like that," Daniel answered. "They only care about themselves."

Viv picked up Millie and headed toward the kitchen. "Come on, sweetie. Let's go get you something to eat then we'll give you a nice bath." He wrinkled his nose at her sour smell. How could Gwen have treated such a precious little girl this way?

Grandma was surprised when Ray and Viv walked into the kitchen. "You seem to have children coming out of thin air... Oh my, doesn't she have young Daniel's eyes?" she said as she again looked at the child.

"Grandma, this is Millicent Jane Marshal. Millie, for short," Viv announced. At the kitchen counter with Grandma, Beth started laughing. "You do realize you could probably end up with four kids under the age of three?"

Grandma gasped, and Beth closed her eyes as she realized she'd let the cat out of the bag.

Opening her eyes again, she smiled. "Yes, we could be having twins, but we're keeping quiet until we're sure."

"My lips are sealed," Grandma said.

She and Beth watched as Viv found something for Millie to eat.

Ray had, moments before, joined them at the kitchen counter. Millie looked at Viv and said "Daddy!" before she snuggled into his neck.

With that one word, Viv felt his heart give over, as she filled a spot reserved only for his children. He pressed his hand against her small back, holding her close. "Yes, I'm your daddy... Well, one of them." He hugged her as he flashed a smile at Ray and said, "I hope you really like kids, because we're about to be run off our feet."

* * * *

Later that same day, Ray took his time as he bathed and shampooed Millie's hair then untangled it. It amazed him when it fell almost halfway down her back.

They still had a couple of hours of daylight left, so Ray and Viv went shopping and got some clothes, a double pram, a baby capsule, and child's booster seat for the car. Ray very much enjoyed shopping for these two small children now belonging to Viv and him. He couldn't wait for the child, or children, Beth carried to join them.

The next morning, Ray was in his element as he sat with Millie on his lap and picked up a brush. Pulling her hair up into piggy tails, he wrapped red ribbon in a bow around each one. Viv was laughing with them each time Ray blew raspberries on her back to make her giggle. Ray couldn't believe how good-natured she and Ben both were.

"You know," Ray said as he started doing the buttons up on her dress, "we'll have to go car shopping. The Mercedes isn't going to fit all the kids in when the next ones come along. I was thinking maybe a seven-seater wagon or one of those van things. What do you think?"

"Whatever you want, love," Viv answered.

Ray set Millie on her feet and began packing the nappy bag.

"Love, what are you doing?" Viv asked curiously.

"I remember whenever I took Girly anywhere, she was always hungry, so I always packed food to take with us. Trust me. I know what I'm doing—always pack food and extra clothes."

Ray saw Viv had tears in his eyes when Viv realized that everyone had decided to attend the funeral with them. Ray's parents hugged them as they got out of their car at the church, and Ray led the way inside. Viv and Daniel were the only ones to attend from their mother's side of the family, and only three people had come from Daniel's father's side. They ignored Daniel and Viv completely, though Gwen did come over and hand Ray an envelope of what he assumed were the medical records she had found. Ray thanked her and put them in the nappy bag as the service began. Both children were sleeping quietly in the pram, and Ray stood with one arm around Viv's waist. With his other hand, he took one of Daniel's and squeezed.

Fury burned in Ray's gut as once again Daniel's family walked away without so much as a goodbye. When everything was being organized for the funeral, they'd opted to have a double cremation. Ray didn't think Daniel would have been able to sit through a service twice. Neither Daniel nor Viv cried during the service, which struck him as odd, though he suspected the tears would come later.

* * * *

Antonio had been busy while they'd been at the funeral. When Ray and Viv went to dump their stuff in the room, they found that a single bed and a crib had been set up. In the parlor, a cradle and a playpen had also been added. And from God knows where he'd unearthed a heap of toys. Millie was happily investigating each one. She smiled over at him and Viv where they sat on the couch.

"Daddy."

"We're here." Viv rose, climbed into the playpen with her and sat on the floor of it as she promptly filled his lap with toys.

"The daddy look really suits you." Ray grinned.

After a while, she grew hungry. Viv picked her up and went to sit on the couch next to Ray, who was giving Ben his bottle. He rummaged through the nappy bag, pulled out a banana and peeled it for Millie to eat. Both looked up as Daniel called out, and Millie started giggling as Beth took a photo of the four of them.

"Your first family photo for your mantel." She smiled.

Ray shook his head. "Then you messed up, because we have two more children. Granted they're a little big to sit on our laps, but they're definitely ours. Come on, Girly, Dan. Get your backsides over here and into our family photo."

Daniel and Girly sat on the floor in front of them. Girly laid her head on Daniel's shoulder as Beth took another photo.

She had tears in her eyes after she took the picture. "Boy, you all look so good together."

Grandma joined them, sat on the settee, and announced that she was moving rooms. "I'm seventy-seven years old. I shouldn't have to be climbing stairs at my age, so I've decided to move into your grandpa's old room." She looked at Ray and Viv. "You two should take my room. The suite's sitting room can be turned into a nursery."

"Grandma, we can't do that." Ray smiled at her.

"Too late. Antonio and the staff are already rearranging things. The movers will be arriving soon.

I've arranged for them to bring the rest of your stuff from the other house."

Ray was stunned. "Grandma, the others haven't decided to move in yet."

"Well, are you going to share custody of these children and shunt them back and forth every couple of days? They need stability. Is Viv going to give up his job and his schooling to look after them full-time?"

"We haven't discussed this yet," Ray said, though he noticed Viv winced at the thought of giving up his job. Ray knew Viv loved his job.

"Well, I have thought about it, and this is how I see things. Viv will still go to work and school, and Ray will be the stay-at-home parent. Neither of you need to work, but I know how much Viv likes his job. Besides, I'll get very lonely if you leave me." She pouted.

"What about us, GG? What are we supposed to do?" Girly looked at her expectantly.

His grandmother didn't even blink as she answered. "Move in here, of course."

Daniel started laughing. "You just want to go skinny dipping in the pool with us."

"What about my house? Am I supposed to let it sit empty?" Ray asked. He needed to be sure his grandmother fully understood what was going on and that she was completely certain she wanted them there full-time.

"We'll find someone to housesit, or maybe you should sell. You don't need it. When I'm gone, you'll have this place."

Ray looked over at Jasper. "Want to buy a house?"

Jasper laughed. "Yeah, like I could ever afford your place."

"It's going cheap." Ray grinned back at his best friend.

"How cheap?" Jasper asked warily.

"You want to tell him, Grandma—or should I?"

"You will pay exactly the same price, and under the same conditions, Ray did when he bought the house from his grandfather."

"Which was?"

Beth burst out laughing. She remembered. "One carton of beer, and if we sell, Ray has first option of buying the property back for the same price."

"Hahn Premium Light, if you don't mind." Ray grinned.

"Then what am I supposed to do with my house?"

Daniel stated the obvious, "Find somebody to rent to, so you can pay the rates on both houses."

Ray couldn't believe everything seemed to be so easily falling into place. He hoped to God things stayed this way.

* * * *

Later that night, as they lay in bed, Ray broached a subject he'd never wanted to bring up again, but with the court case looming, he knew they were going to have to talk things through. He needed to suss out just how Viv was feeling.

"I know that after such a perfect day this may seem in bad taste, but we need to talk about Grace."

"Do we have to?" Viv sighed as he rolled onto his back.

Ray rolled until he was facing Viv. "Yeah, love, we do."

"Okay, fine, what do you want to talk about?"

Taking a moment to sort what he wanted to say in his head, Ray pushed up until he sat on the bed. He took Viv's hand and held it gently. "What do you think will happen to her?"

"Well, Byron says we have a good case against her. I will have to give evidence at some stage, but he's hoping she'll just plead guilty and save us all the trouble," Viv answered.

"Do you think that will be the end of it? That she'll finally be out of our lives?"

"Fuck, I hope so. I'm not sure how much more bullshit we need to wade through. I just want things to run smoothly for once. The sooner this court stuff is over, the better I will feel. Though, to be honest, I don't think I want to air what happened for the rest of the world to see, especially if it means dragging the Connelly name through the mud. I don't want that ever happening."

"We've weathered worse. No matter what happens, we'll be standing at your back. You're our family now."

Ray trembled as Viv slowly ran his fingertips over Ray's chest. "That feels nice," Ray said.

"You want nice? Then come here."

When Viv tugged on his arm, Ray willingly fell into his lover's embrace.

They quickly shed their clothes, and Ray grabbed the lube and tossed it onto the bed.

"I think we should buy stock in this stuff. We sure go through enough of it," he said, trying to lighten the mood.

He didn't even give Viv a chance to decide which position he wanted. Ray took matters into his own hands and started stretching his own arse out. Tonight, he needed Viv to fuck him through the mattress in punishment for bringing that bitch into their minds. Getting on all fours, he dropped his head to the bed and waited. It didn't take Viv long to move in behind him.

The slight burn as Viv entered him was almost overwhelming. In his head, he brought to mind so many unsexy things to stop him from coming before the fun really started. The way Viv filled him was wonderfully erotic, all in its own right. There was no talking necessary. Ray was willing take anything Viv had to offer then afterward, beg for more.

The sound of skin meeting skin, accompanied by the harsh breath of lust and unavoidable moans was like a symphony to Ray's ears—one that would play until the final crashing crescendo of orgasmic bliss.

He didn't have long to wait.

Tumbling to the bed, they drifted into sleep. Ray couldn't have felt any happier than he was at that very moment.

Chapter Ten

Viv lay in bed waiting for Ray to come in, as he thought back over the last three months, especially the parts since they'd found out they were pregnant and the other children had arrived.

In truth, it's totally fucking amazing how easily our lives have changed so completely, and yet it all somehow fits together better than it had been before. Ray is so fucking awesome — he took in two strange kids and claimed them as his own then spent his days playing or teaching them to swim and seems to love every damn minute of it. Ray truly is a beautiful person.

I can't believe how excited Ray got when the doctor confirmed Beth was carrying twins, and how enthusiastically he kissed everyone in the room — twice. When the doctor looked at him like he was a lunatic, Beth smiled and explained Ray really loves kids.

By the end of the first trimester, Ray had busily thrown himself into turning the sitting room into a nursery. Three cribs were set up against one wall, and Millie's bed was against another one. The doorway connecting the sitting room to the master bedroom was fitted with a door to give Ray and Viv some privacy when needed. As Ray explained, there was no need for little eyes to see everything.

There were more clothes than he could poke a stick at. There were so many that they took up half of one wall in closet space as well as four sets of drawers.

Viv smiled when he remembered even potty-training Millie seemed to be fun for Ray. Every night when Viv got home, Ray would get Millie to tell Viv the new word she had learnt. Daniel was Danu, Girly was Ree, Grandma was GG, Ray's parents were Nan and Pop, and he and Viv were both Dad. Ben was the only name she got right, but mostly she called him 'baby'.

Viv was so proud of his little family.

They had, only moments before, put the kids to bed, but Viv knew Ray liked to stand and watch them for a few minutes while they slept. Eventually he crawled onto the bed with Viv, smiling seductively as he did so.

"I love you, my husband."

Viv chuckled as Ray's lips found his. No matter how tired Ray was these days, he always made time for Viv when they first came to bed. If anything, their sex life had gotten even better and hadn't fizzled like so many people complained theirs did.

When Ray finally stopped kissing Viv, he said, "I think your kissing gets better and better every damn day." He grinned. "You wouldn't believe how turned on I am by you right now."

Leaning up on his elbows, Viv watched in awe as Ray stripped off his boxers and dropped them beside the bed within easy reach, in case he had to get up during the night. Tonight Viv found he was also completely turned on by Ray and couldn't keep his hands or his lips off him. Ray seemed to relish the attention. On nights like this, just sex wasn't what occurred — they made love.

Afterward, while they lay in each other's arms, Ray said something to make Viv feel so many wonderful things. If asked later, he wouldn't be able to even begin to explain how he'd felt.

"I think times like right now are making me wish one of us was a girl," Ray whispered against Viv's shoulder.

He tilted his face so he could look into Ray's eyes. "Why do you want one of us to be a girl?"

Ray smiled his crooked smile that Viv worshiped so much.

"Because then I could marry you."

"You want to marry me?" Viv was stunned.

"I would give anything to be able to marry you," Ray moaned, before he once again lost himself in Viv's kisses.

Viv adored having the effect of being able to scramble his lover's mind with only a kiss.

However, he couldn't believe how one little sentence could make him feel like he was capable of anything. In that instant, he wanted to marry Ray. More than anything in the world, he wanted that connection. Once Ray fell asleep in his arms, Viv slowly extricated himself and headed for the kitchen. Ben would be waking up for his bottle shortly, and Viv needed a cuppa — or maybe a shot of something stronger. His brain was on overload as he tried to sort it all out.

He wasn't surprised to find Grandma sitting in the kitchen with her own cup of tea. "What has you up at this time of the night?"

Viv smiled. "Cuppa, Ben's bottle, and your grandson just... He just..." Viv looked at her and couldn't help grinning. "Ray wants to marry me."

"I take it, judging by the smile on your face, you like the idea as well?"

Viv nodded. "I wish it could happen. We'd be a real family then." He made his cuppa then prepared a bottle, setting it aside to warm.

"You already are a real family. You can't get much more real than raising children and loving each other."

Viv thought about it. "I definitely love him. There is no denying that. Ray's such a fantastic father and a wonderful husband. But, you know as well as I do he deserves more. He's a good person, who should always get his heart's desire."

He quickly finished drinking his tea when he heard Ben through the baby monitor. He and Grandma sat and listened as Ray picked him up.

"Shh, baby. Daddy's here. Your other handsomer daddy disappeared. Hopefully, he's getting you a bottle, your big sister a drink, and me a can of Coke. Then we can all love him forever and ever," he obviously joked.

"You heard him." Viv snorted. "I have to go. My waitering services are needed." He snagged a sippy cup full of warmed milk for Millie, and a can of Coke out of the fridge, then grabbed the jug where the bottle was warming. "It was nice talking to you, Grandma. Don't stay up too late." He kissed her cheek as he headed back to their room.

In the hallway, he listened over the monitor while Ray changed Ben then put Millie on the potty. "Good girl, Millie. Who's Daddy's good girl? Soon you will be doing wees in the big girl toilet."

She giggled when Ray kissed her noisily and took her back to bed.

By the time Viv got there, Ray had pulled the rocking chair over beside Millie's bed and sat rocking with Ben in his arms as he sang softly to them both. Viv stood in the doorway and watched. At that moment, Ray looked…perfect. Viv moved the other rocker and held out his hands so Millie could climb onto his lap. Handing Ray the bottle, he sat with Millie while she drank from her sippy cup then he rocked her until she fell back to sleep.

Viv smiled at Ray as Ben finished his bottle. They both placed their bundles into their beds, put the chairs back where they belonged, rinsed the bottle and cup out in the bathroom, closed the door gently behind them and, hand in hand, went back to bed. Ray wrapped himself around Viv. How they went to sleep now would be how they woke up in the morning.

"I love you, Ray."

"I love you too." Ray yawned and pressed his face into Viv's chest to kiss him one last time before drifting off to sleep.

Viv soon followed.

* * * *

Another month passed, and Ray found himself sitting inside the nets of the safety trampoline with Millie as she jumped up and down, squealing. Viv and the rest were outside clapping each time she jumped. Whenever they clapped, she would give Ray a kiss.

"Come on, chicky-babe. One more jump and we'll go and give Dad some kisses."

Kisses was her newest word, and she demanded them from everyone. Ray looked at Viv. "I think we may have to keep our eye on this one when she grows up. If she's this free with her kisses now..."

Millie ran to Liam. "Pop, kisses. Pop... Kisses."

Liam covered her face in butterfly kisses as she laughed. Ray took Ben from Viv when Millie launched herself in Viv's direction.

"Dad... Dad kisses."

This was Millie's second birthday, and it surprised Ray when he found out Viv had invited some of the guys from his job and their families to come and help celebrate. Ray thought most of them were quite shocked to find out Viv was actually gay and his partner was Liam Connelly's son. The wives had invited Ray to join their playgroup, which he loved. This wasn't an official playgroup. Instead, they met at a different person's house every week so their kids could interact. They laughed when he said they had two more on the way. He gestured to where Millie was currently kissing Beth's stomach...kissing their babies.

* * * *

A few months later, Ray, Viv and Daniel sat in the parlor listening as Byron King told Viv and Daniel that they had another brother out in the world somewhere who was ten years old.

Confused, Daniel wondered why their mother didn't say anything to them about him at the hospital? Then again, she hadn't said anything about Millie either.

Byron shuffled through some papers on the coffee table and said, "The boy is currently in foster care. He was made a ward of the state nine and a half years ago. I've made inquiries into this, and they are willing to reunite the family if appropriate. Meaning, if you're both willing to take parental custody. His name is James Henry Marshal." Byron looked at each of them in turn before adding, "And, I'm told he has a slight mental problem."

"What do you mean?" Viv asked cautiously.

"He's been in many homes over the years, and in one of those homes, another foster child hurt him badly. This resulted in him being a little slow — he has learning problems. From what I gather, he takes a little longer for things to sink in, but there are no physical handicaps. He is a very happy child, he..."

Viv looked at Ray and saw pain wash over his face. His heart broke when he thought Ray wouldn't want another child. Five children were too many, especially if James had special needs, so he was surprised when Ray spoke.

"Of course we want him. He should be right here with the rest of his family." Smiling at Viv he said, "Lucky I love kids, don't you think?"

"I'm lucky you love *me*," Viv answered. "I wouldn't have been able to do this on my own." He turned to Byron. "Will the two of us being in a gay relationship be a problem?"

"Not that I'm aware of, but we do have a problem with Daniel's parents' life insurance. A Gwen Burke is contesting the will. She claims that since she had primary care of Millie for nine months, she should receive the money. She says Daniel cut all ties with his parents at an early age."

"I didn't cut ties with them. They threw me away. They were the ones who didn't want me," Daniel snarled.

"How much are we talking about?" Ray asked.

Byron picked up a piece of paper, "Between the two of them, there will be one hundred and fifty thousand. Initially, this was left to Daniel."

"I don't want a damn cent of it," Daniel said softly.

"What about for the younger ones, then? Though, to fight Gwen for the money would probably cost more than the payout."

Ray smiled. "Somehow I don't think we'll be fighting. If Daniel doesn't want the money, give it to Gwen. None of our children will need anything from their past. I want you to look into our adopting them legally, so nobody can ever take these children away from us."

* * * *

At the end of the meeting, Daniel and Viv went to find Girly, who was looking after the kids.

Ray stopped to talk with Byron. "I do have something else you might be able to help me with. I want to keep tabs on Grace Kennedy. I know after her sentencing, she was remanded in custody, but she must have got herself a lawyer because he's been trying to establish contact with Viv — and that, I won't allow. Especially now that we've been informed to make no contact whatsoever. I thought we had a clear-cut case against her."

"Do you think she is liable to cause problems?"

"I don't know, but if I took a guess then I'd say yes — she is definitely up to something. At this stage, I'm not going to tell Viv what I'm asking you to do, because I don't want him pulled into her bullshit yet again. He and Dan have already been hurt too much by her antics. Viv and I have talked about this and he just wants it over. I want to be able to give him that peace of mind."

"Okay, Ray," Byron said as Ray walked him to the door. "I'll see what I can find out, and I'll get back to you."

"Thank you."

* * * *

Viv watched as Ray pushed Millie on the swing set Ray had built for the little ones. The fact Ray was so willing to take in his whole family still amazed him. A week had passed since they had found out about James, and Ray had already started to get his room ready. They were waiting for all the appropriate paperwork to be finalized before they could bring another member of their family home.

Plucking up the courage, Viv asked some of the questions he wanted answers for.

"If they let us adopt the kids, what last name will they have — yours or mine?"

Ray seemed to think about it for a while, "They could have yours if you wanted — or mine — or both. I don't really care, as long as they're legally ours."

"It matters. We're a family, and we should all have the same last name," Viv whispered. He wanted to make sure Ray understood what he was saying.

"And how are we going to do that?"

"I could marry you." Viv's breath caught in his throat while he waited for Ray to reply.

Ray turned and stared at him. "We're gay. Even if we have a commitment ceremony, we still have our own last names."

"Not if I change mine legally by deed poll. If I did that, then we could all have the same last name." Viv didn't add that he had already started the process.

Ray gave the swing a push when Millie called out to him. His mind was apparently reeling with the possibilities. "How did you come up with this idea?"

"The night you said you wanted to marry me. Well, I've been thinking about this, and when I thought my way through the problem, I went to Grandma and talked the idea over with her. I told her I was willing to sign anything she wanted to protect your money. I didn't want anyone thinking I'm after what's yours." Viv reached into his pocket, pulled out and handed Ray a small box. "I'll get down on one knee if you want me to."

Shock registered on Ray's face. There was no other possibility. His hands trembled and tears filled his eyes as he opened the box. Viv dropped down onto one knee.

"Raymond Alexander Connelly, will you marry me?"

The ring was beautiful, and one he knew Ray recognized as his grandma's.

"Grandma said this ring had special meaning to you, so we had it resized, hopefully to fit you." Viv took the box from Ray and pulled out the ring. "Well, a yes or a no would be helpful about now," he said nervously.

"Yes," Ray said breathlessly. "Yes! Yes! Yes!"

He held out his left hand as tears ran down his face. Viv slid the amethyst and diamond ring onto his finger.

"This is the ring Grandma gave to Isobel when she and Larry got engaged, before she did her runner on us all. I thought it got buried with her."

Viv got to his feet and hugged Ray tightly against his body. "I love you so much, Ray," he whispered as he brought their lips together.

Their kiss ended with a very determined Millie, demanding to be pushed.

"One more push, chicky-babe, then it's bathtime for you," Ray said as he wiped his tears away.

* * * *

No more than an hour later, Ray and Viv trooped into the kitchen with the children and took their places at the table.

"Hey! That's Mum's ring," Girly said as she grabbed hold of his hand.

"It's mine now." Ray smiled. "Viv and I just got engaged."

He laughed as Girly screamed and threw her arms around him. Then she did the same to Viv.

His whole body thrummed with happiness every time he thought about what was to come. Soon he was going to be a married man in the truest sense of the word and he wouldn't have changed anything. In the end, he had got what he wanted—Viv.

"We'll have to have an engagement party," she said enthusiastically. "I'll get Tarni to help me organize it—or maybe her mother. Cora's a wiz when it comes to stuff like this. "Who will we invite?"

Ray turned to Viv and studied his fiancé's face. "What do you think? Family only?"

"I don't know. Tony and the guys from the club would be pretty cut if we didn't invite them, and some of the guys from work and their wives would probably like to be here as well."

"That's a brilliant idea. I'd love to have the girls from playgroup and their families here to help us celebrate. We could have a big family barbecue type thing with jumping castles for the kids." Ray's excitement grew with each passing second.

Girly pulled out her phone and called Tarni to set up a date when they could all get together and plan. Even Grandma got caught up in the enthusiasm of the planning of the party. She called Antonio in to give him the news that he would be helping to organize the catering of first the engagement party, then later on the wedding.

In the midst of the weirdly controlled chaos, Viv turned to Daniel and said, "I'm also going to change my last name, so our all the family has the same surname. When we get married, I'll become Christopher Connelly."

"But I still get to call you Viv, right?" Daniel asked.

Ray had to bite the inside of his cheek to stop the bubble of laughter from breaking free.

"Yes. You can still call me Viv. Things will be less confusing for the children if everyone has the same last name."

"So what did Nan and Pop say?" Girly asked.

"We haven't told them yet," Ray admitted. "Viv only asked me a little over an hour ago."

"Um, technically that's not true," Viv stated softly. "I went and told your father after I talked to Grandma about my plan. I wanted to do everything right, so I went and asked for your hand in marriage. Your father was the one who gave me the suggestion of changing my name by deed poll. Liam said Vivvens-Connelly or Connelly-Vivvens was too much for kids to learn to spell."

"What would you have done if he had hated the idea?"

"I probably wouldn't have asked you. I would rather live the way we are than cause an upset within your family. Plus, I wanted to get him to organize a pre-nup to protect you."

"We don't need a pre-nup," Ray said matter-of-factly. Deep inside his heart, he knew Viv would never do anything intentionally to hurt him.

"Yes, we do, Ray. I told your father I would never ask for one cent of your money, but I did have a few stipulations of my own."

"Like what?" Ray asked curiously.

"Well, we'll be sharing custody of all our children. I want to be able to visit them if we ever get divorced, and I wanted all our children to be considered equal," Viv said quietly. "And then I told him about James Henry, but I think Byron must have already told him since he didn't seem really surprised."

Ray leaned over and kissed Viv deeply. "I love you, Mr Connelly." When they broke apart he added, "Thought I'd try your new name out. It does have kind of a nice ring to it."

As the night progressed, they continued talking about the upcoming engagement party. Ray couldn't wait for the real thing.

* * * *

Ray couldn't contain his excitement. A week later he, along with Viv who held Ben in his arms, and Millie, all stood on the back lawn of Grandma's estate and watched while the party was being set up. Between Cora and Antonio, they had done a fantastic job in a very short amount of time. He couldn't believe how organized they both were. Millie was clapping her hands in excitement and dancing at their feet as the jumping castle was inflated. With the arrival of a strange vehicle, Ray's focus was pulled from the party's set-up. It came to a stop beside the house. A woman got out, followed by a young boy who stood behind her. Viv walked in their direction.

"I'm looking for Christopher Vivvens," she said hesitantly as they approached.

"That's me," Viv said as he handed Ben to Ray.

The woman looked at him doubtfully, and Ray wondered.

Eventually the woman said, "By the courts, you have been awarded custody of your brother, James Marshal."

Ray winked at the young boy peeking at him from behind the lady. In return, the youngster rewarded Ray with a shy smile. Ray thought the kid was a beautiful boy. It didn't matter whether or not he had a mental handicap. As of that moment, James Henry was another most welcome part of their family.

"Is this him? Is this James?" Viv crouched so he was eye level with James.

Young James looked exactly like Ray imagined Daniel had at the same age.

"Do you know why you're here?" Viv asked softly.

The boy nodded. "You're my big brother, and now you're going to be my new dad." James visibly relaxed when Viv grinned at him.

"Yes, I'm your brother, and yes, I'm going to be your dad. Would you like that?"

"I'm scared." James stepped into Viv's arms.

Ray's heart dissolved a little more from the love of how his family was growing.

"Don't be scared," Ray told James, as Viv hugged the young boy. He pointed to the party preparations. "This is all for you to welcome you to our family."

"Who's he?" James whispered loudly in Viv's ear and pointed at Ray.

"Well" — Viv glanced at Ray — "that's Ray and he'll be your other dad."

While Viv spoke gently to James, the woman's eyes seemed to bug out of her head. Ray was glad that Viv didn't see her reaction.

"And she's your sister, Millie." Viv pointed at Millie, who now stood beside Ray holding onto his leg. "And the baby Ray's holding is your brother Ben. Then, you have another brother named Daniel. That's him over there." He gestured to where Daniel stood with his arms wrapped around Girly. "The girl with him is your sister Sara. We call her Girly." Viv smiled encouragingly at James. "And soon we'll have two new babies joining the family too, but we don't know if they are boys or girls yet."

"You have seven children!" the woman blurted out in disbelief.

Ray waited until she had regained some of her composure before speaking. "Yes, but only five of them are under the age of eleven, and four of those five are under the age of three."

The woman, who still hadn't given her name to them, sputtered as she tried in vain to work it out. "And how will you provide for all these children? I was notified you were informed James is a special needs child."

Ray didn't want to cause the lady any more stress, so as calmly as he could, he explained. "Look, Mrs..." He waited for her to introduce herself.

"Heatherington." She held out her hand to Ray. "My name is Karli Heatherington."

Ray shook her offered hand. "I'm a Connelly. My family owns the Connelly Corporation and we have more money than we could possibly ever use. I promise you, our children want for nothing."

"Can I have a bike?" James asked shyly, but with a hint of excitement.

"You can have anything you want, little man." Ray chuckled.

"Can I have a red one? Red goes faster," James said matter-of-factly.

"Then a red one you will have." Ray winked at the boy. "Can you swim, James?"

When he nodded, Ray said, "Good. I was going to take Millie and Ben for a swim. Do you want to come with us? We can leave Viv to talk with this nice lady.

Ray asked Mrs Heatherington for James' bags. There were only two small ones, so he called Daniel and Girly over to help and introduced them to their newest sibling. Seeing Daniel and James together, there was no doubt in Ray's mind that the two were related.

Girly picked up a giggling Millie and carried her inside, while James got a piggyback ride from Daniel. Ray carried the bags in one hand and Ben in the other, leaving the one little box of toys for Viv to carry in. They had managed to fit another child's bed into the nursery, as Ray didn't think James should sleep by himself when he first arrived. Being alone might scare him. When Daniel and Girly had left, Ray helped James unpack his clothes, mentally making notes of what he would need to buy for him.

James seemed embarrassed when Ray unpacked some pull-ups. "I wet the bed sometimes so Deena made me wear them. She didn't like having to wash my sheets. She got really angry whenever I wet the bed." His hand automatically went to his bottom in apparent memory of his caregiver's anger.

The boy's action saddened Ray so he hugged him. "Well, we won't get angry if you wet the bed. I don't mind washing sheets and neither does your other dad. So don't you worry about anything. Accidents happen."

"I'll wear my pull-ups. I don't want to make you angry." A frown marred his face. "I don't want to be sent back to Deena's. Sometimes she's mean."

James put the pile of pull-ups in the drawer.

Tears welled in Ray's eyes. He blinked furiously, trying to stop them before James noticed.

"Son, you won't ever be going back to Deena's. You belong to our family now, and we will never give you away." He watched as James changed into shorts, then gasped when he saw the red welts across James' bare bottom. This angered him, but he didn't want to embarrass James any further, so he didn't comment on them. Instead, he changed Millie into her togs and put a waterproof nappy on Ben.

"Are you ready to go swimming?" Ray took the kids into his room while he changed into board shorts, throwing Viv's onto the bed so he would know to come join them when he was done.

Taking James by the hand, he led him down through the house and out to the enclosed pool area. He wanted James to know that here he would be loved. James was now with his family.

Daniel and Girly met them in the pool area, and they all stayed in the shallow end for James as he was afraid of the deeper water. Ben sat in his floaty chair, and Ray held Millie in his arms.

"I called Nan and Pop and told them of our new arrival." Girly smiled. "They're going to bring a little welcome present. I told them how gorgeous he is. Dan's parents sure knew how to make cute babies."

"It's about the only thing they did right," Daniel mumbled.

They were all playing in the water when Viv joined them. Millie made him laugh when she held her hands out to him.

"Kisses, Dad. Kisses."

She squealed in delight, giggling as Viv covered her face in kisses. He stopped long enough to kiss Ray before wading over to James.

Soon Tarni stuck her head through the door and told them they should get dressed, as the guests would be arriving soon. Reluctantly, they all climbed out of the water and, after drying off, they headed back into the house to get ready.

Ray liked the fact that they were having a casual affair, and people could relax and be themselves. The engagement—and now a welcome home James—party was an afternoon event, so the children attending could enjoy themselves. Only family would be there later on tonight. He had to laugh as the guys Viv had invited were the same ones who came to Millie's birthday party. Ray had invited the new families of his playgroup. They all knew he was gay, so they weren't surprised. What did surprise them all was when Ray got up and joined the band on stage and started singing, and when Beth got tired, he replaced her on the drums while Girly picked up his guitar. After a while, the DJ was in control and played music for the rest of the party, and Ray and Viv took turns at dancing with all their kids or just dancing with each other.

Ray was in hysterics when he witnessed his father climb into the jumping castle with James and all the other kids. Tears flowed down his cheeks with each new wave of laughter. His father didn't seem to care that the kids were jumping all over him. He smiled at Ray and said he was getting into practice for when the smaller grandkids got older. Ray realized his dad truly was happy for him and agreed with the new paths his life had taken. Ray was still standing there watching him when Viv encircled his waist. Ray leaned back into his embrace.

"What are you thinking about, love?" Viv asked as he kissed the shell of his ear.

"Honestly, I just realized I'm very happy." He gently rocked the pram with one hand where Millie was falling asleep. In his other arm, he held Ben. "I have a very sexy fiancé. I have five beautiful children, with two more on the way, and I finally—for once in my life—feel complete. You all make me complete."

Viv leaned close to his ear and whispered, "You're turning me on so much right now. I'd like nothing better than to strip you naked and have my wicked way with you."

"Later tonight, after the children have all gone to bed, you can do whatever you want to me." Ray hummed in appreciation when Viv kissed his throat. "Now stop that before I forget I'm a respectable father and an almost married man." He sighed as Viv ignored him. "I love you, Viv."

"I love you too," Viv said as he finally stopped.

From somewhere on their left, one of the guys from the corporation called out to Viv.

"What's up, Don?" Viv asked as they walked to where a group of Viv's workmates all sat talking.

"We were wondering... When the time comes for the wedding, who gets the buck's night and who gets the hen's night?"

Good-natured laughter rippled over the group, but Ray knew their words were not meant harshly.

"That's easy." Ray laughed with them all. "I'm the wife in this relationship, so I get the hen's night. Besides, most of my friends are your wives, but don't be expecting me to wear a dress at the wedding. I just don't go there, though I could totally pull it off if I had to try. I've been told I have a frickin' fantastic set of legs," he said with a straight face.

Don laughed so hard he fell off his chair, which set everyone off again.

"And what a beautiful wife you are." Viv grinned as he kissed Ray smack on the lips.

"I know. I've been telling everyone that for years," Ray joked. "Now, if you gentlemen will excuse me, I think I need to change my son's nappy," he said as a putrid smell drifted their way. "Can I leave Millie here with you, love?" Viv covered Millie over with her rug and Ray kissed his cheek before he left.

* * * *

Joining his friends, Viv's gaze never left his fiancé until he was out of sight. In his eyes, Ray was becoming more perfect with each new day they woke up together.

"You know," Don said, turning to Viv, "I would never have picked you for being gay."

"I didn't think I was until I met Ray," Viv said. "He needed a boyfriend for something, and Daniel and Girly told everybody I was the one. I was so angry about it at the time. But Ray *was supposed* to find a real boyfriend to take my place. Then, one day I finally realized I *was* the real boyfriend. Somewhere along the way, I had truly fallen in love with him. Maybe the amount of kissing and hugging we always ended up doing while we were playing pretend tipped me over the edge." Viv laughed. "It still came as a bit of a shock to me when I finally admitted it aloud."

Don shook his head in something akin to awe. "And now you have a whole bunch of kids."

"Yeah, well, we already had Dan and Girly, but when my parents died, we got Millie and Ben. Then we found out about James, but by then B was already pregnant and we'd found out she's having twins. So now we have a whole lot of kids, and surprisingly, Ray loves every second of being a dad. I think I'm a very lucky man."

"Want two more? Mandy's sister and her kids are with us. Sweet kids really, but they've had one hell of a life. Teddy and Charlotte must be about the same age as a couple of yours," Don said soberly and started to tell Viv the whole story of what his sister in-law and her two children had been through.

* * * *

When the last of the guests had gone home, the family had moved indoors and were relaxing in the sitting room chatting about everything that had happened during the party. James had climbed onto the chair beside Ray and snuggled into his side. Ben was asleep in his cradle, and Millie was again tucked up in the pram. As James listened, his eyelids drooped. In his arms, he clutched the huge, plush Teenage Mutant Ninja Turtle toy Ray's parents had brought for him. He curled further into Ray's side and fell asleep. Ray looked up as Beth took a photo of them.

"You look so into being a father, you make me sick with jealousy," she said as she came and sat beside him.

A chuckle escaped him. "It'll be your turn soon enough. Are you two all moved into the new house?"

"Nearly. Unpacking is the fun part—or would be if I wasn't as big as a house." She patted her stomach. "But strangely, I still think of that place as your home, and our belongings there look so weird."

"That won't last long. Soon you'll feel like you have lived there forever." Ray gently rubbed her tummy and smiled as he felt the babies move against his touch. "I can't wait for them to be born. I think we'll make gorgeous babies."

"With your face, we can't go wrong." Beth smiled. "Well, on that note, I think I'm off to bed. They get cranky if I don't get enough sleep." She kissed Ray's cheek before Jasper pulled her to her feet.

Viv took her place. "You look tired, love."

Ray agreed wholeheartedly, yet he still found enough energy to smile at his fiancé. "I am, a little. We should get the kids upstairs and put to bed. They've had a big day. We all have." Ray lifted James into his arms and carefully stood so he didn't wake him up, then they said goodnight to the family. Viv picked up Ben and pushed Millie in the pram. Managing to pick up one end of the pram, Ray helped with it as they climbed the stairs.

"I don't know how we'll manage this when we have two more," Ray half joked.

Viv chortled softly. "That's why we have two older children. They get to help."

"You always have the best ideas."

"Well, it's another reason why you're marrying me."

"That, and because you turn me on so damn much," Ray joked again.

"Always a plus. Do you think you can stay awake long enough for me to finish what I started at the party?"

Ray grinned. "I'll try, but if I can't, you'll have to use and abuse me while I sleep, then wake me up for my turn."

Ray was glad Viv had insisted on bathing the kids when they first came inside. He gently lay James in his bed and covered him over before kissing his cheek. James smiled, and his eyes fluttered open.

"Don't forget my pull-up, Pa," he said as he sat up on the edge of the bed.

"I won't." Ray opened the drawer, withdrew one of the little paper garments then helped him into the pull-up.

"Night, Pa," he whispered as got back into bed, rolled onto his side, snuggling his Ninja Turtle. Ray kissed his back before standing up.

"He's really taken to you, hasn't he?" Viv whispered.

Ray smiled at him as he changed Millie's nappy and put her into bed.

"I like being a father, and these kids need to know they're loved. I have more than enough love to go around. We'll have to go shopping tomorrow and buy him some decent things," he said as he dragged Viv into the shower. "I just realized we'll have to think of another boy's name now, since we already have a James."

"What about Michael or Jebidiah?"

"I like Jebidiah—Jebidiah Liam Connelly, and we can call him Jeb for short."

"What about Brandon Robert?"

"What about girls' names? I still want Isobel Christine, but we need another one in case we end up with two." Ray kissed Viv on the chest.

"I've always liked Layla Kathleen."

"Beautiful," Ray said as they turned off the shower and dried each other. "Now take me to bed and have your way with me while I'm still alert enough to really enjoy it."

"Your wish is my command."

* * * *

As they lay there afterward, Ray couldn't help but smile. He heard James stirring and told Viv to put his boxers back on. He was sure they would be getting a midnight visitor.

Moments later, Viv chuckled as he felt James pat his shoulder.

"I'm scared. Can I sleep in here with you?" Viv didn't say anything as he made room for him in the middle of the bed. "Night, Dad." James kissed Viv's shoulder. "Night, Pa," he whispered sleepily as he turned and did the same to Ray.

When Ray was sure the boy was asleep, he whispered, "It's moments like this I love being a father."

In the morning, Ray woke with Viv spooning him, and James was wrapped up in Ray's arms. This was how they had gone back to sleep after the midnight toilet run. This boy needed love and he and Viv were the right parents to give it to him.

There was a noise beside the bed and he smiled when he saw Millie's head pop up.

"Hello, chicky-babe." He pulled Millie up onto the bed.

She held a book in her hands.

Ray pushed himself into a sitting position and sat Millie on his lap as he began reading her *Theodore Mouse*. By the time he'd gotten to the end, Viv and James had both woken and were listening to the story as well. Viv rose to attend to Ben, who had begun fussing, and brought him back to the bed. They all listened as Ray read the story through for a second time.

"I think we should all change before we go down for breakfast." Ray put the book aside. "We have to go shopping today. I have lots of spoiling to do."

While everyone got dressed, Ray turned to Viv. "I think we'll probably have to hire a nanny for when you're at work, especially when the next two get here. I love kids, but even I will need help with so many."

Viv was silent for a while then said, "Don was telling me last night his sister-in-law is looking for a job, but she has two kids, a boy and a girl. They're three and ten, I think." Viv drew Ben's shirt over his head. "She just got through a messy divorce, but she did work in childcare for a while. I'm sure Don said she's twenty-nine."

"I suppose we could talk to her, but she would have to be someone I can get on with. I mean, she'll be in close contact with our babies, and I'd have to feel comfortable with her around them. She would also have to get on with the rest of our family and our extended family. Also her kids would all have to get along with ours." Ray handed Viv a clean shirt. "What's her name?"

Viv thought for a moment. "Amanda, I think, but that could be the little girl's name. The little boy is Teddy, for sure, or maybe the little girl could be Fred."

Laughing, Ray replied, "I think you have things backwards. Amanda is Don's wife. But I do know exactly who you're talking about. The woman is Fred, the girl is Charlotte, and yes, the boy is Teddy. They were at the party yesterday. Fred was the pretty redhead with the pixie haircut running around like a mad woman after her kids. Teddy was the little blond boy James followed around," he explained to Viv. "She's come to our playgroup a few times. Maybe you should give Don a call and see if his sister-in-law can come over for an interview. She could bring the kids while we talk with her. We can send the car for her if she needs a ride. Try to make an appointment for this afternoon, as I still want to shop this morning."

Viv guffawed. "Whatever you want, love."

"If you don't know their number, look in my address book under Mandy." Ray pointed to the book on their dresser. "Keep an eye on the kids while I quickly get changed." Ray went into the closet.

When he finally came out fully dressed, Viv was hanging the phone up. "She'll be here at two, so we'll have to be back by then."

"Plenty of time." Ray grinned as he picked up Millie and strode for the door. "Come on, James. Let's go eat."

Viv hooted, to Ben's delight, as they followed Ray.

* * * *

Ray loved the way James' eyes lit up when he realized they were shopping mainly for him. That look alone was so worth the cost of spoiling him. James could hardly contain his excitement when they stopped at the bicycle display. Ray asked the staff to take a red one to the front to pick up later on their way out of the store. Before they left the sporting goods department, James picked out a black helmet with a skull and crossbones painted on the sides.

"Can you ride a bike?" Ray asked. When James nodded, Ray didn't want to leave Millie out so he also added a trike for her to their order.

By the time they'd all had lunch, they needed to head home for their interview with Fred. When they arrived, they found she was already waiting for them. Ray stopped long enough to call Girly and Daniel down to unload the car.

"I'm so sorry, Fred," Ray apologized as he entered the sitting room. "I hope you haven't been waiting long." He placed Ben in a cradle as he sat on the sofa.

Viv entered carrying Millie, and James followed him.

"Viv, this is Fred. Fred, this is my husband-to-be, Chris, but we all call him Viv." Ray smiled as James sat on the floor with Teddy and offered to share the box of cars he was carrying. Teddy ran his fingertips across James' cheek and grinned as Daniel placed the toy garage on the floor in front of them. Viv put Millie on the mat beside Charlotte. The two girls sat staring at each other.

"We've never hired a nanny before, so we're not quite sure what we're doing." Ray laughed.

She shrugged at him in return. "You're meant to tell me about my position, my responsibilities, my dress code, my wages..."

"Well, the dress code is whatever you decide to put on in the morning. The position is as a live-in nanny, but you don't have to live in if you don't want to.

Your responsibilities are to help me out when Viv's at work because, once the twins get here, I'll need help or I'll be forced to turn into an octopus. Finally, wages. They'll be above the award rate." He blushed. "Let's face it, there will be so many kids to take care of between us, it'll get tiresome so I need to entice you to stay. I don't want you to run away screaming when they all start crying at once."

She sat, wide-eyed, considering all that he'd just said.

He added, "The important thing to us is that you must treat our children like you do your own, and also you will have to put up with our extended family. Did I mention James is a special needs child?" Ray wasn't sure if he was saying the right things. Panic started to swirl through him.

Fred blinked, as though clearing away confusion, then patted Ray's arm. "Now you're meant to tell me I'm on a three-month trial to see how I work out."

"Okay," Viv said. "You're on a three-month trial. Now, will you be living in or out?"

"In, I think. Don and Mandy will be glad to finally get their house back to themselves again."

"In that case, let's go and inspect your rooms." Ray stood and held out his hand to help her up as Girly and Dan came down the stairs. Asking them to stay with the kids, he led Fred to go look at the living quarters, allowing Teddy and James to come with them.

"Now, will you want Teddy to have his own bedroom or will you be happy to let him share with James?" Ray opened the door across the hall from theirs. "This is James'."

James and Teddy looked bug-eyed at all the new things they saw, including two beds with

Transformers quilt sets. James returned with his Ninja Turtle and climbed up onto one of the beds with the toy where he lay down. Then he grinned at Ray and Viv. Teddy scrambled onto the other bed and bounced up and down, grinning at James as he did.

"I think they decided to share," Fred said quietly. She seemed a little shocked. "Teddy doesn't... He's usually a loner."

Viv laughed as they left to go to the next chamber. All the kids now explored the new toys they shared. As they walked into the room next door, Ray explained that the girls could share it, but there was still more remodeling to finish.

Viv patted Fred's arm as they led her into their sitting area, which was to remain the nursery.

Ray moved onto the next door. He looked inside and quickly shut it again. "Hold on a second," Ray said as he slipped inside.

"Josh, wake up, man." Ray shook Josh until his eyes opened. "What are you doing in here?"

Josh looked at him in a daze. "I was sleeping."

"This is the nanny's quarters. I don't think she'll be too happy to find a strange man in her bed." As Josh stood, Ray leered. "Especially when he's naked."

While Josh got dressed, Ray quickly remade the bed, making a mental note to have the sheets changed before Fred moved in. This wasn't initially going to be the nanny's personal space but it was close by and usually vacant.

Ray was still grinning as they walked out into the hall. "Sorry about that." Ray snickered as Josh stared at Fred. "Josh, meet Fred. She's going to be our new nanny."

"Nice to meet you. I'm sorry about crashing in your bed. I must have ended up taking a wrong turn last night and ended up in the wrong wing. By the way, welcome to the family." He walked away, whistling to himself.

"What a strange man." Fred giggled, as she watched him leave.

Ray opened the door and showed Fred into what would be her place. "So beautiful!"

Both he and Viv relaxed.

"Then you like it?" Viv asked nervously.

"*Yes*. When do you want me to start?" She ran a hand over the end of the bed.

"Today. I still need to go and organize for James enrollment into the local school. Will Teddy change schools or will you want him to stay where he is?"

"Things will be easier if they're at the same school. At least they'll each know one other person there on their first day."

Viv and Ray escorted Fred downstairs and introduced her to the rest of the family. Grandma liked her immediately and asked Antonio to have Fred's things brought to the house. Surprisingly, Josh even offered to give her and the kids a lift home so she could oversee the move and say goodbye to her family.

Girly snickered behind her hand.

Ray realized they were in for some interesting times as Josh was the only one out of their group of friends who was taking Grandma up on her offer to move in permanently. He now lived in the guest wing.

"So are we ready to go and get your stuff?" Ray asked nervously, only recognizing then how big of a step this really was.

"Um, yeah, now would be a good time," Fred answered. She turned to Teddy, who was still talking avidly to Jamie. "You ready, big guy?"

"Can I stay here, Mum? Girly and Dan said we can build a fort. I want to stay here with Jamie."

"Is everything okay?" Ray asked as he stepped to her side. "He'll be perfectly safe here?"

Fred nodded. "Remember upstairs when I said Teddy was shy. I meant it. I've never seen him so...relaxed and happy."

"Come on, the sooner we get your stuff, the sooner we can come back and you can check on him.

When Josh carried Charlotte out to Viv's old car, Ray had to smirk. Josh was now using Viv's car. Viv was driving Ray's Mercedes, and Ray had opted for a KIA Carnival so there would be space for all the little ones. Ray didn't care at all about Dan and Girly teasing him for buying 'the Mum wagon', and he'd already fitted out the rear seats with two baby capsules and two booster seats for Millie and for Ben.

Ray's thoughts returned to the present when Antonio handed him the phone.

"Okay, we'll be there," Ray said as he hung up.

"Who was that, love?"

"Byron. I don't know how, but he has managed to get us an emergency adoption hearing at nine o'clock tomorrow morning. If all goes well, they'll all be Connellys by lunchtime." Ray couldn't tamp down the surge of excitement filling him.

Viv threw his arms around Ray and kissed him. "I love you!"

"I love you too." Ray laughed, caught up in Viv's enthusiasm. "Now, do you have to ring someone to let them know you won't be in tomorrow? When we're done at the courts, we still have to check out James and Teddy's new school."

Viv took the phone. "I'd better let Marcus know. He's head of our department and will need to fill my spot for the day." Viv walked out of the room.

Grandma said, "I was thinking the old hall would make a good playroom for the children. Come walk with me and we will discuss the possibilities."

The old hall had at one time been a small ballroom. When he and Girly were younger, they used to play in there on rainy days. He laughed as memories came back to him. It was also the spot where he had first kissed Beth and, strangely, it was also the first room where he'd ever kissed a boy. He wondered if Josh even remembered kissing him.

"See? There's plenty of space for them to run around and it's soundproof. Your grandfather made sure of that when Isobel was little."

Ray laughed again. "I think I'll have fun shopping to stock all this up." The good thing was that this section of the house also had a bathroom and a kitchenette. "Your idea is perfect, Grandma, and if they're in here, they won't destroy the rest of the house."

"That thought never even crossed my mind," she said with an innocent smile.

Back in the parlor, Ray discovered his parents were there and Pop was in the middle of a tea party with Millie and the two boys.

As he looked up at Ray, he smiled. "Byron called me with the good news, so we thought we would come around and celebrate."

"Shouldn't we hold off until they're legally ours? What happens if they knock us back?" Ray asked worriedly as he sat beside Viv and took the hand his man offered.

"Byron says you will be up in front of Judge Hayden Pierce, and he's a big believer in keeping the family together as a unit for stability. Byron said to tell you both to wear suits as he's also a big believer in showing the courts respect."

"I just hope everything goes our way," Viv whispered.

"Me too," Ray whispered back.

Chapter Eleven

Nervous, Viv watched Ray slowly pacing back and forth in the hall of the local courtroom. For nearly an hour, they'd been waiting to see the judge. Ray had insisted on bringing all the children with them, though it surprised Viv when everyone else had insisted on coming as well. Ray's family shouldn't still be able to surprise him, yet somehow they always managed to do so. His own family had never been as close. In his family, you had to fend for yourself or die.

Viv sat in awe. Ray looked so beautiful in a dark blue suit, and he wasn't even worried about having a bunny rug thrown across his shoulder as he rocked Ben to sleep.

The sounds of family chatter quieted when they were called inside. Ray didn't even hesitate as he walked in with Ben still in his arms, though the judge looked mildly surprised. Viv followed and stood beside Ray as the bailiff began reading out what they were there for.

The judge looked at them for a long time before he finally spoke. "It says in your papers you're in a homosexual relationship."

"Yes, Your Honor," Viv and Ray answered together.

"Yet the children involved are the siblings of Christopher Vivvens."

"Yes, Your Honor," they both answered again.

"How long have you been together?"

Viv knew he surprised Ray when he calmly answered, "It's almost our anniversary, Your Honor." He knew Ray would have worked out by now that it wouldn't be long until their two-year anniversary. "Soon we'll have been together for two years."

"Can you explain to me how this relationship is going to work, and why being with the both of you is in the best interest of the children if I grant these adoptions?"

With a beaming smile, Viv watched as Ray held up his left hand. "We got engaged, and will be having our commitment ceremony after our babies are born, Your Honor."

The judge shuffled through his papers. "Twins."

"Yes, Your Honor," Viv replied, gesturing back to where Beth sat. "They're biologically Ray's children and will already have his last name. We want all our children to have the same last name."

"I'd like to hear what your beliefs are in having the same surname, Mr Vivvens?"

"I have already begun the application of changing my name by deed poll, so eventually our whole family will have the same last name. We believe this will make it less confusing as our children grow older."

The judge shuffled through his papers again, withdrew another document and seemed to study it for a long time. "Yes, I see you have been granted the change, Mr Vivvens — or should I say, Mr Connelly?"

Viv couldn't help but grin at Ray as the judge confirmed his new name. Ray held his hand for a moment in acknowledgment.

"This is not the first child you've adopted?" He directed his question to Ray this time.

"You're correct. I also have a daughter, Sara." He indicated to her.

She waved back.

Viv jumped as Beth gasped in pain. Her hands flew to her stomach and her gaze locked with Ray's.

"Ray, my water just broke. It's time."

Chaos ensued as the family went into action. In a weird sort of way, Viv thought the whole thing was like some awkward yet beautifully choreographed dance playing out.

"It's time... Oh, my God! It's time!" Ray blurted out as he turned back to the judge and said in excitement, "Your Honor, it's time. We need an ambulance... We need a doctor."

Viv took the still-sleeping Ben from Ray's arms, so he could go help Beth along with the others.

"We need something!" An excited kind of panic filled Ray's voice as Beth groaned again.

The judge called a recess and had Beth moved to his chambers until the ambulance arrived. Beth lay on a couch along one wall, resting as comfortably as she could between contractions. Viv kept vigil on everything, from Jas comforting Beth, to Ray who was conferring on the phone with the ambulance service, then telling everyone what needed to be done. "You need to push."

Viv watched everything in dazed amusement when Ray apologized before he ducked beneath Beth's skirts. "Oh my God, I can see something! The babies are definitely coming out right now!"

A knock on the office door followed quickly by two ambulance officers entering the room, drew everyone's attention.

"I hear we have someone about to become a mummy," one medic stated.

The exasperated look on Beth's face said it all. "Actually I'm the surrogate—these two are about to become daddies." As she indicated to him and Ray, she added, "Mr Excitement here was about to play doctor. Glad you could come join the fun."

If the ambulance officers thought anything odd about the situation, they had the good grace to keep quiet, for which Viv was grateful.

"I'm Viv and this is my partner, Ray Connelly. I'm also glad you could make it," he said as he tugged Ray toward him and out of the way."

"You're doing fine." Ray vibrated with enthusiasm beside him.

"Shut up, Ray," Beth grunted as she pushed the first baby out. A fine sheen of sweat covered her face.

Viv drew a clean hanky from his pocket and handed it to Jasper, so he could wipe her down.

"Just breathe," Ray coached nervously, panting like they had all been taught in Lamaze class.

All the while, Beth glared at him.

"Isobel Christine," Viv said with awe. The ambulance man let Viv cut the cord before swaddling her in a blanket. An EMT handed Ben to Jasper, who calmly stood off to one side throughout the delivery as another medic passed Isobel to Viv.

The second baby came out just as quickly.

"And Layla Kathleen." This time Ray cut the cord and took the offered infant.

"We did it. We're daddies." Tears shimmered in Ray's eyes.

"Thanks to our beautiful friend here." Viv beamed.

The ambulance crew checked both babies over to make sure everything was okay before putting Beth on a gurney to take her out to the waiting ambulance. The moment they walked out of the door, the judge and their family greeted them.

Smiling broadly, Ray and Viv showed off the newest additions to their family. "Meet Isobel Christine and Layla Kathleen," Ray said.

"We need to get these little angels to the hospital, so we'll be moving the party to a new venue." Viv's darkish side popped out to say hello as the family looked at him as though they couldn't believe it. Hell, Viv couldn't even believe it. "It must be the high of recently becoming a father...again."

Before he could say anything else, the judge held up his hand.

"Step back into my office for a moment please, gentlemen," the judge said.

After they'd entered the office and closed the door behind them, Viv's nerves were zinging throughout his whole body. This wasn't at all how he had wanted today to go, and he hoped they weren't about to get bad news. He held Millie in one arm and clasped James' hand while Ray cuddled Ben.

"I see family means a lot to you both, and you also have a very extensive support network, so I will grant the applications for adoption. I know you need to get to the hospital. I'll have someone get in touch with your lawyer and set up a time to sign everything," Judge Pierce said.

Viv found it a little easier to breathe. "Thank you," he said with relief.

Ray was so happy he held onto Ben with one arm and threw his other around the judge, kissing the man's cheek. "Sorry," Ray said as he stepped back.

"Congratulations to you both." The judge's face reddened but a small smile played across his lips, giving away his true feelings.

Ray was beaming as he left the courthouse and put all the kids into the van. "Can you believe we have two beautiful baby girls? Now our family feels whole."

Ray sighed, and Viv leaned over and kissed him.

God, I love Ray more than life itself.

"The truth is, you all make me happy." Ray grinned at him.

The rest of the family had barely beaten them to the hospital, and Beth's room was already overrun with flowers, presents and balloons. Beth seemed relieved when they got there. She introduced them to the nurses on duty and explained that the babies belonged to Ray and Viv. She also explained how he and Ray would be feeding the babies and bonding with them, as her part in this was over. Excitement filled the hospital waiting room when Viv announced, "They're ours... We get to keep them all. Our adoptions have been granted."

Viv soon realized the other children were starting to wane. It was time to say goodnight. He led Ray to the bathroom so they could talk quietly for a moment.

"I think I need to get the little ones home. And we both know, from previous talks with the hospital staff, they are going to let only one of us stay. B is probably one of your closest friends and you *are* the father, so you should be the one to stay."

Ray pouted, "I want you to stay as well. They're your kids too."

"I'd love to stay, but remember, while you are here looking after these two, I will have three of my own sweet babies to look after." Viv spoke as comfortingly as he could. Having only one of them stay was one thing Ray had argued with the hospital against. "We'll be back bright and early. I promise." Leaning in, he gently but thoroughly kissed Ray. There was so much more he would have liked to have done, but with a room full of family on the other side of the door, it wasn't possible.

Ray didn't answer. Instead, he sighed and walked out to kiss and hug each of their children before Viv was allowed to leave with them. Deep down, Viv wished he could have stayed, but sometimes disheartening decisions had to be made, and this was one of those times.

Giving Ray one last kiss, Viv left and, with the help of everyone else, he took the remainder of his family home.

* * * *

Ray was a bundle of churning emotions after Viv and the children had left. Part of him wished he was going with them, but another part was grateful he was still with the two beautiful children who had just been born. Taking a moment to get himself under control, he picked up the bottles the nurse had brought to feed the girls.

When Ray first saw Isobel and Layla all cleaned up, his breath had caught. The two little girls were probably the most beautiful things he had ever seen in his whole life, and he couldn't wait to get them home and into their own beds. He wanted his whole family together.

"Ray," Beth whispered as Ray finished feeding Layla.

"What, B?" Ray gently laid his daughter back in her crib.

"I was thinking. Since we now have a new house, I don't want to have to wait until next year. I want to start trying for a baby as soon as I can." Her voice wobbled a little as she spoke.

Ray wasn't surprised by her request. In fact, he and Viv had seen this coming since about halfway through the pregnancy.

"Well, I'm ready whenever you are. I'll be in your debt forever." He softly caressed Isobel's cheek as he watched over them. "And I was right. We made beautiful babies." Ray climbed onto the bed next to Beth and embraced her. They lay side by side until the time for Ray to feed Isobel and Layla rolled around again.

"You know, I always wondered what our kids would turn out like as they grew. I mean, if you and I'd ever got married—and now I'll know." Ray smiled at her. "Except now I'm gay, and my husband is definitely not you. At least this way…"

Beth giggled softly.

"The love story between you and Viv was great to watch unfold, especially seeing how he denied he was in love with you. That was, right up until I kissed you on the plane. Jas said the look on his face was priceless." She chuckled again.

"At least he admitted it before I went out and found another boyfriend. It would have been a very awkward and embarrassing situation if he had realized at a later time."

Beth reached over and patted his arm affectionately. "Dan told us Viv never shut up about you, and apparently you were on his mind from the first night you met. This drove Dan crazy — or so he says."

"Only because Dan wanted me too. He wasn't sure who he wanted to date, me or Girly." Ray chuckled.

"Would you have gone out with him?"

Ray shook his head. "I don't think so. I could only see Viv. Every time I closed my eyes I saw his looking back at me. They are so green and sucked me straight in. The day I had to take him round to meet Mum and Dad and he found out Grace was there, he kissed me out in the driveway. You know…just to see if he could. I felt like my heart was going to jump right out of my chest. In the beginning, I used to get confused with his kissing. In that moment, I wanted him so badly, but then he told me not to get carried away, as it was still all pretend."

"Oh, darlin', he was never pretending. I knew the first time I ever saw him hug you. The look on his face said 'This is the one, and I'm in love'. I think everyone except the two of you knew how this was going to end."

Ray lapsed into silence for a moment, before he confided in Beth. "The night I went to Flashes he came, got me, and took me back to his house. He wouldn't have sex with me. He let me do whatever else I wanted." Ray didn't go into any further details. He still hadn't told Girly. "We never told anyone, so you have to keep this a secret."

She snorted. "Too late. Dan saw the stamp on his hand and told the rest of us. The photo I took of the two of you the night we had the pizza party is truly beautiful. I'll have to print you out a copy. The way he flirted with you all night was so entertaining to us. You were oblivious and didn't seem to take the hint."

Ray rolled his eyes and groaned. "I thought it was all pretend."

Silence fell between them, and Ray was content to hold his friend as they drifted off to sleep.

* * * *

Ray woke to the sensation of Viv's lips against his cheek. He and Beth were still snuggled up on the bed. His eyes widened in appreciation the second he realized that Viv had brought breakfast.

"Girly is going to come in to look after the twins for a while so we can take James and get him enrolled in school. We also need to help Fred get Teddy enrolled," Viv said as he handed Ray some clothes.

Ray kissed his children before he did anything else. He'd missed them.

Beth was happy to feed Ben while Viv and Ray each claimed a twin to feed. Millie and James were both drinking juice from pop tops.

Ray started talking excitedly. "The doctor says the girls might be allowed to come home later today or tomorrow. He'll let us know after he's been by to do their check-up this afternoon."

"I hope so. What about you, B? Did they give you a release date?"

"Not yet. Hopefully I'm outta here this afternoon. If the doctor says so, Jas is coming to pick me up after he finishes work."

After the twins were back in their cribs, Ray lifted James and Millie onto the end of the bed and opened the basket of food Viv had brought. Ray laughed as Viv handed Beth a huge muffin.

"Antonio sends his congrats on the two new additions to the family."

Beth giggled as she broke off a piece and stuffed her mouth. "Tell him thanks."

They were still eating when Daniel and Girly walked in with a bunch of flowers for Beth and two teddy bears for the twins.

"Fred said she'll meet you at the school at eight o'clock, so you two better get a move on," Girly pointed out as she tapped the watch encircling her slim wrist.

"You can leave Millie and Ben here with us if you want," Daniel added.

Ray shook his head and smiled. "Thanks, but they haven't been with me all night, so I think I'll keep them close," he said as he put them into their pram. Viv pushed the pram while James took a hold of Ray's hand.

The drive from the hospital to the school took no more than fifteen minutes. Fred met them out in front of the school entrance. Josh, standing, waited with her.

"Josh came to help me with Charlotte," she said with a shrug at his and Viv's amused faces. "Uh-huh." Ray smirked in Josh's direction as they all headed inside the building to where the office was located. They sat in chairs that lined the hall and waited to be called in.

As the interview progressed, Ray was glad to find that the headmaster was very sincere and open-minded. The man didn't even bat an eyelash when Viv said he and Ray were in a relationship, though he did react when he was told about all the children who may be attending the school in the future. Ray happily gave him the names of the four younger Connelly children and Charlotte. When the headmaster expressed interest in James having the same name as the library building, Ray explained that his grandfather donated the money to build the library and supplied the workers to do all the construction. The school then had named the building after him.

Ray introduced Fred and said her son would also be enrolling, as she was their new nanny. And he explained how Fred would also be in charge of dropping off and picking up James on some days. At this point, Viv gave Headmaster Wallace a list of people who may be picking up both children, though it surprised Ray that Josh had been added to the list he and Viv had decided on.

When the interview was over and all the correct papers had been signed, a teacher led them on a tour of the school and introduced them to each boy's teachers. They would be in different classes, owing to their last names being on the opposite ends of the alphabet. Headmaster Wallace handed them a flyer about the upcoming fete held the following month and told them to come and join the fun.

Just before they left, another teacher gave them the book lists of what would be needed for James and Teddy to start school, with assurances that by the time the boys got there, a special needs teacher would be ready to work with Jamie. This last bit of information was a huge relief to Ray. He didn't want Jamie to become a statistic. So many children fell through the cracks in school for the pure fact that they were misunderstood or misdiagnosed. At least this wouldn't happen to their son.

Once they were outside again, their plans changed. Josh agreed to take Viv back to the hospital while Ray and Fred went shopping for all the school supplies. Ray loved all of this and was again in his element as he regaled Fred with stories as they shopped. Fred kept insisting that she should pay for Teddy's things, but Ray wouldn't let her. He wanted to do this, and he could afford to spoil them. They laughed as both boys opted for the same in everything, except where James got red, Teddy picked blue. Ray then bought Teddy a blue bike and helmet.

Even the two girls didn't miss out as Ray bought them matching baby dolls and strollers and lastly, Ben got two new teething rings, seeing as he had more teeth coming through.

They stopped for lunch in the mall cafeteria, and Fred started to cry.

Confused, Ray asked, "What's wrong, Fred?"

Through her tears, she explained how her kids had never had anything new. Nearly everything they owned was a hand-me-down. Ray draped his arm around her in comfort. He truly didn't know what to say, so he just held her until her tears subsided. The children ate quietly beside them.

After they'd eaten, Ray bought an extra booster seat for the van so they didn't have to keep transferring Charlotte from one car to the other. It just made sense to Ray. Every now and again, he would see more tears glistening in Fred's eyes. He was happy that Fred and her kids were getting to have a little bit of their own happiness and see that life didn't always have to be dark and bleak.

Once they were home, they took the kids and all the new stuff to the playroom. Here they spread everything out and they organized for the beginning of the next week, for the boys' first day of school. While they sat on the floor covering and labeling everything, they discussed what sort of things to buy for the play space. By the time they were finished, they had a long list of what was needed and the renovations they wanted.

* * * *

When Ray went back to the hospital, he gaped at the scene before him. Viv looked adorable sitting there nursing one of the babies.

"So beautiful." It was only then that he saw all the gifts had been packed up beside Beth. "What's going on?"

"It looks like we all get to go home. Jas is going to meet me at your place."

By the way Viv helped him transfer everything to the van, Ray knew his lover was just as excited as he was to take their girls home.

"Grandma is so keyed up at home that she's been calling me non-stop all day, asking when we are bringing the girls home."

"You and me both." Viv cuddled him close as they made their way back to the room.

"You ready to go?" Ray asked Beth, who already stood there dressed with her bag in hand.

"Yes, I seriously need a decent cup of coffee... Lead on, McDuff." She motioned for them to pick up the girls so they could go.

"Don't we have to sign anything?" Ray asked.

"Already done. The doctor came around just before you arrived. Let's go home and show Grandma what she's been wanting to see."

The drive home seemed to take no time at all.

Grandma was extremely thrilled to have both baby girls placed in her lap so they could have a photo taken. "I want all the rest of you great-grandchildren to come and sit by GG while we get a nice picture. Daniel and Girly, get your butts over here." Grandma chortled, which cracked everyone up.

In moments like this, Ray thought life couldn't possibly get any better. All the bad things they had endured melted away in the love and happiness filling the room.

When Antonio brought in a snack for them all, Ray insisted that the man sit and have his photo taken with all the younger Connelly children. Antonio held both twins while James held Ben, and Millie sat on his other side. Girly and Dan couldn't help themselves as they crouched behind the couch so they could be in the photo too.

Ray looked around the room and spotted Fred and Josh sitting on another sofa. Charlotte and Teddy sat with them. When Ray readied the camera to take a photo of them, Josh put his arm around Fred's shoulders. She blushed.

* * * *

Three weeks later, Ray awoke to the sound of James and Teddy talking through one of the monitors on the bedside table. He woke Viv up so he could listen too.

"Don't cry, my Bear. My pa loves washing sheets, so he won't get cranky at you."

They heard Teddy crying and the sound of James getting out of bed.

"When I wet the bed, Deena would make me pull off the sheets and get changed."

Teddy's tears stopped, and Ray realized by all the giggling that they were stripping the bed in question. Ray and Viv dressed.

"Where am I going to sleep?" Teddy asked.

"You can share with me, just like we will when we grow up and get married."

"Okay, Jamie."

"Goodnight, my Bear. Love you."

"I love you too, Jamie," Teddy whispered.

By the time they got into the hall, they met Fred, who had obviously been woken by the same conversation.

"What do we do?" she asked. "I can't tell them not to share when you and Viv do."

Ray shook his head. "I never actually thought about this. Maybe we get trundles for under their beds in case this happens again. I'm sorry, Fred."

To his surprise, she started to snicker, and pressed her hand over her mouth.

"Sorry," she said when she got herself under control. "But my ex would have beaten the shit out of him if he'd found Teddy in bed with James."

"But they're only kids." Viv sounded shocked.

Also stunned, Ray gaped at her. *How could a parent treat his child that way?*

"Honestly, it wouldn't have worried Damien. You should have heard him when he found out I was going to be working and living here. I was lucky Don was there and made him leave. Actually, this is probably the reason why Teddy wets the bed. He still has bad nightmares about his father."

Worried, Ray asked, "Do you think working for us will cause you problems? I would hate to think of anything happening to you or the children." He steered her and Viv back into the nursery so Jamie and Teddy wouldn't overhear them.

"The only thing he could possibly do to me is try to take my kids, and I know for a fact that will never happen. His current girlfriend is not maternal and doesn't want them." She patted Ray's arm. "Sorry I freaked. Their sharing doesn't bother me at all. I promise."

Ray snuck into the boys' room and took the wet sheets and pajamas from where they were piled on the floor. For a moment, he froze in awe as he watched Teddy and James asleep in the bed, wrapped in each other's arms. He hoped that none of this came back to bite any of them on the arse.

The house was quiet as Ray took the sheets down to the laundry. He threw them in the machine and washed them. They could be hung out in the morning. By the time he got back to the boys' room to finish the cleaning, he found that Viv had already wiped the bed over with disinfectant and left it to dry.

* * * *

Viv leaned against the doorframe and watched as Ray tucked the doona in around the boys. "I'm gonna head down and get the stuff ready for the nursery. You know the other contingent will be awake any second now."

"Okay. Thanks, love." Ray gave him a quick peck on the lips in passing. The sensation sent a warm tingle rippling through Viv's whole system. Before leaving, Viv smiled as he stood in the hall and watched the perfect swing of his lover's arse as he entered their bedroom suite. The smile never left his lips as he went to the kitchen and back. He must have done something good in his life to end up with the wonderful person Ray was. Entering the nursery, he handed Ray one of the bottles.

"Wasn't that one of the sweetest conversations you've ever heard?" Viv asked, as he lifted Layla from her crib. "Didn't James sound so grown up as he explained everything to Teddy? It's hard to believe he's classed as special needs."

"What will we do if he turns out to be gay?" Ray asked, as he fed Isobel, the worry in his voice evident.

Viv thought for a while about the image of them hugging in their sleep. "Well, I guess we would support him with whatever path he follows in life. Straight or gay, it'll be his life, and as his parents, we'll have to respect and love him, no matter what."

Ray smirked at him, but Viv could still see a hint of worry in his lover's eyes as he spoke. "You spoke as beautifully as any proud parent would. I'm proud of you, Mr Connelly."

"Honestly, Ray. I never really understood gay people. For over half of my life I'd heard over and over they were wrong. My dad wasn't a homophobe per se, but like me, he truly didn't understand them. When Dan told me he was bi, I didn't take it well at first, but after a while, I realized he was still Daniel. His being bi hadn't changed him at all. Now I know differently. Sometimes being gay is exactly right." Viv smiled warmly at Ray. "More to the point is that I think you're exactly right—for me. I just can't believe I took so long to realize what you actually meant to me."

"When did you know?" Ray asked.

"I think I knew from the moment you first smiled at me at Declan's. But, having never been gay before, I denied what I was feeling." Viv gently burped Layla. "When did you first realize?"

"Same night. Every time I looked at you, my body would vibrate like crazy. After I got back from picking up Girly and found you were sitting at our table, I nearly had a heart attack. You were so unbelievably beautiful, and the color of your eyes sucked me right in. Before I left, I was contemplating coming over to tell you what a beautiful smile you had, but I chickened out. But it didn't matter, because fate had other plans for us."

Ray put Isobel in her crib. "Your kissing used to confuse me so much in the beginning. I couldn't understand why you would kiss me like that if you were straight."

"I guess I liked kissing you," Viv answered.

"I fell in love with you in a heartbeat."

"When?" Viv asked curiously.

Ray chuckled. "Truthfully, it was the night we came to dinner at your house and you zapped me."

"I knew I liked you as more than a friend the night you went to Flashes—and not because I liked kissing you, though I didn't comprehend I was in love with you until we were boarding the plane. When B kissed you, I was so crazy jealous I wanted to pull her off you. I realized Jasper was staring at me, and I stopped. I couldn't fathom how you could make such a huge decision in our lives without talking to me about it first. Then it hit me. You weren't even aware of the fact I was in love with you."

"Everyone else knew," Ray said quietly. "They all told me you were in love with me right from the very beginning, and I kept telling them they were wrong." Hurt resided in his voice.

Viv had never meant to hurt Ray, and promised himself he never would again. "Well, they were right. I should tell you that the night after our pizza party, when I slept with you in your bed, I felt you up in the morning then was so guilty. I didn't want to own up to what I was feeling."

Ray grinned back at him. "I know. I was awake and thoroughly enjoyed your fondling, though I had to finish the job myself in the shower. Did you know Girly walked in when we were asleep and saw you touching me? That girl has no comprehension of the word privacy. Grandma says it's my fault. After all, I raised her to be that way. Girly ragged on me for waking up a gay virgin yet again, after you had apparently spent all night flirting with me."

"I did not flirt with you."

"Well, B and Girly both seem to think you did. You did hold my hand a lot, and as usual, they tell me I was oblivious to everything."

"I did get jealous in the morning when B hugged you." Viv put Layla in her cot. "Come, my dear. Let's go to bed and make mad passionate love."

"You always have the best ideas," Ray said as he pulled Viv toward their bedroom.

Viv didn't need a hot and heavy encounter. Not really. Even though he had said the words, he knew he would be just as contented for slow and sensual if all they did was kiss and hold each other. He was happy knowing that the man in his arms loved him wholeheartedly. They may have had a few rough times in the beginning but their love was still going strong.

More to the point, Ray's unending love for him held them together. Ray wouldn't have a bar of it when Viv tried to push his lover away after what had happened with Grace. Ray had stood fast through all the court hearings and was there holding his hands as she was sentenced to seventeen months behind bars. His lawyers had argued for more time, but the judge presiding over the case believed in Grace's show of remorse and showed her leniency. Now their lives were finally getting back to normal and he hoped that nothing would come along to rock the boat again.

With the subtle change in his mood, Ray didn't complain as he adapted to what was happening. No longer satisfied with the long lingering kisses, he wanted more and was determined to take what he needed. That fact alone made Viv love Ray even more than he already did. The intensity of their kisses never tapered off as Viv slowly rolled them until he had Ray pinned beneath him. Viv broke the kiss long enough to command, "Hold onto the headboard and don't let go. No matter what, keep your hands right there — and no talking."

When Ray nodded, Viv leaned down and devoured his lover's mouth once more. At the same time, he trailed his fingers down Ray's fuckable body, knowing without a doubt that goose bumps would be breaking out all over his lover's skin.

As the kiss ended, Viv wasn't sure how to express everything he was feeling with words. Instead, he intended to show the man below him exactly what was going through his mind. He needed to show Ray just how much he loved him.

Ray watched him with obvious curiosity but Viv went on without a word. He lowered his mouth to Ray's throat and began nibbling, licking and tasting every bit of skin offered. The sounds coming from Ray were making Viv harder than he'd ever been. His cock was so sensitive to the touch as it rubbed against the bed between Ray's legs.

Reluctantly, Viv moved lower, pausing over Ray's left nipple, sucking it to a hard little peak that fitted perfectly between Viv's teeth. The best part was the way Ray seemed to thrum with everything Viv did to him. Ray's body was made for Viv and for Viv alone. Hopefully he would take Ray over the edge into bliss with him.

As he swapped from one nipple to the other, he almost wished that he'd allowed Ray to speak. He missed all the words that spilled from his sex-addled brain, but it was an easy fix.

"Talk to me," he whispered against the nipple he was gently abusing.

"Viv… Love… You make me… Oohh…" Ray arched below him.

Viv knew what Ray wanted, but he needed to hear the words. "What do you want, love?"

"You. I want you to…to… Damn it."

He bucked his hips as Viv moved lower still on his lover's body.

"Viv, suck me… Please."

That was all Viv needed to hear. In one quick motion, he swooped in and sucked Ray's cock into his mouth so it kissed the back of his throat. Swallowing to relax his muscles, he took Ray in a bit further. Ray gasped as they both stilled — almost as if Viv deep throating him had come as a shock to both their systems.

Somewhere in the fog enveloping Viv's senses, he heard Ray pleading over and over again.

"I want you, please."

Slowly at first, Viv began the sensual act of giving Ray the most intense blow job. He did everything he knew his lover liked — the hard press of his tongue on the underside of the cock on the outward pull, finishing with a loving caress of the slit, then more hard suction applied to bring him back to the start. This was something he willingly repeated many times.

The moment something hit him on the top of the head he knew that Ray had let go of the headboard, but he couldn't be angry with him when he realized it was actually the bottle of lube. By this time Ray was mumbling incoherently, the sign that his lover was close. Out of pure mischief, Viv released Ray from his mouth.

"Put it back. I'm not done yet," Ray demanded.

"Okay, but I was only going to ask if you wanted to finish in my mouth or inside my arse. It's been a while since you've taken the lead... So the choice is yours, love—mouth or arse?"

The myriad of emotions washing over his lover's face was breathtaking to behold. Viv could've come from just watching Ray's naked body as he flushed while trying to decide. In the end, Viv was happy with the man's choice.

"Mouth. I want you inside of me tonight."

Viv never even waited for further instruction as he once again sucked Ray deep into his mouth, setting up the rhythm his lover preferred. At the same time, he flipped open the lid on the lube and coated his fingers.

God, I love this man.

Slipping first one then a second finger inside his lover, he stretched him. Viv had always thought he'd hate this part of sex, but strangely he loved it. The whole sensation of feeling the heat deep within Ray was so intimate, and he was glad he never had to share this with anyone else.

"More, Viv."

Viv added additional fingers, twisting and turning them, touching every part of Ray that he could. When Ray's cock pulsed in his mouth, he pressed into his lover further, aiming for the place that would take Ray to new heights. The second his fingertips ghosted over Ray's prostate, he pulled back just enough to take Ray's load onto his tongue so he could taste the very essence of his man.

As the stranglehold on his fingers eased, he slowly pulled them out. Viv lubed up his cock and moved up

Ray's body. When they were face to face, Viv pressed his hard-on between Ray's arse cheeks and drove home in one deep thrust. The response was immediate as Ray wound his legs round him and held on.

"Gonna fuck you hard and fast," Viv ground out. "Would you like that, love?"

"Yes," Ray hissed.

The tight heat wallowing his cock was too much to bear, and Viv knew he wasn't going to last long. Already little shots of electrical energy zipped around his body to settle in his balls. The more energy they gathered, the tighter they became. Viv sped his rhythm up as his orgasm ripped through his body like a tidal wave ready to wash away everything in its path. The only thing stopping it from bursting free was the barrier Ray's body made. Two deep thrusts and Viv bit down on Ray's shoulder as his release filled Ray's passage.

This was what he had been searching for — pure and unadulterated bliss.

"I love you, Ray."

"Love you too."

* * * *

In the morning, Viv woke to find he was alone in bed. By the coldness of the sheets, he knew Ray had been up for a while. Viv went to the nursery and didn't find Ray there as he had expected. The babies were all still asleep. Hearing Ray talking quietly to Teddy and James over the monitor, Viv decided to join them. Viv stopped in the hall and listened as Ray told both boys how proud he was of them both for stripping the bed the night before. Though, Viv noticed, he didn't mention the fact that the two boys had shared a bed.

"See, Bear?" James said. "I told you my pa loves washing sheets."

Viv chuckled.

"Next time — if there is a next time — it's okay to come and wake me up, and I'll help."

"You're not angry?" Teddy asked in amazement. "You're not going to yell at me?"

"Nope."

Ray chuckled. The very thought of yelling or even smacking someone for something they couldn't control was ludicrous. After a moment or two of small talk, he heard Ray say, "Now go get ready for school. You don't want to be late."

Their morning rituals were starting to take shape. Viv would get ready to leave for work, and he'd kiss each of their children in turn, hugging James and telling him to have a good day at school. He always saved his last and best kisses for Ray, which only made James and Teddy giggle. Though, today seemed different. Grandma didn't seem to be her usual animated self, and Viv was loath to leave Ray to deal with it alone, especially when he couldn't put his finger on what was wrong.

Pulling Ray from the room, he voiced his concerns. "I'm worried about Grandma. Is there something going on that I should know about? She seems off, somehow. Do you need me to stay home?"

Ray walked him to the door. "Don't stress. I know you have that uni final today and I don't want your mind fogged up with what's going on here. I'll get to the bottom of things and fill you in tonight."

Viv gave Ray one final kiss goodbye. Ray could tell him not to stress as much as he wanted, but this was his family too and he did worry about everyone. The family had stuck by him over the last few months and he was determined to do the same for them.

* * * *

Ray walked back into the kitchen and leaned against the counter. He watched his grandma as she quietly sat and ate her breakfast. "You're looking tired, Grandma. Are you feeling okay?"

She smiled and nodded, but Antonio was standing behind her and shook his head.

Ray's heart lurched. He needed to talk with the man as soon as possible to find out what he was keeping from him. He knew his grandma would keep even her own death away from him so he wouldn't have to worry. Somehow, he knew he had to make her understand that they were family and it was okay to share worry. Grandpa wasn't around anymore, and they could make up their own rules to live by. After she'd finished breakfast, he escorted her to the sitting room and made sure she was comfortable before he left.

He asked Fred to watch over the kids as he went back into the kitchen to grab their lunchboxes. The moment he entered the room, Antonio was waiting for him.

"Tell me."

"This morning I went to tell her breakfast was prepared, and she was clutching at her chest. I rang the doctor straight away, but while I was on the phone, the pain eased. I still made an appointment for her to go in and have tests done. Dr Riley says it's better to be safe than sorry. You know how stubborn she is. I wanted to ring your father, but she doesn't want anyone told, not even your parents. She doesn't want any of you to worry."

Tears prickled his eyes. His worry must have shown. Antonio embraced him.

"What are we going to do? Why is she such a stubborn old bat? Do you think it's her heart, and if so, how do we keep her calm?"

"You being here is the best thing for her. Sometimes your presence is like having James back, and she's happy again. She told me once that you are the spitting image of James when he was younger, when they first met."

All day Ray couldn't seem to shake the sadness filling him, yet he tried to hide his feelings when he was around his grandma. She didn't ask, but she had to know something was wrong. Even if she suspected that he knew what was going on, she was stubborn enough to remain silent. He'd always been an open book to her, and she had oftentimes referred to him as her mini James.

In truth, Ray hated the fact that he looked like his grandfather. James Connelly had been a total bastard who had ruled his family with an iron fist. Ray blamed him for the way everyone had turned against Isobel when she needed them the most. If it hadn't been for his grandma, Girly would have been put up for adoption.

Later in the afternoon, Ray sat with James and helped him do his homework. Their agreement was that the homework had to be finished before he could play with Teddy, and Ray knew that Fred had the same kind of arrangement with her son too. That night after Ray had put the children to bed, Viv came home from work and found him sitting in their bedroom crying. Ray tried to hide the fact but he knew it was useless.

"Love, what's wrong?" Viv asked worriedly as he knelt in front of Ray.

Ray could only cry harder as he wrapped his arms around Viv. "It's Grandma." Viv held him tighter. "What's wrong with her?"

"Antonio took her to the doctor this morning and the doctor did tests. She's having problems with her heart, but she doesn't want us to worry so she's keeping it a secret. How can I help her and give her support if I have to pretend I don't know what's going on?"

Viv kissed Ray's tear-stained face. "We'll get through this. She'll have us here with her. If we have to, we will tell her we know." Viv pulled Ray to his feet and led him into the shower. Stripping them both naked, he quickly washed him before drying Ray and leading him back into their room. "You can take comfort in my body if you want to," Viv whispered lewdly as they crawled into bed.

Ray chuckled. "I was planning on it." At least for a little while, he knew he was going to be able to forget everything as he lost himself in Viv. The very fact that Viv was already reacting to just the thought of sex did wonders for Ray's self-esteem. He wondered if it was this way for other couples or if he and Viv were just special.

Leaning over, he yanked open the bedside drawer and retrieved the lube. He coated his fingers liberally before he began to stretch Viv's body. The tightness around his fingers was going to feel even better around his cock.

"I love touching your body. We never seem to have enough time anymore just for each other. I wish..."

Ray swallowed hard. "I wish this night could go on forever."

"Fuck... Ray... That's enough. I need you inside me now... Right now, damn it." Viv hissed as he bucked against Ray's hand, as if telling him to get a move on.

"Pushy damn bottom," Ray grumbled gently as he removed his fingers and pressed the head of his cock against Viv's hole. "Is this what you want?"

"You know it is... So hurry the hell up."

Ray groaned as Viv tried to impale himself on Ray's cock. Ray moved back just enough to receive a frustrated snarl from his lover. Leaning in, he kissed Viv's chin seconds before he slowly and surely breached his lover. The look of wonder on Viv's face each time Ray took him this way was a great big boost to a man's ego. It was a look that told him he was loved.

Before Viv could utter a word, Ray pulled back and thrust forward, deliberately trying to stop either of them from coming so fast. He wanted this to be a night to remember. The smell of their bodies meeting in passion was so wonderfully strong and fueling all his other senses. If he were a jet plane right now, he'd be soaring across the open skies. *Fuck, I love this man. I love everything about him. This is how life is meant to be.*

"Ray... God... So close... Just a little more... Harder... Deeper..."

With each babbled word, Ray upped his pace. The sweat dripping down his face to land on Viv's chest and shoulders was turning him on faster than he could believe. "Touch yourself. I want to see you come. You're so pretty when you come."

Ray held himself up as best he could and watched as Viv tugged his own cock in time with the rhythm Ray was trying to maintain. The second Viv's arse gripped his cock harder than he ever thought possible, Ray watched in a lusty haze as cum painted Viv's chest. Two thrusts were all it took for him to follow Viv into orgasming. His whole body tightened like a vice while pleasure ghosted over his whole body in a heated wave. Collapsing on top of Viv, Ray lay there until they both came back from heaven. "Viv," Ray whispered when they had finished. "Can we get married soon? I want Grandma to be there. I want her to see how happy we are and how much I love you. I want her to know she was right about me all along."

"We can get married as soon as you want to, love. I don't think Grandma is ready to kick the bucket yet. There are procedures to help her heart along. You know what? I'm glad she was right about you. Otherwise, we would never have had the chance to be together." He kissed Ray tenderly.

"So am I."

* * * *

Two days later, Viv had finished packing all the nappy bags to get ready to go to the school fete. This would be their first family outing. Josh had opted to come with them so he could help look after Charlotte. This fact in itself put a smile on Ray's face. Josh was starting to settle down, even if he didn't yet know what was happening to himself.

James and Teddy eagerly introduced them to some of their new friends as they lined up at rides. Most parents' eyes widened as James introduced them as Dad and Pa. Even Millie had started calling them by the different names, and Ray knew the titles were going to stick with all their children.

Actually, most people stared at the amount of small children they had and were amazed that they had time for them all. Ray met a few people he thought he could possibly be friends with outside of the school environment. Surprisingly, one was the principal's wife, Hayley. Ray found her extremely funny to be around, and she didn't seem to have any problem with their sexuality. Hayley explained that her brother-in-law was gay and she loved him very much.

A couple of hours into their day, Hayley had even jokingly asked if he or Viv knew of any nice guys interested in a relationship. Her brother-in-law Seth was currently single and very available, and according to Hayley, he was a touch lonely. Viv started laughing at them as Ray took Seth's phone number. When she showed them a picture on her cellphone of what he looked like, she added, "He's here somewhere. I'm sure if you stick around, you'll get to meet him."

"Hey, Josh, is Angus still single? If so, I think I have someone to set him up with." Ray showed Josh the picture of a young, dark-skinned man with the most amazing gray eyes he'd ever seen.

Josh pulled out his phone and made the call, then nodded to Ray and held out the phone.

"Hey, Angus." Ray chuckled as Viv frowned in his direction. "Sorry, Angus, but I'm off the market. I managed to get my straight guy after all." Ray winked at Viv.

Viv frowned even more.

"Look, would you like to come and meet this friend of ours? His name's Seth." Ray laughed as he listened. After he'd finished, Ray gave him the details of where they were.

"He'll be here in about twenty minutes. Maybe you should find Seth."

Hayley took back her phone and told her brother in-law to come meet them. She excitedly told Seth that they had organized a date for him.

"He's on the Ferris wheel with Jack. We'll see him as soon as it stops."

They sat at picnic tables to have a cold drink as they waited. Ray waved at Angus walking toward them. He introduced Angus to Hayley, before showing off his family. "And these are Viv's and my kids." Ray chuckled as Angus' eyes widened. Viv had claimed his hand as they sat there. Ray knew it was all a show of ownership but he didn't mind.

"Well, where's this hot date you have for me, hmm?" Angus asked curiously, a smile playing on his lips.

"Not here yet. He's on the Ferris wheel with his nephew."

He was interrupted as the young man in question leaned over and kissed Hayley on the cheek.

"Seth, this is Angus," Hayley introduced them.

"Hello," they both said together and laughed.

Ray smirked as Angus' eyes widened appreciatively when Seth smiled at him.

Standing, Angus took hold of Seth's hand. "Let's go for a walk and get to know each other." He pulled Seth away.

Hayley giggled at her brother in-law's bemused expression. "I'm glad Angus made the first move. Seth would have been too shy," she said as she watched them blend into the crowd. "How did you meet Angus?"

"Josh set me up on a blind date with him," Ray answered truthfully.

"Didn't you like him?" She looked worried as she stared in the direction the two men had taken.

Ray patted her hand to reassure her. "On the contrary, I actually thought he was a very nice guy. I would've liked to have found out more about him, but I had a complication."

"What complication?"

Ray chuckled in memory. "At the time, I was madly in love with Viv. Isn't that right?" Ray lightly punched Viv on the shoulder.

"And you were straight?" Haley asked.

Viv nodded. He answered Haley, "I wasn't ready right then to admit I was attracted to another man."

"When did you admit the truth?" Hayley asked.

Viv blushed. "Just after Ray announced to our whole family he was going to be making babies with his best friend's wife. Who, I should add, also happened to be Ray's ex-girlfriend. I finally realized in a bout of jealousy that I'd been having feelings for him from the beginning."

"And these two lovely girls are the result of making babies with my ex." Ray indicated Isobel and Layla.

"And the others?" Hayley asked.

"They are my brothers and sister. My parents died in a car crash, and Ray and I adopted them all. We also have two grown children as well. Dan's twenty-one and Girly is nineteen." Viv sounded almost shocked as his words sank in.

Ray sighed with relief at the pure expression of love in his partner's eyes. "We're a couple because of them. Viv and I finally managed to get together because of their meddling." Ray grinned as James came and sat on his lap then offered Ray some fairy floss. "Dan is Viv's brother, and Girly is my niece—well, she actually was my sister's daughter, but I adopted her after Isobel died."

"Your life is fascinating," Hayley said in awe. "I could sit here and listen to you two all afternoon and never get bored."

"Sadly," Ray said, "I think we'll have to head home soon. We need to start getting the little ones ready for bed. As cute as they all look, taking care of them needs a set regimen to make sure everything runs smoothly."

Hayley nodded in understanding. "I can honestly say you have made my day and I loved getting to know you both."

They started gathering all their belongings when Viv spoke. "Maybe you could come around one weekend for lunch and meet the rest of the family. Grandma would love to meet you."

They exchanged phone numbers. While they were heading back to the car, Ray phoned Josh to tell him they were leaving and to say they had gotten Charlotte and Teddy each an extra show bag. Viv nudged Ray as they began loading everything into the car and pointed to a vehicle parked two rows back and slightly off to their left. Seth and Angus were leaning against the side of the car talking. When Angus leaned in and kissed the guy, Seth didn't seem to mind a bit, which made Ray smile. He was happy and he wanted everyone around him to be happy too.

A hint of jealousy tinged Viv's voice as he climbed in behind the wheel and asked, "Was that how it happened for you? Did you kiss him while standing beside your car?"

"Nope, we didn't even go that far. He knew I wasn't interested in him. If you recall, you and I stared at each other all night. I may have got a kiss on the cheek from Angus and Tomas, but that was all. The only other guys I can ever remember kissing in my whole life are Josh, that guy from one of our gigs years ago, and the guy from Flashes when you came and crashed my date again."

"I was not staring at you all night," Viv insisted. "I was merely watching…" He changed the subject mid-sentence. "Why were you kissing Josh?"

Deciding to answer the questions in order Ray said, "I didn't mind that you crashed my dates. At least you ended up coming home with me each time. I know that night I went out with Angus you were trying to make me jealous and I can tell you it bloody well worked. I was so upset with you, right up until you kissed me out by the car."

Viv chuckled. "But I was always kissing you, so that doesn't count. The night we slept on the couch… When you were asleep I kissed you, and when you kissed me back, I nearly had my way with you right then and there."

Ray looked into the back and smiled when he realized that all the children were dozing after their big day out. Turning back to Viv, he asked, "Turned you on a lot, did I?"

"Let's just say, if we'd have been naked, we would both have lost our virginity that night."

"Wish you would have woken me up then." Ray laughed. He reached out over the console and caressed Viv's thigh as he drove.

"I wish I had too. Don't think I haven't worked out you are avoiding answering my earlier question. So spill it. Tell me all about you kissing Josh."

He laughed as Ray rolled his eyes and began to tell the story.

"I think we must have been around fourteen or so, and B and Josh were sleeping over at Grandma's with me. Grandma was letting me have a party for Josh's birthday and we were in the ballroom—the one we use as the kids' playroom now." Ray blushed. "We were all playing 'Spin the Bottle' and when my turn to spin came up, every time I tried to spin the bottle the damn thing must have been possessed, as it always landed on Josh. After three spins, Josh sighed dramatically before he tackled me to the ground and stuck his tongue in my mouth. I was so shocked that I bloody nearly bit it off."

Viv couldn't seem to stop the laughter bubbling from his chest. Ray was glad Viv wasn't angry about something stupid that had happened so many years ago.

"What happened next?"

"When he finally let go of me," Ray continued, "I shoved him away. One of our friends asked why he had tongued me. Josh shrugged and said he was going to kiss the hell out of the first girl who landed on him. And when it kept being me, he decided to fuck it, he was getting some action. He also went on to tell them all that for a guy, I could really kiss. Everyone cracked up all over again. All night long, the guys kept blowing kisses at me."

Ray smiled. He lifted his hand and caressed Viv's cheek. "When we get home, I want to check with Antonio to make sure Grandma's okay. I may need you to keep her distracted while Antonio and I talk."

After pulling up in the garage, Ray helped Viv lug everything to their room then left Viv with the children as he went in search of Antonio. He found him in the kitchen, supervising the preparations for dinner.

"How is she doing today?" Ray asked quietly.

"Actually she seems to be feeling better today. Dr Miles said she should be okay for now. If she has another turn, I'm to take her in straight away. Next week, I'm taking her in to have tests done to see whether or not she needs a pacemaker. The other option is to find out if they would be better off doing bypass surgery."

Ray nodded. "Does she know I know?"

"This is our secret." Antonio patted his arm. "Before I forget, Byron King has called a few times today looking for you. He didn't want to call your cellphone in case Viv answered. Maybe you should give him a call back."

Ray went into his grandma's study and called Byron on his mobile. "Hey, Byron. It's Ray. I heard you needed to talk to me."

He was met with silence for a second before Byron answered him. "I've been keeping tabs on the Kennedy woman like you suggested. Even though she is currently in jail, we know she won't remain there forever. I got a call from the medical facility at the prison where she's incarcerated and there's a complication where she is concerned."

Thankful he was sitting so that his legs wouldn't give out, he replied, "What kind of complication?"

"She's pregnant, due in a month's time, and you can count backwards as well as I can."

"Viv's the father, isn't he?" Ray swallowed a fire ball, which had consumed all his air so he could barely breathe. "Was this why she was trying to contact Viv since she went to jail?"

"Yes. Ray, I've visited the prison and spoken with her, and the thing is, she doesn't want the baby. Sleeping with Viv was something she did to get back at you for what happened up at the lodge. By the time she even found out she was truly pregnant, she was already incarcerated and it was too late for an abortion. I can tell you this. Grace Kennedy is a real nasty piece of work. She gave me a proposition for you. She says for fifty thousand dollars, the mongrel kid is yours—her words, not mine. If you don't take her up on the offer then you will never see the kid."

"Pay her," Ray whispered. "But she doesn't get anything until after the child is born and in my arms."

"Then what? Should I put the baby up for adoption?"

Anger flashed through him at Byron's assumption that he would get rid of something that was part Grace. Maybe he was hinting that Grace would try to wheedle her way back in after the child was born.

"No. I don't care who the child's mother is. As soon as the baby is born, I'll bring him or her home. I'll name a boy Jebidiah Liam Connelly, or if a girl, then"—Ray thought for a moment—"Eloise Claire Connelly, but I want everything written up legally so after Grace is released, she can never come and take the child from us. I want it written so she is to have nothing whatsoever to do with the child ever again."

"Are you going to tell Viv?"

"No. Not at the moment. I don't want to make him feel guilty and worry him. He'll find out soon enough. At least being in jail will keep her out of trouble, even if we spend another ten grand to keep her in the infirmary until the baby is born."

"I'll get on it."

"I'll call you once a week to check how things are going and I want to be there at the birth. I need to figure out a way to break this to Viv so he doesn't freak out."

Shuffling of papers drifted through the line. "Okay, I'll hear from you next week."

"Bye." Ray hung up to realize he was no longer alone.

"That was a very interesting conversation I just overheard," his grandma said as she came and sat beside him.

"It looks like we're both keeping secrets," Ray said quietly.

Her eyes widened a fraction. "I see Antonio has been telling tales on me." Grandma shrugged sadly. "Don't worry, my dear boy. I'm not ready to kick the bucket yet. Doc Miles says we have everything under control and there isn't any need to start planning for funerals. But she will be happy at least someone besides Antonio knows. Apparently I have another great-grandchild to meet. What are you going to do now there is another baby on the way?"

A soft gasp fell from Ray's lips. "Eight kids. If you had asked me a year ago if I was going to have more children, I would have hoped yes, but I would have never thought there would be eight." Ray shook his head. "At least I have the means to support them all. And in our family, they will be loved."

"Don't you think Dan and Girly are a little old to be classed as children?" Grandma chuckled.

"Yes, but they'll always be my kids, Grandma, just like I'll always be yours. When I first got Girly, you took us in because Dad and Grandpa said I had to be a man and provide for my child. Remember? Antonio used to pay me for doing chores around the house, and I used to pay you rent on our rooms."

"You always did take your responsibilities so seriously," she answered fondly.

"I loved Mum and Dad, but I was closer to you and Isobel." Ray kissed her cheek. "Some days I miss her so much."

"You and me both. Though, soon I'll catch up with her and your grandfather wherever they are, and together we'll all watch over you."

With a teasing tone, Ray said, "Grandma, you know you're going to outlive us all. You're as tough as old boots." Getting to his feet, he added, "I suppose I should go and help Viv with bathtime or they'll have soap suds everywhere." Ray helped his grandma up. "We'll see you at dinner, and promise me there'll be no more keeping secrets from me. I love you, and from now on, I want to know how you are feeling."

"Whatever you think is best, dear." She patted his arm as he went up to help Viv and she headed into the sitting room.

Walking into the bathroom, he stopped when Viv looked up from where he sat on the floor and smiled. "I thought you'd forgotten about us."

"Never." Ray sat beside him and took Millie into his lap as Ben and James finished their baths.

Viv had always insisted that boys and girls should not bathe together, and Ray agreed wholeheartedly. Ben looked so cute as he sat there, giggling and splashing in the water. His actions made Millie laugh and clap her hands. James was busily playing with the bath toys in the adjoining shower. In reality, bathtime for all the children could take up to two hours before everyone was bathed and dressed in their pajamas.

"I got a little distracted talking to Grandma. She knows we are aware of her health problems. I told her not to keep secrets from us, that we need to know how she's feeling."

"Did she agree?"

"Yup." Ray stood, turned off the shower then helped James gather his toys before he picked up Ben. He moved into the bedroom where the clothes were laid on the bed.

By the time Viv came in with Millie, Ray was dancing with James. Viv called out to him. As Ray turned, Ben took three steps, wobble for a second or two then fell over to land on his butt. Ray and Viv started clapping and Ben giggled.

"Let's go and show Grandma. She'll be excited." They finished getting all the kids dressed to head down to dinner. They met Josh and Fred in the hall. Fred held her hands out and took Ben so Ray and Viv could carry one baby each. Josh held the hands of both little girls and James and Teddy ran on ahead.

"Girly and Dan have gone to the club, so they won't be home for dinner," Grandma announced as Viv and Ray put Layla and Isobel into their twin cradles.

Fred buckled Ben into his highchair, and Josh sat both girls on their booster chairs so they could see at the table. Ray smiled to himself as Josh took a seat beside Fred.

"Hold on a second, Fred. Look at this, Grandma." Ray quickly undid Ben, stood him up on his feet.

Viv stood a few steps away and held out his hands. "Walk to Dad, Ben," Ray encouraged.

"Come to Dad." Viv clapped his hands. Ben giggled and took the few steps into Viv's arms amid cheers and clapping from everyone. He was still giggling while Viv buckled him back into his chair.

Ray asked Antonio to join them for dinner, as they would like to discuss the menu for the wedding, seeing as he had helped Cora work her magic for the engagement party.

Grandma's eyes lit up. "Who are you going to have as bridesmaids?"

Ray didn't even have to think twice. "Girly and B, and I think I'll ask Dad to give me away. We would like to have all of our children in the wedding party."

"What about you, Viv?"

"Dan and Tony"—he winked at Grandma—"but I'd like to ask if you would do me the great honor of giving me away. You're the closest person I have to a parent, and seeing as I'm now legally a Connelly, Ray and I thought I could ask you."

Grandma clapped her hands and laughed enthusiastically, which made all the kids giggle. "Where are we going to hold the wedding? Should we hire out a hall?"

Ray was ready for this answer and shook his head. "We were thinking we could have the ceremony in the hall here—I mean, before we finish converting it into the playroom. For once, I would like to see the room used for the purpose it was meant."

"That would be lovely."

"We would like to be somewhere where our children could be nearby in case we're needed. You know I don't like being far away from any of them." Ray chuckled.

"What about when you go on your honeymoon?" Josh asked curiously.

Ray and Viv looked at each other and Viv answered. "We'll go on a honeymoon when the children are older."

"Or we'll sneak off to the guest wing for the night and get you to babysit them all," Ray teased Josh.

"That's doable," Josh answered in all seriousness.

"Where are you planning on actually getting married? The ceremony, I mean," Antonio asked.

"We haven't made up our minds yet. We have a few choices, like out on the lawn under Isobel's tree or on the front steps, and if it rains then we thought we could use the steps in the foyer," Ray said thoughtfully.

"Now the big question is," Grandma began, "when are you planning on getting married?"

Viv pretended to think about it for a minute or two before he grinned and said, "As soon as Antonio and Cora can organize everything. You both did such a good job with the engagement party. We want you both to do the wedding."

Ray saw gratitude fill Antonio's eyes. The man couldn't stop smiling all through dinner.

"What's the color scheme?"

"Cream, burgundy, and gold." Viv shrugged. "Do they sound like they'll go together?"

"How about we leave that up to Antonio and Cora?" Ray laughed.

"Wedding cake?"

"Chocolate," Ray and Viv both said simultaneously.

Ray almost burst out laughing when Josh did a fist pump in the air.

They sat drinking coffee and talked about table settings, music and food choices, until, in the end, Viv stood and announced bedtime for the children.

Josh carried Millie, who had already fallen asleep. Fred once again took Ben. This left Viv and Ray with the twins. Fred and Josh tucked Millie and Charlotte into their beds then did the same for the boys. Viv and Ray went from room to room and kissed them all—even the two who didn't belong to them.

* * * *

Four weeks later, they were having another wedding discussion when Ray's mobile began ringing. He excused himself to answer. When he had finished talking, he poked his head back into the room and told Viv and the others that he was ducking out for a bit and borrowing the Mercedes. Viv looked worried, but Ray said he would be back soon.

He arrived at the private medical facility and was shown into the labor ward where Grace was getting ready to give birth to Viv's child.

"You almost missed it," she spat when she saw him.

Ray walked over to her. She was doubled over in pain as she stood beside the bed. Not knowing what else to do, Ray began rubbing her back, but she swore at him so he stopped.

"The sooner they get this brat out of me, the better. I don't even want to see the fucking thing again for as long as I live."

"Luckily, that's why I'm here," Ray said coolly. "They can hand the baby straight to me and you won't even have to lay your eyes on him or her."

"Have you got my money?" she snarled, amid another wave of pain

Ray's voice turned as cold. "As soon as I take custody of my child, I'll call Byron and he will put the money into your account."

The staff already knew the situation. Ray had made a huge donation to the facility to be able to walk away with the baby. Grace groaned and didn't complain when Ray helped her back onto the bed. He stood off to one side and silently watched as Grace gave birth.

"You have a son." The doctor smiled at Ray.

Ray couldn't help but grin as he cut the cord. The little boy was beautiful, and Ray was unable to stop himself as he walked over with the nurse and waited for her to clean the baby.

"Have you chosen a name yet?" the nurse asked. Ray waited until Grace had been wheeled from the room. He was hard pressed not to notice she was now handcuffed to the bed rail. She was about to be transferred back to the prison infirmary. Sometimes having a shit-load of money helped.

Ray grinned as he answered, "Jebidiah Liam — Jeb, for short."

He gasped when the nurse handed him the baby boy. The child in his arms opened his eyes, and Ray stared into their green depths. For some strange reason, he'd thought all babies were born with blue eyes and they changed in the weeks after birth. How wrong he was.

Ray pulled out his phone and hit the call button. "Pay her." He ended the call. He felt the part of his heart housing his children's love shift to make room for one more.

The nurse smiled as Ray carefully loaded Jeb into the capsule he had brought along for this purpose. "You'll have to bring him back for a check-up tomorrow."

"I'll be here." Ray thanked everyone and left to see the administration officer responsible for filling out Jeb's hospital chart.

By the time he finally got home, it was five o'clock, and he realized he might have made a mistake in not telling Viv earlier about the situation with Grace. There had never seemed to be a good time, and now he was a little worried what Viv's reaction would be. Ray bypassed the main door and headed straight to the kitchen entrance, intending to avoid everyone until he had got a bottle organized for Jeb, but luck didn't seem to be on his side.

Grandma smiled as he walked through the door. He knew she alone would have guessed where he had gone. "Tell me. Boy or girl?"

"Boy. Jebidiah Liam Connelly, meet your great-grandma," Ray said as he lifted the baby out of the capsule.

Grandma gasped. "No mistaking who his father is with those eyes."

Ray froze when his grandma looked past his shoulder. In that very second, he knew that Viv was standing behind him. His chest filled with apprehension as he slowly turned and acknowledged Viv's presence.

"I'm home." Ray moved to the side so that Viv could see the little boy in Grandma's arms. Viv recoiled a step and dropped the two baby bottles he was holding.

Ray took Jeb out of Grandma's arms, walked over to Viv and handed him the baby. "Meet our son. Jebidiah Liam Connelly."

Viv was visibly shaking as he stared down at the tiny child in his arms.

Ray's heart was pounding crazily when he realized that Viv saw his own eyes staring back at him. Guilt, shame, and sadness filled his face. Viv handed back the baby, turned and walked out of the room without saying a word. Ray took the bottle Antonio had passed him and followed Viv up to their room.

"Talk to me, Viv. I need to know what you're thinking," he asked softly, as he sat on the bed beside the man he loved with his entire being.

"Why would you bring that child into our home to be a constant reminder of what happened to me?" Viv whispered softly.

Ray sat there and fed the baby as he waited for Viv's emotions to run their course. "Jeb is part of you. Do you honestly think I could walk away from this baby? Don't you want your son to be a part of our family? Regardless of his mother, he now belongs to us."

"How long have you known about him, Ray?" Viv asked. Anger tinged his words

Ray cringed. He knew he had to answer honestly or else he might cause bigger problems.

"I've known for a little over a month. She didn't want him, and I did. I paid her what she wanted so I could walk away with him."

"So, you're telling me you bought a baby?"

"No, I did not... I paid her to stay away. Jebidiah belongs with us."

"How much?"

Exhaustion hit Ray and he sighed deeply. "Viv, it doesn't matter. We have him here now —"

"I said how much, Ray?"

"All totaled, it was close to one hundred thousand."

Shocked, Viv gasped.

Ray added, "But to me, Jebidiah was worth every cent, and honestly, I would have paid anything she wanted to be able to walk away with him."

Viv looked at the baby in Ray's arms. "He really is mine, then."

"No. He's ours," Ray corrected him, handing Jeb to Viv to finish feeding. "We have to go back to the clinic tomorrow for his check-up. I'd like you to be there with me at the consultation. Grace is probably already back at the prison infirmary, so there will be no chance of you running into her."

"I love you, Ray," Viv whispered.

"Well, I hope so. It makes sense if you do, seeing as you're going to marry me in a month." He grabbed some clean clothes from out of his dresser. "I'm going to have a quick shower then go and kiss all our other children. I've missed them. This will give you and our son time to bond." He stopped what he was doing and smiled at Viv. "You do realize we have matching sets now—four boys and four girls." He cackled as he stopped in the doorway of the en suite.

Viv was still staring in amazement at the tiny little boy. Ray understood that Viv would soon lose his heart to the baby—his son. The infant's little hand reached up toward Viv's face. Viv gently burped him.

Ray continued into the shower and gave Viv the time he needed to come to terms with everything that had been thrust into his lap.

They were still in the same position when Ray came out of the bathroom and headed into the nursery. Viv stood and carried Jeb as he followed.

"We need another crib now." Viv rocked Jeb in his arms.

"We can use a cradle for tonight and have a new crib delivered tomorrow. Stay here and I'll go get Josh to help me carry it up."

Ray left Viv and went to knock on Fred's door to let her know about their new arrival. Josh answered the door.

"Josh, you're just the person I was looking for. I need you to give me a hand for a moment." Ray pulled Josh from the room. "So what, pray tell, are you doing back in the nanny's room?"

Josh shrugged. "We were just talking. Don't look at me like that. James, Teddy, and the two girls are in there as well."

"Uh-huh." Ray grinned as they reached the parlor. "I need you to help me carry this cradle upstairs."

"What for?" Josh grabbed one end and lifted.

"You'll see," Ray answered.

Back at the nursery, Josh nearly dropped his end of the cradle when he saw what Viv held in his arms. "Holy fuck. They're multiplying." He gasped as Viv laid Jeb in the cradle and Jeb's eyes opened. "I have to get Fred. She's not going to believe this." He shook his head in shock as he left the room, only to return a few minutes later with Fred and all the kids in tow.

"Fred, meet Jebidiah Liam. Isn't he beautiful?" Ray announced proudly.

"Oh my," Fred said when she saw his eyes. Her gaze flashed to Viv's face as she did the mental math of when he would have been conceived. Even though Fred hadn't been living with them at the time, they all talked about, especially when the court case was in progress.

Viv must have guessed what she was thinking. "Yes, he's mine."

"Things always have a way of working out for the best." Ray gently caressed Jeb's face. "At least we got something wonderful and amazing out of the whole crazy mess."

Viv wrapped his arms around Ray. "You are wonderful, and so frickin' amazing."

"Yes, I know," Ray joked as he picked Millie up and gave her a huge kiss. "Hello, chicky-babe. Did you miss me?" He handed her to Viv then gave James a huge hug as well. "I've missed you both."

Teddy was watching them shyly from where he stood near his mother. Ray put James down then hugged Teddy too.

"My turn," Charlotte squealed as Ray picked her up and cuddled her. She giggled hysterically then held her arms out to Josh, who took her.

"Man, I can't wait to see the expressions on everyone else's faces when they see him."

Ray looked down at the four sleeping infants as they all lay in their beds. "You know, I think we will have to hire another nanny. Eight kids between the two of us are going to be a stretch."

"Hire me. I'll be your other nanny," Josh said as he placed Charlotte back on the floor. "It saves me from going out and looking for a job. Besides, the kids already love me."

Ray and Viv both burst out laughing, which woke up all the babies.

"What the hell is wrong with you two? They're just kids, for crying out loud. How hard is it to be a nanny?"

Josh rolled his eyes as they burst out laughing again, and this time Fred joined in.

Ignoring them, Josh took Jeb, carried him in one arm, grabbed Charlotte's hand and began walking out of the door. "We're heading down for dinner if you would care to join us." He didn't look back as he left them all still standing there.

"I think he's actually serious," Viv said softly, as he gathered up Ben.

"Give him a couple of days. By then he'll have changed his mind," Ray answered as he captured Layla then took Millie's hand as they went down to dinner.

By the time they reached the ground floor, Josh had put Jeb back into the capsule Ray had brought him home in.

When Ray raised his eyebrow questioningly, Josh said, "We just carried the second cradle upstairs."

Once all the children were placed in their designated spots, Daniel and Girly entered the room. Ray watched Girly count the babies three times then pinch herself as if to make sure she was awake. Then she pinched Daniel to see if he was awake, before she stared at Ray in shock.

"When did you...? Where did you...? Oh, my God!" she finished upon seeing Jeb's eyes. She turned and stared at Viv. "Grace?"

Both Ray and Viv nodded. Daniel was too stunned to talk, but he couldn't stop smiling and rubbing his arm where he'd been pinched.

"What name?"

"Jebidiah Liam," Viv answered.

Girly whistled lowly. "He sure is going to be a heart-breaker when he gets older, especially with those eyes."

"Takes after his dad." Ray beamed.

"Speaking of fathers," Grandma began, "your parents will be over tonight to meet their newest grandson."

After dinner, and with the help of both Fred and Josh, Ray and Viv managed to get all the children bathed and into their pajamas before Ray's parents showed up.

Ray cautiously handed Jeb to his father when his parents sat on the couch. "Dad, I'd like you to meet Jebidiah Liam. Jeb, this is your pop."

The infant stared at Liam and Liam's gaze immediately fell on Viv.

"Yes, biologically he's mine," Viv said, quietly blushing in shame.

"Ours," Ray corrected as he handed his father a bottle. "Make yourself useful, Dad."

"How are you going to manage with six kids? Eight if we count Fred's too?" his mother asked. Grinning from ear to ear, she accepted Isobel and a bottle to feed her with.

"Well, we kind of have two nannies now," Ray replied with a smirk

"Who's the other one?" Liam asked.

"Josh applied for the job, so now he's on a three-month trial," Viv answered with a straight face.

"No, really. Who have you hired?"

Josh shook his head as he fed Layla. "Ye of little faith. I shall show you all how wrong you are."

Girly snickered behind her hand as she watched Layla throw up down the back of Josh's shoulder. The look of horror on Josh's face had Ray giggling right alongside Girly.

Chapter Twelve

On the day of the wedding, Viv couldn't believe how nervous he was as he got ready for the ceremony due to start within the next half hour. While he waited, he nervously paced around the confines of the bedroom. Tony and Daniel kept telling him to calm the hell down, but Viv was terrified something was going to go wrong and ruin their plans. He let his mind drift over everything that had changed so drastically in his life. And he was grateful that nothing else had happened. He didn't know how much more he could take. When he'd voiced his worries to Ray, his lover had just smiled and told him that all things happen for a reason. Sometimes Viv secretly wished they would stop happening.

Then he thought about how everyone had come together to help out where needed. Fred and Josh—who to everyone's amazement had actually turned out to be very good as a nanny—had taken all the babies away for the morning so he and Ray wouldn't get puked on while wearing their suits. Grandma had James and Millie, and had made sure they were in their finery for their parts of the ceremony as the flower girl and the ring bearer.

Right now he wanted so much to see Ray and talk to him for a few minutes, but Girly and B had dragged him off early in the morning.

"It's time," Grandma said as she came back into the room. She looked lovely in a pale lavender dress. She patted Viv's cheek. "Don't forget to breathe. James and Millie are now with Ray."

Viv exhaled loudly. "Sorry, Grandma. I guess I'm a little nervous."

"You're not the only one—so is Ray. Before we head on out, I have to tell you that you both look beautiful," she said as she looked him over.

Their wedding apparel had been handpicked by Cora. Viv wore a black suit with a white shirt and black tie. Daniel and Tony were dressed in dark gray suits with purple shirts and gray ties. Millie was dressed in white, and James was a miniature version of Viv. As the music started, Grandma walked Viv to where the celebrant waited under Isobel's tree with Dan and Tony.

When the music changed in tempo, Viv's searched the crowd until he found who he was looking for. Girly and Beth, both wearing black dresses, walked down the aisle. His eyes filled with tears the moment Ray came into view wearing a gray suit shot through with silver, and a purple shirt with a dark gray tie.

Viv thought his soon-to-be husband looked so beautiful holding onto Liam's arm as they walked toward him. Liam was dressed in black and white like Viv and Jamie.

Viv didn't remember any of what happened until the celebrant said they could kiss. Halfway through the ceremony, he vaguely remembered reaching across and wiping the tears out of Ray's eyes. As they broke apart, the celebrant announced them to the waiting gathering of family and friends.

"I would now like to introduce Mr and Mr Connelly."

Antonio and Cora seemed to be in their glory as they showed people in for refreshments while the wedding party had photos taken. They had the traditional wedding party pictures then Viv and Ray wanted family portraits done as well. Viv had already heard more than one person comment and ask about the event organizers. He knew Antonio and Cora would soon be having requests for party planning.

Their first official dance after committing to each other was to *Loving You* by Paolo Nutini—the very same song he and Ray had listened to so long ago in his bedroom when Ray and Girly had come to dinner.

The nanny service Cora had arranged to look after all the children in attendance was set up in a suite of rooms in the guest wing. Ray and Viv disappeared more than once to the nursery with their children. Even on their special day, Viv needed his family close, and Ray shared that feeling.

By midnight, Viv and Ray were ready to bid their guests goodnight. Viv headed off to take their children to their own rooms. Ray gave him a lingering kiss before going down to the kitchen for bottles. Stepping into the hall, Viv saw Josh coming out of Fred's room, his clothes slightly mussed.

"What are you doing in the nanny's room again?" Viv smirked.

Josh looked at Viv, at first in embarrassment then he shrugged. "This is the nanny's room and I'm a nanny? I moved in a month ago when you hired me."

"What does Fred think about all this?" Viv asked as he indicated for Josh to follow him. "How did I not know this?"

"It took a bit to convince her, but in the end, she saw things my way. She's too scared to tell you in case you might fire her." Josh gauged Viv's reaction. "And the reason you didn't know is because you work so much and miss a hell of a lot that goes on around here."

Viv didn't answer for the longest time. Instead, he realized that Josh was right. He really did miss so much with his career.

His silence made Josh nervous.

"You won't fire her, will you? I can move back out if it's a problem."

"Don't be stupid. Who else would we find to put up with the craziness that's our family?" Viv playfully swatted his friend. "So I guess you're quite fond of her?"

"Yeah, you could say that. Fred's not at all the type I'd usually go for, but there's just something that attracts me to her. And the kids... Well, they're the best, and a complete added bonus. Who would have thought Josh McAddams would ever settle down?"

"Settling down is the easy part. The hard part is taking the first step. Have you two done it yet?" Viv asked curiously.

Josh shook his head. "She's not ready yet, and I'm prepared to wait until she is. I think her ex-husband terrified her when they were together. To some extent, I think he still does. I have to...be the opposite of him, and show her that loving someone else is okay. I want her to see that not all men are like him. Does that make sense?"

"Actually it makes perfect sense. I believe if you persist long enough, you will work things out, and you'll get what you want in the end. Look at Ray. He persisted and eventually he got me, and now we have all these great kids."

By the time they had gotten back to the nursery with a baby cradled in each arm, Ray had beaten them there. With a shake of his head, Viv placed the babies in their beds before going back for Ben and Millie. As awkward as it was to carry both children, he didn't want to leave one behind. Once again, Josh came with him and had taken Charlotte. Jamie and Teddy were still awake and they willingly left the nannies and headed for their own room. Viv couldn't put his finger on it, but there was something off with Jamie. And once he had finished feeding the babies, he was determined to get to the bottom of it. They took Charlotte and Millie to their room before heading back to Ray.

Josh pushed the door to the nursery open for Viv and saw Fred standing inside talking quietly to Ray as he changed one of the infants. Josh followed Viv into the room. They all took one baby and fed them.

"It was a beautiful ceremony," Fred said as she rocked Jeb.

Josh yawned loudly. "Your dad had tears in his eyes when he gave you away. I was standing next to Antonio and Magen and even they were teary."

Ray turned and smiled at Viv.

Viv thought his husband glowed. Truthfully, he couldn't wait until they were alone in bed to take full advantage of his mood. More in love than he had been in his whole life, Viv was ecstatic that Ray was so willing to keep on sharing his body with him.

"What are you smiling about?" Josh asked as he focused on Viv.

He winked at Josh. "I'm thinking about all the things I'm going to do to my husband once you two bugger off back to your own bed. Thinking is almost as good as doing, but not quite."

Josh snorted as Fred froze.

Ray's eyes widened and a smile formed on his lips.

"Well, as soon as this lot's back in their cribs, you can take Mr Wonderful to bed and get freaky with him all you want," Josh said.

"I'm planning to do so." Viv leered at Ray as he stood and placed Ben back in his crib. Walking over to the built-in stereo, he turned the CD player on low. David Bowie was barely audible, but Viv and Ray both liked the idea of getting the kids used to him early, as over the years they would be hearing him a lot. "I'll check on the others and be right back." He sang softly to the music as he left the room.

Once again, Charlotte had kicked off all her coverings, so Viv pulled them back up and tucked them in around her. Millie lay sound asleep, and Viv kissed her cheek before going in to the boys' room. James was in the same bed as Teddy, cuddling the other boy. Now positive that something had indeed happened to upset his son Viv planned to find out what it was.

"What are you still doing awake, little man?" Viv murmured. Surprise slapped him as Jamie climbed into his arms.

"I'm scared."

With those words, Viv realized that Jamie was crying. He rubbed his child's back in comfort. "Why are you scared?"

"I don't want to go back to Deena's. Please don't make me go. I don't want to leave Bear. I love him."

He cuddled closer, wrapped his arms around Viv's neck and wept.

"What are you talking about?"

"Kelly said I wasn't a good boy. She said I was disgusting, and you don't want me anymore. She said you want to send me back to live with Deena. She said you don't want me, that I'm always naughty. She said you don't like it when I hug Bear, and you only keep me here because the judge said you had to."

Viv froze in anger. "Who's Kelly?"

Jamie clung tighter to him and wept harder.

Sitting up in his bed, Teddy answered. "She's one of the ladies who came to look after all the little kids. She said some really nasty stuff to Jamie."

"She's Deena's best friend." Jamie sobbed. "Dad, I'm sorry for being naughty. I won't hug Bear anymore if you don't want me to."

Viv stood, lifting Jamie into his arms, and walked out of the room. He stopped long enough with the others to grab Ray and filled him in on what James had just told him. He hoped Kelly was among the women still at the house as some had already gone home. Teddy followed them.

At the makeshift nursery, Teddy pointed Kelly out to Viv and Ray.

Furious, Viv stalked over and demanded her to step out into the hall. She took one look at James and realization dawned on her face. Viv also asked the woman in charge to come with them. If they were going to do this, then he wanted witnesses who weren't family or friends.

The head woman asked, "What's going on?"

Viv glared at Kelly. "I would like this woman to apologize—firstly to our son, then to us. Afterward, I want her to get the hell out of our house. I will also be recommending her termination."

"I do not apologize to children," Kelly said defiantly.

Jamie flinched in Viv's arms.

Viv saw that she had wanted to say something else but had changed her mind at the last moment.

"Oh, yes, you damn well will," Ray spat right back at her.

Viv wanted to cheer his husband on.

"Will somebody please tell me what is going on?" the head woman asked.

Viv coaxed Jamie into telling the woman in charge what Kelly had said to him. Tears streamed down his face by the time he had finished and he hugged Viv around the neck.

Shocked, the head woman fired Kelly on the spot and demanded that she apologize.

"Kiss my arse," Kelly shouted as she headed for the front door. She turned back and looked at them all. "Faggots shouldn't be allowed to raise children. You take them away from perfectly good foster homes to bring them into this den of sin. The next thing we'll hear is that you've had your way with him. It's bad enough he spent the whole night holding hands and hugging the other little boy living here."

Viv snapped. Handing James to Ray, he strode toward Kelly, grabbed her by the upper arm, yanked her to the front door and pushed her out into the night. The woman in charge was very apologetic about the whole situation, but Viv was too pissed off to listen to her. He knew the party was still going on, so he walked past them and headed back into the hall. When he returned, he had Byron King with him.

The woman in charge, who he found out was named Ellen, described the scene and what everyone had said. Viv informed Ellen that he was going to serve Kelly with papers about defamation of character, slander and for the mental anguish their son had endured while under her care. Viv assured Ellen that in no way would this affect her business. She willingly gave Kelly's full name and address to Byron and agreed to be as helpful as she possibly could. She apologized again as Viv and his family readied to leave and go back to bed. She wanted to assure them that the narrow-minded comments Kelly had made were not shared by the rest of the company.

Once upstairs, Jamie was still very upset, so Viv carried him into their bed while Ray filled Josh and Fred in on what had happened. Viv heard them rush from the room to be with Teddy. Viv lay on the bed with Jamie when Ray finally came in and lay down beside them.

He watched as Ray tilted Jamie's face until he could look into his eyes. "Now you listen to me, James Henry Connelly. You're not a naughty boy, and we will never send you back to Deena's. We're not keeping you because the judge said we have to. We're keeping you because you now belong to us and we love you *very* much. You are an important part of our family." Tears filled Ray's eyes as Jamie finally calmed down enough to fall asleep.

"Do you want me to carry him back to his own bed?" Viv asked quietly.

Ray shook his head. "Would you be too disappointed in me if I wanted to keep him here with us tonight?"

"Never, love." Viv lifted James off the bed long enough for Ray to pull the covers down. "I'll go and get his Ninja Turtle." Ray moved Jamie enough so Viv would be able to spoon him when he came back. Viv put the toy turtle in Jamie's arms before he and Ray had a quick shower and got back into bed.

"What would make a grown woman say something like that to a child?" Ray whispered, his voice cracking with emotion.

All Viv could do was pull his husband back against his chest and offer comfort.

"Jealousy, love. We took him out of welfare and gave him a better life than they themselves are living. They'll always be poor, and one day he'll be wealthy."

Ray couldn't seem to stop his tears from falling. "I'm sorry, Viv. I didn't want this to spoil our wedding night."

He kissed the nape of his husband's neck. "Love, our children's needs will always come before our own. We'll have plenty of time to consummate this marriage. We'll probably consummate it over and over again." He ended with a suggestive kiss against the nape of Ray's neck.

Ray's chuckle through his soft sobs was magic to Viv's ears, especially when he said, "I'll hold you to that."

Ray encircled Jamie with one arm as Viv snuggled into his back.

"I love you, Christopher Connelly. You're one of the best things to ever come into my life."

Viv placed butterfly kisses on Ray's shoulder. "I hope you still think so when we're old and gray."

"You know I will." Ray yawned. His tears had finally stopped. He kissed James on the cheek before succumbing to sleep.

Viv couldn't help but watch over his family while they slept, promising himself he would protect them from all the nastiness life would throw their way.

* * * *

When Viv woke in the morning, Ray had turned in his arms and lay draped around his body. James was still asleep and hugging his Ninja Turtle. Viv smiled as Ray's eyes opened and he was rewarded with a very enjoyable kiss.

"Good morning, my husband," Viv whispered.

"Good morning, love of my life," Ray answered.

"What were you dreaming about?" Viv wanted to know what was running through his lover's head.

"Honestly, I was thinking about the wedding and how everyone looked. In my dream, B looked a little bit pregnant. This is odd, as we haven't even begun to try yet. Then I thought to myself, B really did look a little more, I don't know...well-endowed yesterday."

"No way," Viv whispered, his mind automatically running back to B at the wedding. Ray was right.

"Do we still have some of those pregnancy kits we bought for when we were trying for Layla and Izzy?" Ray said as he pushed himself off the bed.

"They're in the bathroom, I think." Viv got up, followed him and watched as Ray pulled out a box, checking the expiration date and heading out of the room.

"Do you know which room they're sleeping in?" Ray asked.

Knocking on Fred and Josh's door, Viv poked his head into the room. Josh was still dead to the world.

"Morning, Fred. Ray and I need to go see B for a minute. Could you keep an ear out for the kids and James? He's still in our bed. We'll be back as soon as we can." He didn't even comment on the fact that Josh and Fred were both naked, and had obviously, at some stage during the night, been busy, but he couldn't stop the smile from spreading across his face.

"I think they might have consummated our marriage for us." Viv chuckled, as he took Ray's hand and walked to his old room. They knocked once on the door as warning before they opened it and walked in.

Viv was hard pressed not to laugh as Ray jumped on the bed, crawled up in between their friends and patiently waited for them to wake up. This didn't take long, mainly because Ray kept poking them both in their ribs.

"Ray," Beth began, "if you haven't woke me up for a very good reason, I'm going to knock the ever-living shit out of you."

"I've woken you up for a very good reason," Ray blurted. "I need you to go and pee on a stick."

"What?" She pushed herself into a sitting position and looked at the pregnancy test. "Ray, I can't be pregnant. We haven't done anything yet."

"Just humor me." Ray handed her the stick and pushed her out of bed then pulled Jasper into the center of the bed so Viv could sit on his other side. They both slung an arm around him as they waited. "Holy crap!" was all they heard through the bathroom door.

Jasper jolted fully awake and jumped up, but Beth was already back in the bedroom before he got to the bathroom door. She handed him the test and his face went totally blank. Viv fist-pumped the air as Ray let out a loud cheer.

They watched as Jasper stared at the stick in his hand for a long time before he looked at her. "How...? Who?" He seemed incapable of further speech.

"You," Beth said, stunned.

"But I can't," he stuttered and tried to hand back the positive pregnancy test.

"But you did." Beth glowed. Her hands shook as she held them out to him. "Dr Emerson said your count was too low, but I guess he was wrong."

Viv couldn't help himself as he said, "Obviously you had one determined little bugger who defied the odds and found a way home."

Jasper couldn't speak as he embraced his wife. Tears flowed down their faces as they held each other tightly before letting go.

"Sorry, I'm so emotional," Jasper whispered as he stroked his hand gently over his wife's stomach.

Viv couldn't help but marvel at the beauty of it all.

Jasper turned to Ray. "But this doesn't let you off the hook for when we want more. We gave you two, so fair is fair."

Beth giggled. "Unless, of course, I decide I want green-eyed children then I'll be hunting after Viv."

She laughed even more as Viv gaped at her

Finally, he found his voice and answered, "We'll give you one each if you prefer. We owe you big time."

"I'll hold you to that," Beth said as she hugged Jasper again. "Come on! Let's go and tell Josh he's going to be an uncle."

Ray laughed. "Well, you'd better go to the nanny's room. That's where we found him this morning and, according to a little birdie, he's been there for the past month."

"Josh and Fred? No way." Beth grinned. "Josh doesn't settle down. He has a different girl every week."

"Not since he met Fred," Viv replied. "He's been home every night for the past couple of months. I think the whole settling down thing kind of sneaked up on him."

"I've got to see this for myself." Beth didn't wait for them as she quickly walked through the halls to Fred's room. She knocked once before entering, without an invitation.

The rest of them followed closely.

Since he and Ray had visited this morning, Fred had pulled on clothes. She'd obviously been to check on the children. Josh, on the other hand, was still naked and asleep. Fred began blushing

Beth burst out, "Holy crap!" Then she must have realized that she was being rude. "Sorry. Morning, Fred." She grinned as she walked over and shook Josh until he woke up.

"I'm awake, for crying out loud." He rolled over and wrapped his arms around Fred. "What do you want, love?"

"I'm not the one who woke you up. She did." Fred pointed at Beth.

He looked over his shoulder at their visitors. "Hi, guys. You're all up nice and early." He reached over the side of the bed and grabbed his jeans before he stood up and pulled them on. "What can I do for you, sister dear?"

"Oh, nothing really," Beth said casually. "Jas and I wanted to tell you you're going to be an uncle." She looked at Fred. "And if *this* keeps happening then you will be an aunty. We—"

Josh pulled her into a hug and spun her around in a circle. He turned to Ray. "You never said anything about trying again so soon."

"I didn't. I mean, I'm not the father." Ray grinned.

Frowning, Josh asked. "Then who?"

His gaze fell on Viv, who only snorted and shook his head. He was not getting the credit for this child.

"Me!" Jasper said proudly, puffing out his chest. "I knew all the sex would have to pay off sooner or later."

Josh let go of his sister before hugging Jasper and kissing him soundly on the lips.

The babies began to wake up, their sounds filtering through the monitors. Josh held Fred's hand as they walked into the nursery.

Viv went down to prepare the bottles and to see what was for breakfast. When he came back, he wasn't alone.

"Hey, Angus, what are you doing up so early?" Ray questioned.

Viv handed him a bottle to feed Jeb, quickly picked up Izzy and sat next to Ray.

"Seth and I wanted to say goodbye. We're heading off to Sydney for a couple of weeks." He held onto Seth's hand.

"And we wanted to thank you for introducing us," Seth added shyly.

"I'm glad you hit it off," Ray answered.

When Seth and Angus had left, Ray turned to Viv and asked, "You weren't jealous, were you?"

"Well, he's very good-looking. Maybe one day you'll wake up and realize what you gave up to be with me," he answered sincerely.

"Yes, but look what I've gained by being with you. I could only have got all of this" — Ray leaned over so he could kiss Viv — "with you."

When they pulled apart, Jamie stood in their bedroom doorway watching.

"Good morning, little man." Viv held out an arm so James would come to him and gave Izzy to Beth so he could pull Jamie onto his lap. "Are you feeling better this morning?"

James nodded as he hugged him back.

"Come on. Let's go and get you dressed."

Viv stood and went with Jamie to his bedroom so Ray could fill Jasper and Beth in on what had happened last night.

By the time they had all gone downstairs, a breakfast barbecue was already underway. Liam and Claire called for Jamie to join them while Viv and Ray organized their kids' breakfasts. By the amount of attention his parents were lavishing on Jamie, Viv concluded that Byron had filled the rest of the family in on what had taken place the night before. He was glad he didn't have to tell them. He was still too angry about the whole thing.

But Jamie was definitely enjoying the attention. It would go a long way in reassuring the boy that he was very much wanted.

When Viv and Ray got to the table, his father and Jamie were talking about jobs. Liam was asking Jamie what he was going to be when he grew up.

"I'm going to work for you, Pop, with Dad then I can save up money and marry Bear," James said as he took a bite of toast.

Chuckling, Liam turned to Ray. "Remember when you were little and you wanted to marry Mr Squiggle?"

Viv bit his lip to keep from laughing at this new bit of information about his husband.

Ray blushed as the others laughed.

"The guy could draw, okay?" Ray defended himself. "And I was three. I wanted to ride in his rocket ship. Besides, Dad, Bear isn't a toy. Bear is Teddy."

"Jamie has called Teddy 'Bear' since the first day they met," Viv added.

Nodding in agreement, Jamie looked serious.

"Oh," Liam said, "and what does Teddy want to do?"

"He's going to work for Dan and Girly and marry me," Jamie said matter-of-factly. He moved over, making room as Teddy walked over to the table and climbed up on the chair beside him. "We're getting married, right, Bear?"

"Yep." The table fell silent as Teddy hugged Jamie before adding, "Mum said we could."

Fred ducked her head in the light of all the attention aimed at her. "I figure they'll eventually grow up and may change their minds." She shrugged. "When I was young, I wanted to marry my cousin because he could walk on his hands. I grew out of it. They're just kids and —"

"I was seven when I fell in love with my first boy," Daniel said quietly. "I never grew out of it."

Rolling his eyes, Josh asked, "What's the big deal? Who cares if they're gay? We're going to love them anyway. They're still Teddy and Jamie. They'll *always* be our kids."

"Spoken like a proud father," Claire said.

Josh beamed at her.

Standing, Jasper proudly announced that he was going to be the father of his very own biological child. "Then Viv and Ray will help out on the next time round," he ended with a smug grin.

"I peed on a stick," Beth said when the family looked at her. "Who says miracles don't happen?"

Chapter Thirteen

Ray sat in a chair and growled in frustration. The two months following the wedding had been stressful and Ray was about at his wits' end. He'd never truly understood how much Kelly's hurtful words were going to affect his family—especially Jamie, who had withdrawn into himself. Ray couldn't figure out how to make things better. Even his nightly chats with Viv didn't seem to help. This was why he'd gathered the whole gang in the new playroom. He hoped it would shake the blues. Plus he wanted help putting some of the toys together. A job that was easier said than done, Ray concluded when he listened to Josh grumble.

"You know, you would think these things would come with better instructions." Josh scratched his head before adding, "What are we meant to do with all the extra bits?" He looked from the newly constructed play furniture to the small but steadily growing pile of extra screws.

"You could always put them in empty milk containers and turn them into maracas," Brent said jokingly from where he and Tarni were putting together some doll cribs.

Giggling, Beth sat filling the little kitchen hutch with plates and cutlery. Both Ray and Fred had made sure that all parts and pieces were too big to be swallowed.

"Don't worry so much. The kids will love the play set, whatever it ends up looking like. When I worked in childcare, they always loved playing in the home corner."

Ray looked over at Teddy and Jamie where they sat on huge floor cushions bouncing the babies in the bouncinettes while the girls reclined off to one side, reading books.

"See what I mean?" She indicated the boys.

"Do they worry you with the way they act?" Beth asked as she absentmindedly rubbed her baby bump, which was getting huge, although the pregnancy looked good on her.

Ray turned, listening. It worried him as to what Fred might say.

"At first," Fred began, "I freaked when I thought Teddy might be gay. Mainly I was worrying what Damien would say. If he found out, he wouldn't think twice about flogging him." She looked at the two boys, who now sat close together reading from the same book. "But honestly, I'm for whatever makes my child happy, whether a girl or a boy. Josh is right. If he turns out to be gay, I'm still going to love him, no matter what. Besides, it's too hard to keep them out of the same bed."

Relaxing, Ray knew deep down that he'd worried that she might blame Viv and him, and he knew that Viv had been anxious about the same thing.

Josh burst out laughing. "I'm going to laugh my arse off the day they realize they're too big to fit in the same single bed and come asking for a bigger one."

"You're a sick and twisted man, brother," Beth said with a smile. "So you plan on still being here, then?"

"Of course," he answered instantly. "Fred can't get rid of me so easily, and as soon as the waiting period for her divorce from that loser has passed then the sooner I can marry her and make her mine."

"You want to marry me?" she asked.

The look of astonishment on her face nearly sent Ray into a laughing fit.

"Why wouldn't I?" Josh retorted as he blew her a kiss.

The second she burst into tears, Ray watched on in morbid fascination as his friend jumped up to comfort her.

"Don't you want to marry me?" Josh embraced her as she cried even harder. "Well, this wasn't actually the response I was hoping for. Okay, we don't have to get married. I won't bring up the subject again."

"No! The thing is, I *do* want to marry you, but I'm afraid of Damien. I'm scared of what trouble he might cause."

Ray's heart twisted over at the anguish his friend was going through and, in the thick of what was happening, he didn't have a clue what to say to make things right. He wished he did.

"Do you think he might try to take the kids?" Viv asked.

Fred nodded. "His new girlfriend is different from the last. What if she wants them?" She stepped away from Josh and sank to the floor next to Ray.

He grabbed her hand in comfort.

"I mean, I know he wouldn't want them permanently. He'd think they are too much trouble, but if Teddy tells him he wants to marry Jamie, Damien might hurt him."

Ray sucked in a much needed lungful of air as he prepared to speak. He knew that what he was about to say would be met with resistance, especially from Teddy and Jamie.

"Do you think we should separate them? Maybe even give them different bedrooms? We could put Teddy in the one on the other side of the girls."

"Maybe that wouldn't be such a bad idea," Fred reluctantly agreed.

This is so not going to be fun. Ray stared over at the two frowning boys.

* * * *

Frustration overwhelmed Ray. The separation of Teddy and Jamie wasn't going as smoothly as he'd hoped. Both boys had been crying almost constantly for about two weeks. Thank God they were in the middle of school holidays and home. More often than not, they went to bed separately and woke up together. Viv was no help since he was always at work and constantly tired, cranky and distant when he got home.

Six months down the track, Ray watched as Fred threw her hands in the air in exasperation announcing that she was giving up.

"They win! Two eleven-year-old boys have beaten me. I'm tired of telling my son no and making him unhappy."

"What are you saying, love?" Josh asked.

Fred handed him a piece of paper.

Josh read aloud. "Dear Santa, I want to marry Jamie, so tell my mum so we can share our room again. I don't need presents this year. All I want is Jamie. Bear XO"

"How am I supposed to fight that?" she asked.

"I'm sorry, Fred," Ray said slowly. "I don't know what else to try."

"Let them share," Grandma declared as she came in to join them all at the dining room table.

It worried Ray that today she wasn't looking one hundred percent. Usually she stayed in her rooms when she wasn't feeling well. He jumped up and made her a cup of green tea.

"Are you okay, Grandma?" He kissed her cheek.

"I'm fine, but you all need to stop tormenting those boys. Let them live their lives." Grandma called to Teddy and Jamie who were sitting at the other end of the table. "Boys, do you want to share your room again?" she asked them kindly.

They both nodded. "Yes, GG," they said in unison.

Jamie took hold of Teddy's hand. His eyes shone with excitement. Something Ray hadn't seen for a long time.

"Then move back in together. This is *my* house and I'm telling you I'm okay with you being in the same room."

Teddy looked over at his mother and Josh to see if he was allowed to get excited yet.

"Can I still marry Bear?" Jamie asked her.

"Sure." Grandma waved at them. "And don't you let anyone tell you no. You can do anything you set your mind to."

She smiled as both boys turned to each other and hugged each other tightly.

"Grandma," Ray said once the two boys had left the table, "maybe this isn't such a good idea."

His grandmother stared at him for a very long time. By the time she had him squirming in his seat, she finally answered.

"Look at it this way," she began. "You let them be together in this house and when they grow up, I'm pretty confident they'll want to be together outside of it too. That's what they want, and the outside isn't going to be as understanding as this family should be. Yes, those boys might grow out of this childhood love, but if they don't, they should be allowed the freedom to be who they are." She casually took a sip of her tea. "I never once told you not to be who you are. I even encouraged you. Now, I'm telling you—leave those boys alone. This house is where they are meant to feel safe, secure and loved." She let her gaze wander over Ray and the rest of the family. "If any of you have a problem with the boys sharing a room then I'm going to tell you all to grow up. At least they love someone. Do you think just because they are so young that they don't know their own minds?"

She looked so serious that Ray couldn't help but laugh, and soon the others found the laughter contagious.

The boys returned to the room, their faces beaming.

"Now what do you boys want for Christmas?" she asked, smiling.

"A big bed like my dad's, so Bear won't keep falling out," Jamie replied innocently.

With those few words, Josh burst out laughing again. "I'm sorry, but I knew it was coming. I told you this would happen." He wiped the tears from his eyes and hugged Teddy and Jamie. "I guess you'll have to be good and see what Santa brings you."

"Uncle Josh, you do realize Santa isn't real. Bear told me," Jamie stated.

"If you think that's true, then why did you write to him?" Grandma asked Teddy.

"We're too big to believe in Santa, but just in case he is real, Jamie thought we should write to him asking for help," Teddy answered. "It doesn't hurt to try."

Grandma had one condition.

"If you boys want to share a room again, then you're to do the moving yourselves. Do I make myself clear? No one can help you."

"Yes, GG," both Jamie and Teddy answered quickly.

Teddy tugged on Jamie's sleeve. "Let's get started or we'll never get finished by bedtime."

They spent the afternoon moving Teddy's things back into Jamie's room. Antonio was overseeing the transition and reported that the boys had a very smart idea and were using the two red wagons that usually held their toys.

Later that same day, Ray lay on the bed reading when Viv came home.

"You're late, love."

Viv was quiet for a long time.

Ray began to worry. "Is something wrong? Have I done something to upset you?"

Walking around the bed, he stopped and pulled Ray to his feet, embracing him.

Ray could feel Viv's body trembling. "Love, what's wrong?"

"Ray, I…" He hesitated for a moment then started again. "Ray, there's this guy at work."

He stepped away from Viv and looked him in the eye. He wanted to see what was written on his husband's face, making sure there were no mixed signals. "What guy?"

"His name is Shane." Viv ran his hand through his hair.

Getting upset, Ray needed reassurance that there was no need for concern.

"Ray, I don't know what to do." Viv looked worried.

"About what?" Throat dry, Ray could barely swallow.

"Shane won't leave me alone. He keeps talking to me in a sexual manner and touching me when no one else is around. I've repeatedly asked him to stop, but he laughs and says I enjoy what he's doing—when I don't. Now, when I see him heading in my direction, I start feeling sick. I don't know who to turn to for help."

Ray relaxed somewhat and took Viv's hand. "Have you told anyone? Maybe, if you had a chat with Uncle Matt—or Don."

"I told Don, but I can't tell Uncle Matt. Ray, Shane is Byron's son. He started working with us not long after the wedding, and he's been harassing me ever since. I don't know how to make him stop. At this stage, I don't even want to go to work."

It upset Ray that this was happening to Viv, but he was also happy that this wasn't as bad as he'd thought. It was something that could be fixed. "So this is why you have been so cranky lately?" He caressed Viv's cheek. "I was worried you had grown sick of me and the kids and wanted out."

Viv looked at Ray in shock. "Don't be stupid, Ray. You are the best things ever to happen in my life. I will never grow sick of you or the kids. Love, that's just impossible." Viv kissed Ray deeply before adding, "Don't you know by now, every time I look at you I want to take you to bed?" He slid his hands down to cup Ray's arse and pulled him close. "My body belongs only to you."

Ray shook his head to clear it from the erotic visions Viv had placed in his mind. "I hadn't realized Shane was back in town. The last I heard of him, he was in France. I bet Brent isn't happy. They've hated each other since we were all kids."

"Ray, how do I make him leave me alone?" Viv hugged Ray tight.

Ray held him just as fiercely. "Uncle Matt will probably bring him to the Christmas party," Ray said thoughtfully. "Leave it to me, love. I'll make the idiot leave you alone."

"How?" Viv asked.

Ray shook his head. "It's best you don't know. If I tell you then you'll only try to stop me." He kissed Viv. "Trust me. By the time I'm finished, Shane won't bother you again."

Viv finally began to relax. "So what's been happening at home today?" he asked brightly. "Tell me what exciting things you and our children have been doing?"

"Teddy moved back in with Jamie," Ray began, launching into the story of the letter to Santa.

Even though Viv was chuckling, his face still held a look of worry. "What did Fred say?"

"Not much, really. Josh was laughing his arse off, and no one wanted to disagree with Grandma. She told them if they wanted to live together, then they had to move all Teddy's things by themselves—and they did. The boys took all afternoon, and they were exhausted when they were done. I haven't checked on them yet, but I bet they're in the same bed. I think we finally have to admit they're probably going to announce in a few years that they're gay."

Viv hugged Ray closer. "But they're our boys, and we love them. How are you going to get around the one bed thing?"

"We explained to them that at the moment they need to keep the two separate beds as a big bed wouldn't fit into their room." Ray shivered when he realized that Viv was slowly undressing him. "Josh told them if they still want to get married at eighteen, then they could have a big bed. They smiled and said okay then announced to everyone that when they were eighteen, they would move into my old room. They..."

He lost his train of thought when Viv pushed him backward onto the bed and climbed on after him. Viv was so determined in what he was doing, he didn't even realize that his mobile was ringing.

"You'd better answer that," Ray whispered. "It could be important."

"Hello," Viv said.

Ray saw the color drained from his husband's face when he heard the other person speak.

"What do you want, Shane? How did you get my number?"

Holding out his hand in anger and annoyance, it surprised him when Viv handed the phone straight to him without complaint. Ray listened silently as the arsehole on the other end of the line explained in detail exactly what he wanted Viv to do for him. Shane fell silent when Ray burst out laughing.

"And would that be before or after he has finished making love to me?" Ray said politely before he hung up and returned his attention to the man above him. "Now, where were we? I believe you were about to ravish my body," he whimpered as Viv once again began to carefully stretch him.

The fierce heat enveloping Ray let him know he was even more alive, and the look in his husband's eyes portrayed how very much Viv loved him. As Viv added additional lubed fingers after the first one, Ray groaned as he pushed out and impaled himself further. The tingle that had started in his nipples suddenly surged outward until the sensation engulfed his whole body. His cock ached and the feeling of the pre-cum sliding down the length of his shaft was going to tip him over the edge long before Viv would get inside him.

"Viv... Please... I need... On fire..." He wasn't even sure if his ramblings were actually being spoken aloud or were all inside his head.

The look of lust that filled Viv's gaze had Ray panting in need. He truly loved Viv with his whole heart. Ray needed more and rolled them until he was sitting on top of Viv. Lifting himself slightly, he paused as Viv caught up with what Ray wanted. Ray bowed his back with the first touch of Viv's cockhead against his hole. The slight friction forced Ray to push back, and he did with great relish. His gaze locked onto Viv's face as Viv's rigid cock entered him. Ray moaned as he slowly took in more until Viv was balls-deep inside him. Ray relished the miraculous feeling as they stayed frozen in time and nothing and no one else in the world existed, except for them.

"I need you to move, Ray."

Viv hissed as Ray lifted then dropped suddenly. Slow up and fast down sounded good in Ray's mind, especially if the pleasurable noises coming from Viv were any indication of how the man was feeling.

His own body was on fire with every movement. Having his body breached was such a powerful thing, and Ray wanted more. Grinding down, he was ready to explode like a firecracker. Everything was all mixed up. He felt so light yet intense at the same time. Each orgasm his lover gave to him was somehow better than the last, and Ray relished them all.

Even though it was the wrong time to think about what was running through his mind, Ray couldn't help but make a comparison between what he had once had with Beth and what he now had with Viv. This with Viv won by a long shot. Never in his whole life had he ever felt so complete.

"I love you, Ray." Viv groaned as he dug his fingers into the flesh of Ray's hips.

"Christopher Connelly, do you realize just how much you turn me on when you say those words to me?" Ray leaned forward and pressed his face into Viv's shoulder. He gently bit the juncture where Viv's shoulder and neck met and held on with each upward thrust of Viv inside him.

"You're so beautiful, Ray," Viv whispered into his hair.

"I bet you say that to all the pretty boys," he joked as he sat up and witnessed hurt wash over Viv. "Sorry, love." Ray sighed. A groan fell from his lips when Viv shifted to his waist as he intensified his motions.

"You're the only pretty boy I care about." Viv pulled Ray down into his embrace and Ray lost it all when he felt Viv release into him.

"Remember when we were too scared to try this?"

"The best thing we ever did was get tested so we could lose that thin piece of rubber. Feeling the real you is unbelievable," Viv stated between kisses. He sighed as the phone rang again.

Viv looked at the number. "Hello? Jas, we're on our way." He hung up and reluctantly shifted Ray. "B's in labor."

They jumped up and pulled clothes on without taking the time to shower. Ray grabbed bottles, formula and food as Viv packed nappy bags. By the time he got back, Josh and Fred were up and organizing the kids. He would have asked his grandma to look after them but he knew she would want to be at the hospital too, seeing as she claimed the whole band as family.

Eliza Jane Briggs was born at twelve fifty-three am on a Wednesday morning. Jas and B were over the moon. The baby was definitely going to be one spoiled little girl. And according to her proud father, she was blessed with her mother's good looks.

* * * *

Viv was nervous as they waited for the guests to arrive for the company Christmas party. This year, at Grandma's request, it was being held at her house.

Shane was going to be there too, and Viv hated knowing that the pain in the arse would be anywhere near his family. He didn't want to put himself or Ray through the stress of what the arsehole might cause.

"Love" — Ray kissed him tenderly — "don't worry about this. I told you I'd take care of all your troubles with Shane."

"You haven't had to listen to him all week, Ray, explaining how he is going to get me drunk and have his wicked way with me at this party. I spent two days hiding in a vacant lab to get some relief." Viv rubbed a hand over his churning stomach. "I think I need some Mylanta."

"He won't have a chance to get close to you. I promise." Ray smiled sweetly.

He wanted to believe Ray, but he knew how full-on Shane could be.

Antonio had hired the same nanny service they had used for the wedding to look after the children for the night. This time they'd sent three capable women out to do the job. Viv and Ray had given in to all the pleading and were allowing the boys to attend the party for a while.

When they headed down to the party, Ray was smiling a little too much. That fact somehow made Viv worry more. Most of the guests were already there, so they had no problems locating Shane. Ray had been right about that as well. All they had to do was look for the largest group. Shane always liked to be the center of attention

"Ray," Shane said with a smile as he saw them approach. Viv's eyes widened in shock as Ray hauled back and punched Shane straight in the mouth, knocking him backward onto his arse.

"What the fuck, Ray?" Shane spat a mouthful of blood on the floor.

"Keep your fucking hands off Viv," Ray retorted calmly, "or next time I'll do some real damage." He turned as his father approached them.

"Who the hell is Viv?" Shane spluttered

"My husband, so stay the hell away from him." The anger in Ray's voice should have been a warning, but it seemed that Shane wasn't listening.

"What's going on?" Liam asked.

"Your son has lost the plot," Shane accused as he got up off the floor. "I haven't even met his fucking husband."

"Whatever," Ray said. He walked over, drew Viv close and slung his arms around Viv's neck, kissing him. "Come on, love. Let's go get a drink."

Shane stared at them.

As they left, Viv heard Liam state, "I wouldn't advise trying to steal Viv away from Ray. As you can see, he is very protective of his family."

"Viv... He's Chris?" Shane asked stupidly.

Viv heard Brent laughing. "You're such a wanker sometimes, Shane." He was still laughing as he came over and joined Viv and Ray at the bar.

Both mad and relieved, Viv realized that Shane was not going to be a problem any longer. He looked at Ray. "Did you have to punch him in front of everyone?" he asked quietly.

"Yes, he did," Brent answered then ordered a drink. "Being punched in the mouth is the only thing that wanker would understand."

"Where's Tarni?" Ray asked as though to change the subject.

"Upstairs with B, Fred and Girly. They're having girl time with all the kids."

"They're all getting clucky," Daniel said as he and Josh joined them. "Next thing you know, we'll all have babies."

"You mean Fred, Girly and Tarni are, because I don't think Ray and I will be jumping back into the daddy pool any time soon." Viv chuckled. "Here's to being a father." He raised his glass to Jasper as he neared them.

"I love being a daddy." Jasper grinned. "I can't wait till we have more." He looked at Ray. "Bear and Jamie just told us all that you punched someone in the face."

"Shane," Brent stated.

"Ahh, enough said." Jasper chuckled.

"Okay, someone explain?" Daniel asked curiously.

"I told you Shane's a wanker. He seriously believes he's God's gift to everyone." Brent stopped, deep in thought for a moment. "I wonder if we should introduce him to Grace. I mean, after she gets out of prison."

Viv and everyone else cracked up laughing.

They all turned as someone tapped Ray on the shoulder.

The smile left Ray's face when he saw Shane standing there. "What do you want?"

"I'd actually like to apologize, Ray. I didn't know. If I had known Chris was Viv then I would have left him alone."

"Even though you knew he had recently got married, you thought sexually harassing him was okay? Even when he asked you to leave him alone?" Ray asked.

"He was fair game." Shane shrugged. "I wasn't hurting anyone."

"Fair game to you maybe, but not to anyone who has morals," Ray snarled.

Shane glared at him. "It wasn't as though I was getting anywhere. I wouldn't have done anything to him."

"Then why did you explain to him what you were going to do to him tonight once he was drunk, and why did you talk on the phone about screwing him, which I must say was quite entertaining. Though, I have to tell you some of those suggestions are anatomically undoable. Viv and I sure gave them a good try, though. What I really want to know is—how you didn't think it wouldn't hurt Viv or impact our family?"

"I said I'm sorry, Ray," Shane whispered.

"I'm not the one you should be apologizing to," Ray spat back.

Shane turned to Viv. "Chris, I'm sorry for everything I've said and done that made you feel uncomfortable. I will refrain from doing so again in the future."

"Thank you," Viv said.

Although he didn't want to forgive the man, he knew it was the right thing to do. Promptly dismissing him, he turned his back on Shane as Jamie and Bear ran up to them.

"Dad." Jamie jumped up onto the stool beside Viv and Teddy climbed onto Josh's lap.

"What's happening, boys?" Viv asked.

"Nothing. Girly told us to come and annoy you, as the babies are all going to sleep," Jamie answered.

"Sounds like Girly." Daniel laughed. "Speaking of her, I think I'm ready to ask her to marry me."

Ray choked on his drink as he spun and looked at Daniel.

"You know," Daniel continued, "make things all nice and legal...just in case she does want to have babies with me. I'd like us to be married first."

Viv thought his brother looked slightly green.

"Do you think she will say yes if I ask her—or laugh her arse off at me?"

"Ask her and find out," Brent said as he pointed to the four girls as they descended the stairs.

Daniel shook his head. "I'm too much of a chicken."

Falling silent with everyone else, Viv enjoyed the scene as the girls joined them. Girly cuddled Daniel and kissed him.

Before Brent even opened his mouth, Viv could tell by the mischievous look on his face that he was going to give Daniel a much needed shove. "Hey, Girly." Brent grinned wickedly. "Daniel's too scared to pop the question in case you laugh at him."

She stepped away from Daniel and stared at him as his face flamed bright red.

"Thanks, Brent," Daniel whispered.

"No worries. What are friends for?" He clapped Daniel on the shoulder.

"Well?" Tarni asked. "What's your answer?"

"When?" Girly questioned.

Since Daniel looked confused, she elaborated.

"When are you planning on us getting married? There's a lot to organize before we get hitched." She turned to Tarni. "You'll be my bridesmaid, won't you? And you as well, Fred, and B will be my matron of honor, seeing as she's the only married one, and Dad will give me away." Her face lit up. "We've got to tell GG."

"I know a faster way." Ray walked up onto the stage and took the microphone from the stand they had earlier set up for the speeches.

Stunned, Viv listened with his mouth ajar.

"Attention everyone," Ray began. "Could I please have your undivided attention? I would proudly like to announce my beautiful daughter Sara Jane Connelly, better known as Girly to the rest of us, has only moments ago accepted Daniel Lee Marshal's hand in marriage." He held up his glass and toasted them both. "Here's to the happy couple."

A cheer rose through the room.

In that moment, Viv's heart plummeted when Ray dropped his glass. His husband's gaze focused on someone in the crowd. When Viv turned, he saw Grandma. She was clutching at her chest then collapsed.

"Grandma," Viv screamed. Forcefully pushing his way across the room, he dropped to his knees beside Ray, who now held his grandma in his arms.

The crowd gathered around them as Grandma's eyes fluttered open and focused on Ray's face. "James, you came for me. I've missed you so much."

Ray pulled her into his arms. "Ahh, Chrissie, my love, you knew I'd be waiting for you." He put on a slight Irish brogue.

Someone in the background called triple zero.

Viv listened in heart-breaking silence. His sole focus was on his husband and the grandma he loved.

"It won't be long, Chrissie, my love. Help is but a moment away. I need you to hold on for me, darlin'. Your time in this world is not over."

Viv's tears fell as Chrissie's eyes closed.

"Hang on, my sweet Chrissie," Ray whispered as he rocked his grandma in his arms.

* * * *

Ray couldn't even look up as his family dropped to their knees around him. Jamie and Teddy were crying somewhere nearby. Guilt hit him. He couldn't even comfort them right now. His heart broke as he listened to his grandma's last breath. They did CPR until the ambulance arrived. He thought his life was over until he heard one of the paramedics.

"We have a pulse!"

The EMTs treated Ray for shock. Even though Grandma wasn't dead, he knew he'd come close to losing her. He didn't know what he would have done if they hadn't been able to revive her. She had been the one sure thing in his entire life.

Nothing anyone said consoled him. As the guests went home, he sat in the nursery, even pushing his family away. He crawled onto a child's bed, where Millie lay, and cried then he moved enough to let

Jamie climb on with them. Ray held his children and wept.

"Pa, please don't cry," Jamie whispered and clung to Ray. "GG wouldn't want you to cry like this. She would tell you to suck it up, princess, and get your arse to the hospital."

Ray clung to his son and listened to the truth in his words as his tears abated. Getting up, he kissed Jamie's cheek. "I love you, Jamie." He held out his hand and took Jamie back to the room he shared with Teddy then ruffled his hair as he waited for him to climb into bed beside the other boy, knowing that everyone needed comfort tonight. "I'll see you in the morning, little man. I will be better then. I promise."

"I love you, Pa. Now go to the hospital and see if GG is okay," Jamie whispered as Ray shut the door.

Ray turned to find Viv standing in the nursery doorway watching him. Tears blinded Ray again as he made his way into the comfort and safety of his husband's arms. Viv led him into their room, but they weren't alone. All their friends and family were there.

"I need to go to the hospital."

Ray felt so lost he didn't know what he was supposed to do, but Jamie was right. He had to get his head back in the game and be by his grandma's side. His family needed him to be strong, even if that meant sitting in a waiting room for hours on end. He would do it. Deep down he knew his grandma would do the same for him.

* * * *

Four days later, everything was almost back to normal. In the wake of Grandma's heart attack, some interesting tidbits had been unearthed. Viv could not believe how big of a secret Grandma had been holding onto for so long. Everyone in the whole family seemed to be reeling from it. To be honest, Viv couldn't understand why the truth hadn't come out years ago. The family seemed too shocked to even talk to each other. When Viv found himself alone with Grandma, his curiosity got the better of him.

"Why didn't you ever tell them?"

Sorrow filled her face as she replied, "I made a promise to my husband that I would keep his secret until the day I died."

"Then why drop the bombshell on them now?" Nothing made sense to Viv.

A sly look crept over her. "I kept my promise. Technically, I died right here in this very home. Was it my fault they revived me? Once I died, I was free to tell you all. Do you think they hate me now?"

"They would never hate you. More than likely, they're pissed off because you kept this from them. From the reaction Antonio had at the hospital, he already knew."

"Of course he did. When he was younger, he looked too much like Liam for him not to see it. Liam, of course, was already married by this stage so he never really took notice of the little boy who belonged to our housekeeper. James never wanted to be reminded of his indiscretion, but I forced him to do right by his son—both his sons, Liam and Antonio." Her gaze faded as if she had stepped back into her memories.

"Antonio stayed in this house after his mother passed away. Although we play him as being our butler, he and I have always known the truth. Why do you think we are so close? Hell, I've even put his kids through school. His wife never knew the truth, but that wasn't my doing. Antonio didn't want to cause waves in the family."

"What's going to happen now?" Viv pondered his own question. He didn't really expect an answer and was surprised when Grandma gave him one.

"Now we wait and see how things are after everything calms down. I know my family will do right by each other. It's Ray I worry about the most, as he is the one family member who stresses about everything."

Viv snorted. "I don't think you need to worry about Ray. Before I came in here, he was headed to find Antonio. He told me he was determined to learn everything there was to know about his uncle."

Grandma chuckled. "Poor Antonio."

* * * *

"I'm going to miss this place like crazy," Antonio said as he sat beside Ray.

"What are you talking about?" Ray asked.

"Now that everything is out in the open, things will be different. What do you want me to do?"

"What do you mean?" Ray asked. Why were things going to have to be different? Even if the dynamics of the family had been altered, it didn't mean that their lives would have to change so much. To Ray, all it meant was that their family had gotten a tad bigger.

"Would you like me to look for new staff for here?"

"You're not leaving me, are you?" Ray grabbed his hand. "Please, Antonio, don't do this." Ray saw the answer in his uncle's eyes and knew that he had to try harder. His grandma's heart attack had brought home to him how much he needed his family.

"I think my presence here now wouldn't be what your family wants. I mean, after what Chrissie told you all."

"You belong here with the rest of your damn family." Ray glared at him. "You're only... What? Thirty-nine? You're like my big brother. I need you here with me and my family. You know what a spaz I am. You cannot leave me here to my own devices." Ray bit back his smile. He was going to get his uncle to admit he wanted to stay if it was the last thing he ever did.

"Ray." Antonio patted his hand.

Ray could see the man was trying not to smile.

"Is your family trying to get you to leave? I don't believe that excuse for one minute," Ray stated firmly. "'Cause I was thinking maybe now that the truth was out in the open, you could all move onto the estate, and maybe Magen would think about being Grandma's caregiver? I know they've always got on like a house on fire and sometimes I think Grandma could do with another woman to talk to. She told me a couple of months ago how much she enjoyed the weekly visits she had with Aunt Magen."

"That's part of the problem. I don't want Liam and Claire believing my family is trying to take what belongs to Liam."

"Please don't go," Ray whispered. "I know some of the staff are coming up for retirement, and Mrs West is moving back to England at the end of the month. I really want you to think about moving in here. We have plenty of room in the guest wing. You could turn it into your family home. I certainly don't mind. I know Lily is at uni and Sean is still at school. Please, Uncle Antonio. Please talk to your family about this and see what they say — or is the real reason that you don't want to stay because I'm gay? I'll understand if so. I'll miss you but I'll understand."

"You know better than that, Ray." Antonio sounded almost offended. "Your sexuality has never been an issue for me and mine. I'll talk about this with my family then let you know what we decide. It's your dad I'm worried about."

Ray decided that he was going to talk to his Aunt Magen. There had to be a way to make all the awkwardness go away and bring the whole family together.

Surprisingly, he found Magen and her two children on their way to visit Grandma and he couldn't stop his grin as he took in the wide-eyed expression of his cousins. Sean was seventeen and Lily was turning twenty.

"Hello, guys, can I talk to you a minute?" Ray asked as he gestured for them to step into the nearest empty rom.

"What can I do for you, Mr Connelly?" Magen asked politely.

"Please call me Ray, Aunt Magen." Ray grabbed a hold of her hand. "I asked Uncle Antonio to move in here with you all, but I get the feeling I have upset him in some way."

"You want us to move into your home?" Her eyes widened in surprise.

"This house is very big, Aunt Magen."

"Do you expect us to work for you?" she asked as she studied his face.

"I expect Sean to finish school and be a kid, and Lily can do what she likes. They are free to use anything they want in the house. They are family, after all. I expect you to eat dinner along with the rest of us. We're a family and that's what a family does."

"What about me, Ray? What am I supposed to do?"

"How about you get to know the rest of us as family now that we all know the truth." Tears trickled down his face. "I know that's what I want. Grandma told us now for a reason. I believe she wants us to be a family."

Magen's eyes widened even more. "Ray, I don't know. Ant—he seems a little touchy where this is all concerned."

"Don't you think we should at least try?" Ray smiled at her. "I know you stopped coming to see Grandma as much when we moved in and I wondered why. I've always wondered if the fact that Viv and I are gay affected your decision."

"No," she said instantly and closed her eyes for a moment. "Ant's mother had an affair with your grandfather, and he's the result. I didn't want to intrude into your lives—in case the truth came out. At first, I didn't know then Ant said some things that got me to thinking. Chrissie confirmed all my suspicions. Now everything just seems complicated."

Ray was stunned at her honesty. "The truth is already out. Now all we can do is move on with our lives. I can't get Uncle Antonio to tell me what he truly thinks."

"That it makes me illegitimate," Antonio said from the doorway. Hurt laced his voice. "And nothing more."

"No."

They turned as Liam spoke roughly from behind Antonio. Ray hadn't even realized that his father was in the house. "That makes you my brother. Why didn't you tell me, Antonio?"

"Would it have mattered? I promised our father I would never tell you."

"Yes, this matters a lot," Liam said. "I'll speak to Byron tomorrow."

"I don't want your money," Antonio said defiantly. "I never have."

"I don't care about the money. I care about you." Ray's father smiled. "What would make *you* happy?"

"I don't know," Antonio answered.

A thrill of excitement ran through Ray as his father grabbed Antonio up in a bear hug and embraced him tightly. "Come and get to know me and Claire." He shook his head. "I know you already know us, but now you need to know us as family."

"I already know you." Antonio chuckled as he left with Liam, taking Magen with them.

Ray looked at Sean and Lily after their parents had left. "Did either of you know?"

They both shook their heads. They seemed as stunned as he was about all these revelations.

"So we're really cousins?" Lily whispered then flew into Ray's arms and hugged him. "I always wanted to be a part of your family. I remember playing with Girly when we were kids."

Sean sat on the edge of the couch and stared at his hands. "So we're like...rich now?" he asked softly, more to himself than anyone else. "I've always hated rich kids."

"Do you want to meet my babies?" Ray asked with a grin when Lily put her arm through his. "Come on, Sean."

Sean jumped up and grabbed Ray's hand as they walked through the crowd. Ray smiled in passing at Antonio as he led Lily and Sean toward the playroom.

Ray laughed at Viv lying on the ground surrounded by crawling babies. Teddy and Jamie lay in a beanbag together reading a book. Girly and Dan were in the kitchenette making cuppas.

"Love, I would like you to meet my cousins, Lily and Sean Duval." Ray introduced them as though they'd never been in the house before.

"Cousins—I always wanted you guys to be family." Girly looked through the partition at them, a huge smile plastered on her face.

"Yup," Sean tried to say as casually as he could.

"Fantastic," Girly exclaimed. "Another girl in the gang." She put her cuppa up on a shelf and hugged Lily. "Someone to shop with too."

"Not me. I hate shopping," Lily said, slightly embarrassed. "Sean's the one in our family who loves to shop."

"A boy who likes to shop." Girly stared at Sean. "I usually have to drag Dan or Brent along kicking and screaming."

"Dad," Jamie called to Ray, "when Bear and I turn eighteen and move into your old room, can we have blue and red sheets?"

"Jamie, you still have years to wait." Ray chuckled.

"Six years, three months and ten days," Bear answered. "We worked the time out."

"Two thousand, four hundred and eighty-five days." Jamie grinned. "We made a calendar."

"They've decided to get married when they grow up, and Josh told them when they turned eighteen, they could share a queen-size bed. For now, they squash into a king single together," Ray explained.

"They're gay?" Sean asked curiously.

"See, you *will* fit right in." Lily gently pushed Sean's arm.

"Are you gay?" Girly asked.

"Yes," Sean said, "but I don't have a boyfriend or anything."

"Do your parents know?" Viv asked. As he sat up on the floor, Layla crawled into his lap.

"Yes, I told them when we came to your wedding."

"The only reason he came out was Dad caught him kissing one of the bar staff."

"He wasn't bar staff. His brother was your best man or something."

"Penn?" Daniel said in surprise.

"I didn't find out his name because Dad laughed so hard he embarrassed the guy and he wouldn't talk to me for the rest of the party."

"Live here and you'll see Tony a lot. Penn lives in Sydney, but comes up all the time and visits. Even sleeps over some nights," Daniel said with a grin. "Penn likes to swim, so we usually have a pool party while he's up."

"Does Tony know his brother's gay?" Girly asked as everyone got comfortable on the floor cushions.

"Yes," Daniel said. "I told him. Penn didn't know how to. I forgot to tell you Tony will be here soon. He had to stop off at the club before coming."

"Actually, Tony may be moving in with us for a couple of months," Viv said. "His apartment block is being renovated and they have asked the tenants to vacate for the next two months or so."

They sat there talking and as the afternoon wore on, all their family and friends found their way to the playroom. Mrs West had been left in charge of the house as Liam dragged Antonio and Magen in with him. Ray didn't think his dad was planning on letting go of Antonio any time soon.

"You should have told me sooner," Ray said to Antonio. "I'm very put out with you."

"It wasn't my secret to tell," Antonio answered softly. "I loved my dad enough to do as he asked. He didn't want any of you to know."

"Dad was a jerk," Liam snapped.

"Yes, we know," Ray joked.

Lily giggled from where she sat with her back propped against the wall next to Ray. "I think we all agree that Grandpa wasn't always that nice. At least now nothing else can go wrong, seeing as all our secrets are out in the open."

"The best part," Beth said, "is even though this is a horrible time with Grandma's heart attack, it's also a frickin' fantastic time because you found family."

"Hey, Josh?" Ray called. "Did you know Bear and Jamie are counting down the days until they are eighteen?"

"Of course I do. I helped them make a big calendar. And when I say it's a big calendar—I mean huge."

"What's this about?" Liam asked. He laughed as Josh explained the whole conversation with Grandma about the boys moving back in together and still wanting to get married.

"What are you going to do when they turn eighteen?" Magen asked.

"Let them move into a queen bed together, but honestly, they will probably need to have one before they get much older. Bear keeps falling out of the one they have now."

"You don't care if they're gay?" Magen asked curiously.

"No," Liam answered. "Gay or straight, they're still our family."

"Sean's gay," Lily said. "I thought I'd get that out in the open."

"How do you feel about black men?" Viv asked with a smile as Tony walked through the door. "Tony is moving in for a couple of months. I ran it by Grandma and she said it was okay."

While Viv spoke, Ray noticed that Tony wasn't alone. An older teenager was with him, dressed in gothic attire and everyone stared at him.

"Maybe less if they start on my floor first. In the meantime, this kid needs to talk to you," Tony said as he sank to the floor then picked up Jeb.

Ray stared openly at the boy. His eyes were the same color as Viv's. "I'm looking for Christopher Vivvens," the boy stated.

"That's me." Viv put Layla aside and stood.

"Then… I think you're my father," he said softly.

Then and there, Ray knew what else life had in store for them.

About the Author

NJ needs to write like she needs to breathe. It's an addiction that she never intends to find a cure for. When you don't find NJ writing about the wonderful men in her stories you find her reading work by others who she greatly admires. NJ lives in the SE of Qld, Australia with her family who all encourage her writing career even if she does occasionally call them by her character's names. NJ thinks that anyone taking the time to read her stuff is totally awesome.

N.J. Nielsen loves to hear from readers. You can find her contact information, website details and author profile page at http://www.totallybound.com.

Totally Bound Publishing

Home of Erotic Romance